The
HOPE
WITHIN

—— Heirs of Montana ——

The HOPE WITHIN

TRACIE PETERSON

BETHANY HOUSE PUBLISHERS
Minneapolis, Minnesota

Published by Bethany House Publishers
11400 Hampshire Avenue South
Bloomington, Minnesota 55438

Bethany House Publishers is a division of
Baker Publishing Group, Grand Rapids, Michigan.

Printed in the United States of America

ISBN 0-7642-2772-6 (Paperback)
ISBN 0-7642-0046-1 (Large Print)

Library of Congress Cataloging-in-Publication Data

Peterson, Tracie.
    The hope within / by Tracie Peterson.
        p.   cm. —(Heirs of Montana ; 4)
    Summary: "1886 Montana stands on the brink of statehood, and Dianne Selby finds her world turned upside down in this conclusion to Tracie Peterson's Montana saga. Through the twists and turns of life and nature, Dianne comes to realize that the hope within Jesus Christ is the only hope that lasts"—Provided by publisher.
        ISBN 0-7642-2772-6 (pbk.) —ISBN 0-7642-0046-1 (large-print pbk.)
        1. Women pioneers—Fiction. 2. Ranch life—Fiction. 3. Montana—Fiction.
I. Title II. Series: Peterson, Tracie. Heirs of Montana ; 4.
    PS3566.E7717H67   2005
    813'.54—dc22   2004024190

To those who struggle in sorrow,
weighed down by the trials
and fears of this world.
There is a hope beyond this world,
a hope in whom we can take rest—
His name is Jesus.

Books by Tracie Peterson

www.traciepeterson.com

The Long-Awaited Child • *Silent Star*
A Slender Thread • *Tidings of Peace*

BELLS OF LOWELL*
Daughter of the Loom • *A Fragile Design*
These Tangled Threads

LIGHTS OF LOWELL*
A Tapestry of Hope • *A Love Woven True*

DESERT ROSES
Shadows of the Canyon • *Across the Years*
Beneath a Harvest Sky

HEIRS OF MONTANA
Land of My Heart • *The Coming Storm*
To Dream Anew • *The Hope Within*

WESTWARD CHRONICLES
A Shelter of Hope • *Hidden in a Whisper*
A Veiled Reflection

RIBBONS OF STEEL†
Distant Dreams • *A Hope Beyond*
A Promise for Tomorrow

RIBBONS WEST†
Westward the Dream • *Separate Roads*
Ties That Bind

SHANNON SAGA‡
City of Angels • *Angels Flight*
Angel of Mercy

YUKON QUEST
Treasures of the North • *Ashes and Ice*
Rivers of Gold

NONFICTION
The Eyes of the Heart

*with Judith Miller   †with Judith Pella   ‡with James Scott Bell

TRACIE PETERSON is a popular speaker and bestselling author who has written more than sixty books, both historical and contemporary fiction. Tracie and her family make their home in Montana.

CHAPTER 1

Virginia City, Montana Territory
June 1886

"I HATE THIS TOWN," DIANNE SELBY SAID AS she looked down on Virginia City from their front porch on the hillside above the town. From there, Dianne could very nearly see every building and buggy, every weather-worn board, every decaying signpost.

"I've known far worse," her aunt replied. Koko Vandyke was beginning to show her age with streaks of gray in her otherwise ebony hair. The gray was deceiving, however. Koko seemed just as energetic and spry as she had when Dianne had first met the half-Blackfoot woman over twenty years ago.

"Yes, we've all known a much harder life," Koko's brother, George, threw in.

Dianne didn't appreciate the fact that neither of her friends appeared to be on her side. "You can say that and not give it another thought," she said with a sigh. "You're going home tomorrow."

"It won't be that long before you join us. Maybe another two months at the most," George said, giving her the first encouraging word she'd heard that day.

The Diamond V was Dianne's home, and she'd been separated from it for nearly five years. The fire that had laid waste to the ranch house and outbuildings had also devastated Dianne's heart and dreams.

"I don't know whether to believe that or not, George." She returned her gaze to the desolate streets below. "Cole is always changing his mind about when we'll return. Even now he's talking about waiting until next spring. The freighting business is doing so well, he's certain the extra time will mean all the difference to us." She turned her back on the town and looked to Koko and George. "We don't need extra time—we need to be home."

Koko reached out and took hold of Dianne's hands. "You will be. Don't fret over this. Cole is just being extra cautious. The fire took everything. He wants to be sure he can replace the comfort you were used to."

"But that doesn't matter," Dianne protested. "I don't need a comfortable life. I need to be back on the ranch where I can raise my children. The boys are miserable here—they hate it. Luke always asks when we can go home, and Micah still asks to return to his special fishing hole. John is unhappy because the others are unhappy, and Athalia hears her brothers talk about horses and animals and longs for what she's never known.

"I'm telling you, I can't take much more." Dianne fought back tears. "I try to be understanding about this, but five years have slipped away in understanding. The first year was completely reasonable. I knew we wouldn't be back at the ranch overnight. Then more time slipped away, and Cole ended up breaking his leg in that accident late the second year."

"No one could have foreseen that wagon breaking loose," Koko interjected. "It wasn't as if your husband arranged the accident so that he could force you all to remain here in Virginia City."

"I know that, but then when he was completely recovered, the freighting business seemed too good to leave. Cole was too busy bringing in building supplies for other men's houses. Had George and Jamie not pushed to get back to rebuilding, we'd have no hope of returning this year. Even so, I must say my hope is dwindling. It's already June, and Cole isn't making any plans. Every time I talk to him about ordering cattle, he changes the subject. When I try to mention finding a buyer for this place, he talks of the blessing this house has been. When I talk of purchasing a herd, he tells me we haven't the time to both build and restore the ranch and tend cattle."

"And he's right," Koko said softly, "about the house, anyway. It has been a blessing. Where would any of us have been without it? Then, too, how would we have cared for livestock and focused on building the cabins and barns?"

Melodious sounds drifted out the open parlor window. Ardith, Dianne's widowed sister, was again comforting herself in music. It was uncanny the way she had taken to the piano. She could hear a song and replicate it without any difficulty. Seeing her interest, Dianne had found Ardith a teacher. But Ardith had soon surpassed the woman. Once she'd learned to read music there was no stopping Ardith in her determination to learn.

"This house has been a blessing. It's given us time," Koko said softly. "Time to heal and time to renew."

Dianne thought back to their descent upon the small city. The fire had devastated them—taking not only the ranch house and barns, but nearly all of their belongings. They had escaped with very little as the fire moved more quickly than anyone could have imagined. The large house in Virginia City had accommodated them nicely, providing room for Cole and Dianne's family, as well as Koko and her children, George, and others. They were fortunate—blessed to be alive and safe, for death had touched them as well. Dianne's sister

Ardith had lost her husband, Levi, to the fire. He had been a dear friend to them all and a wonderful foreman. She didn't know who would ever replace him—if they ever even needed a foreman again.

Bitterness welled up in her heart. "It's just not fair."

George nodded, his eyes filled with sorrow. He understood. He had once gone by the name "Takes Many Horses" and had lived with his Blackfoot relatives, enjoying the liberty and freedom of the Indian way of life. It wasn't fair that he should have to give that up in order to keep from being pushed onto a reservation with his friends and family. It wasn't fair that he had to deny his heritage in order to keep from losing his life.

Dianne bit her lip. Ardith's sorrowful serenade was causing Dianne's spirits to sink ever lower. *I thought music was supposed to soothe and comfort.* But comfort had deserted her long ago.

"We have to trust that God knows what's best for each of us," Koko said. "George and Jamie will work hard to see your cabin completed. Susannah and I will make curtains and rugs. You'll see. It will come together before you know it."

"I'm not concerned about the physical presence of a home," Dianne said in an exhausted sigh. "I'm worried that Cole will

never allow us to return. It wasn't his home—
it was ours."

"It was his as well," Koko said reassuringly.
"He's trying to do right by his family. Dianne,
you know that God is good and that He will
guide this family's steps. You mustn't let this
temporary delay cause you such pain and sorrow."

Dianne knew she was right, but it was so
hard. Hard to watch them pack their belongings. Hard to know that Koko and George
would soon spend their nights in the quiet
comfort of the Madison Valley.

Ardith concluded her playing, and Dianne
could hear her speaking in hushed tones with
Winona. The child had been misplaced along
with the rest of them. Ardith seldom spent
time with her daughter, feeling unable to bear
the child's constant stories and memories of
Levi. Dianne knew the pain Ardith bore was
more than she could share with anyone. She
had dared to open her heart only to have
another tremendous loss pierce her. Now the
child she once took comfort in was only a sad
reminder of that pain.

Dianne sighed. At least Cole was safe and
alive. She shouldn't be so angry, so bitter. She
needed to rest in the Lord and trust Him for
answers. But it was so hard. It was the kind of
thing she could never do in her own strength,

so trusting God for help in this matter was her only hope.

On Sunday Dianne sat beside her husband, listening to an aging Ben Hammond give a sermon on prayer. He spoke as a man convinced of the power his subject rendered. He had known answered prayer. He had seen the results and was there to testify that God still listened when His children prayed.

"'And when ye stand praying, forgive, if ye have ought against any: that your Father also which is in heaven may forgive you your trespasses. But if ye do not forgive, neither will your Father which is in heaven forgive your trespasses.'" Ben paused and looked at the congregation. "Some of you here hold grudges against others. Some of you are mighty angry because of wrongs done you. You may feel betrayed or cheated."

Dianne squirmed in her seat and Athalia, or Lia, as they called their four-year-old daughter, crawled onto her lap. Ben always had a way of making her feel as though he were preaching just to her.

"I knew a man once who held his father a grudge. The man had promised the boy the family farm and livestock as an inheritance. He regaled the boy with stories from the time he was old enough to understand their meaning. Stories about how great the farm would be, how wondrous it would feel to own his own plot of land, to work the soil with his own two hands. The boy spent night after night growing those dreams in his mind. Then one day the sheriff came and directed the family to leave the farm. The father had been unable to make his payments. The livestock were sold one by one to pay the father's debts."

Ben paused and closed his Bible. He looked from face to face as if seeking to know they understood the importance of what he was about to say. "This boy had a reason to hold a grudge. The father had filled his head with promises, even as he lost the family's money in gambling. He knew he would never fulfill the promises he offered his son, yet he continued to promise what could never be. And that was what hurt the boy the most. He hadn't really cared about the land or the animals. He cared about the lies, the betrayal, the broken promises from a man he trusted.

"The boy left his family, unable to stand the sight of his father. Every time he looked at the man, he wanted to scream out against him, but he remained silent . . . and little by little his heart hardened against his father until there was no possible hope for forgiveness. And the father wanted forgiveness. He begged for it. He swore off his gambling ways and went straight. He found peace in God's word— accepted salvation through the blood sacrifice of Jesus Christ. He restored the family as best he could, taking a job cleaning printing presses for a newspaper publisher and delivering papers. He found a little house for his family and never again did he allow temptations to cause such grief to his loved ones."

Ben sighed and stepped down from behind the pulpit. "He tried hard to reach out to his son. He wrote letters and asked friends to speak to the young man, and even as he lay on his deathbed, he pleaded for his son to forgive him. But the son never came home. He never opened the letters and he never forgave his father. The father died and the boy figured it was just as it should be. The old man had finally gotten what he deserved. After all, he'd killed the very heart of his son."

There were murmurings across the con-gregation. Dianne had long since stopped squirming and was caught up in the story. How could anyone be so heartless as to refuse forgiveness when it was asked for? She couldn't even imagine knowing such a person. That's why Ben's words hit her so hard as he continued.

"I was that boy. I was hard and unforgiv-ing, because you see, I didn't know the Lord's love. I didn't know, and in my ignorance I let my father go to his death with a grudge between us."

Dianne's breath caught in her throat. Surely Ben jested. He was such a kind and loving soul. There couldn't possibly be any truth to this story—yet she'd never known him to lie.

" 'And when ye stand praying, forgive. . . .'" Ben let the words trail off. "There's a powerful hurt that's running deep through the hearts of some of you. You don't feel like forgiving because the other person doesn't deserve your forgiveness—because their wicked ways have caused great destruction. Or maybe they've mended their ways, but you can't seem to mend your heart. I'm here today to tell you that Jesus can do the mending if you do the forgiving."

Dianne scarcely heard the rest of the service. She felt the boys grow restless beside her as they waited for the final hymn. She felt Lia nestle her head against Dianne's shoulder and start sucking her thumb. But her primary focus was her need to talk to Cole. She had to ask him to forgive her anger against him. She had to give him her forgiveness for the delays and the way he'd ignored her hurting heart.

After church the family began their walk home. Luke and Micah raced each other while John begrudgingly held Lia's hand and walked at her speed. Dianne reached for Cole's hand as the rest of the family progressed toward the house.

"I need to talk to you."

He raised a brow at the seriousness of her

tone. "Going to make confessions?" he asked with a grin.

Dianne nodded, her sober expression causing his smile to fade. "Cole, I've been very angry with you—holding a grudge against you. I want your forgiveness, even though I don't deserve it."

"What are you talking about?" He seemed genuinely perplexed.

"The ranch—us living here. All of it. I've been so angry, especially when Koko and the others left for the ranch. It hurt so much and the pain was almost more than I could bear. So instead of enduring it, I turned it into resentment against you."

Cole stopped her there in the middle of the street. "But why? You know I've been working to get us back on the Diamond V. You know it's important to me to provide you with the things you had before."

She shook her head. "No. I don't think I did understand that. All I knew was that you stood in my way of going home."

His expression dropped. "Is that how you truly saw it?"

A warm breeze fluttered the ties of Dianne's bonnet. She hated having hurt him with her confession, but she hated having lies between them even more. "I've tried to see it your way. I've tried to be patient about the delays, but every time I saw you freight another load of lumber for someone else's house or bring in an order of windows, or talk about how the valley was returning to its old state of glory, I held you a deeper grudge." She looked away shaking her head. "I never meant to—it was just my defense against the pain."

"I never wanted to cause you pain," he said. "I only wanted to be realistic about our return. After all, there were the children to think about."

"That's part of the reason I'm so grieved. The boys hate it here. They are constantly picked on at school, and they miss their ponies and the days we spent out of doors. Lia hears their tales and asks me why she can't have a horse or learn to fish."

"And I suppose you tell them I'm to blame."

Dianne's head snapped up and she narrowed her eyes. All of her good intentions to let go of her anger faded in that single statement. "I'm not that cruel. I've never spoken against you to the children. I will confess that I spoke to George and Koko the day before they left. I told them how I felt—how hard it was to watch them go home while we have to remain behind. George promised me that he and Jamie would work to put our house in order so that you would feel comfortable moving us there this fall, but I told him I saw no sign of your being willing to do that."

It was Cole's turn to be angry. "I told you when the time was right, we'd return. It would be foolish to rush back. Do you want the children living exposed to the elements—to wild animals? We have a good life here. Our friends are here."

"Well, my heart is there!" Dianne declared and began to walk away.

"I thought I was your heart," he called after her softly.

Dianne stopped in midstep. Her confession had not gone well. She was angry again. Angry and hurt. She turned and looked at her husband. "And I thought I was your heart."

He sighed and came to where she stood. "You *are* my heart—my life. But I don't want to argue this out in the middle of the street."

"I didn't ask you to argue with me, Cole. I merely wanted to confess my wrongdoing and receive your forgiveness." Her tone was clipped, edging on sarcastic. "I suppose you won't give it now—now that you know how I felt."

"Feel."

Dianne looked at him for a moment, unsure what he meant. "What are you saying?"

"You still feel this way. It isn't in the past at all. This isn't a matter of how you felt—it's a matter of how you still feel."

Dianne started to deny it, then nodded and began walking toward the house on the hill.

Why can't I let this anger go? Why can't I forgive him and forget it—just release it here and now?

"'But if ye do not forgive, neither will your Father which is in heaven forgive your trespasses.'" She heard Ben's words ringing clear in her heart. It was all just too much to deal with.

The last thing Dianne wanted to confront was a houseful of people upon her return from church. But that was exactly what she got. Morgan, one of her older brothers, had come with a group of several people he'd taken on tour through the Yellowstone National Park wilderness.

"Hello, sis," he said as Dianne came into the house. "I have some people here I think you'll enjoy meeting. I thought you might be willing to put us up for the night as well."

Dianne looked at the group of four men. Clearly they were city dudes out to take in the country air. It was a scene she'd seen several times with Morgan. He seemed to enjoy acting as tour and hunting guide these days.

"The two rooms at the far end of the upstairs hall are free. You're welcome to them. There's also a room just off the kitchen."

"I can take that one," Morgan said, giving Dianne's shoulders a squeeze. "I'll get our guests settled upstairs. Can you feed us as well?"

"We'll manage," she said as she removed her bonnet.

"Wonderful. Here, let me introduce you." Morgan took Dianne by the hand and pulled her over to meet her guests. "This is Mr. Stromgren. He's from New York City, as are his companions, Mr. Wayne, Mr. Winters, and Mr. Mullins. Gentlemen, this is my sister Mrs. Dianne Selby."

Cole came into the room and Morgan included him in the introduction. "And my brother-in-law, Cole Selby."

The men had already gotten to their feet for Dianne, but they extended their hands in welcome to Cole. After he'd shaken each man's hand, he turned to Morgan. "Are you needing rooms?"

"Yes, and we've already spoken with Dianne about the matter. I hope that was all right," Morgan said, looking rather sheepish.

"You know it is. You're always welcome."

From the next room, Ardith began playing the piano. It was a beautiful Chopin piece, one Dianne had come to recognize and love.

"Where is that glorious music coming from?" Mr. Stromgren asked.

"That would be my sister. She's playing in the parlor next door." Dianne went to the paneled sliding doors and pushed them back. "Ardith, we have guests, and they are very much enjoying your music. I hope you don't mind."

Ardith looked up as she continued to play. "I don't mind."

"You are truly skilled, my dear," Mr. Stromgren said as he came to stand beside Dianne. The other gentlemen joined him. "This is the kind of talent I've been looking for. Why, people would pay a fortune to hear her in New York." He looked to his companions, and they all nodded in agreement.

"It isn't all that often," he continued, "that you find a beautiful woman with such talent. The audiences are all about appearance. The visual is very important."

"I don't suppose I would know anything about that," Dianne said.

"Well, I do. It's my business to provide audiences with talented artists. Your sister must have played since she was very young."

"Actually, no. She has only played for about the last five years."

"A truly amazing feat. Why, she masters Chopin as if she were part of the music."

Ardith completed the piece and rose. "Thank you for your compliments, sir."

"Christopher Stromgren," he said, stepping forward boldly. "I know we've not yet been properly introduced, but we must speak. I have a proposition for you. I would like to take you to New York and present you to the awaiting audiences there and in other cities around the country."

"You've only heard her play one Chopin serenade," Dianne protested. "How do you know that she can play anything else?"

Stromgren's gaze never left Ardith. The man, with his curly red hair and thick, bristly mustache, seemed enthralled. "I just know these things."

Ardith smiled—a rarity to be sure. "I need to help with dinner, but perhaps we could speak afterward."

Her attitude completely took Dianne by surprise. Her sister was generally very reserved and had nothing to do with strangers.

"I will count the minutes," he replied. "May I at least have your name?"

"Ardith. Ardith Sperry."

Dianne excused herself and made her way to the kitchen. Pulling on her apron, she couldn't help but address the matter the moment Ardith stepped into the room.

"What are you thinking? You don't know that man. Why, he could be nothing more than . . . than . . . well, you know. A man who entices innocent young women for ill purposes."

"I think he seems rather charming," Ardith said as she took up her own apron.

"Who is charming?" Mara Lawrence asked. The young lady had stayed with them since the time of the fire.

"Mr. Stromgren," Ardith replied before

Dianne could say a word. "He wants to take me to New York City to play piano for audiences there."

"How interesting."

"What about Winona?" Dianne questioned, hoping the mention of the child's name would bring her mother back to her senses.

"I suppose we'd simply have to discuss that at the appropriate time."

Dianne shook her head. "You can hardly drag the child all over the country. Winona needs you here. Not in New York."

Ardith turned a cold expression on her sister. "Mind your own business. I'll live my life as I see fit. And I'll care for Winona in whatever manner I believe best."

CHAPTER 2

CHESTER LAWRENCE WAS A HARD MAN. A man of determination and purpose, he was ruthless and unforgiving. He was also the richest man in all of the Madison Valley. By his standards the world was in good order. He no longer had to compete with the Selbys and the Diamond V for beef contracts, and he had a healthy, growing herd to see him through hard times. Of course the summer drought had made cattle ranching more interesting, to say the least, but with the help of his hired hands and his sons Jerrod and Roy, Chester felt that the world and all its treasures belonged to him.

He shifted in the saddle and looked out across the river valley. He'd never seen a more beautiful piece of country. The rich ground was perfect for grazing, and despite the drought, the Madison River ran free and clear. There were really only two thorns in his side that continued to haunt him. One, that the Selbys still owned the land adjoining his, and two, that his daughter Mara had betrayed him to take up a life with the Selbys.

"Traitor. She always was different. Just like her brother." He tried not to think of Joshua or Mara, but at times like this they had a way of creeping into his thoughts. Mara was a grown woman now; almost twenty-two years of age, if he remembered right.

She was nothing like her mother or father. In fact, Chester couldn't think of anyone in the family that she took after. He had raised his children to be strong, hard, and determined to succeed. But with Mara and Joshua, the lessons refused to take. He couldn't figure out what had gone wrong.

Chester didn't like to admit that their desertion bothered him. He still had Jerrod and

Roy, and they were mean enough to get anything accomplished that needed doing. Then there was Elsa. She'd just turned twenty in the spring, and Chester had plans for her. Plans for himself, really. He would marry Elsa to the old rancher who lived to the north of their property line. Herbert Denig was older than Chester, but he fancied Elsa and had agreed to sign over control of his property upon his death to Chester. The price: Elsa.

Chester thought it a reasonable deal. The only problem would be convincing his daughter. And now Mara was interfering with all of his plans. She'd invited her sister to come live with the Selbys in Virginia City.

"Those cursed Selbys. Stealing my children."

He turned his gelding toward home and rode for nearly an hour thinking only of how to convince Elsa to stay and marry Denig. He certainly couldn't appeal to her loyalty, for the girl had been unnaturally distant when he took a second wife after her mother had passed away.

He sometimes worried that she'd known her mother's death had come at the hands of his new bride, Portia Langford. But since nothing was ever said about such matters— and because he knew that if his children had any real proof of the murder, they would have been happy to mention it—he couldn't figure out Elsa's hostility.

Now Portia was gone as well, having been found burned to death on Selby land. He couldn't figure out why she'd been there that day, unless she wanted to gloat over the destruction. He missed Portia but was also relieved by the loss. He'd always known that had she not died first, she would have eventually tried to kill him off. Just as she had her other husbands.

He almost laughed out loud remembering how she'd given him an account of her deeds—proudly, almost as if she were near to bursting for the desire to tell someone her accomplishments. She told him she was confessing so he would know he had nothing to fear from her. After all, she certainly wouldn't have come clean with him had she ill plans for his future.

Chester didn't believe her. He thought her more in need of proving to him that she was dangerous—that he needed to watch his step. After all, he knew his demeanor was intimidating to most folks, Portia included. He could easily see at times that he frightened her. It kind of excited him to know that. So her little confession didn't have the effect she had hoped for. He merely regarded her as a dangerous animal—a she-bear living within his home. He was always on his guard. Always cautious of her actions. But still, he liked the woman. She'd been his equal in many ways, and for that reason, he was sorry she was gone.

The sound of a rider approaching from behind caused Chester to rein back his horse and turn. He felt the dust dry his throat to an intolerable tightness as his youngest son rounded the bend and came into view.

"Joshua." He muttered the name almost as a curse.

Joshua approached on the back of a large black gelding. The horse had clear indications of Arabian blood and carried himself well. Pity he'd been cut. The animal would have made a beautiful sire. The beast whinnied as if agreeing with Chester's thoughts.

"What are you doing here?" Chester growled out.

"That's not a very kind greeting for someone who hasn't seen his son in nearly five years."

"That's because you aren't welcome here."

Joshua appeared unfazed. He was taller and more filled out than Chester remembered. He wasn't as big as his brothers, but still there was nothing shameful about his appearance. No doubt the women found him handsome, but Chester wondered if the boy was capable of a hard day's work.

"I thought perhaps we could talk."

"Talk has never done anything for me.

Besides, I have a meeting with your brothers. I don't have time for this."

"Could I just wait for you at the house?" Joshua asked. "I won't take long, and I promise to leave before dark."

Chester was curious about what would bring the boy back to the ranch he had so hated. "All right. You can wait for me, but I want you gone before night."

"I promise you, Father, I will be long gone."

————

"So the prodigal returns?" Jerrod Lawrence said to his brother Roy. He nudged him and pointed to the house, where Joshua was dismounting.

"Never thought we'd see him again," Roy said, spitting to one side. "Think he's come for money?"

Jerrod laughed. "He'd know better'n that."

Their father rode up to the barn. "You finished with that shoeing yet?"

"These premade shoes just ain't as good. We oughta take the horses into town and have 'em properly fitted. Better still, we oughta hire us a decent smithy," Jerrod said, putting aside his tools.

"I'll be the one to decide what we need and what we don't need. You two are no better than

Joshua if you can't follow my instructions and treat me with respect."

Jerrod straightened and looked his father in the eye. When Jerrod had been a boy, the man had absolutely terrified him. Now Jerrod simply saw the fading glory of a once strong and powerful man.

"You get all the respect you deserve. Don't try to bully me around."

Their father narrowed his eyes. "You two are always thinking yourselves too good to take orders. I don't need the grief."

"We've taken your orders and taken care of your ranch, but we've just about reached our limit. That's why we called this meeting. Me and Roy are leavin'."

Their father's expression remained fixed—stoic—but Jerrod noticed him pale ever so slightly.

"What in the world do you think you're doing spouting such nonsense to me? You two have a past that you don't need folks finding out about."

"A past that clearly implicates you, old man," Jerrod said, pointing his finger at his father's chest.

"You can't prove that."

"You'd like to believe that, but it ain't true." Jerrod pushed his hat back off his forehead. "There isn't a court in this land that would find you innocent when Roy and I start talking. So before you think to threaten us into staying on this ranch, think again. We know who set that fire five years ago."

"Set the fire? That fire came on the heels of a dry thunderstorm."

Jerrod laughed. "That fire came at the hand of your devious bride, Portia."

Chester shook his head. "She would have told me if she'd had such plans."

"Well, apparently she figured you didn't need to know. Roy and I followed her out that day. We figured she needed a dressing down— she'd gotten us in too much hot water with you. You believed her story about us beating her when we hadn't even laid a hand on her. So we figured we'd teach her a lesson—give her a scare."

"Like that woman could be scared of anything."

"Oh, she looked pretty frightened when that fire came over the mountain."

Chester's expression changed. "You were there? When she died?"

"Yep, we were there. Her horse fell and trapped her underneath. We figured it fittin' and left her to burn. We also figured she was doin' your bidding. That fire was set directly in line to burn the Selby ranch. She carefully calculated the wind and the location. That fire was deliberate, and we'd happily tell the court that you instigated it—even helped her accomplish it."

"You would turn traitor on your father?"

Roy laughed. "Like you wouldn't sell either one of us any day of the week and twice on Sunday if it meant makin' you cattle king of Montana."

"You're calloused and without loyalty," their father accused.

"And just where do you s'pose we might've learned that, old man?" Jerrod asked. "You've only lived it by example every day of our lives. You taught us that holding anyone or anything too dear was a weakness. You taught us to think of ourselves first—and others never."

"So go then. If it's all that important to you. I can hire two more men to take your place. You mean nothing to me more than that."

Jerrod wouldn't let the old man know that his words cut. He'd worked hard all his life to feel nothing—to care about no one. He refused to let himself desire his father's approval. It didn't matter now, because he wouldn't let it matter.

"Good. Glad you see it our way. Who knows, maybe you can convince old Joshua to stay home now—do his part."

"I don't need any of you." The older man turned, then paused and looked back. "Don't be expecting any money from me. You can take what belongs to you, but don't think you'll be getting any part of an inheritance."

"We've already taken what we want and have the money we need," Jerrod said, leaning casually against the fence of the corral. "You oughta know by now that we're perfectly capable of fending for ourselves."

"So you've been robbing me blind as well. I guess I should have known that."

"There's a lot of things you should've known," Roy muttered.

They eyed their father for a moment, and then Jerrod shook his head.

"Are you leaving today?"

"No," Jerrod replied. "But soon. In our own time. Just wanted you to know. Figured we wouldn't sneak off like Joshua did or desert to the enemy like Mara."

"At least they didn't steal from me."

"Don't be so certain of that. You remember those papers you paid to have removed from the courthouse in Virginia City? The papers that would have helped you steal the Selby land? Well, I'm fairly confident our little Mara was the one who stole them back," Jerrod said. "So don't think us so different. She foiled all of your plans. We're only walkin' away with what we deserve."

"You deserve to hang," their father muttered.

"No more than you. Do you honestly

suppose anyone would be surprised to know your part in the Farley murders? Do you suppose it would be that hard to convince a jury that you were there?"

"Shut up," the old man declared, crossing the distance with surprising speed. "If you know what's good for you, you'll shut up and clear out as soon as possible."

"I'll go in my own time, old man. Don't threaten me." Jerrod was nose to nose with his father. The hatred shone clear in his father's eyes.

"You'd better watch yourself, boy. You have to sleep sometime." The man's words were cold and poisonous. Jerrod could almost feel the chill of death in his father's stare.

"So you're back," Elsa said as she served Joshua a cup of coffee.

"Not to stay here, but to get you."

She straightened and looked at him with surprise. "Truly?"

"Are you willing to leave?"

"Of course, but he won't be willing for me to leave. Still, I'll be twenty-one next year. I can take my freedom then, although I scarcely have the funds to make my own way."

"I figure to provide for you, although it won't be much. That's why I never could send for you before now," Joshua admitted. He'd made his sister a promise the night he'd left that he would free her from this ranch. Now he was back to fulfill his obligation.

"I know I can't give you a life of wealth or keep you in these kinds of luxuries," he said holding up the china cup.

"Who cares about such things?" Elsa said. She sat down opposite her brother. "Would you really take me away from here?"

"Of course. That's the only reason I came back."

She leaned back against the brocade of the settee. "I can't imagine being free of this. Free of the hatred and anger—the lack of love. I've nearly wasted away longing for some tenderness." Tears came to her eyes. "Do you know what it is to live completely isolated from everyone who is capable of showing kindness and love?"

"Doesn't Mara visit?"

"She tried to come here, but Father threatened to shoot her. Virginia City is so far away, she'd never be able to do it on her own, and up until this year there wasn't much rebuilt at the Diamond V."

"Are they back at the ranch now?"

"No. There are some workmen there and a few cowhands. I heard the Vandyke family would be back soon. That was a week or two ago, so they may well be there now. Otherwise, they're in Virginia City. Mara still lives with the

Selbys, and it causes Father no end of complaint."

"I'm sure," Joshua said, sipping the steaming brew. It was really much too hot to drink coffee, but it seemed rude to reject his sister's efforts.

"If I can convince Father to let you go, will you come with me?"

"Of course. Where will we go?" Elsa questioned.

"Virginia City for starts. We need to find Mara."

"And how will we live?"

"I'll find work."

"There isn't much available. The drought has been hard on everyone—not just the ranchers. The Selbys do own a freighting business. Maybe they'd take you on."

Joshua shook his head and put down the cup. "I have a profession. I'm a preacher."

"You're a what!" his father bellowed from the doorway.

Joshua wasn't sure how much his father had overheard, but he steeled himself for an attack. "I'm a preacher. I share the Word of God with lost souls and saved."

Chester Lawrence strode across the room and threw his hat atop a small table. "You can't be serious. That's the most ridiculous thing I've heard yet."

"I felt the Lord's calling on my life, Father.

It's not ridiculous at all. I studied under some wonderful men and learned a great deal about the Bible. I have helped to preach at a small church in Philadelphia, and many people came to the Lord while I was there. I was hoping to share God's plan with you, Father. I thought you might be ready to hear the truth about hell and eternity without Jesus."

"Get out!" his father yelled. He approached Joshua as if he would bodily throw him from the house.

Joshua got to his feet. "I came here with another purpose as well. I'm sorry you don't approve of my profession, but I would like you to hear me out."

"No. There's nothing you could say that would interest me. You're dead to me, boy."

"Father!" Elsa said, jumping to her feet.

"You stay out of this, girl. You have no say in it."

"But Elsa is part of the reason I'm here. I promised to come back for her."

His father stepped back as if Joshua had slapped him. "Come back for her?"

"She wants to leave the ranch, and I told her I would take her to live with me."

The older man looked from Joshua to Elsa and asked, "Is that right? Answer me."

She nodded, and Joshua could see the way she fairly cringed at their father's demanding voice. "I want to leave."

"No. Now get out," he said, turning to Joshua. "Your sister is staying here. I've got plans for her. She's my responsibility—at least for the time being, and she will do as I say."

"But she isn't happy here," Joshua protested.

"I don't care if she is happy. She's not going anywhere. But you are. Go!"

Elsa began to cry in earnest, and Joshua knew he'd best leave rather than further upset their father. "I'll leave for now, but I'll be back. I think if we talk about this calmly and rationally, you'll see that it's a better life for her in the city than out here in the middle of nowhere."

"If you don't leave now, I'll throw you out of here," his father barked, stepping forward in a menacing manner.

"Go, Joshua. Go before there's trouble," Elsa sobbed.

Joshua nodded. "I'll be back. I promise, and you know I'm a man of my word."

CHAPTER 3

"HERE, HAVE A CHEW AND JOIN ME FOR A talk," Marcus Daly said as he came upon Zane Chadwick. He extended a plug of tobacco, but Zane shook his head and hoisted a wooden crate into the back of the wagon.

This accomplished, he pulled out a hand-kerchief and wiped his forehead. The heat was making things miserable, as were the fumes and smoke from the local smelters. The air, some said, was poisonous to breathe. Zane figured it not too far from true, given the fact that most of the vegetation was dying or had died. It was said that the sulfur and arsenic content from the refining ore inevitably filtered into the air. Zane had even seen a cat drop over dead after licking itself. No doubt it had been the victim of a heavy dose of arsenic dust.

Tucking his handkerchief back into his pocket, Zane smiled. "I'll forego the chew but will enjoy the talk. So what brings you here today?"

"Just felt the need for some conversation with sane folk."

"Sounds like you must have had a run-in with Mr. Clark."

"That man is always causin' me grief," Marcus replied, his Irish brogue thick.

Zane understood the long-time irritation between his business associate and William Clark. Their competition around Anaconda and Butte was well known. Both men fancied themselves the copper king of the area, and both intended that they alone should take the throne and rule.

"If we can just get those crazy Michigan instigators to stop fighting us on the price of copper," Marcus began, "my little hill could realize me some thirteen million dollars this year. Half of that will be from copper alone. But if the prices don't rise and if my competition doesn't stop gluttin' the market . . . well, it won't be William Clark who grieves me the most. Still, I'd like to be riddin' this country of him. If it's not one thing, 'tis another."

Zane smiled. Marcus hated Clark through and through. Clark felt the same toward Marcus—of that there was no doubt. Clark made it clear that he saw Marcus as an Irish buffoon with few manners and fewer recommendable qualities. Marcus Daly in return saw Clark as a wealthy moneygrubber who intended to succeed on the backs of his workers, friends, and family. Their battles were notorious and were likely to only grow in intensity.

Zane decided not to focus the conversation on Clark but rather on the pricing problems related to copper. "So what's the worst of it now? Will the prices per pound continue to drop?"

"Copper is down to ten cents a pound," Marcus replied woefully. "And just think, it was sixteen only three years ago."

"So those Michigan-Boston men are depressing the market to teach us a lesson?"

"They think they can squeeze us out, but I won't go. We'll keep producing." He sighed and looked to Zane. "Well, we may have to shut down for a time. I hate to say it, but I'm thinkin' I may have to close the Anaconda until those ruffians back East come to their senses and realize they no longer have the only offering of copper."

"Closing the mine would be a desperate act. Are you certain there's no other way? What about your thirteen million?"

Marcus shook his head. "That's product that has mostly been realized. Between the silver and copper ore—both of which show no signs of playing out—we could be the center of all copper production."

"I hope you won't have to make the decision to close. Especially as we head into autumn and winter. Folks need to have a living to endure the harsh elements."

"And don't I know it." Marcus seemed

momentarily defeated. "I'll know for sure by August."

Changing the subject, Zane addressed a matter near to his heart. "I'm going to take a load of goods over the mountain and then head on back to Virginia City to see my family. I thought I'd best let you know in case you missed me." He smiled broadly at the man.

Marcus spit a stream of brown and asked, "How long will ya be gone?"

"I'm not sure. Business isn't what it used to be for me, and I'm considering what to do with my future. I'm not sure I want to stick around here. The place reeks of death."

"Oh, that's just Clark," Marcus said with a big grin. His despair seemed to pass.

Zane laughed. "Be that as it may, I'm not so sure I want to be here anymore."

"Don't give up on us yet. This copper war will settle down and the price will soar. You'll see. Anaconda will make a fine capital for this territory once it becomes a state."

"You sound certain that you'll have your way and push through Anaconda, when Clark is equally determined to have Helena remain the capital."

"I am certain. I have me plans."

Zane nodded. "And he has his."

"Now don't be talkin' like that, me boy. Clark has his plans to be sure. He fancies 'imself a politician now, don't ya know. But never mind that. He'll be just as miserable at that quest as he is at others."

"Seems to me he's not doing that poorly for himself."

Marcus spit again and wiped his mouth. "He doesn't know what's in the heart of the people. He doesn't understand their needs, their desires. I do. I'm down here with them—one of them."

Zane laughed. "One of them who will earn thirteen million dollars this year and possibly dismiss the entire mining staff of the great Anaconda mine."

"But I'll be helpin' them who haven't the same opportunities. I use my profits to see to givin' honest men work—at least as best I can, considering the conditions. Clark is only interested in helpin' himself. He doesn't care that copper is at ten cents a pound."

Zane was already tired of the comments. He tried hard to have a good opinion of everyone, William Clark included. It didn't bother him in the least that the man was rich and had political ambitions.

"Say, could ya be arranging some timber for me on your trip east?" Marcus suddenly questioned. "We're eatin' it up at an alarming rate in the mines. And the government is pressin' me something awful regarding the federal woodlands."

"I'd heard they were none too happy about

you taking trees. Taking the laws a little more seriously, are they?"

Marcus shook his head. "I don't care what they want. I need that wood. The Anaconda uses some thirty-five thousand board feet per day. I have braces to put in and supports are needed to insure the safety of my men. See if you can't arrange some shipments for me. Talk to your family and friends. Your brother-in-law should know a good many fellows who might be willin' to help."

"I'll do what I can, but transportation may be an issue. Getting those logs to the railroad is hard and dangerous work."

"I'll pay enough to make it worth the effort. I'll write you up some figures and give you an idea of what to offer. Just don't let them rob me blind."

"I know you have arrangements with the railroad, but what about buying some land yourself? You've got plenty of money, so it's not like you can't afford it," Zane threw out. "There are some great forests to the north and west of Butte, out by Missoula. I saw them in my soldiering days."

"It's a worthy notion. I'll take it up and give it some thought. But for now will you do this for me?"

"Of course."

Mara Lawrence tried to concentrate on her quilting stitches as the other women in Dianne's living room openly chatted about a variety of subjects, none of which really interested Mara. Her mind was focused on thoughts of a husband and family. There was no one in particular who brought those thoughts to mind for her, but Mara was seeing her life slip away—even though she was only twenty-one.

"Well, you can't say that the church social won't offer us a good time," Charity commented. Mara was unsure what had brought about this remark and decided to pay better attention.

"I didn't mean to imply that at all," Dianne said, her needle weaving in and out rhythmically. "I merely said this town offers nothing of entertainment or positive influence. It appears quite the contrary. My boys, for example. They never got into such fights when we lived on the ranch. Now it's not unusual for one or the other to come home once a week with a blackened eye or torn clothes."

"I have to admit," Ardith threw in, "Winona has learned more bad habits during our time here. Perhaps it's because we were so isolated on the ranch."

"And the life there was better. We had more control and influence over our children because we schooled them instead of a stranger."

"Well, this town offers good along with the bad," Faith declared. Mara knew that the former slave was often ill-treated by the whites of Virginia City, so it surprised her that Faith Montgomery should defend life in town.

"If it weren't for the hospital and doctor, I have no doubt my Lucy would have died from the croup a long time ago. Then there's something to be said for having so many conveniences at your fingertips."

"We never lacked for anything when we lived on the ranch," Dianne said, her voice getting louder. "And while I realize we went from time to time into Madison before it burned to the ground, it wasn't like being in a town of this size."

"It could be worse," Charity said with a smile. "We could be in Bozeman where there are plenty more people and problems."

"Or in Butte," Faith said, "where I'm told every blade of grass has died and withered away because of the fouled air from the mines."

"Of course, things could always be worse," Dianne agreed.

Tension filled the air, making Mara uncomfortable. She'd been with these same people now for nearly five years. They were the closest people she had to real family. Her own father wanted nothing to do with her. He considered her a traitor—worse than that even. He considered her nothing . . . nothing at all. Her brothers were worthless, except for Joshua, but she hadn't heard from him in years. Then there was Elsa, her little sister. Mara longed to help Elsa escape the ranch.

The silence fell heavy, and Mara could no longer stand it. "I would like very much for you to pray for me," she said softly.

"Why, child, whatever is wrong?" Charity asked.

Mara smiled and paused in her stitching. "Nothing is wrong. I simply want you to pray that God will bring me a husband. I want very much to marry and have a family. The prospects here have been many, but not very well suited to my desires or needs. I know that God wants me to marry and raise a family, because He's put that longing in my heart."

"Marriage is a rough and rocky road," Dianne said with a sigh. "A great deal of hard work that requires every bit of hope and strength you can give it. Be sure you are ready for such things before jumping in."

"I saw my parents and their marriage, so I know all about the ugly side of it," Mara admitted. "They held no real love for each other. I'm actually not certain what ever brought them together. They seemed more miserable than happy for as long as I can remember."

"Marriage is pain," Ardith said softly. "Life is pain. You can't count on anything, and nothing ever turns out the way you hoped it might."

"But marriage is also joyous if it involves the right people. Don't tell me you didn't share happy times with Levi," Charity said, looking tenderly at Ardith. The girl had been like a daughter to the older woman, and Mara knew Charity's love for Ardith ran deep. Charity even acted as grandmother to Winona.

Ardith stopped her stitches and grew thoughtful. "There were good times, yes. But there were bad times. A miscarriage. A death. Those things, put in the balance against the good times, are much more overwhelming."

"Would you trade the time you had with Levi?" Faith asked softly.

Ardith picked up her needle again. "If it meant never experiencing this pain, then yes. Yes, I would wish I'd never met him."

Again the silence permeated, invading Mara's peace of mind. She wondered at these women. All had different outlooks on what marriage meant to them. The good and the bad, the difficult and simple, it all added up to leave its scars and memories for each one.

"I will pray that God will send you the right man," Charity said to Mara. "I will pray it right now." She stilled her hand and bowed her head. "Father, I ask for your mercy on this child. I ask for your blessing—the blessing of a husband and family. I ask that her heart might be strong enough to endure the things to which she will be called to face in marriage and motherhood. I pray too for Ardith. I ask that her pain might be lessened and taken away. That the joy of what you gave her in marriage to Levi might indeed be more precious . . . more lovely . . . more desirous than remembering the misery and sorrow. And I pray too for Dianne and Faith, that they might grow in love and hope through you and that their marriages might be strengthened and made joyful as they draw closer to you. Amen."

"Amen," Mara said with a smile as she met the older woman's gaze. "Thank you. I suppose some would say I want what I've never seen or experienced. Some might think me a wishful thinker or a dreamer, but I need to believe that love is out there for me."

Dianne nodded. "I'm sorry, Mara. I didn't mean to imply that it wasn't. I merely hoped to make you understand that it isn't all flowers and laughter. It's sometimes very hard. I just didn't want you to go into it unaware."

"I'm not a fool," Mara replied. "I know nothing in life comes easy. What happiness I've known, I've fought for. Even living here with you—knowing love and the real meaning of family for the first time in my life—has been so wondrous. But it certainly didn't come easy."

They were all looking at her now, and Mara suddenly felt very self-conscious. Still, she couldn't stop the flow of words. "All of my life I lived with lies. No one ever said what they really meant. They were hurtful and mean, self-seeking in every way. There were no birthday celebrations or Christmases like you know them. There was no compassion or sympathy. My father always said, 'Sympathy is for fools who wish only to continue in their misery.' I'm sure he felt compassion was the same.

"Living here with you, getting to know you and how much you care for each other . . . well, it's given me hope. Hope to believe that God might someday allow me the same privileges."

"And He will," Charity said softly. "I believe it."

"I believe it too," Faith declared, and Dianne nodded slowly.

Mara watched Ardith go back to her handwork. There would be no acknowledgment from her. The widow was still much too unwilling to give life another chance. Mara felt bad that Ardith should still mourn so deeply. She'd watched the sorrow separate Ardith from her child, and it made Mara uncomfortably aware of memories from her own past. Times when her own mother had hardened herself against her children. Mara vowed she'd never treat her loved ones in such an ill manner.

"So what kind of a man are you looking for?" Faith asked with a grin.

Mara was rather taken aback by the question. She thought for a moment, however, and offered an answer. "He would have to love God, first and foremost. He should be honest and trustworthy. Gentle, loving, good natured, good humored, and kind." She looked up and smiled. "I think those are the most important things."

"Those are all wonderful traits," Charity said. She put aside her sewing and got up to stretch.

"Why don't we rest and have some tea," Dianne suggested. She, too, put aside her needle and thread and got up. "I have some cake for us as well."

"If you'll excuse me," Ardith said, pushing back her chair. "I'm quite tired. I'd like to lie down before Winona comes home."

"Certainly. Take your rest," Charity encouraged. "When she gets back from playing with her friends, I'll see to her."

Mara watched the woman walk away. *It could happen to me*, she thought. *I could end up a widow—a mother without a father for my child. I could end up alone and bitter . . . hopeless.* The thought frightened her to the marrow of her bones. *I don't want to be like her. I don't want to feel such loss.*

"Are you coming?" Charity asked as she moved toward the kitchen.

Mara smiled and secured her needle. "Yes. I was just daydreaming."

"Keep dreaming. One day, when you least expect it, your dream may very well come true."

Mara laughed. "That's what I'm counting on. I just haven't found the right man to fit the dream," she said as a knock sounded at the front door. Mara looked up, realizing she was the reasonable one to answer it. "I'll see who it is."

"Then come join us in the kitchen," Charity said as she turned to go.

Mara smoothed down her blue calico print gown and touched her fingers to her dark hair. That morning she'd tied it back very simply with a blue ribbon that matched the color of the dress. It felt like everything was still in order. Without giving her conversation another thought, Mara opened the door only to be stopped in midsentence.

"Good after . . ." Her voice faded into silence.

The man standing on the other side of the door laughed heartily. She knew this man—not well, but nevertheless she knew him. She didn't remember him being quite so tall—or so handsome. She saw his twin, Morgan Chadwick, from time to time, but Zane was often absent.

"Welcome, Zane," she murmured and opened the screen door.

"How do you know it's Zane and not Morgan?" he asked.

"You two have your differences—if you know where to look." She immediately grew embarrassed at having answered so boldly.

He seemed amused. "Truly? You'll have to elaborate someday and tell me your secret for figuring us out." He peered past her into the house. "Is Dianne home?"

Mara could only nod. Up until now she hadn't found a single man who struck her fancy. Up until now she hadn't felt the flutter of butterflies in her stomach and the rapid palpitation of her heart at the sight of a man. Up until now, she'd never considered Zane Chadwick as a potential mate. But that had just changed.

CHAPTER 4

ON FRIDAY, WORD CAME FROM COLE'S mother that his father was near death. For Cole, the news was devastating.

"They've never seen the children," he said, shaking his head. "I just never thought to make that trip to take them back. I always figured there'd be plenty of time."

"It's too far to up and go on a whim," Dianne said, trying to comfort her husband. "Besides, we had the ranch to worry about."

"Yes, the ranch kept us busy. Maybe too busy."

Dianne cringed at the comment. Was this Cole's way of condemning their former home and way of life? "I think," she began, "we should see how close George and Jamie are to completing the cabin. Maybe once we're moved back onto the Diamond V, you could take the train to Kansas and see your father."

"Did you not understand what I read to you?" Cole asked, pushing back errant brown hair. "He's dying. He may already be dead."

"Which is exactly why you can't go getting

all excited about this and rushing into anything. He very well may be gone," she said,
trying her best to be sympathetic. Her biggest
fear at this moment was that Cole would use
this as an excuse to take her farther from the
home she loved. "I just don't think we should
act hastily. Why don't you send your mother a
telegram and get more information?"

"She can't afford to be telegraphing me
back, and I can't afford to waste any time,"
Cole replied. "If this were your father, would
you wait?"

She shook her head. He had a good point.
If it were her family member, she'd move
heaven and earth to be at their side. "No, of
course you're right. Why don't you go back
and—"

"We'll all go," Cole declared. "I want them
to see the children."

"But it's an awfully long trip."

"Not by train. The train will make it seem
easy. You'll see. I'll go wire for tickets and a
schedule. You get our clothes packed and
ready everyone for the trip," he said as he
moved to take up his hat. "We'll have one of
our freighters take us to the station at Dillon,
and we'll head south from there."

Dianne struggled to sound sympathetic. "I
know you want your mother and father to see
the children, but Cole, please hear me out.
This isn't the best situation to thrust upon the

children. They might not be able to handle this."

"Then we'll help them handle it," he said, looking her in the eye. "Dianne, I need you to help me through this." His voice was low and soft, yet there was an undertone of pleading.

She nodded and went to him. She felt bad for the way she'd treated him. They held each other close for several moments. Dianne couldn't begin to tell him the fear in her heart. What if they went back to Kansas and had to stay for an undetermined amount of time? What if they never came back to Montana?

She pushed the thoughts aside even as she pushed away from her husband. "I'll let the children know. I'm sure they'll be excited about their first train trip."

"Thank you." He turned to go. "I'll arrange everything so that we can leave immediately."

Dianne watched him leave, and her heart sank. She felt despair wash over her and threaten to strangle the breath right out of her body. It was bad enough to live in Virginia City, but at least it was only twenty-five miles from the ranch. Kansas was an entire world away. She blinked back tears and bit her lower lip to keep from crying.

The ranch is my home. I should be there now. In her mind she could see Koko and Susannah working around the house and grounds. She imagined Koko tending a garden and nurturing life out of the soil. She thought of Jamie, now nineteen years old. He had a real pride in working his father's land. He loved working with the cattle and the horses. Especially the horses.

"Mama, what's wrong?" Lia asked as she came into the room. "Are you sad?"

Dianne looked at her daughter and nodded. "Yes. Yes, I'm very sad. Grandfather Selby is very sick."

"Is he gonna go live with Jesus?"

"I don't know. He might," she said, struggling hard to quickly rein in her emotions.

The boys came bustling in behind Lia. "We saw a man with a bloody arm," Luke said in complete awe. John and Micah nodded. It was clear that they were as impressed as their brother had been.

"I have some news for you all," Dianne said, hoping to steer their minds away from the image of violence. "We're going on a long trip."

"Back to the ranch?" Luke asked.

Dianne saw the hopefulness in his eyes. She might have started crying for real were she not worried about her children. She wasn't often given to tears, and when she did cry, it upset the children.

"No, not back to the ranch," she explained. "Your grandfather Selby is sick, and your papa wants to go back and visit him in Kansas. Papa wants his mother and father to see you children and know what fine little people you are."

"How long will we be gone?" Micah questioned. "Who will take care of Barky?"

Dianne smiled down at her son. He was the only one of the boys with hair the same color as her own—a sort of golden honey wheat. Lia also had this same coloring, but on her brother it was most striking. "I don't know how long we'll be gone, but I'm sure Aunt Ardith will care for the dog. We're going to ride the train." She tried to make it all sound wonderful.

"The train!" the boys said in unison.

"A real train?" Luke asked.

"A real train," she assured. "Your papa has gone to arrange the tickets, and our job is to get ready. We must wash up the clothes and get them packed so that we can leave quickly. You must also clean your room."

The boys frowned. "Do we have to?" Micah asked.

"Yes. We can't leave without having everything in good order. Now you get to work, and Lia and I will start the wash water."

"We're going on the train!" Luke said as they turned to head for the stairs.

"Will it be loud?" John asked.

"Real loud," Luke confirmed as if he knew firsthand.

Dianne shook her head and smiled in spite of her broken heart. Her children were her life's blood. They never failed to make her day brighter.

By evening everyone in the house knew of the Selby trip. Cole had returned with a schedule and confirmation of tickets. They would leave for Dillon the next day. It seemed too soon to Dianne, but she said nothing.

"We'll be perfectly fine here. Don't worry about us," Mara said, trying to assure Dianne. "Ardith and I can manage everything. Besides, Faith and Malachi are just down the road and Charity and Ben are only a few doors down."

"That's right," Charity said. "In fact, if it makes you feel better, we can come and stay with the girls."

"I doubt anything would make me feel better," Dianne admitted. She glanced over her shoulder to see that Cole was caught up in giving Ben the details of their trip. "I don't want to leave."

Charity patted Dianne's hand. "There, there. By the time you get back, your cabin will be ready. You'll have a new home."

"It will be better than sitting around here," Ardith said. "I keep thinking about Mr. Stromgren's proposition to come to New York. Travel might well be the best thing for all of us."

Dianne attempted to hold her tongue but

couldn't. "Ardith, please don't go doing something foolish. Wait until I return before making any hasty decisions. Please . . . I need you to care for the house and for the dog."

"I can't promise. I have to do what's best for my family—just as you have to do what's best for yours."

"Never fear," Charity said in a soothing tone. "Ben and I will take care of everything should Ardith become determined to leave."

"Thank you." Dianne met the older woman's loving gaze and nearly broke into tears. Charity had long been a motherly companion, and sometimes she seemed to be the only one who unselfishly supported Dianne in her hour of need.

Zane came in about that time with a young man that Dianne thought looked very familiar. Mara jumped up and ran to the man. "Joshua!"

Dianne watched the brother-and-sister reunion with some interest. Would Mara leave them now? If so, that would leave Ardith and Winona all alone in the big house. Perhaps Dianne could use this as an excuse to forgo the trip to Kansas.

"I can't believe you're here," Mara said, her voice breaking with emotion. "I've missed you so much. Why didn't you write?"

"I couldn't for a while. There simply wasn't enough time. I was working one odd job after another and generally fell into bed every night more tired than the night before. After a while, I just lost track of time. Then when I found myself free enough to send word, I wasn't sure where you were. I wrote to Elsa, but apparently Pa burned those letters and kept her from seeing them."

"Sounds like Pa. So what are your plans?"

"I've come back to stay for a time. I don't know for sure where the Lord is leading me."

Mara turned to Dianne. "Could he have a room here with us?"

All thoughts of using the departure of Mara and her brother as an excuse fled Dianne's mind. "Of course." She looked to Cole. "That would be all right, wouldn't it?"

Cole got up and shook Joshua's hand most enthusiastically. "It would be more than all right. It would be answered prayer. You see, I was somewhat apprehensive about leaving your sister and Ardith here alone."

"Alone?" Joshua questioned, the confusion evident in his expression.

"I'm taking my family back to Kansas for a time. My father is dying, and we must leave immediately."

"I'm sorry to hear that, sir."

"Just call me Cole."

"I'm glad to be answered prayer," Joshua said with a smile. "I've been called a lot of things in the last forty-eight hours, but that's not been one of them."

"Well, be assured that's exactly what you are. You can be the man of the house while we're away. Now I won't feel any need to rush back."

Dianne opened her mouth in protest, then closed it quickly. Though she didn't want Cole to think her unfeeling about his concerns or needs, the situation absolutely filled her with terror.

No need to rush back.

No need to come back at all.

Morgan returned to Virginia City with his hunting group the day after Dianne and Cole departed for Kansas. Zane greeted his twin with a seemingly casual indifference, yet each man knew he was happy to be in the company of the other.

"So how did you do?" Zane questioned after the other men had gone to clean up and rest.

"We got buffalo. That was what they wanted," Morgan said with a shrug. He poured himself a cup of coffee and leaned back against the wall. "Mr. Stromgren couldn't stop talking about Ardith. When we were here before the hunt, he heard her play the piano, and now he thinks she should move back East. He's talking to her right now. He's convinced she's the kind of performer he needs to impress the high society of New York."

"That hardly seems likely." Zane poured his own coffee, then added a generous spoonful of sugar. Stirring slowly, he shook his head. "We know nothing about this man—at least nothing important."

Morgan grinned. "He's good with a rifle. Used to be a time that merited a man enough favor and, coupled with his horsemanship, could get him just about anything he wanted."

"I suppose he's a superior horseman."

Morgan laughed. "Good enough. I don't know, Zane. He appears to be well thought of. The other men in our party hailed him as well respected and recognized in certain social circles."

"Yes, but which social circles?"

"Do you suppose Ardith would listen to advice from us anyway? She seems to be used to making her own decisions and choices. And who can blame her after all she's been through?"

Zane couldn't argue with that. "She is independent, and I know she hasn't exactly had an easy life. Still, that doesn't mean this can't be yet another bad situation. I just wouldn't want her to get hurt."

"Neither would I," declared Christopher Stromgren as he bounded into the kitchen. "I was on the back stairs and couldn't help over-hearing your conversation. Forgive me for eavesdropping, but this matter is of the utmost importance. Your sister has a natural ability—a gift. It should be shared with the world."

"She has a young daughter," Zane said, a bit uncomfortable with the man's brazen temperament. "What do you propose she do with Winona while she's impressing the world?"

"I was told that the girl could stay here with family until Ardith was established. There's no reason the child couldn't join us at some future time."

"Join *us*? That makes it sound awfully cozy." Zane narrowed his eyes and stared the stranger down. "I don't know you, Mister, and yet you want me to accept your proposition to take my sister away from her home and child. I'm not sure exactly what arrangements you're suggesting, but it doesn't set well with me."

"You misjudge me, sir. I'm certainly no molester of women. I have only the utmost regard for the weaker sex. Part of the reason I find your sister's talent so fascinating is that it stems from such a pure and unspoiled heart. She is a breath of fresh air. Unassuming and lovely in her simplicity."

It was Morgan's turn to jump in. "Is that a nice way of saying she'll impress your uppity society folk with her low-scale way of life?"

"Not at all." Stromgren seemed indignant.

His face flushed to a red only a few shades lighter than his hair. "You both seem to believe it my desire to make sport of your sister, while in truth I want only to honor her and bring her the fame and glory she deserves."

"What's all this about?" Ardith asked as she joined them in the kitchen. "I could hear you all the way down the hall."

"Then you know this conversation is about you and whether you should go to New York," Zane said.

Ardith's features hardened. "Well, that's really for me to decide, now, isn't it?"

"I didn't suggest it wasn't. I merely questioned the reasonability of it and the responsibilities you already have to your daughter."

"Winona is strong—like me. She's also capable of understanding change. She's endured a great deal of change in her life." Ardith turned to Stromgren. "Why don't you come into the parlor and I'll play for you. I have some great new pieces to show you."

"Wonderful!"

They turned to go, with Stromgren leading the way. Ardith paused at the doorway. "Stay out of this. This is my life, and I won't have anyone interfering with my decisions."

The twins stood silent for a moment after she'd gone. Zane shook his head. "She can sure get herself all worked up. Just like Ma used to do."

"I was thinking the same thing." Morgan put down his cup. "Look, I wanted to let you know that I'll be back fairly soon. I'm taking a man to the Idaho Territory to hunt mountain goat. His name is Roosevelt. Theodore Roosevelt. He's a rich man from New York, but lately he's lived over Dakota way. He has a ranch there."

"Ah, one of those city fellows playing on the frontier?"

"No, not as much as you might think. He really enjoys getting his hands dirty. I liked him. I think you will too. He's very excited at the prospect of hunting the mountain goat. Guess he's quite the sportsman."

"Well," Zane said, putting his cup aside, "I doubt I'll be here. I need to get back to Butte. I've been working to line up some timber for Marcus Daly, but as soon as that's settled I need to return. If you're coming back through that way, why don't you look me up?"

"Sounds good," Morgan admitted.

"Hello," Mara Lawrence said as she came into the kitchen. She struggled to hoist a basket filled with shopping goods to the table.

Zane came immediately to her side and took the basket. "Hello, yourself." He smiled at her, thinking she was about the prettiest girl he'd ever known. "Looks like you bought out the mercantile."

"I heard that you liked berry pie. We were

out of lard and a few other things, so I thought I'd do the shopping and then get your pie started." She swirled away from him in a blush of pink fabric. Pausing momentarily, she looked over her shoulder and smiled.

Zane looked at her oddly. Was she flirting with him? He was much too old for her to consider in such a way, but it seemed that's what she was doing. He looked to Morgan as if for confirmation, but his twin only laughed and headed out the back door.

"Why don't you sit here and talk to me while I put together the dough?" Mara called as she pulled a bowl from the cupboard.

Zane felt a sudden flush of heat under his collar. "I . . . ah . . . I have things to tend to, but thanks . . . ah . . . just the same."

She placed the bowl on the counter. "Why, Zane Chadwick. You sound positively terrified. Surely you aren't afraid of socializing with me."

He swallowed hard. He wasn't about to let her think him afraid, but in truth, he was. "I hardly think we have anything to be socializing about. You'd be better off talking to one of my sisters."

Mara leaned back against the counter. "But it's you I want . . . to talk with."

For a moment Zane lost himself in her stare. She had beautiful brown eyes trimmed in dark lashes. Her cheeks were rosy and her lips . . . He shook himself from such thinking. "I . . . uh . . . I gotta go." He couldn't leave fast enough.

He heard her giggle as the screen door slammed behind him.

What was that Lawrence woman up to?

———————

"I'm glad you're at least open to the idea of coming to New York," Christopher Stromgren said as he walked with Ardith.

"I'm open to whatever will be most beneficial to myself . . . and to Winona."

"She's a beautiful little girl."

"She is that."

"I notice some darker . . . features." His voice was hesitant, as if prodding a wound gently.

"She's half Sioux," Ardith said without hesitating. She might as well confess all of her skeletons. "I was raped by a Sioux warrior, one of the men at Little Big Horn. Does that put an end to our relationship and possible business venture, Mr. Stromgren?" She stopped and stared at him hard.

Though his eyes widened in surprise at her bold statement, he said, "Not at all. If anything, it gives me an even higher regard for you. How terrible that you should have borne such misery at the hands of savage captors. How did you come to be with them?"

Ardith sighed and began walking again. "It really isn't relevant. It is sufficient that you understand that it happened. I wouldn't wish for the information to come out later and then shame you and your company."

"That kind of thing might only serve to bring in bigger crowds. Curiosity seekers, if you would. Custer's battle still works audiences into a fervor. It might be quite interesting to use that as a billing tool."

"No. I don't want to be seen as such," Ardith declared. "I have lived with that since being rescued. People have been kind but also guarded and uncomfortable. I would much rather be seen for my ability to make music."

"But of course," he said, seeming shocked that she would suppose it to be otherwise.

"If we cannot keep my secret, then I would rather not consider this proposition any further."

"My dear Mrs. Sperry, you have nothing to fear from me. My lips will be as silent as the grave concerning your past."

CHAPTER 5

ARDITH WAS UNCOMFORTABLE WITH THE relative emptiness of the house after Morgan moved on with his travelers and Zane headed back to Butte. She thought constantly of Christopher Stromgren and his ideas for promoting her piano talents. She wondered if it were the best choice for her life.

Living in Montana didn't seem to be the best for her. She'd known nothing but misery in Montana. She finished making her bed and continued to brood.

If I go to New York, she thought, *I cannot take Winona.* The child was precious to her, but she was also testing Ardith's patience with painful questions and memories of Levi.

Levi. She couldn't even speak his name aloud. She had been so convinced that theirs was a love that would last a lifetime. And it was. She just didn't count on Levi's lifetime being so short.

She plumped the pillows and stacked them neatly at the head of the bed. Her anger toward God kindled with new intensity. *If you hadn't taken him from me, I might be happy now. I wouldn't have to consider going to New York.* Yet it wasn't an unpleasant contemplation. Ardith had listened to Stromgren's stories of the city that seemingly never slept. She found it amazing to hear of parties that would last well into the wee hours of the morning. And not parties for the riff-raff or hoodlums, but fashionable society. Upper-crust matrons and their powerful husbands. These were the people, Stromgren related, who made the rules of society. Ardith found it all quite fascinating.

She opened the door and slipped downstairs, hoping that no one would come to pester her. When breakfast was over she had hurried upstairs to avoid any discussions with Mara and her brother Joshua. But she had promised to do the breakfast dishes after she tidied her room, and now that task lay before her.

With Dianne and her family gone, it was like a great silence engulfed the house, and yet it wasn't quiet at all. She could hear Winona in the front room, chattering at a rapid pace with someone. Probably Mara. Ardith's daughter found it curious that Mara was sewing a wedding dress. Ardith thought it merely silly.

Ardith noted that all of the dishes had been washed. Apparently Mara thought to do her the favor, but frankly Ardith would have rather had the work to keep her mind occupied.

"Can I be of help?" Joshua asked as he came into the kitchen.

Ardith had her back to him and scowled. Why couldn't he leave her alone? He seemed compelled to practice the religion he felt was so important. But frankly, his counsel was not something she desired. Yet she knew he'd offer it.

"I thought maybe you'd like to talk about Mr. Stromgren's proposition. I sensed that your brothers were very opposed to your leaving. Perhaps there is some merit in their concerns."

She turned to face him. "I think there is better merit in minding your own business."

"Perhaps your thoughts are clouded on the matter and it would help to discuss it with someone," he offered.

He was hardly more than a boy at twenty-two. Ten years her junior. Who was he to suggest she didn't know her own mind?

"I'm merely thinking of your daughter," Joshua said as he pressed his point home. "She needs you here with her. Not in New York City. Do you even have any idea what that town is like? I do. I've been there."

"Good for you," Ardith said, finally losing her patience. "I suggest you go back there or leave me alone. Either way, I don't want to hear any more about this. You are hardly the one to be giving me advice." She picked up a damp dish towel and started to fold it.

He frowned. "What do you mean by that?"

"You're barely a man. I had lived a hundred lifetimes by the time I was your age." She held his gaze with a hard stare of her own. "You have no idea what I am capable of doing or not doing."

"Maybe not, but I know that little girl. She spends hours each day with me because you won't!" Joshua said sternly.

He came to where Ardith stood, dish towel in hand. She was glad she didn't have hold of a plate or she might have busted it over his head. "How dare you!" She leaned forward until she was nearly nose to nose with the man. "You aren't even a father. You know nothing about parenting."

"I'm beginning to wonder if you do."

She had never been treated in such a manner. Levi had always been so careful and tender with her, and even Dianne avoided upsetting her. Ardith's throat ached in that awful way it often did when she couldn't cry and she couldn't calm herself. She tried to speak but the words stayed lodged deep inside.

"Look," Joshua began, his tone more gentle, "I just don't want you to make a mistake and throw away the most important person in your life. If you go away, things will never be the same between you two."

Still she could say nothing. She backed

away, twisting the towel in her hands. She wanted to run and leave this conversation, but Joshua stood between her and any means of exit.

"Winona talks to me about her father," he said. "She misses him. She wants to know that she'll see him again. She wants to know that you won't die and leave her too. She has a million questions to ask you, but you avoid her. Why?"

"Because she has a million questions." Ardith barely squeaked out the words. She looked to the towel and realized she'd nearly knotted it in her frustration.

He nodded and stepped back. "I know you're struggling. I can see that you're still in pain, even after all these years, but you can't make the pain go away by ignoring your child."

Ardith regained a bit of her composure. "You're twenty-two years old. You've spent the last few years studying to become a pastor. You've been preaching God's Word and saving souls. I suppose it's natural that you think you have all the answers—that you can save me too."

"Only Jesus can do that," he said with a smile. "I can't be your savior or Winona's."

"I'm glad you realize that. I feel bad that I cannot answer Winona's questions or comfort her. However, do not think to give her false hope or to put ideas in her head that might be better avoided."

"Ideas?" he asked. "What ideas are you talking about?"

She cast the towel to the counter. "Ideas about replacing Levi. She's looking for another father—for someone to fill the void in her heart. I'm not. I don't want another husband, and I certainly wouldn't consider a child such as you even if I were."

Joshua's mouth dropped open, clearly stunned by her words. Ardith took that opportunity to push past him and run for the sanctuary of her bedroom. In her heart she harbored bitterness toward Joshua for his interference . . . and Levi for his desertion. But most of all, she reserved her rage for God—the one who could have kept it all from going so terribly wrong.

———

The trip to Kansas hadn't been an easy one. The boys constantly wanted to roam the train and talk to everyone on board. John, especially, seemed prone to getting into trouble, while Luke and Micah worked just as hard to keep him under control. Lia found train travel made her sick to her stomach, which in turn made her tired and grumpy. Between chasing after her sons and cleaning up after

Lia, Dianne was ready to forget the entire trip and return home.

Of course, I was ready to do that before we ever set out, she reminded herself as she rocked Lia in her arms. The train lurched and bounced as it made its way ever closer to Topeka. They were supposed to be in the city limits very soon. After that, the conductor assured them it would only be another few minutes before they could exit the train. Dianne sighed. It couldn't come soon enough.

Cole had barely talked to her during the trip. His mind was clearly preoccupied with what he would find in Kansas. She knew he worried that his father would already be dead—that he'd have no chance to show him the children or to say good-bye. She knew, too, that Cole worried about his mother. He'd already mentioned not knowing what she would do after his father passed on. Dianne had suggested she move to the Diamond V, but Cole had quickly put that idea aside, reminding her that if their old house were still standing that might very well work, but his mother couldn't live in a rustic cabin.

She had then suggested his mother could live in the Virginia City house when they moved back to the ranch. Cole hadn't responded immediately to this, and she thought for several miles that the idea merited some positive reaction. Then he up and declared that his mother would never want to leave his sisters and be separated from her grandchildren.

Dianne didn't remind him that their children were her grandchildren as well. She simply didn't care enough to press the issue. She was tired and dirty and more than ready to leave the train.

"Look, Mama, the city!" Luke declared, his nose pressed to the glass. They'd had the window open earlier only to find the ashes from the smokestacks more unbearable than the humid heat.

"I see it," Dianne said, trying hard to match the excitement of her ten-year-old son. Everything was an adventure to him, while to her it was just one more reminder that she was very far from home.

"Do you see it, Pa?" Micah questioned.

Cole nodded. "I do."

Lia stirred in Dianne's arms. "Are we there yet?"

"Yes," she assured, smoothing back her daughter's damp hair. "We'll be getting off any minute."

"And then we'll see Grandma and Grandpa Selby, right?" Luke asked.

"Grandma and Grandpa Selby," John parroted.

Dianne thought Cole might respond, but he just turned within himself and frowned.

"Yes, but remember, Grandpa is very sick," she told them.

The boys nodded solemnly. Dianne encouraged Lia to sit up. "We're nearly there. Let me fix your hair."

"I wired Ma that we'd rent a team and buggy," Cole said as though he'd not already told this to Dianne.

"I think that's a wise choice," she murmured. Dianne sensed a growing distance between her and her husband. She knew she was mostly responsible for it, but now it seemed Cole was adding to it.

"I'm sure they can extend the lease for as long as we need," he said.

Dianne supposed it was his way of warning her that they might be here for some time, but she refused to let herself consider that.

With Lia's ribbon readjusted, Dianne helped her daughter onto the seat, then turned to her husband. "I know you're worried about what you'll find, but please remember that I love you and I'm here by your side."

Cole patted her hand. It was really the first sign of affection he'd given since their trip began. "I know. I know this is hard for you as well. I'm grateful that you're here."

Dianne cherished the moment and in an uncharacteristic show, she leaned over and kissed Cole on the cheek. A matronly woman from across the aisle gave a loud "harrumph" at this public display, causing Dianne to almost giggle out loud. If a woman nearing forty, mother to four children, couldn't give her husband a little kiss on a train without raising eyebrows, Dianne didn't know what the world was coming to.

Still, all across the western mountains and prairies, Dianne had seen the world civilize itself more and more. She saw the fancy traveling suits of other women. Heard the refined speech of a couple's conversation. She knew her children were considered to be complete urchins, with one woman even suggesting Dianne give them a healthy dose of laudanum to ease the journey for all.

I'm not going to like this end of the world, she thought with a sigh.

———

"It looks just like I remember," Cole said as they drove into the farmyard. "Pa's done a good job of keeping it up."

"It's very nice," Dianne admitted. "I can't say that I like this humidity, though." Her clothes felt as though they were sticking to her body, and the air was so heavy that she wondered if she'd ever be able to draw a decent breath.

"Do they have a dog?" Luke asked, hanging over the side of the open buggy.

"Yes, at least they did when I lived here. He

was a very nice dog too. I'm sure you'll have fun with him."

"Does he look like Barky?"

Dianne smiled. The family's collie had been dubbed Barky Dog-dog by Luke when both were very young. The name had stuck and since been revised to just "Barky."

"No, he's not a collie like Barky. He's big and black," Cole said as a dog came bounding off the porch, barking up a storm. He wasn't black, however, but rather a mottled mixture of brown, white, and gold.

A woman came out onto the porch and called to the animal. "Jake! Jake, come!"

The dog reluctantly heeded his mistress's call.

"Ma!" Cole stopped the horses and jumped down from the buggy without even setting the brake.

Dianne quickly corrected this problem, then turned to her children. "Be on your best behavior. It's important that you mind your manners, as Grandpa's sickness has made it hard on everyone. He might even be with Jesus now, and that will make Papa very sad."

The children all nodded, wide-eyed and obviously intrigued by their new circumstance and surroundings. Dianne managed to descend from the buggy without help, then reached up to take hold of Lia. The boys bounded out without hesitation, seeming to enjoy every moment of their adventure.

Dianne looked to see that Cole was listening to his mother. The woman seemed to be talking in a rapid but hushed voice. Whether she did this because she didn't want Dianne and the children to overhear or because this was her nature, Dianne had no idea. There was nothing here that she knew—nothing that she understood.

Dianne cautiously approached the porch with her children, wondering if she should have waited in the buggy. Cole's mother said something, then stepped back from her son. Cole turned.

"Dianne, this is my mother, Mary Selby. Ma, this is my wife, Dianne, and our children." He noted each one, telling their names and ages.

Mary Selby was not a handsome woman. She was rather stern faced and severe, in fact. Dianne thought she might look less so if she were to arrange her hair differently. Her gray hair had been pulled back tightly and arranged into a no-nonsense type of bun that rejected any sign of an escaping wisp.

"Hello, Mrs. Selby. I'm so glad we could finally meet." Dianne tried to sound pleasant without making it seem joyous. After all, the circumstances were not what anyone would have wanted.

"Pity you didn't come when Hallam was

well," Mary said in her first greeting.

Dianne was uncertain what to say, so she said nothing. She was tired, hot, and sticky and longed only for a bath. She knew Lia would also feel better if given a chance to bathe and cool off. Still, Dianne didn't want to set the tone for their visit by making demands.

"Ma was telling me that Pa is barely holding on. The doctor says it won't be long. We got here just in time."

"What can we do?" Dianne asked.

"There's nothing *you* can do!" Cole's mother snapped. "He wants to see his son."

Dianne tried not to appear shocked. "I merely wondered if we might help with the housework or cooking—maybe the laundry and yard work, so that you would be freed up to sit with your husband."

Mary sneered. "I don't expect you would know much about farm life."

"I doubt it's that different from ranch life," Dianne countered, unable to hold her tongue. "And laundry is pretty much laundry wherever you go." She smiled, hoping to soften the retort.

"Your wife is rude," Mary told Cole without even attempting to hide her comment.

Dianne bristled. "My suggestions were not meant to be rude but rather to offer insight. I'm very capable of helping out."

"I don't need your help. I have daughters

for that. Just keep your children out from underfoot." With that she turned and opened the door. "You know where his room is," she told Cole. "You should go to him immediately. The others can wait in the front room."

Cole seemed to remember his family's exhaustion, much to Dianne's surprise. "Do you have room for us here, or should I take them back to a hotel in town?"

Mary looked back at Dianne and the children and frowned. It was almost as if Dianne could read the woman's mind. She would obviously like it if Dianne and the children were not a part of the arrangement at all. *Well,* she thought, *at least there we agree. I wish I were home working with the horses and checking the new calves.*

"I have room. You needn't take them into town. Although the children mustn't be noisy and disturb your father."

"We understand," Cole replied. "I've already told the children they must be on their best behavior. Why don't I get our bags and you can show us to our rooms. Then Dianne can settle the children and I can see Pa."

Mary seemed to consider this for a moment, then reluctantly said, "Very well."

"Go ahead," Cole told Dianne. "I'll get our things and find the way. Come on boys, you help me."

Mary gathered her dark brown skirt and

trudged up the stairs. Dianne could feel the woman's disdain but had no idea why she should so hate her daughter-in-law and grand-children. When they reached the top of the stairs, Mary turned abruptly to the left. Dianne and Lia followed in silence.

Without ceremony, Mary opened the door to a room. "You and Cole will be in here." The room was small but serviceable and clean. "Thank you, it looks lovely," Dianne said softly.

Mary didn't respond but instead crossed the hall and opened another door. "The children can stay here."

Dianne looked inside. There were two small beds and a dresser, but little more. The room smelled musty, as if it hadn't been aired in some time. The shades were pulled, making it dark and dingy. Dianne tried not to be upset by the sight. "Thank you. It should serve us well."

"I would hope so," Mary snapped.

"It's dark," Lia said, peeking from behind her mother's skirt.

Mary was clearly not pleased with the comment. "There's light enough."

Dianne decided she couldn't make the woman any more angry, so she braved a request. "Might we get some water for cleaning up?"

"The room is perfectly clean," Mary said,

her disgust with them evident.

Dianne smiled. "I didn't mean for the room. It's quite in order. I meant so that the children and I could wash up. We've been on the train for some days, and we're very dirty and hot."

"There's a pump out the back door. A bucket too. You're welcome to fetch water." The words seemed to pain Mary to even speak them. "There's a tub on the back porch if you feel the need for a bath. You should know, however, we're suffering a drought and water is a precious commodity. We aren't fancy folk, and I won't tolerate you bathing every day."

Dianne thought to push aside propriety and ask Mary why she was treating her so ill, but thoughts of Hallam dying held Dianne in check. She wouldn't be herself if Cole were as sick, so she could hardly expect this woman to be happy and gracious.

"Thank you, Mrs. Selby," she said as Cole and the boys started up the stairs with the baggage. "We'll be mindful of the water."

Dianne showed the boys where to put their things. "You boys will share this room with your sister." She could see that Mary was speaking again to her son. No doubt complaining about Dianne's desire for water. Dianne was most relieved when the woman departed. Cole took their bags to the room across the hall, leaving Dianne alone with the children.

"It's hot in here," Micah said softly. "And smelly."

"And dark," Lia added.

Dianne raised the shade. "There, see. It's not so dark. And we'll put up the window and let the breeze come in. That will help with the heat." She pulled on the window until it complied.

"You put away your things, and then we'll fetch some water and clean ourselves up. It will soon be lunchtime, and we don't want to be dirty."

She left the children to their chores and went to find Cole. He had deposited the bags but was nowhere to be found. No doubt he'd gone to see his father. Dianne sighed and sat down on the bed. There was no way this was going to be easy. She sighed again and leaned against the iron footrail.

"Are you all right, Mama?" Lia asked as she came into the room.

Dianne lifted her face and smiled. "I'm just tired, sweetheart. Weary of the road we've been on."

CHAPTER 6

"I HAD NO IDEA THAT YOU WERE SICK," Cole told his father. He was shocked at the emaciated appearance of the man. Cole glanced around the darkened room. It depressed his spirit. There hung a smell of death that made him shudder and wish that he could run away from all of it. "You should have let me know sooner."

"Came on kind of sudden-like," Hallam told him. "Doctor says it started with my heart and now other parts of my body are wearing out."

Cole nodded and pulled his chair closer to the bed. It was difficult to understand his father's raspy words. "And there's nothing to be done?"

Cole's father closed his eyes momentarily, then opened them. "There's plenty that needs to be attended to, but nothing can be done for me. I'm glad you came. I've been wanting to talk to you about the farm."

"What about it?" Cole figured his father would ask him to sell the place.

"I'd like you to take it over. I'm leaving it to you in my will."

Cole knew his face registered surprise. "You want me to run the farm?"

"It would be a real blessing to me to know that your mother wouldn't have to worry about anything. We've had help from the neighbor in harvesting, but we can't expect that to continue." Hallam began to cough. Cole reached for a glass of water at his bedside and helped his father to sit up enough to drink. The coughing subsided, but it was clear his father was weak—in no condition for debates about what needed to be done with the farm.

"When you feel up to it," Cole said, replacing the glass on the nightstand, "I'd like you to meet my children and wife. I'm mighty proud of all of them."

"I'd like that," his father acknowledged.

They were silent for several minutes. Cole wiped sweat from his brow, as the heat of the room seemed unbearable. "Are you too warm?" he asked his father, hoping for an excuse to open a window.

"No. I'm cold all the time. Doctor says it's because my heart isn't working properly." There came another silence, but then Hallam pressed the issue of the farm again. "I need you here, son. It's a good farm. Good ground. You can grow most anything in river bottom land. It's what I've always wanted," he explained. "To leave you something of value—something of me."

Cole was torn. Dianne would never approve of living in Kansas. She was already longing for the mountains. She hadn't said as much, but he knew it nevertheless. "I'll think on it, Pa, but you need to remember, I have a ranch to run."

"That's your wife's property, isn't it? I'd be giving you this as an inheritance. It'd be yours."

Cole hadn't expected his father to hit the one nerve in him that kept him from complete happiness in Montana. He constantly felt as though he were tending other people's land and property. At least the freighting business had been his own, and it had done well. He was proud of his work there. Of course, he'd been proud of his work at the ranch too, but now that George and Koko were back at the Diamond V, and Koko's son, Jamie, was nearly a man, it seemed only fair to let them run the ranch. Of course, he knew Dianne didn't see it that way.

She realized her uncle's ranch would have belonged in full to Koko and her children had they not been part Blackfoot, but Cole knew too that the land had won her over. Dianne's heart was in Montana. It wasn't here in Kansas, nor was it likely to be.

"I'll think on it, Pa" was all Cole could

manage. He wanted to offer the old man comfort in his time of sickness, but he couldn't lie to him. There would be no easy way to convince Dianne to live here—even if Cole desired it for himself.

"Your ma isn't doing all that well. She isn't dealing with my sickness as I'd hoped. She's afraid, and I can't die in peace knowing that she's fearing her future."

"She'll always have a home with me; you know that."

"But her home is here. I moved her from one place to another all our married life. I want her to have a place to call home. A place she can grow old in. Cordelia and Laurel are both here with the grandchildren. She won't want to leave them."

"Maybe she could live with one of them— or else they could come here."

Hallam shook his head. "I wouldn't count on that."

"Pa," Cole pleaded, "I have a family. Dianne loves Montana, and her family and friends are there. I love it there too. I can't say that I would easily trade it for Kansas."

"Please consider this for me. I know I haven't always been the best father, but now I finally have something to leave you—an inheritance." His words were growing more faint.

"You rest now, Pa. We can talk more about this later." Cole leaned over and pulled the covers up around his father's shoulders. "I'll see you tomorrow."

That night Cole couldn't talk to Dianne about the conversation he'd had with his father. He knew she would be upset, and because Cole had had so little time to process the request and consider the situation, he decided not to bring it up yet.

The next day seemed no easier, as his mother commanded his attention early in the day and then he went to spend time with his father. By the time he was alone with Dianne the following evening, it was late and the heat had made them both irritable.

"I've hardly seen you since we've arrived," Dianne commented as she ran a damp cloth over her neck and face.

"It's been difficult." Cole sat on the edge of the bed and wondered how to best explain his father's desires. "I've wanted to talk to you, however. My father has been asking me to do something for him."

She stopped washing. "What does he want?"

He drew a deep breath. "He wants me to take over the farm. To inherit it upon his death and care for my mother."

She held his gaze. "And what did you tell him?"

"I reminded him that I had established

myself in Montana—that we were happy there."

She sighed. "Well, I'm grateful for that."

He shook his head. "He needs me, Dianne. My mother needs me too. I'm not sure what's to be done."

"You can't be seriously considering his request."

"I must. This is my family."

"The children and I are your family."

"Yes, but I can hardly leave my mother without help. I can't turn away from them now in their hour of need."

Dianne walked slowly to the opposite side of the bed, forcing Cole to turn if he wanted to continue the conversation face to face. She pushed aside the covers and sat down with her back against the pillows. "I knew you'd find another reason to keep me from the ranch."

He stiffened. "This isn't about that. It's not about you or the ranch."

She nodded, tears streaming down her cheeks. "That much is evident."

Cole immediately felt bad for his words. "Dianne, you know that I love you. You know that I want to make you happy. I'm sorry we haven't moved back to the ranch, but I wanted and needed things to be in order before we returned. I didn't want you and the children living like you did when you first came to the territory."

"Don't you understand?" Dianne questioned, looking to him with such an expression of sorrow that Cole longed to take her into his arms. "I'd rather live in a tent in the middle of the Diamond V than live in a palace here in Kansas. I'd rather have nothing more than a ranch shack in which to raise my children than to endure this place with its heat and humidity and hate. Can't you see how hard it is for Lia? She's not well. She can scarcely breathe properly. She coughs all the time now, and it's only been a couple days."

"She's probably just caught a cold," he replied. "If it worsens we'll take her to the doctor. Look, I'm sorry this is difficult. It's hardly easy on me."

She wiped her tears with the back of her hand and turned to him. "I know, and I'm sorry. I've lost my father and mother—I understand what loss is and how it devastates and clouds one's judgment."

"And you think my judgment is clouded?"

"I think you've lost sight of what our dreams were."

"Maybe I've just lost sight of what *your* dreams were. Maybe I'm only now finding out what mine are." He hadn't intended to take on the harsh tone, but he'd had more than he wanted of this conversation. "Look, it's hot and I'm tired. I want to go to sleep. We can talk more about this tomorrow."

Dianne rolled over on her side. "Just so long as you realize one thing. I cannot live here. I won't stay here."

Cole lay awake for a long time after that. He wasn't sure if it was her words or the heat that caused his stomach to sour, but he felt sick for most of the night. Dianne wouldn't stay here, and his mother wouldn't leave. How was he supposed to meet the needs of both women without hurting one or the other?

Lord, this won't be easily solved, he prayed. *Please give me wisdom.*

The days went by so slowly that Dianne thought she could actually count time in the number of labored breaths she drew. The air seemed so thick that she could scarcely fill her lungs enough, and Lia had developed a chronic cough. Dianne told herself it would be all right—that she could endure this short time for Cole's sake. But nothing was right about this place.

Standing over a tub of dirty laundry, Dianne was hard pressed to find anything good or uplifting about her circumstance. She tried to pray, even as she worked, but the words wouldn't come. Lia was hardly herself, sitting on a blanket nearby. She didn't want to play or even help, as she often begged to do at home in Montana. The boys seemed the least affected. They were running in circles around the yard, playing with Jake and enjoying the day. Dianne was at least grateful that they were happy.

"Mama, when can we go home?" Lia asked.

Dianne straightened. "I don't know. Papa needs to be here for a little while to help Grandma and Grandpa Selby. When things are better, we can go back to Montana."

Lia sighed and picked up her doll. Dianne felt the same hopelessness that seemed to engulf her child. They weren't needed here. They weren't even liked. It was clear that Mary Selby wished Dianne and her children had never come. Dianne tried to talk to Cole about it, but he told her it was all her imagination, that his mother was simply worried about her husband.

Dianne could understand that, but it didn't make her treatment any easier to bear. Cole's sisters were an entirely different matter. Laurel had arrived that morning, bringing her spoiled daughters. Josephine, who was sixteen, made it quite clear that she wanted nothing to do with her rowdy cousins. She sneered down her nose at the boys and rudely questioned why Dianne would allow Lia to run around half dressed. Dianne explained that they were unaccustomed to the heat, but it didn't matter to Josephine or her mother. Laurel's other three daughters were equally obnoxious, even laughing at Dianne's gown and asking if people in Montana didn't care about fashion. Dianne told them in a clipped tone that people in Montana worked hard to stay alive and didn't have time for frippery.

Perhaps the thing that bothered Dianne the most was the girls' closeness to Mary Selby. They clearly ruled the roost and had their grandmother's affection. It made Dianne sad for her own children, who immediately noted the change in their grandmother. Mary Selby fussed and doted on each of the girls, clearly ignoring Dianne's children.

Cordelia and her two girls arrived about an hour after Laurel. Eva, age ten, seemed interested in the boys, but Cordelia quickly put an end to that. She forced Eva and her little sister, Lydia, to remain with Laurel's daughters and have nothing to do with Dianne's children. In fact, after the briefest of introductions to Cordelia, Dianne was clearly dismissed by Mary Selby.

"I'm sure you have things to occupy your time," Mary had stated curtly.

It was then that Dianne had gathered her brood, along with the laundry, and headed outdoors. Dianne had remained outside all morning, hoping fervently that Cole's sisters would leave before lunchtime.

"Mama, that mean lady is coming," Lia suddenly warned.

Dianne looked up to see Cordelia making her way across the yard. "You boys are entirely too noisy. Stop playing with that dog at once and go sit down."

Dianne watched the boys freeze in their place, shocked that anyone should make these demands. Deciding it was time to establish some control, Dianne went to Cordelia. "If you have a problem with my children, come to me, not to them."

Cordelia was only a few years Dianne's junior, but she clearly thought herself superior in this situation. She touched a gloved hand to her chest as if surprised by Dianne's attitude.

"I'm only thinking of my father."

"Your father's room is on the front side of the house. We are here in the backyard, clearly away from the house. I doubt seriously the noise can even be heard in the kitchen, much less in his room."

"You are just as rude as Mother described you."

"If telling the truth or standing up for one's family is rude, then yes, I'm very rude. I don't know what I've done to put you or your mother in such ill tempers, but I won't let you take it out on my children."

"Your boys are positively heathens. They need discipline."

"They need to be back home," Dianne snapped.

"Well, that isn't going to happen now, so you'd best learn to deal with them. We're civilized here, and their lack of manners won't be easily tolerated."

Dianne felt a chill for the first time since arriving in Kansas. "I'm uncertain as to the manners and behaviors of this part of the country, but treating people as though they are no better than dirt to be swept aside is considered rude and ill mannered where I come from. You walk around here with your airs and attitudes, your sister and children just as uppity as you are, and yet you condemn my family?"

Dianne gave her no time to respond. "I came here to support my husband in his time of grief and have been treated with nothing but disdain since setting foot on this property. Cole wanted to show off his children—children that he is very proud of, I might add. And those same children have been treated with contempt such as I would not impose upon a dog."

Cordelia sneered. "You weren't needed here. Cole was. He still is and always will be. Our mother needs him to take over this farm and to care for her."

"Cole has a place to run—a ranch in Montana. He has a wife and children to whom he's now obligated," Dianne countered. "This farm is not his home."

"Don't be so sure. Our father has already asked him to stay and take it over once he's gone."

"Yes, I know that. Cole discussed the matter with me and we came to the conclusion that such a thing simply wouldn't work. We have a home in Montana, and that's where we'll return after the funeral."

Cordelia seemed taken aback by this news. "You are a selfish woman. Taking a man away from his grieving mother."

"She has you and Laurel to see to her needs. She has your children and Laurel's and clearly wants nothing to do with mine." By now the boys had gathered around their mother as if to protect her from Cordelia's barbs. Dianne didn't wish for them to be a part of this, however.

"Boys, take Lia to the pump and clean up for dinner." They immediately did as they were told, much to her relief.

Cordelia seemed to be surprised by this but said nothing. Dianne, however, had plenty she wanted to say now that her children were out of earshot. Leaning toward Cole's sister, she put aside propriety.

"Cole is my husband, and he knows his responsibility to his own family comes first. I won't allow you, your sister, or your mother to interfere with that. We aren't staying here in Kansas, and you might as well get used to it."

Cole rounded the milk house just as Dianne finished speaking. To her surprise, Cordelia burst into tears and ran to her brother.

"Your wife is so cruel!" She threw herself into Cole's arms.

"What's this all about?" he questioned.

Dianne opened her mouth to speak, but Cordelia immediately commanded the situation. "She's been berating me for mentioning how grateful we were that you were here and how we were hoping that you would stay on to comfort Mother after Father passes on. She feels we're trying to make unfair demands on you."

Cole cast an accusing glance at Dianne.

"I've merely been telling your sister than I don't appreciate the manner in which the children and I have been treated. She came out here commanding our boys as if she were somehow in charge."

"Dianne, the situation is not easy for them," Cole said, looking at her as if she had broken all the rules of proper protocol.

Cordelia sniffed and dabbed at her eyes with a lace-edged handkerchief that seemed to appear out of nowhere. "We're none of us ourselves," she said softly, clinging to Cole. "It's been so difficult watching Father . . . fade."

"That's still no reason to make children feel bad," Dianne countered.

"Dianne, you must show more compassion," he commanded. "I'm certain Cordelia meant no harm."

"She says you'll leave right after the funeral. Please tell me that isn't true," Cordelia sobbed. "I don't know what we'll do without you. I don't know how we'll make arrangements for everything."

Cole frowned. "I have no intention of leaving while I'm still needed here."

Dianne narrowed her eyes and met her husband's gaze. She was glad that Cordelia had once again buried her face against Cole's shoulder. Her rage was barely controllable. How dare he take his sister's side over hers?

"Cole, please hitch the buggy for me. The children and I are going into town . . . where I'm sure we'll be treated with more warmth and welcome than we are here."

Dianne gathered her things and stormed away. "Children, go comb your hair and make yourselves presentable for town. We will leave in fifteen minutes. I need to change my clothes."

She tried not to give in to her anger, but the moment she went through the bedroom door, Dianne threw the basket and contents across the room. She let out an exasperated cry and began nearly tearing her clothes from her body.

"I can't believe he could treat me like that

in front of his sister. He can't help but know how that would make me feel," she muttered. She dropped the lightweight calico gown on the floor and stepped out of it. Going to the wardrobe, she opened it and pulled out a serge suit of amber and black. Cole came into the room as she pulled on the blouse, fumbling to secure the buttons.

"I don't want you to go to town alone."

"I don't want you to make decisions about living in Kansas without consulting me," she snapped.

"Dianne, this isn't an easy situation."

"No, it isn't. You don't see how you are being manipulated by those women."

"My mother and sisters are only looking for strength—encouragement."

Dianne pulled on her skirt and tucked in her blouse before buttoning the waist. "If those women had any more strength, they'd be men! What they need from you—what they are demanding from you—is your very life, and mine."

"That's not true. You've been unfair about them since we first arrived. You didn't want to come and now you're blaming them somehow for having to be here."

She pulled on her jacket. "The only thing I blame them for is trying to turn you against your family."

"No one could do that," Cole replied.

"Well, it seems to me they've already accomplished that. You took the word of your sister over mine only moments ago."

"She was in tears," he protested.

Dianne finished the final button on her coat and looked hard at her husband. "Is that what one has to do in order to get a little compassion from you? I've cried a bucketful since we've arrived. Does that count?"

Cole came to her. "Look, I'm sorry. I know I haven't been myself, but what can you expect? Look at what I'm trying to deal with."

Dianne felt the fight in her die away. She could see in his eyes that he was genuinely sorry for what had happened. "I know it isn't easy, but I can't help you bear this when you push me away at every turn."

"I can't deal with the condemnation you give me. I know I've failed you in so many ways, but I can't bear anything more at this point. Seeing my father die . . . well . . . it just makes me all the more aware of how frail life is. How I haven't accomplished anything that I'd hoped to do." He reached out and put his hands on her shoulders. "Please don't go to town alone. I know you're upset, but I don't want anything bad to happen to you or the children."

She drew a deep breath. "Very well. I'll stay."

He smiled and pulled her into his arms. "Thank you."

She bit her lip to keep from saying any-thing further. He wouldn't understand and might not even hear her. She sighed when she thought of trying to make dinner and deal with Cole's sisters and mother. Still, there was noth-ing else to be done. She'd already promised him she would stay. She'd set her own punish-ment.

CHAPTER 7

HALLAM DIED TWO WEEKS LATER. DIANNE felt almost a sense of relief in his passing. Still, he was the only Selby who had treated her with any kindness, so she felt some loss along with the relief. Cole said little to her about his father's death, and Dianne didn't press him. She was barely on speaking terms with him since the incident with Cordelia, and now that Hallam had passed on, it was clear she wasn't needed.

Arrangements were made for the funeral, with Cole helping his mother from dawn to dusk. People began coming by to offer their condolences. Most brought some type of food, and soon the kitchen and dining room overflowed with cakes, puddings, vegetables, and meats.

Dianne kept her children upstairs or out back most of the time. No one seemed interested in meeting them, and the family didn't wish for them to be around.

"Why does Grandma hate us?" Luke asked his mother.

Dianne wanted to respond in a catty manner but held her tongue. If she worked to put up walls between the Selbys and her children, she'd be acting the same as they were. "Grandma doesn't hate you. She's grieving, and that makes people say and do strange things. Just pray for her, Luke. Pray that God will comfort her heart."

Her eldest nodded and went back to playing with his brothers.

"Is Grandpa going to stay dead?" Lia asked when her brothers were occupied once again.

Dianne smiled at her daughter. "His body is all that died. His spirit belonged to Jesus, so he will live forever in heaven."

"Like Winona's papa?"

Dianne thought of Levi. "Yes. Like Winona's papa."

"Will my papa die?"

Dianne saw the worry in Lia's expression.

"Oh, Lia, everybody dies someday, but I think your papa will be around for a long, long time. You mustn't be afraid of death, though. Jesus said, 'I am the resurrection, and the life: he that believeth in me, though he were dead, yet shall he live: And whosoever liveth and believeth in me shall never die.' When our trust is placed in Jesus, we only die to our earthly life—but we'll live forever in heaven."

"But Grandpa died and Levi died," Lia replied.

"Only their bodies. They both loved Jesus, so their spirits will never die. They will go to heaven and live with Him forever."

"I'm glad. Winona wants to see her papa again. She told me so."

Dianne smiled. "There will always be people we'd like to see again." *Places too,* she thought. *I long for Montana and the people I love there. Lord, it's so hard to be here. I feel so alone except for the children.*

She tried hard, however, to be pleasant and kind. She didn't want her personal feelings to be a topic of criticism. There were already plenty of things her mother- and sisters-in-law found fault with. No need to give them any more ammunition against her.

With Hallam buried and the funeral behind them, Dianne began to look for some sign that her husband would take them home to Montana. But as August slipped away and September loomed, Dianne began to fear the worst.

Occupying the boys with some primers she'd brought, Dianne left them reading and went downstairs to attend the task of ironing. Lia was sleeping and the heat had subsided a bit. It seemed a good time to see to her chores. It also seemed a good time to think through the situation and come to some decisions.

I must convince Cole that we need to return home. She tested the iron and began to work out the wrinkles in one of the boys' shirts. *If only he would listen to reason. If we wait too long, winter will come and travel will be too dangerous. Maybe if I remind him of the children—especially of Lia's health—he'll be willing to make the arrangements.* But in her heart, Dianne worried that nothing would ever convince her husband to leave his mother's farm. She had prayed for strength and understanding, but neither one seemed to be hers. There was no peace for her here. Her children were rejected and she was despised. How could Cole continue to desire living here when his wife and children were so clearly disliked?

Dianne had managed to iron nearly half of the things she'd brought when Mary Selby appeared in the kitchen. She said nothing to Dianne in greeting but immediately went to work. It looked as if she intended to bake, so Dianne quickly began to gather her things. She wanted there to be no excuse for Mary to be unhappy with her.

Moving quickly and quietly, Dianne had managed to collect everything and start for the back stairs when Mary suddenly halted her.

"Why do you hate us so?"

Dianne turned, basket in hand. "I beg your pardon?" She couldn't possibly have heard the woman right.

"You have been nothing but mean spirited and hateful since you've arrived."

"That isn't true and you know it. From the moment we first came, I've offered to help you. I asked several times what I might do to be of use to you, and you dismissed me."

Mary stiffened and straightened her shoulders. "You've offered no help. You've only worked to turn my son against me. Against us. His father wanted him to stay. He's left Cole this farm. It was always his dream to leave something of value to his son."

"And now he's done that and gone on in peace," Dianne reminded her. "I'm glad that he could accomplish what he wanted."

Mary gave a snort and shook her head. "Glad? You are no such thing. Would you add lying to your list of troublesome deeds? You've made it clear you hate us and this place."

Dianne tried hard to figure out the woman. Her comments were so convoluted, however, that it was difficult to have patience with her.

"I have no hate for you, Mother Selby. I have been hurt by you, as have my children. But I do not hate you."

"How in the world have I hurt you or your children?" Mary asked, seeming genuinely stunned by her comments.

"You ignore my children but fuss all over your daughters' girls. Do you know how much Cole longed to show off his children to you—to have you see them and be proud? But instead, you've scorned them, had nothing to do with them. They've been hurt by this, asking me why you hate them. So if hatred is to be discussed, perhaps you should consider your own heart. Why do you hate us?"

Mary Selby's eyes narrowed. "You took away my son once before, and you want to take him away again. I need him here, but your selfish heart won't allow you to yield in obedience to your husband's desires."

"My husband has given me no indication that staying here is his desire," Dianne said, trying hard to calm her nerves. "He told me of his father's wish for him to take over the farm, but Cole never once said it was something he wanted to do. He's worried about you, of course, but he also realizes that he has a family to care for."

"He could care for that family here."

"He barely sees that family here," Dianne snapped. "You seem to go out of your way to occupy his every waking moment. His boys miss him fiercely. Cole used to play with them every day, and now they seldom even get a moment to speak to him alone."

"Children should be disciplined and trained, not played with," Mary countered. "School will soon be starting, and I've already directed Cole as to where he should enroll the boys. They won't feel so concerned about their father's actions once they are back in school."

"My boys are not going to school here in Topeka. They will go to school in Montana."

"That's not what Cole and I discussed last night." Mary sneered and walked to the cupboard. "You need to understand that Cole is my son and he realizes his obligation to me. He will remain here with me—because it's the right thing to do. If you were a Christian, God-fearing woman, you'd understand this."

"Because I am a Christian, God-fearing woman, I realize just how wrong this is. The Bible says it is fitting for a man to leave his mother and father and cleave unto his wife!" Dianne declared. "If I were you, I'd be cautious of trying to tear apart what God has brought together."

Mary stood speechless. *Good*, Dianne thought, *let her consider that for a time*. She clutched her basket tightly and nearly ran up the back stairs. She wanted to scream. She wanted to pack all of her things and declare to the entire world that she and Cole and the children would be on the next train out of town— even if they had to ride in the freight car.

But of course, she couldn't say any of those things. Hurrying to the sanctuary of her room, she slammed the door behind her and let her tears begin to fall.

"Father, this is so unbearable. What am I to do? How am I to endure this woman and her hatred? I don't want to cause Cole further grief, but this misery is wounding my children. Being here has only caused us pain."

Dianne fell across the bed and sobbed. She was completely without hope. *No,* her mind protested, *you have Jesus, and in Him is all hope.* She struggled to sit. "But you seem so far away. I'm alone here and afraid. Please help me."

Dianne managed to stay out of her mother-in-law's way for the rest of the day. That evening they gathered for dinner, but no one said much of anything. Even the children were subdued. When dinner concluded, Dianne quickly instructed the children to carry their dishes to the kitchen, then ordered them to their rooms.

"I'll be up to read to you as soon as I have the dishes cleaned up," she promised.

Reluctantly the boys headed for the back stairs, but Lia began to cry. "I want to go home, Mama."

Dianne knew if she tried to comfort her, it

would be her own undoing. "I understand, but right now you need to go upstairs. We can talk about this later."

"I don't like it here," Lia protested. "I want to go home."

"Go upstairs now!" Dianne said more harshly than she'd intended. Lia's lower lip quivered and tears poured in earnest. Dianne couldn't bear it. "I'm sorry, Lia. Mama's got a powerful headache. Please just go upstairs and I'll be there soon."

The child did as she was told, and Dianne focused her attention on the dishes. The pain in her heart was nearly as fierce as the headache. *Something has to change,* she thought. *We cannot keep going like this—angry and sad, longing for home.*

Later, she sat on the edge of the bed Lia shared with John. Luke and Micah had come to sit on the bed as well while Dianne read to them from the Bible. Her heart wasn't in it, and she was certain her children realized this. Still, Dianne knew they needed to see her take her comfort in the Lord—even when comfort seemed so far away.

She prayed softly with them, listening to their prayers and offering her own as well. Then she tucked them in and kissed them. "I love you so much," she whispered.

"Does Papa still love us?" Micah asked.

Dianne felt the stabbing pain of that question. "Of course he still loves you. He's just very busy."

"And sad," Luke added softly.

She nodded. "Yes. He's very sad, but he still cares about us."

But she had a harder time convincing herself. As she made her way across the hall to the room she shared with her husband, she couldn't help but wonder if Cole had any thoughts of them whatsoever.

Dianne dressed for bed, pulling a light-weight sleeping gown over her head. She sat down to brush out her long hair and ponder the situation. She needed to speak to Cole—to convince him to return immediately to Montana. Winter would soon be coming to that part of the country, and they needed to arrange to move back to the ranch.

With each brush stroke Dianne tried to imagine how she might approach the subject. She was still angry with Cole's mother and knew it would never do to try and confront Cole with what had happened. In fact, she was beginning to doubt he'd even believe her.

She finished with her hair and still Cole hadn't come to join her. Deciding to sit up and wait for him, Dianne picked up her Bible and slipped into bed. She leaned over and turned up the lamp in order to read, then opened the Bible to the Psalms.

By ten o'clock Cole was still nowhere to be

found. It wasn't like him to be up so late, and it worried Dianne. Getting out of bed, she pulled on her robe and decided to go in search of him. He might be sitting alone, wondering what to do. He very well might need her. At least Dianne hoped he still needed her.

She went down the back stairs, thinking he might be in the kitchen, but he wasn't. Dianne slipped through the house, investigating each room, but found them all dark and silent. She was about to give up when she caught the sound of voices coming from outside. Apparently Cole and his mother were talking on the front porch.

Dianne went to the open door, thinking she might join them. But she halted as Cole's voice seemed to fill the quiet night.

"Dianne won't be happy with my decision," he began.

"She's your wife," Mary Selby countered. "It's time she learned her place, son. A wife should go where her husband leads, not the other way around."

Dianne seethed. Cole had made a decision—obviously to stay—without so much as discussing it with her. She held herself in check, longing to burst out the door and declare them both insane. How could he do this to her?

She hurried back through the house and up the stairs. Her heart was racing, pounding in a fury of anger. She hugged her arms close. *I won't stay. I won't stay here on the farm. I'll take my children and go back home. I'll do it tomorrow if need be.*

She paced her room for what seemed to be hours before Cole finally appeared. She said nothing, hoping maybe she'd misunderstood the entire scene.

"I'm surprised you're still up," Cole said as he began to unbutton his shirt.

"I thought it might be important for us to talk," Dianne replied. She plopped into the only chair in the room and watched her husband carefully.

"Yes, I need to talk to you about the farm and about being here," he admitted. "I was just speaking with Mother about it."

"I thought husbands and wives were supposed to discuss things first. I thought we were supposed to make these decisions together."

Cole frowned. "Sometimes a man has to make decisions alone, Dianne. Sometimes it's difficult to include too many other people in some plans."

"But you could include your mother, is that it?" she said as she stood up and started pacing across the small room.

He took off his socks. "You need to hear me out."

"Well, it's nice of you to finally bother speaking to me. I suppose I should be grateful," she said sarcastically.

"Dianne, you're acting childish. You need to stop it now." Cole's tone was the same one he used when getting after one of their disobedient children. Dianne resented being treated this way and was about to stress that fact, but Cole held her in check.

"Just listen for a minute and keep silent. I'm tired of your anger and bitterness. I can hardly stand to be in the same room with you for ten minutes because of it."

Dianne was shocked by this revelation. Shocked and wounded. She stepped back as if he'd slapped her.

"I'm sorry if I've hurt you with my words, but honestly I don't know how to cope with this anymore. My family is in need—my mother is alone. I can't simply leave her to fend for herself."

She remained speechless. She was still trying to understand Cole's comments about her bitterness. Never had she felt so empty and lonely.

"When your family was in need, I was there for them. Now I'm asking you to do the same for mine. My father is dead and my mother is trying as best she can to endure. The farm needs attention that she cannot give it."

Cole came to within a foot of where she stood. His eyes seemed to implore her to understand. Dianne knew to say anything against his mother would be insensitive. She could see that he was torn—even hurting.

"Dianne, please help me in this. I can't bear your anger anymore. This isn't some trick to keep you from the ranch and your beloved mountains. It isn't a husband asserting his authority in order to establish control over his wife. It's a simple plea for help—for assistance."

She had never heard him like this—he was very nearly begging. "What do you plan to do?" she asked softly. "What are you asking of me?"

"I've told Mother that we'll stay," he replied.

She felt an iron band tighten around her chest. She could scarcely draw a breath. Feeling lightheaded, she reached for the chair and dropped into it. Cole came to her, kneeling at her feet. He took hold of her hand, but she barely felt his touch. He meant to keep her here—a prisoner far from all she loved. There were no words.

"Dianne, it's only for a time—just through winter. By spring I'll convince my mother that selling the farm is the prudent and wise thing to do. Hopefully she'll see that she can move with us to Montana or live with my sisters and still be happy. Right now, nothing seems suitable to her, because of my father's passing. She feels lost and has told me so. The thought of the long winter months alone frighten her."

Dianne shook her head as sorrow washed over her. She couldn't even look at him. He had betrayed her. He had chosen his mother's manipulation over her needs. Nothing would ever be the same between them.

"Dianne?"

She got to her feet, nearly knocking him aside. In a manner borne out of routine, she slipped the robe from her shoulders. She carefully placed it across the foot of the bed, then climbed into bed. Leaning over, she blew out the lamp, leaving only the lamp on Cole's side of the bed to light her husband's way.

"Dianne, talk to me." He came to her and added, "Please."

She lifted her head, finally meeting his eyes. She recognized the longing there—longing for her communication and understanding, but she didn't have any to give. "There's nothing to say," she finally murmured. "You've already made your choice . . . and it wasn't me."

CHAPTER 8

Butte, Montana Territory
September

"ZANE CHADWICK, I'D LIKE YOU TO MEET Mr. Theodore Roosevelt of New York City and lately of the Dakota Territory," Morgan introduced. "He's the man I mentioned back in Virginia City."

Zane extended his hand. "Pleased to meet you, Mr. Roosevelt."

"And I you, Mr. Chadwick. This is quite the territory. Yes, sir, quite the territory."

The man's squeaky voice detracted from his otherwise rugged look. He'd dressed in hunting clothes, obviously ready to give chase at a moment's notice. His eyes seemed ever searching, almost as if he were trying to analyze everything at once.

"My brother tells me you've come to hunt mountain goat," Zane began. "I wish you the best. Goats are not easy to take down. They have a way about them. Just when you think them cornered with no place to go, they defy gravity and all that is normal and head straight up rock walls and granite cliffs."

"Sounds like a New York politician," Roosevelt countered with a great guffaw. "Of course, I know firsthand about such matters."

Zane grinned. "Nevertheless, you're in for the hunt of your life."

"So I've heard," he said. "The goats intrigue me greatly, and I look forward to the hunt."

"Mr. Roosevelt," Morgan offered, "is running for mayor of New York City."

"That sounds like a daunting job."

Roosevelt laughed. "That doesn't even begin to describe it. Corruption runs rampant and must be stopped. There are criminal types who believe themselves immortal and above the law. You show them the error of their thinking—show them the very laws they've broken—and they simply throw the book out the window and ignore you. I intend to see that changed."

"Well, I wish you the best in that hunt also," Zane replied. He liked this man, Roosevelt. He didn't act pretentious or put on airs. He simply seemed to be the kind of man who saw a problem and set about to resolve it.

"We thought you might join us for supper. It's nearly that time, you know," Morgan said, pulling out his pocket watch. "Actually, it's well past. It's already six-thirty."

Zane nodded. "Supper sounds good. There's a great restaurant nearby."

"Wonderful," Roosevelt said. "Lead us."

Zane enjoyed his evening very much. The supper was more than satisfactory with thick beefsteaks so tender they could nearly be cut with a fork. Zane couldn't remember food this good since leaving the Diamond V.

"My own ranch in the Dakota Territory produces beef every bit as flavorful," Roosevelt declared, "but I dare not say as tender."

"My sister's ranch produced quality beef as well," Zane responded. "I was just remembering how hard it was to strike out on my own and leave those wonderful meals behind."

"And where is your sister's ranch?"

Zane glanced at Morgan. "It's in the Madison Valley—or was. A fire some years back destroyed most of it. She and her family live in Virginia City as they prepare to return to the ranch. I hope it will once again become a great ranch."

"Have they stock?"

"Not much," Zane told him. "They sold off a good number prior to moving to town. They've invested the money, taking some of it to create a freighting business. They have done quite well in this and have put money aside to replace the stock when they move back to the ranch this fall."

"I could make arrangements to sell them several hundred head." Roosevelt reached for his coffee. "Put them in touch with me."

"I will," Zane promised, then turned to Morgan. "You've been very quiet this evening."

Morgan laughed. "Mr. Roosevelt has already heard most of my stories. We figured you'd be our entertainment tonight."

Grinning, Zane picked up his own coffee cup. "I don't know how entertaining I can be, but talking has never been a problem."

"Tell me about the copper industry," Roosevelt requested. "Tell me about the troubles you're facing here in Butte."

Zane put down the cup. "It's not good. The prices have dropped dramatically due to the large quantity of ore being mined. In turn, some of the best mines have had to let workers go and close. Digging copper is not without its expense. Not only do you need workers, but you must have machinery to pump water from the mine and transport the ore in and out, along with the men. There's also the lumber situation. Mines use a great deal of lumber."

"And how is this resolved? Your landscape has been quite defoliated."

Zane nodded at Roosevelt's comment. "Marcus Daly is a good friend of mine and very successful in the copper industry. He has struggled with this issue as well. He made a pact with the Northern Pacific Railroad, which holds vast tracts of forested areas. He's also managed to make agreements with western lumber barons. Still, he keeps searching. He sent me earlier this summer to arrange additional possibilities for lumber."

"Seems a pity to destroy forests for copper," Roosevelt said thoughtfully. "I'm a strong believer in protecting the land. I've been most impressed with this part of the country. I'd like to see it remain as wondrous for the generations to come. This town must surely have held beauty at one time. Mismanagement has destroyed its appearance."

"I agree," Morgan threw in. "I hate seeing the destruction. This area was once quite lovely and now it's hardly fit for man or beast."

"Unfortunately, if the copper prices don't recover, we may see this town suffer great loss and it won't matter what kind of lumber we can lay our hands on or how lovely it is or isn't." Zane tossed back the last of his coffee. "Already we've lost several hundred people. They've moved on, afraid that the job losses will never be recovered. I don't believe that personally, but it's hard to convince a man who has hungry mouths to feed that he should be patient."

"True enough," Roosevelt agreed.

Zane had no desire to continue focusing on the sad state of the town. "So, Mr. Roosevelt, what made you decide to run for mayor?"

"I've been involved in politics since I was twenty-three years old. In fact, it was a great interest when I was in attendance at Harvard College. Honest men cannot stand by and allow for corruption and destruction of all that is good. They must take a stand."

Morgan nodded solemnly, toying with his cup. "Honest men should do what they can, but at times it isn't enough."

"He's right, you know," Zane said. "I consider myself an honest man, but when faced with the ugliness and corruption of my superior officers while serving in the army, it seemed a hopeless battle. I eventually resigned, unable to make a difference for the good."

"The battle isn't simple or easy, to be sure," Roosevelt admitted. "But much like hunting mountain goat, the task cannot be forsaken based solely on difficulty. I intend to see New York changed. I intend to see the world changed and not simply in my dreams. No, sir, I will see this reality."

Zane smiled. No doubt this man could make that happen.

———

"So what did you think of Mr. Roosevelt?" Morgan asked Zane later as they readied for bed.

"He's a man with ambition, to be sure."

"I liked him from the first moment we met. He has a spirit about him that suggests great things."

Zane sat down on the edge of the bed and yawned. "Did you get him settled in at the hotel?"

Morgan nodded and threw his boots to the corner. "He seemed well enough pleased, as did his traveling companion. He has his ranch foreman coming along with us. The man's name is Merrifield. Anyway, I told them I'd call for them at five. We need to push on if we're to get him back to New York by October."

"I almost forgot," Zane said, getting up. He went to the dresser and held up a letter. "News from Dianne. She's not very happy."

"What's going on?"

"You can read it for yourself if you like."

"Nah, just tell me about it. My eyes are nearly crossed as it is. I haven't been this tired in some time." Morgan stretched out on the bed, not even bothering to cover up.

"She says Cole's father has passed away and Cole feels it's necessary to stay through the winter to help his mother."

"That can't set well with Dianne."

"No. She sounds pretty upset. Not at all happy. She's worried that winter will pass and then of course it will be time to plant crops and Cole will decide to stay on to help with that. She says the boys are miserable. Cole's insisted she put them in school, and they hate it."

"I can well imagine. Remember what it was like for me? I thought I'd never learn to read, and then when I did, it still wasn't up to the standards of everybody else. School can be hard."

"She also says Lia isn't well. Apparently the air is bad for her. Can't be as bad as Butte," he said with a laugh. "I feel sorry for them. She wishes I would write to Cole and ask him to return. Tell him how much we need them back here. What do you suppose I should do?"

"Stay out of it," Morgan said, never even bothering to open his eyes. "Cole's the man of the house, and Dianne needs to let him make the decisions."

Zane replaced the letter and came back to the bed. He shook his head at Morgan's outstretched body. "You're going to want those covers by morning. I'd suggest you get back up and let me pull them down."

Morgan groaned and rolled off the bed. "You've always enjoyed causing me pain."

Zane laughed. "Hardly that. You seem to impose that on yourself."

They crawled back into bed and Zane turned down the lamp. As the darkness engulfed the room, Zane heaved a sigh. "You know Mara Lawrence?"

"Sure. She's the one living with the family in Virginia City. Her pa is that mean old cuss who Dianne thinks murdered her friends."

"Right. Well, she's made it pretty clear that she has feelings for me."

Zane could feel Morgan shift to his side. Leaning up on his elbow, Morgan asked, "And what about you? Do you have feelings for her?"

"I can't deny enjoying her company. But I'm twice her age."

"Age shouldn't matter. If you like her, why not court her?"

Zane closed his eyes, seeing Mara's face in his mind. "It doesn't seem that simple."

"Why not?"

"It just doesn't."

Morgan fell back against the bed, his voice completely sober. "I can tell you from experience, if you like her, you need to act on it."

"You're thinking of Angelina, aren't you?" His brother had been in love with a young woman only to lose her to their older brother, Trenton.

"I try not to think of Angelina."

"But that's why you said that, isn't it?"

Morgan blew out a loud breath. "I should have told her from the get-go that I was in love with her. Maybe if I'd spoken my piece, she wouldn't be married to our brother now. So if you're in love with Mara Lawrence, I suggest you forget about the age difference and get to telling her the truth of it."

"I suppose it couldn't hurt to at least discuss it," Zane said. He wasn't known for being overly cautious, but this was a matter where brawn and brains couldn't help him. Matters of the heart were not only confusing, they were downright scary.

"Would you do it over?" Zane asked. "If you could turn back time, would you do it differently—knowing what you know now?"

Morgan was quiet for several moments before replying. "I can't honestly say. I know Trenton loves her and that they're happy together. How could I deny my own brother that kind of happiness? It would take a pretty selfish man to wish that gone only so he could have it for himself. Now, if you don't mind, I'd rather not talk about this anymore."

"I understand, but I need to know something. I mean, if Mara is the right woman for me, that's one thing. But maybe she's not and I'd be denying her happiness with the right man."

"Women seem to be pretty clear on letting their heart lead them. If Mara's heart has chosen you, then you'd probably be better off just giving up."

Zane stared at the ceiling trying to imagine life with Mara. He thought of her here in this bed, sleeping next to her rather than his brother. He tried to imagine her in his arms . . . the taste of her lips on his. He even envisioned her holding a baby—his baby. He wanted and needed a family more than anything else he could think of, and he had to admit, Mara

Lawrence had wormed her way into his heart. But then so had other girls, and they hadn't turned out to be the right ones. How could he be sure about this?

"Morgan?"

"Hmm?"

"What if I'm wrong? What if my feelings for her aren't strong enough?"

"Ma always said that love and marriage were ten percent feelings and ninety percent hard work. I'm thinking you shouldn't rely too much on what you feel for her. Think instead on whether you can spend the rest of your life with her—if you can work side by side, raise a family, things like that."

Zane knew that Morgan was right. Feelings would fade. He thought of Dianne and how hurt she'd been by her husband's decision to stay in Kansas. He'd once thought he'd never seen anyone more in love than Cole and Dianne. But here they were struggling and suffering. They had been having hard times ever since the fire and Cole's decision to remain in Virginia City. Did he want to endure those kinds of difficulties with Mara Lawrence? Would she willingly follow him no matter where he led?

If I don't pursue this, Zane thought, *will there be another chance? Will another woman come along? A better woman?*

"Morgan."

Morgan yawned. "What's a fellow gotta do to get some sleep around here?"

"Just answer me this, and then I promise to leave you alone."

"All right. What do you want to know?"

"Has there ever been anyone else—after Angelina? You know, another woman who made you feel as special? A woman who you felt you could spend the rest of your life with?"

Morgan said nothing for several minutes. In fact, Zane thought perhaps he'd fallen asleep. Then without warning, he spoke and the sorrow in his tone made Zane sorry he'd asked.

"No, there's never been anyone else, and I really don't expect there will be. Losing Angelina was a very hard thing. Losing her to my brother was even worse. Now she's in the family, but she'll never be mine. It kind of makes me glad that Trenton had to leave the area and remain dead to the world."

Zane thought of their elder brother's past. Trenton's outlaw days had never caught up with him, but it had been awfully close, especially when Mara's stepmother learned of his past deeds. Of course, Trenton had been guilty by association more so than anything he'd actually done by his own hand. Still, he'd broken the law, and now he would have to either give up his life and face the penalties for that or remain in hiding. And with him, Angelina would bear the same sentence.

"I'm sorry if I caused you pain," Zane said, rolling to his side. "I just needed to know."

"And now you do. So tomorrow I'd suggest you go back to Virginia City and find your lady, and Mr. Roosevelt and I will move on to the Idaho Territory and find our goat."

Zane laughed. "The sport will probably be similar in difficulty."

"Not at all. Your prize wants to be caught."

CHAPTER 9

"I'M SO GLAD TO FIND YOU LADIES AT home," Faith Montgomery said as she joined Ardith and Mara in the front sitting room. "I wanted to bring you this cake and see how you were doing without Dianne and Cole."

Ardith took the cake and placed it on a side table. "I'm guessing this is one of your special burnt sugar cakes. I'll be happy to serve it with supper."

Mara had enjoyed this delicacy before and shook her head. "Oh, we surely don't have to wait, do we? Couldn't we have a slice with tea?"

Faith's round brown face expressed her delight. "I can't stay all that long. School will be ending for the day and I need to get back home."

Mara thought the former slave to be one of the most beautiful women she'd ever met. Faith had beautiful dark eyes that seemed filled with joy and laughter. The woman had known horrible times, but her love of God seemed to conquer even those sad memories.

"My brother Joshua will be sorry he missed you, Faith. He tells me you two had quite a discussion after church on Sunday."

"Indeed we did. He has a strong desire to reach out to all people, even black folk. He wanted to know about my people and some of the life I'd lived prior to the War Between the States."

"That's what he told me. He said you were quite informative. He truly has a passion for service. He doesn't intend to stay here in the West, however. I believe he hopes to settle in a larger city, perhaps have a church with all types of people."

"It won't be well accepted on either side," Faith said. "He'll have much to overcome."

"The city seems more forgiving than the small towns of the West," Ardith interjected. "Folks out here aren't too happy with people whose skin is colored other than white. The Chinese have suffered terribly, as have the

Mexicans who've ventured this far north, and of course anyone of Indian blood."

"Has Winona suffered because of her heritage?" Faith asked.

"She looks Indian—how can she not suffer? Children are cruel. They don't care that Winona had no choice in her father. People don't care that I had no choice. It's simply a matter of prejudice."

"And fear," Faith added. "People don't understand, and so they're afraid. People see folks who are different and fear that those differences might somehow harm them."

"But how can they take it out on a little girl?" Mara asked. "Winona is completely defenseless. It isn't right."

"It would be better if we were back on the ranch," Ardith admitted. "Or at least if Winona were back on the ranch."

Faith looked puzzled. "What are you saying?"

"Christopher Stromgren has written to me again. He's the gentleman who wants me to go to New York. This time he's included a train ticket."

Neither Faith nor Mara could hold back their surprise.

"When did this arrive?" Faith asked.

"What do you plan to do?" Mara asked enthusiastically. She had heard Ardith speak about the offer to play piano in New York for some time. It was hard to imagine that she would actually take up the suggestion, but Mara couldn't help but notice a certain look in Ardith's expression. It was a look Mara had never seen before.

"The letter came two days ago. I've been thinking about nothing else since it arrived," Ardith admitted. "It would be a wonderful change of life for me."

"But what of Winona? If the people are cruel here, how will they be in the city?" Faith questioned. "You can hardly believe they would simply overlook her heritage."

"I wouldn't take Winona with me."

Mara could scarcely believe her ears. "You'd leave your child behind? But who would care for her?"

"Dianne would give her a home. Winona needs to be back on the ranch. She misses Koko and Susannah. Koko is someone Winona can relate to . . . someone who understands what Winona is enduring."

"But Dianne isn't here and Koko is on the ranch, twenty-five miles away. How would you get Winona there?" Mara asked.

Ardith shrugged. "There are ways. My brother-in-law owns the freighting company, after all. I could always ask them to take us on the next delivery to the ranch. I could arrange with Koko to watch her until Dianne is able to return."

"But Dianne has already stated that it will be spring before Cole even considers coming back. That's a long time," Faith said, her expression grave. "I hope you'll put this to prayer and consider what you're doing before you act on it."

Ardith was obviously upset with the turn of the conversation. She got up quickly, the gray wool skirt swirling around her feet as she turned abruptly and began to pace. "Neither of you understand what I am bearing. I cannot remain here."

Mara felt sorry for the older woman. She had seen Ardith deal with the sad loss of her husband and knew the widow was often overwhelmed with her child's questions.

"Music has been a solace for me. It has helped me to overcome my sorrows in ways I never thought possible," Ardith said in defense of her earlier comments. "I've been gifted with a musical talent that Mr. Stromgren believes should be shared with the world. I can't help but think of how much this might bless both me and Winona."

"And how would that be?" Mara asked softly.

Ardith stopped and stared at Mara for a moment. "I think it would be a blessing to be rid of this place for a time. Coming west has only served to harm me. First by nearly drowning in the river, then by being taken by

Indians. I could write a long list of the wrongs done me, but it wouldn't change a thing. But now I can change where I live . . . and my future."

"But won't your sorrows and memories simply follow you?" Faith questioned.

"You think you have all the answers," Ardith retorted. "You think you know what's best for me. Dianne always thinks so too, but she doesn't know me . . . none of you do. I'm not at all the woman you think I am."

"Maybe we don't know your heart completely," Faith said softly, "but we know pain when we see it, and I've never known a pain you could outdistance yourself from. Pain is something that you'll take right along with your bags. Not only that, but by leaving Winona behind, you'll add guilt."

"No I won't. I won't feel guilty for doing what's best for her."

"How could it be best to lose her mother?" Mara asked. "My mother was cold and indifferent, but still I loved her. I miss her terribly at times."

This seemed to take Ardith aback for a moment. "She would . . . well . . . Dianne would be a better mother."

"But Dianne isn't here," Faith reminded her.

Ardith let out an exasperated breath and began pacing again. Her arms flailed as she tried to explain herself. "I have done the best I can. Can neither of you understand that I'm ready for a change? That I need something different? I need something that isn't here. Winona will just have to get by and understand that I cannot be a good mother for her until I deal with this awful emptiness inside me."

"Child, only God can fill that emptiness, not crowds in New York City." Mara nodded at Faith's words.

Ardith shook her head almost violently. "God doesn't figure into this . . . not now . . . not ever. He left me to fend for myself so many times. I kept crawling back to Him, thinking I was the one who was wrong, but now I know that it's just not true. I did nothing to merit losing Levi. I did nothing to deserve losing our baby."

Faith got up and went to where Ardith paced. Reaching out, she stilled the younger woman by taking hold of her arms. "Ardith, I believe you, and God knows the truth of it. Those things just happened as a part of life. We can't stop bad things from coming our way. It doesn't mean that we've necessarily done anything wrong when trials come. Jesus said there would be trials, but He also said we could take heart because He's overcome the world."

"He's God; of course He's overcome the world," Ardith said sarcastically. "But I'm just a woman, and I don't seem to be much capable of overcoming anything."

"But—"

"No, Faith. I don't want to hear anything more on the matter. I know what I have to do. I just need to find a way to accomplish it."

Mara could take no more of the painful conflict. "I have to tell you both something." She smiled. "I know it might sound silly . . . but I'm in love."

Ardith's eyes widened and Faith's mouth actually dropped open to form an O. Mara could see she'd captured their attention and hurried on to explain.

"Ardith, I'm in love with your brother Zane. I know he's twice my age, but I don't see why that should matter. He's a good man with a loving heart, and I can't help myself."

Both women stared at her. They were speechless, and the looks on their faces made Mara want to laugh out loud. Instead she got up and went to pick up the cake. Taking it to Ardith, she pushed the plate into her hands. "Why don't we talk about this some more . . . over cake?"

Faith chuckled, finally gaining her voice. "I see nothing wrong with a man being twice your age, if you love him."

Ardith seemed to get her wind. She put the cake down, shaking her head and muttering. "You've heard nothing I've said. Love is pain. . . . I can't in good conscience encourage you to pursue my brother or any other man. Now if you'll excuse me, I have a horrible headache and need to lie down before Winona comes home."

Ardith hurried off without another word, leaving Mara feeling guilty. "I hope I didn't hurt her feelings. I didn't mean to." She looked to Faith. "I only wanted to change the subject and quell her anger."

"Child, she must find her way through this sorrow. She needs to give it all over to God, but she's convinced He doesn't care."

"How can we help her?" Mara said, feeling close to tears. Ardith's sadness was almost contagious.

"We can pray for her. We can pray and trust that God will do the rest."

Mara thought about Faith's words long after the supper dishes had been washed and put away. Joshua had gone off to visit with Ben Hammond. He wanted very much to get a community revival planned, and Ben was the one man who could help him accomplish his goal.

Ardith and Winona had disappeared upstairs shortly after supper, leaving Mara alone with her thoughts and feelings. Her parents had lived such a loveless marriage, passing that lack of emotion on to their parenting. Mara had never once felt truly loved and cared for, except by Joshua. Even then, it wasn't the kind of love she needed or desired. Then Dianne Selby had told her about God's love. It seemed too impossible to be true. How could God love a silly little girl . . . the daughter of a ruthless man?

But He does love me. He loves me and He has taken me out of that desperation and given me hope. A hope within . . . a hope that never failed her. So it seemed perfectly acceptable that in faith she could seek God out and ask for love . . . and He would give it to her.

And He had, at least as far as Mara was concerned. Zane Chadwick might not yet understand how it worked, but Mara knew she could bring him around in time.

Checking to see that the kitchen was in order, Mara made her way through the house and stepped out onto the front porch. There was a definite chill in the evening air. No doubt the snows of winter would soon come.

"I know you have it all planned out . . . you know my future," she whispered in prayer. "I just need to trust you and be patient. But I'm not good at either thing . . . at least not as good as I wish I were."

She leaned on the porch rail and sighed. Closing her eyes, she continued to pray. *I feel so sad, Lord. Sad for Ardith and Winona. Please help them. Please let Ardith find contentment again. Let her know peace and happiness. Let her find joy in her child. And help Joshua to know where you're leading him. Give him clear direction and let him bring many people to the truth.*

And, Lord, there's Elsa. She's so trapped right now. Our father is being very underhanded about her, and we don't know why. Lord, you know Josh has been out there so many times trying to convince Father to let her go. Still he refuses, and Elsa's afraid. Help her, God. Help her before something bad happens.

Mara prayed for the people around her, for the Selbys and for those at the ranch. It seemed there was a never-ending list of folks to pray for, but Charity always said that when your own problems seemed to overwhelm you, you'd find the burden lifted as you bore other folks and their problems to the Lord in prayer. *It's true,* Mara thought. *Already I feel better.*

But after exhausting her list of people and their needs, Mara found herself right back at her own longing. She couldn't help but let the image of Zane come to mind. She could almost reach out and trace the edges of his face. She could even imagine herself telling him how much she loved him.

"You look like a woman with a lot on her mind."

Mara opened her eyes, surprised to find

Zane standing on the bottom porch step. "I am."

"I don't suppose it would be safe for me to ask what you're thinking about."

She grinned. "There's no reason to ask. You already know good and well what I'm thinking about."

"That's what I figured," Zane said with a look that seemed to register somewhere between relief and resignation. "Not safe at all."

———————

Word came from Charity and Ben that Gus Yegen, the Diamond V's first foreman, had passed away. Dianne cried quietly in the confines of her room, unable to put to words the grief she was feeling. Gus represented the last of the old life she had known. Gus had been her uncle's friend and right-hand man, and after Uncle Bram had been killed by a grizzly bear, Gus had become her trusted friend and valued employee.

Gus had taught Dianne so much about horses and cattle. He had been a gentle and informative teacher . . . always patient, never cross or belittling. And now he was gone.

Dianne knew she would have to share the news with Cole, but right now she didn't want to. It was her own private news, her own sorrow. And as strange as it sounded, she was determined that no one take it from her.

"Everything has changed," she whispered. "Nothing is as it was. I thought my life was well planned out for me. I thought I would live and die on the Diamond V." Gus probably thought so too. Charity said he'd died in Bozeman. Gus must surely have hated that. It had always been his desire to live out his days on the Diamond V and be buried there.

"Well, at least they're seeing to his burial in my absence," she said, glancing again at the tearstained letter. Charity mentioned that Koko and George had already arranged for the funeral to be held in Bozeman, but that they would then take the body to the ranch for burial. Looking at the date of the letter, Dianne realized the funeral and burial were long behind them. Funny how Gus had died and Dianne hadn't even realized it—hadn't known that such a dear friend was gone.

Dianne wiped her eyes and glanced at the clock. It would soon be time for the boys to come home from school. How she missed them. She felt as though she'd betrayed their trust by sending them to the city school. Luke pined daily for the mountains and Barky. Micah had lost weight and seemed to always cower and hide in his room. John, resilient as ever, hardly seemed to notice his ill treatment. He just went through life letting insult and misery roll off his back like rain on a slicker. But even John could understand the misery of his siblings and mother. He often tried to play the clown in order to pick up their spirits.

It was Lia who worried Dianne most, however. The child was not thriving. The doctor said the problem was something called asthma, which he described as a constriction of the airways. During one particularly bad spell, the doctor had given Lia a small dose of ether. The ether had calmed her coughing and wheezing attack but had rendered the child unconscious. Of course, the doctor hadn't bothered to explain that this would happen and Dianne had been almost hysterical when Lia went limp in her arms. The doctor had quickly ushered Dianne from the room, and it was some time before the nurse came to retrieve her. The doctor could offer no reason for the illness, but he prescribed a medication for her to take four times a day, along with a tablespoon of strong coffee. It seemed to help, but Dianne knew in her heart that going back to Montana would help even more.

Cole was unmoved, however, by any of this. He rarely spoke to Dianne, probably because he knew her sadness would only cause them to fight. He came to bed late in the night—after he was sure Dianne was asleep. At least that's what she suspected. It was taking its toll on them. Cole wore a haunted expression with dark circles under his eyes. He showed little interest in the boys or in Lia, making only minimal conversation at dinner. Dianne had convinced herself that it was his guilt that kept him from being able to spend time with his sons. They never failed to tell of how miserable they were at school . . . how the other children hated them . . . how they disliked their teacher and the discipline.

Dianne herself had tried to help the boys deal with their frustrations, promising them that soon, very soon, they would go home to Montana. But was it fair to promise them something she couldn't even begin to hope for?

Folding the letter, she drew a deep breath and blew it out rather loudly. The sound reassured her that life had to go on. Lia would soon awaken from her nap, and the boys would be home within ten minutes. Dianne could only pray that they could have a peaceful evening without any disparaging remarks from her mother-in-law.

CHAPTER 10

SUNDAY SERVICES WERE LONG AND LABORI-ous for Dianne. In the past, she had looked forward to spending time in church, but not here in Topeka. The people seemed cold and indifferent. They were friends of Cole's mother and sisters, which meant they certainly could not be her friends as well. As the final hymn concluded and the last prayer was offered, Dianne breathed a sigh of relief. Soon they would go home and her obligations to the community would be concluded for another week.

"I'm hungry, Mama," John said, wrapping his arms around Dianne.

"I know, sweetie. We'll soon be home and it won't take much time before lunch is ready."

"Will you make us some cookies?" Micah asked.

Dianne tousled his hair. "We'll see. If there's time, I just might. Now come along. Papa has already started for the door." Dianne herded her boys down the aisle filled with peo-ple, doing her best to follow Cole. He had taken the news of Gus's passing hard. Perhaps not as hard as his father's death, but Dianne thought it to be a very close second. Cole did manage to say that he had always seen Gus as a sort of father, that the man had helped him to learn a great deal about ranching. Dianne had agreed. It was the first peaceful conversation they'd had in months. Now, however, Cole seemed to be back to his old disinterested self. He had taken hold of his mother's arm and escorted her out of the church, leaving Dianne and the children to fend for themselves. His actions hurt Dianne, but what could she say? She lowered her gaze to the floor. He was helping his aging mother. Who wouldn't see that as a son's duty? She kept her gaze fixed to the polished wood aisle, hoping no one would question her about anything.

"Mrs. Selby," a tinny voice sounded from in front of her.

Dianne knew the irritating call belonged to Mrs. Weatherbee. Looking up, Dianne forced a smile. "Hello, Mrs. Weatherbee." Dianne knew that good manners dictated that she stop and wait for the woman to speak, but with four restless children at her side, Dianne prayed the woman wouldn't desire a long discourse.

"I was particularly moved by today's sermon. I'm sure you could say the same."

Dianne frowned. "It was quite in keeping with what I've come to expect on Sunday."

"I thought it particularly meaningful, especially the part about the hypocrites," she said, as if her words should hold some special meaning for Dianne. In truth it did. The pastor had spoken of Christians who were hypocritical. People whose words did not match their actions.

"I do agree with you on that matter, Mrs. Weatherbee. I've known a great many people who were happy to proclaim themselves to be living by the Bible's teachings but whose lives showed it to be to the contrary."

Mrs. Weatherbee's head bobbed up and down so rapidly that Dianne feared the woman might actually hurt herself. "I know it must have been convicting."

Dianne smiled. "I'm sure there are people who are positively trembling in fear as they leave the service today."

Mrs. Weatherbee frowned. "Yes. Well, let us hope that the right people are stirred to obedience."

Dianne nodded. "Indeed. Now, if you don't mind, I must get home and help put on lunch." Mrs. Weatherbee said nothing more. Dianne knew her intention had been to convince Dianne of her need to repent, but honestly, she felt no guilt in that area. The attitude she had now was mainly one of staying out of everyone's way. Her mother-in-law said very little to her on any given day except to criticize.

Still, Dianne was determined to live out her sentence, and to be sure, that's what it was. A sentence of time to serve. Nothing more. There was no joy in this situation. No heart-warming moments spent with her mother-in-law. No nights gathered around the fire to hear stories of when Cole was young. There was nothing to hold Dianne here . . . nothing but her husband's wishes.

Exiting the church, the pastor greeted Dianne with what resembled a pained expression. Perhaps his gout was acting up again or perhaps he just didn't like having to deal with that woman Mary Selby's son had married.

"Good day to you, Pastor Bruening. Thank you for the service." She could offer nothing more complimentary.

"May God bless you, Mrs. Selby."

"He has many times over," Dianne replied and hurried her children along before anything else could be said.

Cole frowned as they approached. "I wondered where you were. We've been waiting to go home."

"It's completely inconsiderate," Mary Selby pronounced in judgment.

Dianne held her tongue and helped the children into the buggy. Lia began coughing, but Dianne knew there was little she could do to help the child. Cole helped her into the buggy, and Dianne took Lia in her arms.

"Poor baby," she cooed. "When we get home I'll get some compresses for your chest."

"You indulge that child entirely too much," Mary Selby said from her place beside Cole.

Dianne gently pounded on Lia's back to help her breathe better. It seemed this action always helped. "I would hardly think," Dianne said softly, "that caring for a sick child would be considered indulgence by anyone."

"She's spoiled. She merely puts on these shows of illness to get attention," Cole's mother said. "I've heard about asthma before. It's mostly a state of emotion that children work themselves into. When they don't get their way, they put themselves into a state of asthma."

"I tend to disregard rumors told by people less knowledgeable than the doctor."

"A doctor was the one who said this," Mary answered curtly. "You'd do well to punish her—send her to bed without dinner."

"Mother, I hardly think Lia is faking her sickness," Cole finally interceded. "The doctor said it's quite dangerous. I don't think a child her age could fool a doctor."

"Perhaps not, but there are other ways she's overindulged."

"Could be," he said, not defending or disregarding.

Dianne felt her anger stir, but exhaustion with these continued arguments kept her from bringing it to the surface. No doubt it was best this way. Her emotional state had run the full gambit from fierce intensity to fading resignation.

Dianne was grateful that the boys remained silent throughout the ride. Lia's coughing abated somewhat, and Dianne had managed to keep from arguing when her mother-in-law made snide comments. It wasn't easy, but despair seemed to make it less important.

At home Dianne hurried her children upstairs, saw to their change of clothes, then went to the bedroom to ready herself for getting dinner on the table. When they had first arrived in Kansas, Dianne had helped Mary prepare the Sunday meal, but Mary never appreciated her efforts and had come to leave the entire responsibility on Dianne's shoulders in order to spend her Sunday afternoons visiting with Cole. Dianne, in turn, had taken to fixing most of the food the night before, making it necessary to just warm things up. It was her own little rebellion, and even when she was exhausted on Saturday night, Dianne would put in the extra work hours just to make sure that Mary's discussion time alone with Cole was limited.

Dianne hated herself for acting this way, but it was her only means of defense. Mary Selby seemed to be doing everything within her power to pull Cole away from her and the children. Dianne didn't even bother to talk to Cole about it anymore. He always accused her of misunderstanding the situation, of believing his mother to have some kind of evil intent.

"It might not be evil," Dianne muttered as she reheated the chicken and dumplings, "but it's definitely selfish."

Ten minutes into warming the food, the children joined her for their chores. Micah and Lia set the dining room table while Luke retrieved extra water for the stove's reservoir. This would be heated sufficiently by the time the meal was over and would give them enough water to wash the dinner dishes. Meanwhile, John helped open two jars of green beans and one of peas. Dianne had already decided she would serve them without garnish, simply warmed with butter and a touch of salt. She took them from John and quickly poured them into separate pans on the back of the stove. It wouldn't take long before they were hot.

Peeking into the oven, Dianne saw that the biscuits were nearly brown. There was also a peach cobbler that was crisping nicely and would be ready about the time they'd finished with the dumplings.

"Table's set, Mama," Micah said as he and Lia came into the kitchen.

"Good. Pour some water for each person and then let Papa know we're ready to eat."

Dianne pulled the biscuits from the oven and arranged them in a serving basket and covered them with a cloth. "Lia, take the butter and jelly dishes to the table."

Lia didn't say a word but did as she was told. Dianne could tell that her daughter wasn't feeling well, but Lia had learned to bear it well. The poor child had heard every word her grandmother had ranted about asthma and the child only pretending to be sick. How could a grandmother do that? Talk like that in front of a child—a sick child. The doctor had even told Dianne that children died from this condition. Perhaps it was time Dianne shared that news with Mary Selby.

After the food was arranged on the table, Dianne took her seat and directed the children to do likewise. Mary studied the table critically.

"I see there are no pickles."

"I wasn't certain that anyone would want pickles. Especially since there really isn't anything to eat them with," Dianne replied. "If you like, however, I can fetch some."

"Goodness, no. This is already taking a good portion of my winter reserves. I won't waste additional food."

Dianne looked to Cole. She wanted so much to mention that if they weren't forced to live at the farm, Mother Selby wouldn't need to worry about the food reserves. But she said nothing. Instead, she waited for her husband to offer grace.

Cole's prayer was simple and to the point. There was little passion in it, but at least he was willing to offer it.

They ate in silence. The children had learned to say nothing at the dinner table. Early in their stay, Mary Selby had told Cole emphatically that children should be silent in gatherings that included adults. Dianne knew her husband didn't approve or agree, but he also refused to defend his family. Dianne had long ago given up arguing the point. Meal-times used to be a great pleasure at the ranch. The family would gather and discuss the day's work to be done or what had been accomplished. The children would join in talking about their studies or what they'd seen down at the creek.

The dumpling stuck in Dianne's throat as she let the memory wash over her. How happy she had been. Could it really be possible that she might never enjoy such a life again? *I can't let that happen. I have to fight this lethargy. I have to get my family home.*

She looked across the table to her husband. "How is the harvest going?"

Cole seemed surprised that she'd actually taken interest in the farm. "Despite the drought, it hasn't been that bad. Ma should realize a good profit."

"That will enable us to plant more acreage come spring," Mary said.

Dianne looked at Cole, hoping he might broach the subject of their return to Montana in the spring. But he didn't have a chance. Luke piped up instead, breaking the rule of silence.

"We're going home in the spring."

Everyone stopped eating and looked at him. His siblings seemed astonished that he had dared to talk at Grandmother Selby's table, while Cole looked embarrassed. Mary Selby, however, narrowed her eyes and looked to Dianne instead of Luke.

"You've been filling his head with lies, haven't you?"

The accusation was the only spark Dianne needed. "I've told my children no lies. Their father said we would stay through the winter, and so we will. We will return home in the spring."

Mary looked crestfallen as she glanced from Dianne to Cole. "Surely this isn't the truth."

Cole drew a deep breath. "Ma, let's not argue over dinner. I have responsibilities back in Montana. I've never said otherwise."

Mary put her napkin on the table. Drawing her handkerchief from her pocket, she pressed it to her eyes. "I can't believe you'd desert me. You know I've come to depend on you."

"We depend on him too," Dianne said, unable to hold her tongue, "but that seems of little importance to anyone here."

"This is just too much for me. I'm going to lie down." She moved quickly to exit the room before anyone could try to stop her.

Dianne stared at Cole, wondering if he might comment on his mother's reaction, but instead he focused back on the meal.

"Papa, we *are* going home in the spring, aren't we?" Luke asked.

Cole looked up. "Son, we'll do our best."

The answer left Dianne chilled to the core of her soul. There was no affirming promise— no positive response. Just a noncommittal *"We'll do our best."* To Dianne it sounded an awful lot like no.

Cole couldn't bear the look on his wife's face. Knowing the food would only sour in his stomach if he ate another bite, he pushed back from the table. "I need to check on something in the barn."

He knew Dianne would follow him out, so he turned to add, "I'd like to be alone."

He hated the rift that had grown between them over the past five years. He knew he had put off going back to the ranch, and he knew it hurt her. Still, it was hard to explain to Dianne that he feared the ranch. Feared starting over. What if he were unable to make it all work? What if he failed miserably? He'd known little about ranching when he'd first arrived in Montana, but now that he did know more, it was almost more terrifying.

I can never give her what she had, he thought as he pulled back the door to the barn. The musty, sweet smell of new hay filled the air. Cole had worked hard to get that hay harvested. There was a sense of pride that filled him at the sight of his accomplishment. The drought had lessened the crop to be sure, but he still felt confident there would be more than enough to see them through the winter.

Climbing up into the loft, Cole took a seat on an old wooden stump. "I don't know what to do," he whispered aloud.

It made him ache within to see his family in its present state. Dianne had lost a great deal of weight, and there was a perpetual sadness to her. It was like watching something precious die. He'd wanted to talk to her about it a million times, but many of the times when he'd started to approach her, she'd said something caustic and his compassion and concern had gone right out the window. Other times she just seemed too depressed . . . and her only solution was to return to the land she loved. When Cole would try to explain why he didn't feel they could do that, Dianne would nod knowingly and give him a look that suggested he'd just signed her death warrant. Neither response was one he could deal with, so most of the time he avoided her altogether.

The truth was, he wasn't much happier here on the farm than she was. He didn't like farming. He didn't like harvest time. The wheat rust burned and irritated his eyes and skin for days on end. The corn stalks were scratchy and gave him a constant itch until bath time. The humidity had abated somewhat, but the fierce heat of August had lingered into September, and neither was to his liking. Kansas farming simply wasn't in his heart.

"But neither is failing to rebuild the Diamond V to its former glory." In Cole's mind he could only imagine the constant comparisons to the old way Uncle Bram had set things up and the new way in which Cole would rebuild. It was the reason he'd happily turned over the plans to Koko and George. When George had suggested he and Jamie could put together a cabin for Cole and his family, it was easy to say yes.

But now . . . If he returned to the ranch and tried to rebuild, he would probably make Dianne more happy than sad. But what of his mother? He could hardly leave her here on the farm, and on the few occasions when he'd actually tried to approach the idea of selling, she'd quickly refused to consider it.

I feel torn in two, God. I want to do right by

*my wife, but my mother is alone and needs help. I
feel bad for the way my children have had to
endure life here, but at the same time, I know
they'll be stronger for it someday. I need to know
what to do, and nothing is coming clear.*

Burying his face in his hands, Cole sighed.
Nothing had gone right since coming to Kansas. His father had died, his mother had set
demands upon him that seemed impossible to
live up to, and the only people he knew he
couldn't live without were quickly becoming
strangers to him.

"Oh, God, help me."

CHAPTER 11

MORGAN COULD EASILY SAY THAT OUTSIDE
of family, he'd never met a man he liked more
than Teddy Roosevelt. The man had a passion
for living that Morgan found contagious. After
days in the woods, tracking goats and enduring
grueling climbs up sheer cliffs and down razor-
like rocky paths, Morgan had figured the man
who hoped to soon be mayor of New York
City would give up. But he didn't. Neither

Roosevelt nor his man Merrifield was inclined to stop.

The first two days, incessant rain poured from thick dark clouds. The only good thing about this was that it put out a small fire that a group of Flathead Indians had started in the woods nearby, possibly to clear some brush. The smoke had been a bitter companion on the first leg of the journey, so Morgan wasn't all that upset with the rain.

When the rain finally stopped, it hardly made a difference, as tall stands of spruce, fir, and hemlock nearly blocked the sun from their sight at times. It made tracking difficult, although Morgan knew no respectable goat antelope would be down this far. They came across tracks of cougar and bear, and vast herds of deer could be seen for the taking. They ate well on venison steaks each night, but the goats continued to elude them.

They camped one night along a glorious stream that plunged and danced in foamy white rapids as it made its way to the valley below. Here, Morgan pointed out water wrens—thrushlike birds that actually made their home along and in the shelter of this brook. Roosevelt was greatly impressed with them.

"They warble sweetly," Roosevelt said, "yet they live right in the torrent."

Morgan thought it rather an interesting

point. "Perhaps they thrive on the excitement and exhilaration of that torrent." Some folks were like that too. He thought of his sister. Dianne always seemed to be at her best when the chaos of the world was dealing its worst. He'd seen her in their younger days happily helping with a cattle drive, completely calm and collected even when facing a stampede.

"Well, these moccasins are done for," Roosevelt declared as he looked over the tattered pieces. "When I hunted in the Big Horn Mountains, moccasins such as these were sufficient. But this territory is quite unforgiving, and my feet have paid the price."

"I hope you brought some boots with you," Morgan said, feeling bad that he'd not made himself more clear on what to expect.

"I do have a sturdy pair of shoes with a nice stout sole that has been studded with nails. Merrifield, however, is less fortunate. He has only a pair of cowboy boots. Sufficient for our days on the ranch, but certainly no good for climbing."

"I would offer you my spare pair, but I can tell Merrifield's foot is much larger than mine, and they'd never fit."

"We shall bear it the best we can," Roosevelt said, still not discouraged by the conflict that had been presented.

When they broke camp the next day, Morgan knew they would need to move rapidly to higher ground. From here on out the journey would only get harder, and it might not be long before snows set in. They packed a light lunch in their pockets and gathered their rifles.

"I thought we would have at least found tracks by now," Morgan told Roosevelt. "I've been here before and the goats are definitely native to this land."

"This place is quite beautiful," Roosevelt said. "It makes the hunt all that more acceptable. I shall be disappointed if we find no goats, but I shall not fault this land. Although I must say this task is as hard as any I have ever undertaken."

"I couldn't agree more," Merrifield said.

They continued to climb higher up the rocky mountainside, skirting ledges and helping each other across crevices. From time to time a rocky slide would start because of their disturbance, but always they managed to secure themselves to something solid to avoid being swept away.

By now, Morgan actually feared he might not be able to locate any game for Roosevelt. The northern reaches of the Coeur d'Alenes were well known for the quarry they sought, but the trip was becoming increasingly more difficult, and the Idaho temperatures were turning brisk. Especially at night.

Morgan was about to devote himself to prayer on the matter when he finally spotted a goat on the rocks above. He examined the ground around them. "Look here!" He pointed to the large rounded hoof prints at the edge of the trail. "We're on the right path."

The deeply worn path had been created by the herds in search of the clay licks. The goats loved the salty taste and would continually come back to these places for as long as they proved safe. Morgan was encouraged by the signs around them.

They moved up the path for another hour before coming to a tremendous slide where rock and gravel lay strewn across the path, along with the trunk of a large pine.

"We can rest here a bit," Morgan suggested, hearing the winded breathing of his companions. The men quickly agreed, and Roosevelt dropped to the ground to ease his back against the tree.

"Ah, a comfortable chair to be certain."

Morgan smiled. He loved the man's spirit. A noise above caught Morgan's attention. He glanced cautiously, not making any sudden move. It was a goat.

"There!" he said in a low whisper.

Roosevelt was in no position to fire, but he strained to see the animal and then to adjust his position. Pebbles broke loose beneath him and the goat startled.

Roosevelt managed to fire off a shot, but it went low, missing all vital organs and instead only hitting the leg of the goat. It seemed not to matter to the animal at all, as it scampered off quickly, seeming to head straight up a smooth-faced rock wall. Morgan was not one to leave an injured animal to fend for himself, so he took off after the beast, and to his surprise, so did Roosevelt.

They must have scrambled after the goat for over an hour before the animal showed any signs of slowing. Morgan was able to track the blood let off by the animal, so he slowed his pace just a bit in order to let Teddy regain his breath.

"We'll get him," Morgan promised.

"Indeed we will," Roosevelt said in a manner that suggested any other option was not acceptable.

By the end of the day, however, they had only managed to get another shot fired at the tenacious beast, and again, Roosevelt only managed to skim the animal, this time slicing through its back, apparently missing the spine. A night of rest put them in good spirits to track the wounded goat and capture it once and for all. And the following morning that was exactly what they did. Morgan had never seen a man prouder of his accomplishment.

"It's a fine specimen," Roosevelt announced, and Merrifield agreed.

Morgan enjoyed their camp that evening. With at least one goat kill under his belt,

Roosevelt was more confident, even cocky in his actions and attitude.

"I consider this a good sign," he told them as they built up the fire for the night. "It didn't come with ease, but good things seldom do. I believe I'll return to New York and win that election. I'm the right man for the job—none better."

"None better to be sure," Merrifield said with a nod.

"And will you make great changes there?" Morgan asked, trying hard to suppress a yawn.

"I intend to see the city completely remade. I'm tired of and sickened by the corruption. We'll make it a better place, I assure you, Mr. Chadwick."

Morgan smiled and stretched out beside the fire. No doubt the man would do just what he said, for Morgan couldn't imagine anyone saying no to Teddy Roosevelt.

Roosevelt smiled. "I will be as those wrens in the stream. Conscious of my surroundings but unwilling to be defeated by them."

———

"Why can't we talk about Papa?" ten-year-old Winona asked her mother.

Ardith rubbed her head. "I told you, I don't want to discuss him. He's dead and gone and that should be that. I won't have you continuing to pester me with questions."

"But sometimes I can't remember him," Winona said, her face crestfallen. She pushed back her long black braid. "I can't remember the way he looked."

"Good," Ardith snapped. How she wished it might be so for her. Levi's image still managed to haunt her sleep most every night. She saw Winona's wounded expression and regretted her tone. Softening the edge to her voice, Ardith continued, "It's best you just forget. Forgetting will help ease the pain, and your papa would not want you to hurt over him anymore."

"But I don't want to forget," Winona said, jumping up from her bed. "I loved Papa. I wouldn't want him to forget me if I died."

"But you didn't die. He did." Ardith forgot all intent to be tender. She knew her voice had risen to a level that could probably be heard by Mara and her brother, but she no longer cared. She was tired of the child's constant desire to drag her into discussions about the dead man. "He's dead," Ardith said, unable to stop herself. "He's dead and gone and never coming back. The sooner you get over his memory, the happier we'll all be."

Winona's lips trembled as her face puckered and tears began to fall. "You're a mean mama. I hate you!"

Ardith slapped her daughter across the face. It was the first time she'd ever laid hands on her in this manner. The action caught them both by such surprise that they fell silent for several minutes. In her heart, Ardith wanted to apologize to Winona. But truth be told, the look on the child's face had reminded her too much of Winona's father. The thought caused her to tremble so violently she had to move to the chair in order to support her shaking body. Easing down, Ardith drew a deep breath to steady her nerves.

"I wanted to break the news to you in a more gentle way, Winona, but I'm going away. I'm going to New York City and you're going to stay with Koko on the ranch until Aunt Dianne gets home from Kansas."

Winona rushed across the room and threw herself at Ardith's feet. "Don't go, Mama. I didn't mean it. I don't hate you. Please don't go."

Ardith could see the red imprint where her hand had hit her precious daughter's face. "I have to go, Winona. I'm no good to either one of us like this. I can't offer you comfort about your papa because I have no comfort for myself. I can't answer your questions, and I can't bear to hear you crying at night because you miss him. Because I miss him too."

"I promise I won't cry anymore, Mama. I'll be a real good girl, just please don't leave me."

"I can't stay," Ardith said, feeling as though her wind were being cut off. She struggled to draw a decent breath. "I . . . can't." *I wish I could.* She pushed Winona back and jumped to her feet. Straining to breathe, she rushed for the window and opened it.

The cool air helped Ardith to regain her composure. She panted, longing to be at ease . . . at peace.

"Mama, don't go. I don't want to live with Aunt Koko or Aunt Dianne. I love you. I want you, Mama," Winona said as she wrapped herself around Ardith's waist. She clung so tightly that Ardith thought it would be impossible to break the child's hold.

"Winona, look at me," Ardith commanded.

Winona raised her head, her expression hopeful. "Yes, Mama?"

"I know you don't understand. I can't say that I understand either. But I have to go away. I can't stay. You have to be brave and strong about this. I have to go away so that I can get better. Maybe when I'm feeling less angry, I'll send for you and you can live with me in New York. Would you like that?"

Winona pushed away, the look of betrayal on her face more painful to Ardith than her looks of sorrow. "No. I wouldn't like that. I want to stay here. I want to live with you here."

"I'm sorry, Winona. I can't."

The child looked as though she might say something more; instead she turned and fled. Ardith wanted to go after her, but in truth, she was glad to finally be left alone. Ardith rubbed her temples.

"What's wrong with me? Why can't I be like Dianne? She's such a good mother. She has so much love to give. Why can't I give love? Why must I only cause pain?"

———————

"You worry too much," Mara told Zane as they walked. Autumn leaves fell into the creek and rushed away in the rippling icy water. Overhead, a pale blue sky peeked out from webs of thinly spun clouds. Zane knew it signaled a temporary change in the weather, while the woman at his side signaled a much more permanent change.

Mara smiled at him, and the look nearly did him in. She was so pretty in her green dress. Zane couldn't imagine why such a charming and youthful woman would want to saddle herself with an older man. Yet for weeks now they'd been discussing the situation, and she refused to hear his reasoning.

"I worry because it's reasonable to do so."

"Worry is a sin," Mara stated flatly. "Charity said it's like saying that God can't take care of a matter. Well, I'm not going to sin over this, and I'm sure not going to take back what I said. I meant every word."

He swallowed hard. She made him feel like a schoolboy again. "You're awfully young to even understand the full meaning of what you said."

She stopped and put her hands on her hips. "Zane Chadwick, I'm old enough to know my heart, and my heart says that it loves you."

"But think of the consequences. I'm forty years old. If we had a family, I'd probably be dead and buried before they were raised."

"And if that happened," Mara began, "then I would have to believe that the good Lord had some further plan for us. But I don't think that would happen. You're too ornery and stubborn to die."

Zane laughed at the way her expression seemed to dare him to contradict her. "I wouldn't talk if I were you. You have the queen's share of stubbornness. Most women would have walked away from me long ago."

"Most women don't possess the same love for you," she said softly. "And love conquers all. All problems, all difficulties . . . all sorrows."

He realized his mind was made up. It was senseless to fight her and his own heart. "We'd have to live in Butte or Anaconda," he said, knowing that it was the same as a proposal. "Marcus has been pestering me to move."

Mara smiled, and the look on her face was one of such self-satisfaction that Zane realized he'd been caught—roped and tied and soon to be branded. "I'll live with you anywhere so long as there's a ring on my finger."

"Butte is not a pretty town, and the air is something awful. The mining makes it bad. I can't say that there's much in the way of entertainments or anything that would appeal to a lady." He shook his head as the reality of it all sunk in. He was going to marry this woman. Marry her and perhaps even start a family. "I don't intend to stay there forever, but for now, I have business there."

"Then I'll have business there as well."

They continued walking as Zane casually discussed the rest of their life. "I don't intend to leave the territory. I like it here."

"Suits me fine."

"I like freighting too, and it takes me away sometimes. Could be I'd be gone for weeks at a time."

"But you'd come home to me," Mara said, looping her arm through his.

Her touch made him tremble, but he kept moving and talking. They were standing at the back porch by the time he finally faced her and asked, "Are you sure about this?"

She laughed. "I've been sure ever since you showed up on my doorstep months back. Sure enough to start sewing my wedding dress. Sure enough to memorize all your favorite dishes and practice cooking them."

Zane drew her into his arms. She came

willingly and fit his body perfectly. He wondered if she could feel the pounding of his heart as she put her hand upon his chest. "I just want you to be sure about this. I don't want to hurt you," he said softly.

"You won't hurt me." She stretched upward and Zane met her lips with his.

"What's the meaning of this?"

They both jumped back at the sound of Joshua's voice. Laughing, Mara went to her brother. "We've just agreed to marry. I want you to be the first to know."

Joshua looked past his sister to Zane. For a second, Zane actually wanted to run. Surely Joshua would think the age difference too great. Why hadn't he thought to talk to her brother and get him to convince her that he was too old for her?

"I don't know if that's a good idea," Joshua said slowly.

"I suppose I should have come to talk to you, since your pa wouldn't hear any of us speak on the matter," Zane offered.

"I don't have a problem with you marrying my sister," Joshua replied. "It's just a matter of the timing. Right now I really need Mara's help with something else."

"What?" she asked.

"With me," Elsa said, coming from the corner of the house.

"Elsa!" Mara ran to her, and Zane watched as the sisters embraced.

He looked back to Joshua. "What's going on?"

"I managed to slip onto the ranch when everyone was gone driving the cattle to winter range. I had her come with not much more than the clothes on her back. I figured, at least I hoped, she could stay here for a spell."

"But your pa is sure to come looking here first thing."

"Pa won't be back for at least a week," Elsa announced. "We've got a little time to figure out what's to be done."

"Probably not near enough time," Zane muttered. He could only imagine Chester Lawrence and his boys riding in, shooting first and asking questions later. "I think we've got some real trouble here." He looked at Elsa and then Mara. The look on Mara's face made him realize without a doubt that she wasn't about to let her sister go back to their father's care. Zane was about to be caught up in much more than he'd asked for.

"And to think, up until this morning I was a happy bachelor," he muttered.

———

Charity was the last person Ardith wanted to see. She knew that Winona had no doubt gone and told the old woman all about the fight. And now Charity had come to chastise Ardith and demand she not go . . . at least that was what Ardith figured.

"She's really hurting, Ardith. You can't just leave her like this."

Ardith was taken aback for a moment. Maybe Charity realized it would be futile to suggest Ardith not go. Maybe she'd only come to talk Ardith into taking Winona with her to New York City.

"I can't take her with me. Christopher . . . Mr. Stromgren said it would be impossible to give her a decent life at first. I'll be doing a great many performances, some of them quite late into the evening. I'll need to learn new music and to have hours alone for practice. Then he also mentioned dress fittings and shopping for the right things to make my appearance fit the image he desires."

"If your heart is set on making this choice," Charity began, "I know I can't change your mind. I just can't bear for you to go off like this. At least wait for Dianne to return home."

"That won't happen until spring, and from her letters we both know it's possible that it might never happen. Cole may change his mind and refuse to return to Montana. And then what? If I don't go soon, I'll lose my chance to ever do this. I've already refused one train ticket. I can't refuse this second chance."

"But, Ardith, think about what this will do

to Winona. She's only a little girl, just ten years old. She'll never be able to endure the loss."

"I endured it." Ardith walked to the window, refusing to let Charity see her cry. The memory of that fateful day when she fell into the river and was swept away from her family was always painful. "I was the same age when I nearly drowned."

"I remember it well," Charity told her. "I was one of the folks to comfort your family."

Ardith wiped her eyes with a quick swipe of her cuff and turned. "Then you shouldn't have any trouble understanding what I'm about to say. I lost everyone. There was no one to comfort me . . . no one familiar to me. Winona won't lose everyone. She'll have you and Ben and her cousins and her aunt and uncle. She'll have friends. People who care about her."

"But she won't have the one who is most important to her. She won't have you."

Ardith shook her head. "She hasn't had me for years. Not since Levi died. I might have been here physically, but I certainly haven't been here for her in any other manner. You know that's true. Why would she care if I went away?"

"I suppose because she loves you."

"She won't for long. Not if I stay. If I don't go, Charity," Ardith said sadly, "I know I'll hurt her more in staying."

Charity came to Ardith and embraced her. "Oh, my poor darling. Levi wouldn't want you to grieve so much. He wouldn't want you to hurt like this."

Ardith bristled and pushed her away. "Then he shouldn't have died. He shouldn't have lost his way in the fire and left us here alone."

Charity frowned. "And this is to be your final answer? You won't stay until spring?"

"I can't stay. I'd prefer to leave Winona with Dianne. I know Lia and the boys would be a comfort to her. She's pined around here for them since they went to Kansas. But I can't force them home."

"Then perhaps you should pray them here," Charity said, straightening. "Because that's what I intend to do."

"You go right ahead. God hasn't listened to me for years. I don't imagine He'll start up now."

Charity went to the door. "I don't imagine He will either."

Ardith was surprised by the old woman's words, and her expression must have shown as much, for Charity only smiled and opened the door, adding, "You have to talk to Him first in order for Him to hear."

CHAPTER 12

"HE WANTS ELSA TO MARRY HERBERT Denig," Joshua told Zane and Mara as they gathered around the kitchen table.

"Isn't he rather old?" Mara asked.

Zane turned to Mara. "He's the rancher to the north of your father's place, right?"

She nodded, but it was Joshua who continued the conversation. "He took the land over from his brother. Father was furious when he wasn't allowed to buy it upon Jim Denig's death, but the brothers were co-owners of the homestead. After Father realized he couldn't talk Herbert Denig out of the property, he settled down to making friends with the old man. At least as much of a friend as Father ever made with any man.

"Apparently they've concocted a plan over the years, and Elsa is the prize to be had."

"But I won't be had," Elsa stated clearly, crossing her arms against her chest. "I won't marry Herbert Denig. He's old enough to be my father."

Mara sent a quick grin toward Zane,

causing him to shift uncomfortably. More than once he'd told Mara he was old enough to be her father, but the girl refused to listen to reason. Now she seemed to find the entire matter an amusing contrast.

"I don't blame you for not wanting to marry an old man, Miss Lawrence," Zane began, "but this will be the first place your father comes looking. I suggest we work quickly to find you another place of lodging if you're to elude marriage."

"I am troubled that we can't just reach some sort of comfortable agreement with Father," Mara admitted. "I don't want to further his grief or anger."

"Father's anger won't be abated by anything we do or don't do," Elsa said, shaking her head. "He's been mean-tempered all his life, but even more so since Mother's death. I suppose he and Portia deserved each other. At least I know they seemed to fuel each other's bad moods."

"But Mr. Chadwick is right," Joshua interjected. "Father will come here first. We need to figure out a plan to keep you safe. You aren't yet twenty-one, and I don't know how strict the law will see things when Father demands you return to the ranch."

"I don't care how strict the law is—I won't go back!"

Zane blew out a heavy breath. The

Lawrence family had been nothing but trouble to him and his family. At least this was a noble cause . . . saving a damsel in distress. And the idea of marrying Mara, although not without its concerns, was a pleasurable trouble. But Mr. Lawrence wasn't going to take kindly to another Chadwick-Selby interference. Zane worried about the retribution that might be heaped on his family.

"Well, we have a little time. Not much, but hopefully enough to figure out what we can do," Zane said, pushing back from the table. "Why don't you three talk it over and see what comes to mind. Maybe we can make some decisions after supper."

He walked from the house, heading out across the porch and down the stairs. Much to his surprise he found Koko's brother coming up the dirt road, riding a brown- and cream-colored Indian pony. It was a day for surprises.

"George," Zane greeted, "what brings you to town?"

"Winter's coming on, and we figured to get supplies and mail at least one more time. Thought I'd talk to Cole and see about helping him get moved out to the ranch. Is he around?" He slid from the horse and extended his hand.

Zane responded with a hearty handshake. "Didn't you hear? Cole has decided to stay in Kansas through the spring. His father's death left the farm without a caretaker, and his mother was beside herself. Or to hear Dianne tell it, her mother-in-law was quite demanding that Cole take over his father's place on the farm and forced them all to remain in Kansas."

"That couldn't have set well."

Zane shook his head. "No, it hasn't. Dianne is grief-stricken, her letters full of sadness and longing. I wish I could figure out a way to help her, but like Morgan said, it's probably best we stay out of it."

George seemed to consider this a moment. He bowed his head and toed the dirt with his boot. "I'm sorry to hear it. I know this must hurt Dianne."

Zane didn't know what to say. He knew that George had been in love with Dianne since they'd first met. The man had always been a gentleman about the situation, however. Zane couldn't fault him for that. His love for Dianne was more an unspoken thing—a loving admiration for something that he knew could never be his.

"She's hurting," Zane said, "but she's strong. She'll figure her way through it and take matters in hand. I've yet to see her refuse to overcome her circumstances."

George looked up with a smile. "Not Dianne."

"So I guess you'll be spending the winter out there on your own. Will that bode well for

Koko and the children?"

George chuckled. "They're hardly children anymore. Jamie will be twenty next year, and he can very nearly outwork me. I swear that boy has the strength of ten men. He knows what he wants and goes after it."

"And what is it that he wants?"

"The ranch restored. His father's dream renewed."

"I can well understand that. It hardly seems fair that the laws are against him inheriting his father's place."

"It's something that's out of his control—especially now. The ranch is clearly in Cole and Dianne's hands. There's nothing Jamie or Susannah can do about that."

"Are they bitter about it?" Zane questioned. He'd seen those with Indian heritage done wrong so many times. The memories of his days in the army reminded him of the injustice he'd witnessed. Even their half-breed scouts were treated poorly. There was absolutely no respect for a man of Indian blood.

George shrugged and tied the horse to a hitching rail. "I don't think bitter is the best word. I think they regret the loss. I know they live only to bring their father's name honor, but no one wants the honor of a Blackfoot."

"But they're only a quarter Blackfoot. That should count for something."

"It does," George replied. "It counts for

being Blackfoot and not white. If Koko weren't such a strong woman of faith, it would probably be much worse for all of us."

"Why do you say that?"

George was silent for a long moment, seeming not to want to answer. Eventually he began. "I've tried hard not to be angry or bitter, as you say, about my circumstance. But at times it's impossible. I feel like the worst kind of traitor to my mother's people. I should be living on the reservation with the rest of the Blackfoot. Starving and growing sickly and bitter with my friends and family. But instead, I'm living a good life in the beauty of the Madison River valley. Despite losing everything, the ranch house and buildings and most of the stock, I still have something they don't have, nor will they ever have it."

"What's that?"

"Freedom," George replied sadly. "They will never know a free day in their lives. They will die on that reservation because it's been mandated that that is the only acceptable place for them."

"I remember having to round up tribes," Zane said reluctantly. "It wasn't pleasant. I wanted to be useful to the Indians as well as the army, but you can't serve two masters."

"It would have been different if more men would have had your heart."

Zane shook his head. "I don't know how

you can possibly not hate me, George. Even if you are the brother of my uncle's wife. I've killed your people at times."

"I've killed yours as well. Do you hate me?"

Zane met the man's dark eyes. He'd only known respect, even love, for Takes Many Horses—George. "You know I don't."

"The same is true for me. Hatred would serve no purpose. It wouldn't bring back the days when we traveled freely for weeks to hunt the buffalo. It can't bring back our way of life, our dreams. There are so many who are angry—who talk of uprisings and war against the whites. But deep inside I think they know they're defeated. They know of the talk and push for statehood. They know it means more white men, and they already know there are ten times more white men here now than were here twenty years ago when you first came to the territory."

Zane knew it to be true. He often thought of the days he'd spent helping round up the renegades as well as chasing down rebel tribes. He still bore a bit of a limp from his encounter at the Battle of the Big Hole, although it seldom bothered him these days. But way back in the early days, there weren't enough white men to fend off brutal attacks. The army's intercession had been absolutely necessary.

"I've always figured if we tried hard enough,

there ought to be a way to live together," Zane said. "But I don't see it happening now."

"No, I don't either. I don't see too many whites who want to live with Indians. But it isn't one-sided. I don't know too many Indians who want to live alongside whites. There are wrongs on both sides. Crimes enough to punish whites and Blackfoot. But whites hold the power, and they will continue to remember the Battle of the Little Big Horn for a long time to come. To whites, one Indian is pretty much the same as the next. They're all guilty of the wrongs done to Custer and his men by the Sioux and Cheyenne."

"I know what you're saying is probably true." Zane sighed. "I've often wondered what folks back East thought of the Indian wars. Those folks pushed the Indians out so long ago that the conflicts out here probably seemed nothing more than a fight in a faraway land. Still, there was some additional interest in General Custer. Folks figured him to run for president the year he was killed. I know it only managed to stir up the animosity of white settlers and eastern city dwellers. They won't remember that Custer was a bit of a . . . well . . . . I shouldn't speak ill of the dead, but he was a rather defiant man where authority was concerned. In some ways, he made his own end."

"I can't condone what happened to Custer and his men, but neither can I condone what happened on the Marias when the army slaughtered helpless sick women and children, thinking they had captured the Blackfoot guilty of killing white settlers."

"They didn't think they'd captured the killers. They knew they had the wrong party. I was there," Zane said bitterly. "I wish I hadn't been. The army knew they were attacking the wrong band of Blackfoot, but it didn't matter. My commander's battle cry was 'Kill them all. Nits make lice.'"

George shook his head, his brows knitting together. "Meaning what?"

Zane frowned. "Meaning that children . . . babies would grow into adult Blackfoot who would need to be fought and controlled."

"Ah. I see." George drew a deep breath. "We had similar thoughts toward the whites. We figured if we killed enough of them, we could eventually wipe them out altogether. We honestly thought if we caused enough problems—warred enough and such—the whites would lose interest in the territory and leave. We were fools, but we didn't understand the heart of the white man."

"Neither did we understand the heart of the Indian. I'm sure we still don't."

"Likewise."

They stood in silence for several moments

while the later afternoon sun moved further to the west. Zane was surprised that he felt somewhat of a burden lifted in talking to George. It was the first time he'd ever had a chance to really discuss his thoughts on the matter.

"Well, can you stay with us or are you heading right back to the ranch tonight?" Zane finally said, breaking the stillness.

"I'd like to stay here tonight if I can. I have a wagonful of goods to haul back, and I'd rather not just get started only to have to make camp for the night. And you know they won't rent a hotel room to an Indian." He smiled and Zane couldn't help but laugh.

"I've never checked on that, but I believe you. It's a lousy hotel anyway. You're very welcome to stay. I'm here for a few more days myself. It'll be good to talk to you about the ranch and see how things are going."

"I'd like to hear more about Dianne and Cole. Maybe you could tell me about Cole's decision to stay."

"We'll discuss it tonight after supper." Zane couldn't help but believe George really wanted more information about Dianne, but he was being polite and not overly forward on the matter. "You can put your horse in the corral. There's not much to offer him in the way of space. There are already a couple of horses in there, but we've got some good feed hay, so he shouldn't complain too much. You can wash up at the pump, then come on in and I'll find out which room the gals want you to take."

Just then Zane got an idea. He turned and looked at George. "Wait a minute, George. Do you have the cabin for Dianne ready?"

"Sure. That's why I came. I figured to help Cole make plans for the move."

"I have something else in mind. We have a little gal we need to hide out for a time. I think you just might have the place for me to stick her for a spell."

Two days later George was back at the Diamond V. Sitting down to a strong cup of coffee, he wondered how much he should tell his sister regarding Cole and Dianne. He knew the letter in his pocket, a letter from Dianne to Koko, probably explained everything, but still George felt uncertain.

"You've said very little since coming in," Koko declared as she placed a bowl of beef stew in front of him.

"I know. I've had my mind on a great deal. The signs don't look good. I think we're in for early snow—maybe heavy."

Koko nodded. "I've seen the signs as well. Susannah and I finished putting up the last of the vegetables and fruit. Jamie found us a wonderful berry patch and stood guard over us while we picked the last remnants for jam."

"I went ahead and purchased some extra provisions. Seemed the right thing to do."

"What did Cole say when you told him about the coming winter? Did they decide to stay in town?"

He drew a deep breath. "Cole wasn't there. He and Dianne are still in Kansas."

"What?" Koko came to the table and took the seat opposite George. "Tell me everything."

He pulled the letter from his pocket. "Start with this and then we'll talk."

She took the missive and read it quickly. "Oh, this isn't at all good. Poor Dianne. She sounds very defeated."

"That's what Zane told me. He said that Mrs. Selby, Cole's mother, isn't treating the family very well. She doesn't like Dianne or the children."

"Yes, Dianne mentioned that as well. Still, this letter was written some time back. Do you suppose they might have worked through their problems?"

George shook his head. "Zane said Ardith had received a letter not but a few days ago. It was worse than ever. Dianne said that Cole's mother is going out of her way to cause problems between Dianne and Cole. Zane doesn't know what Dianne will end up doing."

"Knowing Dianne, she'll take her children and come home."

George looked hard at his sister. She was completely serious. "Leave her husband?"

"Not permanently maybe, but I wouldn't put it past her to think it the wiser choice. She even implies it in her letter, wondering if we would be receptive to her return here on the ranch."

"She knows this is her home," he protested. "She needn't ask to return."

"She's always put me above herself," Koko said softly. "She has never once made me feel that the ranch was anything other than my home . . . my domain. Bless her heart, she's proven Bram's trust in her to be the right choice."

"She's a good woman," George said, still unnerved by the thought that Dianne might well leave her husband. "There's something else as well."

Koko looked at him oddly. "More bad news?"

"Could prove to be, but hopefully not. You know Chester Lawrence's younger daughter, Elsa?"

"I do remember the girl. What of her?"

"She's needing a place to hide." George toyed with the stew. "Seems Elsa was to be married to old Henry Denig, and she isn't of a mind to go through with it. Her brother helped her escape while the men were driving the cattle to winter pasture, and now they want to hide her here."

"Here? Why here? The Lawrence ranch now adjoins the Diamond V."

"I know and that's kind of the thought. Zane figured to hide her in the one place her father would never think to look . . . right under his nose."

"I wanted to share this letter with you as soon as I could. It came yesterday, but I was much too busy finishing some canning to see you," Charity told Faith as they met in Faith's parlor. "It seems things have taken a bad turn in Kansas. Dianne is quite angry. I believe she's considering things that will only bring her further harm."

"Like what?" Faith asked as she tried to skim through the letter and carry on a conversation at the same time.

"Like leaving Cole."

Faith's head snapped up. "Leave her husband? That doesn't sound like Dianne at all."

Charity nodded. "I fear she just might. She's bitter, angry, and unhappy. I've never known Dianne to sit still for long in that kind of misery. I think we need to pray for her, Faith. Even Ben is worried."

"I have been praying, but I see what you're saying. This letter doesn't sound at all like our

Dianne. Perhaps there are things entirely too painful for her to tell us on paper. We both know she wasn't happy leaving Montana."

"We must agree to bathe this in prayer day and night. Ben will be praying and fasting on this—in fact, he started yesterday." Charity paused and tears came to her eyes. "I fear for her . . . for her and the children. I even find myself burdened with sorrow for Cole."

"Poor man is caught between the devil and the desert," Faith said sadly. "He loves Dianne, but she's been unhappy with him since the ranch burned down. Now this. I'm sure he feels the situation is impossible."

"It feels impossible to me," Charity admitted, "but I know God holds the future and all things are possible with Him."

"Are you sure this is the safe thing to do?" Mara asked Zane as they packed some things for Elsa in his saddlebags.

"It's the best we can hope for right now. Maybe after we're married we can take her to live with us in Butte."

"You'd do that for her . . . for me?" Mara asked. The expression on her face revealed how deeply this had touched her heart.

He shrugged. "It would be the right thing to do . . . or at least offer. Your sister will be my sister."

Mara went to him and embraced Zane tightly. "You are such a good-hearted man. I know we'll be so very happy."

"If wishing would make it so," he began, "then I'd know it too."

"Are we ready?" Elsa asked impatiently. "If we don't hurry up, we might meet Father on the trail."

"Remember what I told you?" Zane asked. "You're to take your bags and walk down the street to the freight yard, making sure that you're well seen. Then you'll get on one of the wagons leaving for Corrine. Hopefully the local gossips will talk about this enough to give your father the wrong impression of where you've gone."

Elsa nodded. "I'll do it. I just think we'd better hurry or it's not going to matter. He was due home from the cattle drive today."

"Yes, I know. I also know a few back roads and trails. He won't find us, Elsa. I promise you that."

"If he does," she warned, "he'll shoot first and ask questions later." She shook her head. "I take that back. He won't ask questions at all."

Mara clung to Zane. "Please be careful. I worry for you."

"See what falling in love has done for you?" he teased.

"It's done more good than harm," Mara

replied. "I don't see anything wrong with caring about a person's well-being. I'll be praying for you all the time you're gone." She rose on her tiptoes and he kissed her lightly on the mouth.

"We'll practice this some more when I get back," he whispered in her ear.

Mara blushed as Elsa came to her. "If Father shows up here, you'll have to stall for time. Joshua will surely know what to do."

"We'll be fine—don't you worry."

"All right, Elsa," Zane said. "Go get your things and take your walk. I'll be heading out and maneuver around so I can meet up with you just south of town. I've instructed the men to wait with you until I get there."

He longed to kiss Mara again. He felt a brief sensation of worry as he realized how dangerous the trip could prove. If Chester and his boys had returned early to the ranch, they would be approaching town even now. "I'll see you soon," he told Mara, then mounted his horse.

"I love you," she said, unashamed.

"I love you too." It was the first time he'd spoken the words to her. It warmed his heart to see Mara break into a radiant smile. He knew she would always cherish this moment. But in truth, he would cherish it as well and fondly remember the day he had made Mara's face light up in pure delight.

CHAPTER 13

"SHE'S GOING TO BE NOTHING BUT TROU-ble," Jamie said as George introduced Elsa.

"I beg your pardon?" the young woman responded. She glared at the nineteen-year-old. "I'll have you know I'm quite capable of tending to my own needs. I'm certain I'll not trouble you."

Jamie shook his head. "Women your age are always trouble."

George wanted to laugh out loud but didn't. "Now, Jamie, that's no way to treat our houseguest." His nephew was a no-nonsense kind of man who liked things to stay even and routine. George had known bringing Elsa Lawrence to the ranch would be a risk to everyone, but he knew Jamie in particular wouldn't take well to the idea.

"She isn't staying in our house. Ma's put her in the Selby cabin."

"Nevertheless, she's a guest on the ranch and needs our help. Her father can be pretty cruel; you know that full well."

"That's what I said, she's going to be trouble." Jamie turned to go, hitting his dusty pant legs with his gloved hands.

"You have no right to accuse me," Elsa called after him. She stormed over to where he'd stopped and turned. "I'll have you know that this wasn't my idea. I'm not any happier to be stuck on this no-nothing ranch with you than you are to having me here. However, I'm in a fix and your family generously offered me the solution." She was nearly nose-to-nose with Jamie, and George thought he'd never seen anything quite so funny.

Jamie pressed his face toward Elsa's. "I don't care who invited you—you're trouble and that's just the way it is. Mark my words. There's going to be more problems having you here than getting Montana into statehood."

"Oh!" Elsa barely gasped the indignant exclamation out. "Of all the . . . well . . . all the—"

"Insults? he asked smugly. "I don't want you here. I don't want old man Lawrence coming to hunt you down and causing trouble for my family. I don't want to see my sister or my mother killed in the wake of one of your father's tirades."

"Jamie, enough," George declared. "Both of you stop acting like wild cats tied up in a bag. If all goes well, Mr. Lawrence isn't going to know anything about Elsa being here. After all, why would she come here? It would make more reason for her to join her brother and sister in Virginia City. When Mr. Lawrence sees that she's gone from there and hears the rumors of how she took a freight wagon south to Corrine, perhaps he'll give up."

"But she didn't take a freight wagon south to Corrine," Jamie protested. "She came here."

George grinned. "Only after she was clearly seen riding a southbound freight wagon out of Virginia City."

Jamie shook his head. "I suppose I have no say in this. I've never had a say in anything." He stomped off, causing the dust to rise.

Elsa turned to George. "Is he always like this?"

George nodded. "Sometimes he's even rude." They both broke into laughter.

Dianne was glad that September was over. The heat of Kansas had abated, and the nights were quite chilly. With the cooler weather, Lia's asthma seemed to lessen in severity. She breathed easier and gained a little color back into her cheeks. That had done much to rally her spirits, but there was still the awful truth of facing a winter away from home. This, coupled with the fear that they might never return to Montana, continued to wedge itself between Dianne and Cole.

Dianne was putting away the last of Cole's

freshly ironed shirts when he appeared at their door. She looked at the clock and noticed it was bedtime. "I didn't figure to see you here this early." She tried to keep the sarcasm from her voice.

"I know. I was hoping maybe we could have a sort of truce," Cole said softly.

Dianne looked at the hopefulness in his expression and her anger melted. "I'd like a truce."

Cole closed the bedroom door behind him. "I'd like to talk, if you feel up to it."

"I don't want to fight," she admitted. "I haven't the energy for it."

"I've noticed you're wasting away. It's had me worried. I don't remember ever seeing you this thin. Even Ma commented on how your clothes are just hanging on you."

Dianne started to react to that comment but forced her retort back down. "I'm sorry I've worried you, but it's been very hard to care about food with so many other things on my mind."

"I know," Cole said, nodding. He pointed to the chair across the room. "Why don't you sit there and I'll sit on the bed."

She went willingly to do as he suggested. She could tell he wanted very much to share his thoughts with her. It was the first time in a long, long while that he had made any move to open the lines of communication between them.

"Dianne," he began as he took his seat on the edge of the bed, "I've never meant to hurt you. I only wanted to do the right thing . . . to be a good man and care for those who needed me. I know you're unhappy here. I know you were unhappy in Virginia City. I'm sorry on both accounts."

She sighed. "I know I didn't make it easy on you. I feel like I spend so much of my time getting angry and repenting that little else gets done."

"My choices haven't always been right . . . but, Dianne, I need to be the man of this family. My mother believes you to be interfering and dominating, and I know that is sometimes the case." He held up his hand as she started to protest. "Please hear me out. I defend you constantly to my mother. You don't hear it, I know, but I'm always telling her to stay out of it. I tell her you're a good wife and mother, and I point out all the help you've been to her."

This took her by surprise. She honestly didn't think he ever defended her to his family. She folded her hands together and allowed herself to ease back into the chair. "Go on."

"My mother has her way of doing things. She has always been the one to run our family. She was never satisfied with my father's decisions, and she constantly undermined his authority. We children had little respect for our father because it was clear he had little respect for himself." He looked up and met her gaze with an intense expression. "I can't let that happen in my own family. I can't see my boys raised to feel toward me what I felt toward my pa."

"I've never told the boys you were anything but a good man and father. Sometimes they don't understand why you've turned away from us," Dianne said. "In fact, sometimes they think you don't love them anymore."

Cole frowned. "With my father's death and then the harvest . . . it was hard to have much time for them. But now that winter is coming, it should be easier."

"But with winter coming, why can't we just go home?" Her voice was soft, pleading. She didn't want to anger her husband and break the tender truce, but the question had to be posed.

"My mother needs us. I can't just leave her. Dianne, can't you see how torn I am? I know you want to go home. I know the children want to go home." He got up and began to pace. "God knows I want to go home."

"You do?" She couldn't help but ask. She'd honestly believed that he had come to think of this farm as his home.

Cole stopped and looked at her with an expression that suggested disbelief. "Of course

I want to go back. I don't like it here any more than you do."

She felt tears come to her eyes. "You could have at least told me that. I might not have felt so alone then."

"It seems I tried to tell you at least a million times. But every time I started to share, you got mad at me and started arguing about leaving."

Again Dianne wanted to protest, but she held her tongue. The Lord was convicting her of the truth in his statement. She had been argumentative and harsh. She hadn't wanted to hear a word he had to say on any matter, with exception to one, and that was when they would return home.

"I've needed to talk to you about all of this, but I didn't feel like I could. Ma demanded I talk to her, and while I try not to speak to her about things that concern you and me, she has a way of getting information out of me."

"She has a way of controlling everything she touches," Dianne said, holding back any display of emotion.

"She does indeed. I can't argue with you that my mother is a very controlling woman. She has her thoughts and plans and doesn't like anyone coming along to change them."

"But she's cruel in the process." Dianne couldn't help but think of all the times Mary Selby had been horribly mean to Luke or

Micah or John. Lia pretty much steered clear of her grandmother, choosing instead to hide behind Dianne's skirts any time the woman came into the room, but the boys weren't of such a mind. And because of this, they were always paying the price.

"Do you have any idea," Dianne began, "how she treats your sons?"

He drew a deep breath and went back to sit on the bed. "No. Why don't you tell me about it."

"They can do no right. If your sisters' kids are here, it's obvious that your mother loves them and desires to spend time with them. She barely even speaks to our boys except to reprimand or criticize. The other day, Micah brought home some art from school. He'd drawn a picture of the ranch, even though he could only remember it from our visits out there in the last couple of years. Your mother told him it was a foolish thing, that boys his age should not be given to drawing and wasting their time, but rather they should be learning to work at their father's side."

"She said that?" Cole questioned. "Why would she do that?"

Dianne shrugged. "There's so much more than that. She tells them their manners are atrocious, that their beds are never made correctly, though why she concerns herself with that when I am seeing to it, I'll never know. She tells them their posture is bad, that their hair is unkempt, that they chew too loudly. She constantly criticizes their endeavors. John and Micah set the table the other day and your mother spent fifteen minutes chastising them for placing the silverware too close to the plate."

Cole's face took on a blank look. "I had no idea."

Dianne felt sorry for him and softened her heart even further. "She continues to believe Lia is somehow inventing her illness, even though the child is much better and rarely has an attack these days. Seems to me if Lia were doing it for attention, we'd still be dealing with her coughing fits and inability to breathe." Dianne realized she shouldn't limit this conversation to the wrongs done her by Cole's mother. "We're coping with everything, but we miss you and we miss home."

He nodded. "Dianne, I never meant for this to happen. I figured we'd come here, see my father before he died, and then leave after the funeral. I honestly didn't set out to keep you from your mountains . . . from Montana."

She saw the sorrow clearly written on his face. "I know," she whispered. "I know, too, that I said things that implied otherwise. I'm sorry."

"I don't want to stay here any longer than we have to. I promised Ma we'd be here through the winter. She constantly tries to bring up issues related to spring, but I promise you I reject discussion of anything to do with spring and the planting that will come. Instead, I try my best to talk her into selling the place or at least hiring a full-time man."

"Can she afford a man to work here?"

"She should be able to offer one room and board. There's a nice room off the back of the barn. I could easily set it up for someone to live in. Wouldn't take much work at all. I suggested it to her, but she said she needs me. I feel so bad for her. I know she's got to be grieving, but I can't take my father's place in her life."

Dianne felt the first inklings of optimism since coming to Kansas. "As long as you realize that, I have hope. Hope that wasn't there even moments ago."

"It's what I've tried to tell you over and over. I don't plan for us to stay here, no matter what you hear my mother say. Sometimes I let her ramble because I don't want to fight with her. If I start fighting, she'll just find ways to make me feel even more guilty, and I'm bearing all I can right now."

Dianne got up and went to where Cole sat. She reached out and touched his face with her hand. He placed his hand over hers and pressed it tight to his cheek. "I'm sorry for the anger and lack of love. I do love you. You must know that."

He looked up and pulled her onto his lap. Cradling her against him, he breathed into her hair and sighed. "I've longed for you. I've needed so much to find refuge in your arms. You have no idea what this separation of bitterness has done to me."

"If it's been half as destructive to you as it's been to me," she said, choking back tears, "then you must be devastated."

He stood, lifting her in his arms. "You are my life . . . my love. I cannot stand for things to be as they have been. I cannot live with barriers between us."

She nuzzled her mouth against his ear and whispered, "Let there be nothing between us but the love God always intended." She didn't even bother to wipe away her tears as they fell against his face and neck. As Cole began kissing her with a passion that had been missing for so very long, Dianne seriously doubted he was even aware of her tears . . . or of anything else but the overwhelming emotion of the moment.

———

Dianne went about her morning chores with great gusto and enthusiasm. She had spent a wondrous night with her husband, and the love they had shared had renewed her will to live . . . to fight for what was hers and hers alone.

The boys and Lia noted the difference as she readied them for school. They seemed to absorb her joy, and for the first time she could remember, they went out the door with smiles on their faces and exuberant talk about what the day would bring. Even Lia seemed content to work at cleaning up their room and making the beds while Dianne finished the breakfast dishes.

Humming to herself, Dianne thanked God for the peace that had been made between herself and Cole. It was hard to believe how much time had passed since she'd really prayed.

I'm sorry, Lord. I'm sorry for being so distant. I'm still frightened about the future—I can't lie. She wiped out the cast-iron skillet and oiled it with a bit of bacon grease to ready it for later use. *Please help me, Father. I know things haven't changed with Mary. I don't know how to deal with her.*

As if on cue the woman stormed into the kitchen. "What kind of lies have you been telling my son?"

Dianne stared at the woman in dumbfounded silence. She put the skillet down lest the temptation to throw it across the room grow too strong. "I don't know what you're talking about."

"You vicious little hussy. You think to turn him away from me, but you have another think coming." Mary's pinched face loomed threateningly in front of Dianne. "I know what you hope to accomplish, but you cannot win. I won't give up this fight." She pressed her finger into the middle of Dianne's chest. "You are nothing to me. Your brats are nothing to me. But Cole is my son and I need him. I will not allow you to divide my family by stealing him back to that godforsaken land you call Montana."

Mary turned to leave the room, and Dianne struggled to find some composure for her thoughts. She wanted to say something harsh to hurt the woman as much as she had hurt Dianne. But at the same time, thoughts of Cole's tenderness and love from the previous night buffered her from the worst of Mary's attack. *God can make this right,* Dianne thought.

"I know He can make this right," she whispered.

"What was that?" Mary asked, whirling on her heel at the doorway.

Dianne smiled. "I said God can make this right."

Mary laughed and sneered. "To be sure He can. He has a way of dealing with sinful women like you."

CHAPTER 14

DIANNE DIDN'T KNOW HOW SHE MANAGED to keep her mouth shut, but she said nothing as Mary stormed from the room. Later that afternoon, Cole's sisters showed up, and before Dianne could realize what was happening, they had congregated with their mother in the kitchen, where Dianne was baking cookies. It was to be war, and Dianne quickly realized she was the enemy.

"Why can't you just mind your own business?" Cordelia began. She was careful to avoid the counter where Dianne was working, turning her nose up at the mess of dough and greased pans.

Dianne looked to each woman and was about to comment on this strange assault when Laurel narrowed her eyes and said, "You have been nothing but heartache to this family. I'm sickened by the way you treat my mother."

"She's mourning the loss of our father and yet you constantly go out of your way to further the wound by suggesting Cole desert her," Cordelia interjected.

Dianne wanted to give them all a piece of her mind. She wanted to lash out with cruel words and bitter regard, but instead she prayed silently and offered them cookies. "I've a fresh batch just out of the oven. They should be cool by now," she said, indicating a tray that sat on the windowsill.

"Haven't you heard a word we've said?" Laurel questioned.

Dianne turned back to face them and folded her hands in front of her. "If you truly wish to address this matter, I will discuss it. However, I would point out to each of you that I seriously doubt if you were in my position that you would take kindly to such an attack."

"But they aren't in your position," Mary Selby countered. "They are respectful wives who are obedient to their husbands."

"And how, Mother Selby, would you say I've been disobedient to my husband?"

Mary puffed up, seeming only too happy with such a question. "You've done nothing but make demands of him from morning until night. You question his decisions and chastise him for his choices. Since deciding to stay here and help me, a good and respectable thing if ever there was one, you've grieved him by demanding to return to Montana."

"That's right. I've heard you," Cordelia said. "We've heard you." She looked to her sister for confirmation. Laurel nodded.

"What transpires between me and *my* husband has little to do with any of you. What I have seen is that you three have purposefully gone out of your way to make me feel unwelcome and make my children feel as if they were unimportant."

"A good Christian wife would do as she's instructed," Mary said. "The Bible says you are to be obedient to your husband. An obedient wife is not one who questions her husband when he instructs her to do things a certain way."

Dianne knew the verses on wifely obedience as well as anyone. She had been convicted on several occasions for not being more openly cooperative with Cole's desires. Still, her pride wasn't about to confess this to his mother.

"You have done nothing but try to hurt our mother since coming here," Laurel said, sneering down her nose at Dianne. Her dark blue gown with its tailored jacket and bustle seemed far too elaborate for kitchen talk. Laurel hadn't even bothered to remove her bonnet or gloves and appeared more ready for a ladies' social than arguing.

"I'm sure you ladies might feel better," Dianne said, forcing herself to remain cheerful, "if you were to partake of some refreshments. Why don't you go into the sitting room, and I will bring you tea."

"We aren't here for tea," Cordelia snapped.

"We're here for resolution."

Dianne nodded. "I would very much like resolution myself. You see, I disagree with your notion that I've been trying to hurt your mother. Despite your mother's lack of civility toward me and my children, I've taken over most of the work that she previously held responsibility for. Is that not true, Mother Selby?"

The old woman stammered, obviously surprised by this approach. "Well . . . that is to say—"

Cordelia patted her mother's arm. "Do not worry yourself with such matters, Mother. It's only fitting that she take on the chores. It's her little monsters who make the biggest messes and cause such destruction."

"I beg your pardon. My children have done no harm to this house or to your mother. They have worked alongside me to ease the burden."

"But you disagree with your husband's desire to stay here," Cordelia argued.

"But it isn't my husband's desire to stay here," Dianne countered. "He told me as much last night." She felt her prideful nature rearing and fought to control her anger.

"How dare you lie about such a matter," Mary Selby said, stepping forward. "My son has told me over and over that he would love nothing more than to remain here farming in his father's stead. It's your lack of willingness—obedience—that grieves him and causes him pain."

"'Wives, submit yourselves unto your own husbands, as unto the Lord,'" Laurel said with an authoritative air.

"Exactly," Mary said. "And it further states, 'For the husband is the head of the wife, even as Christ is the head of the church.'"

Dianne was rapidly losing her struggle to contain her emotions. "It also says, 'Husbands, love your wives, even as Christ also loved the church, and gave himself for it; that he might sanctify and cleanse it with the washing of water by the word, that he might present it to himself a glorious church, not having spot, or wrinkle, or any such thing; but that it should be holy and without blemish. So ought men to love their wives as their own bodies. He that loveth his wife loveth himself. For no man ever yet hated his own flesh; but nourisheth and cherisheth it, even as the Lord the church: for we are members of his body, and of his flesh, and of his bones.'" She lowered her voice for emphasis and continued, "'For this cause shall a man leave his father and *mother*, and shall be joined unto his wife, and the two shall be one flesh.'" Dianne drew a deep breath and set her jaw.

"Long winters in Montana leave you with little but washing, sewing, and memorizing

Scripture. If you want to have a holy war of words, throwing out verses to support your hateful ways, I'm more than happy to answer the call. However, be advised, I don't merely quote the words of God, I believe in following their meaning as well."

"Well, I never!" Cordelia said, stepping back a pace.

"I didn't suppose so," Dianne said, knowing her tone was insulting. "My point here is exactly this: Cole and I are married. We are one flesh. God brought us together, and God will severely punish the person who seeks to drive apart what He has joined together."

"You don't frighten me with your memorized Scripture," Mary announced. "You are no woman of God or you wouldn't act in such a manner."

"I do admit," Dianne began, "that there have been times when I've been less than charitable. For those times, I ask your forgiveness. However, I have had nothing but good intentions toward you, and still you reject my kindness and help. God knows the love I've offered you has been cast aside as worthless."

The older woman folded her arms against her chest. "I don't know what you're talking about."

"I've invited you to come live with us in Montana. I've encouraged you to stay with us and enjoy your latter years in rest instead of work."

"I have no desire to live in Montana. I couldn't leave my daughters."

"That's right," Cordelia said, her pink striped gown swishing loudly as she whirled around to take hold of her mother's arm. "We need her here. We enjoy her company far too much to lose her."

"Then let her come live with one of you," Dianne suggested. "It's obvious she cannot farm this place alone."

"That's why Cole should stay," Laurel answered haughtily. "Mother knows she's welcome to live with either of us, but she loves the farm. It reminds her of Father."

Dianne nodded. "Then let her take on a hired man, as Cole suggested."

Both girls seemed surprised by this and looked to their mother, whose face contorted in anger. "This is my son's inheritance. He now owns this farm, and he should be the one to live here and work the land. Not some hired man. Besides, I couldn't begin to afford a hired man."

Dianne was ready for this. "Then Cole and I will pay for him."

Laurel and Cordelia were speechless, but Mary had little trouble in answering. "I wouldn't take your money."

"Maybe not, but you think to take my

husband. You think to steal away the father of my children." Dianne knew her temper was getting the best of her. "Now, if you'll excuse me, I have to finish baking these cookies and start supper. The children will be home from school shortly, and I'd appreciate it if you would act civilly toward them instead of insulting them from their first appearance."

"Oh, you are such a rude, ruthless woman!" Cordelia declared. "My brother shall hear of this conversation."

"I would expect as much," Dianne said, preparing the cookie dough. "Just remember, God is overhearing each word you speak. He knows what transpired here, and He won't allow the righteous to suffer forever."

The trio stormed from the room with that. Dianne realized she was nearly panting for breath. Her anger had set her heart to racing, and her head felt as though it would burst. "Lord," she whispered, "I am trying so hard not to argue with them, but they sought me out and, well, you already know what happened, so I won't go over it again. I'm begging you for help, Father. I'm a willful woman with a temper, and it's hard to remain soft-spoken."

Elsa Lawrence had had about as much of Jamie Vandyke's temper as she could stomach. The man was constantly harassing her, very nearly denouncing her character. His attitude at breakfast had been the final straw, and she now intended to call him to answer for it.

Marching across the yard, her yellow-plaid dress dragging along the ground due to her failure to wear a bustle, Elsa was determined to put Jamie in his place once and for all. Why her brother thought this the safest place for her to hide was beyond her reasoning. For all intents and purposes, Jamie was nearly as much trouble to live with as her father.

Elsa approached the corral where Jamie was working and demanded his attention. "Come here at once. I've had all I will tolerate of your insults. Your behavior at breakfast was abominable. You criticized me for everything from the clothes on my back to my love of potatoes."

Jamie rolled his eyes. "What in the world is this all about? Can't you see I'm working?"

"I see you standing around while that stallion gets the best of you," she retorted.

Jamie threw down his rope and climbed over the corral fence. "If you think you can do a better job, be my guest."

Elsa was never one for backing down from a challenge. "I'll prove to you once and for all that I can earn my keep and be just as good at ranch work as you are. I've been ranching all my life. I know plenty." She hiked her skirts and crawled between two lower rails of the fence.

"Get out of there," Jamie commanded. "You're gonna get hurt."

Once inside the corral, she eyed the angry horse. "You have to gain his trust, and you must never look him in the eye."

"My uncle wouldn't agree with you," Jamie answered from behind her. "He thinks such notions are silly."

"Then he doesn't know horses as I do."

"Ha! He was the pride of the Blackfoot village. They called him Takes Many Horses because of his ability to steal ponies from his enemy."

"Stealing ponies and making them into good saddle horses are two entirely different things." Elsa approached the stallion from the side, making sure he could see her, and began talking to him in a low tone. "I won't hurt you, fella. I'm your friend."

"That's a laugh. You haven't been friendly to anyone since you arrived."

She ignored him and focused on the animal. "I won't hurt you." She didn't raise her hands or head, but rather watched from hooded eyes. The bay calmed. He was no longer laying his ears back, but instead he turned to watch her, shifting his ears to hear her.

"Good boy," she murmured. "You know I won't hurt you."

Elsa rejoiced as she finally stood in front of the horse. He seemed mesmerized, transfixed. Elsa let him nudge her gently, then she carefully touched his shoulder with her hand. "Easy. I won't hurt you."

"He doesn't understand a word you're saying," Jamie declared, jumping up on the fence. "Now get out of there before he decides to stomp you into the ground."

The bay startled at Jamie's actions and backed up. When he came in contact with the fence, he began to snort.

Elsa wanted only to calm the animal, but already Jamie's presence in the corral had broken the mood between her and the bay. She turned abruptly to reprimand Jamie, only to realize the horse had put a hoof down on her skirt. Fighting for balance, Elsa was unimpressed when Jamie rushed forward to catch her.

Unfortunately, the speed with which he approached caused the bay to rear. He whinnied loudly, stomping and snorting in protest. His flailing hooves barely missed Elsa's face.

"Get out of here," Jamie said, pushing her toward the fence.

"Don't tell me what to do," she protested as she regained her footing. She turned to say something more, but just then the bay's left hoof made contact with Jamie's forehead.

Elsa screamed, frozen momentarily by the sight of blood as it splashed down Jamie's face. She ran forward, waving the beast off. "Back! Back!" she cried over and over.

Jamie staggered. "I knew you'd be nothing but trouble," he muttered and fell to the ground. The bay wanted no part of either of them and began to rear again.

It was George who saved the day. Elsa was never so grateful to see anyone as she was to see Jamie's uncle.

"What are you doing in there?" George demanded as he jumped into the corral. He grabbed Jamie's rope and expertly threw a loop around the stallion's legs. Pulling the rope tight, George dug in his heels. Elsa watched in fascination as the horse lost his footing and dropped to the ground.

"Get Jamie out of here," George commanded.

Elsa went to where Jamie lay. He was unconscious and the head wound bled in frightening consistency. *This is all my fault. I caused this. If I hadn't been so angry at him, I would never have risked either of our lives to prove something that didn't need proving.*

Elsa took hold of Jamie's arms and pulled with all her might to drag him to the edge of the fence. *For such a tall, skinny man, he sure weighs a lot,* she thought. George continued controlling the stallion as Elsa crawled back out between the rails and somehow managed to pull Jamie out under the bottom rung.

"We're out!" Elsa shouted to George. "Please hurry. He's bleeding badly."

George released the horse and leaped over the fence in a single bound. He came to where Jamie lay and scooped the boy into his arms as though he weighed nothing. "Go get Koko. She'll know what to do."

Frantic to not make another mistake that might further endanger Jamie's life, Elsa hiked her skirts and ran as fast as she could to the Vandyke cabin.

"Koko! Koko, where are you!"

Susannah and Koko appeared from the pantry. "What is all this commotion about?" Koko asked.

"It's Jamie. The horse . . . struck him," Elsa said between gasps for breath. "George . . . George has him."

At that moment George came into the cabin with the unconscious Jamie in his arms. Koko cleared the table. "Put him here," she instructed. "Susannah, get some hot water and my herbs. Elsa, go to the chest in my room. You'll find an old sheet. Bring it and we'll tear it for bandages."

Elsa hurried to the room, admiring Koko's ability to put aside the fact that her son was bleeding and tend to only what was necessary. Rummaging through the chest, Elsa spotted the sheet and hurried to take it back to Koko.

"It's all my fault," she muttered as she caught sight of the bleeding lump on Jamie's head. "I've killed him."

Koko looked at her oddly. "Nonsense. The horse barely clipped him. He'll be fine."

"He doesn't look fine," Elsa said, tears streaming down her face. "He was trying to rescue me. I was in the corral and I fell. He caught me. Then when the horse tried to trample me, Jamie threw me to safety while leaving himself open to danger. Oh, I can't bear this. If he doesn't make it, I will have killed him."

Jamie moaned and Koko chuckled. "If he dies from this, he's not as tough as I thought."

Elsa sobbed into her hands. "I'm so sorry. I'm so very sorry. It was my pride that did this. I had to show him that I was better than he was at working with horses. I was just so mad at him because he thinks I'm nothing but a ninny. Oh, maybe I am."

"It was foolish to be sure," George said. Elsa looked up and met his compassionate gaze. "But I doubt you've killed him."

"Jamie is always doing something like that," Susannah offered. Her expression was as loving as her uncle's.

Elsa stood amazed that they weren't hateful and angry with her. Her own father would have whipped her for such foolishness, even though she was a grown woman. Elsa moved to where Koko tended her son. "Let me help. It's the least I can do."

Koko simply nodded. "Tear the sheet into strips."

––––––––––

"She hasn't left his side," Koko told George as she came into the kitchen.

"She'll make a good nurse."

Koko laughed. "Or a good wife."

His head snapped up. "Wife? They can't stand each other. All they do is fight."

"I have a feeling things will be different after this," Koko mused. "I have a feeling this might go far beyond nursing a sick man to health."

George shook his head. "I'll never pretend to understand women. Just when you think you know where everybody stands, a woman will up and change the situation every time."

She laughed. "We only change things until they suit us."

––––––––––

Zane listened with only moderate interest to his twin's tales of adventure while hunting mountain goat. Normally he would have found Morgan's supper conversation to be refreshing, but things had changed since Mara entered Zane's life.

"Roosevelt actually managed to bag

another two goats before we headed back. He's really quite a determined man. He's overcome great adversity, including sickness. He's struggled with a weak constitution all his life."

"That must be hard," Zane muttered. Truth be told, Zane's mind was absorbed with the fact that he was to be married. He hadn't even had a chance to tell Morgan yet, and he worried that perhaps the news would be discouraging or depressing for his brother. Still, he had to tell him.

"You might say that my hunt went well too," Zane finally threw out. "I bagged me a wife."

Morgan's forkful of steak stopped midway to his mouth. "You what?"

Zane laughed. "Maybe it would be more accurately said that Mara Lawrence bagged me. We're to be married." He sobered and looked hard at Morgan. "I didn't know how else to tell you. I hope I haven't . . . well . . . you know."

Morgan ignored this and put down the fork. "When? Where?"

"Virginia City. Before the first of November."

"That doesn't give much time for a wedding," Morgan said, rubbing his bewhiskered chin. "Am I supposed to be there?"

Zane laughed. "I kind of hoped you'd be my best man."

"I suppose that means I'll need a bath and a haircut."

"I'd appreciate that. I think Mara would too."

"Married," Morgan muttered. "I can't believe you've gone and gotten yourself caught and hitched."

"Well, the hitching hasn't exactly taken place yet, but yeah, I guess I'm pretty well caught."

"Do you love her?" Morgan questioned, his brows drawing together. "I mean, really love her?"

"I do," Zane admitted. "She's all I can think about. I still think I'm too old for her, but the thought of her with any other man makes my blood run cold."

Morgan drew back and cleared his throat. "Yeah, well, I guess I know how that goes."

"I'm sorry." Zane leaned forward. "I didn't think about what I was saying. I sure didn't mean—"

"I know you didn't mean anything by it, Zane. Don't give it another thought. You should be happy about your marriage to Mara. It's a good thing, and I'm not sorry about it. I'd have to be a pretty petty fellow to begrudge my brother the same happiness I would have eagerly taken for myself."

Zane eased back against the ladder-back chair and sighed. "You don't have to be my best man—not unless you want to. It wasn't very thoughtful of me to impose that on you."

Morgan shook his head. "We're brothers. And besides, I'm doing fine. Trenton and Angelina are happy. That's all that matters. If the good Lord has another woman for me, she'll come along in due time. I don't expect it will happen, but I won't say no if it does."

Zane brightened. His brother had always implied before that there was no other woman in the world for him. Zane had actually envisioned his brother growing old and dying alone. "Great. I'm heading back to Virginia City in a week. Will you stick around and go with me?"

"Guess so. It'll take me that long just to scrub off the dirt and get myself looking respectable." Morgan touched his hand to his shoulder-length blond hair. "Guess you better point me in the direction of a good barber."

CHAPTER 15

"YOU HAVE TO DO SOMETHING ABOUT Dianne," Cordelia declared to her brother.

Cole had just finished mending one of the

harnesses when his sister bounded into the barn. He put the piece aside. "What's wrong now?"

She shook her gloved finger at Cole. "You should know very well what's wrong. She's hateful and mean. She has deeply wounded our mother by her constant threats of returning to Montana."

"But Cordelia, we are returning to Montana," he said softly. He watched the expression on his sister's face change instantly from anger to sorrow.

"You cannot mean it. You simply cannot leave us. Mother has so come to depend upon you, and if you leave it will be the end of her."

"Oh, come now, Cordelia. Mother isn't quite that fragile."

Cordelia bit at her lower lip and looked to the ground. "I didn't want to say anything, but . . ." She paused and after a long pregnant silence looked up. "The doctor told me that Mother isn't well. Her nerves were tested during Father's illness, and now with you being uncertain about staying . . ."

He shook his head. "But I'm not uncertain about staying. I've already told Dianne we'll leave in the spring, and that is what I intend to do."

Despite the fact he was covered in dirt and straw bits, Cordelia took hold of him and embraced him tightly. Cole found it rather

remarkable that she would risk her stylish out-
fit. She usually seemed so completely bound
up in worries over fashion and elegance that he
was surprised she'd even come out to the barn.

"You aren't going to change my mind,
Cordelia. My home is in Montana. I've already
promised my wife."

"Then this is all her fault," she snapped,
practically pushing him backward as she let go
of him. "I told you she was mean."

"Dianne's just tired and lonely. She's told
me how hard she's tried to befriend you all and
how you snub her. Why would you do that,
Delly?"

Cordelia frowned, clearly irritated at the
use of her childhood nickname. "I told you not
to call me that, and I've done nothing wrong.
It's your wife who refuses to act in a decent
manner. Haven't you even noticed that no one
at church can bear her company? Why, you
haven't been invited to any of the important
parties, and all because of her."

"I haven't even been invited to your house,
Delly," he said, emphasizing her name. "You
and Laurel both seem to think yourself well
above inviting the likes of a Montana rancher
and his family into your homes."

"Well . . . you must understand," she
began, "it's your children. I have expensive
pieces in the house; so does Laurel. Your boys
are not known for their manners. They are

constantly breaking things, and it's a blessing Mother doesn't have valuable pieces or she'd be sure to lose them."

"What have the boys broken? I'm happy to replace anything they've been responsible for destroying." He watched his sister as she darted her glance from side to side. It was clear she wasn't comfortable with giving him examples.

"I cannot say what's been broken. Mother was the one who spoke about it. I fear it would only further her grief if you were to mention it, however."

"Still, you brought it up. There must be something of importance there or you would not have wasted your time."

"Cole, please hear me out. Dianne is manipulating this situation, and when you aren't around she is vicious and ill tempered. Mother is quite afraid of her."

He laughed. "Now I know you're lying. Mother isn't afraid of anyone."

"I'm not lying," she declared, stomping her foot. "When you aren't around, Dianne is positively horrid. I fear she'll one day unleash her temper and then we'll all suffer for it."

"If she's that bad, then I should get her out of here—leave and go home to Montana right away before she does someone harm," Cole began. Cordelia's face fell and she opened her mouth to speak, but he waved her off. "But you told me you wanted us to stay. Insisted that it was the only way Mother would keep from falling victim to some state of apoplexy. So now I'm completely confused. Are you demanding we stay or go?"

"I'm simply telling you that your wife is unruly and harsh. She needs to learn her place, and you need to put her in it before she hurts someone."

"Cordelia, I have work to do. I'll speak with Dianne tonight and see what she has to say about all of this, but honestly, I think I know my wife well enough to realize she isn't capable of treating Mother with the kind of brutality you've described."

Cordelia gave a loud huff and turned. "You'll rue the day you didn't intercede," she called over her shoulder. "Mark my words. You'll see."

Her skirts swept the dirt as she stomped out of the barn.

Cole watched Dianne throughout that evening. She was nothing but gentle and kind to his mother. But could there be some element of truth to Cordelia's words? He knew Dianne was unhappy, and in the past he had heard her deliver rather harsh words to his mother. But generally speaking, those were in response to his mother's pointed comments.

By the time they retired for bed, Cole had tossed the subject around in his mind until he was sick to death of it. He felt like Dianne had changed so much since they'd lost the ranch, and yet who could blame her? Her entire way of living—a way she cherished—was gone. She had no chance to recover that loss because he had been unwilling to risk failure. He sighed and added more guilt to his already growing list of inadequacies.

"You were awfully quiet during dinner," Dianne said as she came into the bedroom.

"I've had a lot on my mind. I wouldn't mind discussing it with you, if you have a moment."

"Of course," she replied, appearing surprised that he should suggest such a thing.

Cole knew the days when they'd shared everything in lengthy discourse before retiring for the night were only vague memories. He missed that closeness and wished they could somehow recapture it. Maybe this was the way to start.

"My sister Cordelia came to me today. She was unhappy about the way you treat Mother yet was determined to talk me into staying here. She wants us to drop the idea of leaving in the spring."

Dianne appeared to wrestle with her thoughts for a moment. She quietly went to the edge of the bed and sat down. "And what did you tell her?"

Cole was surprised that she didn't offer any

argument. He smiled. She truly appeared to be trying hard to keep her temper in line. "I told her we were going home in the spring." Dianne smiled and looked to her folded hands while Cole continued. "She told me the doctor feared for Mother's well-being if we left, but I find that hard to believe. Mother is quite healthy, and I see no reason to fear for her life."

"They are awfully desperate. I suppose it might have something to do with the fact that you now own the farm," Dianne said softly.

"But they know they have nothing to fear about that. I think they've decided how it should be and now they want me to toe the line."

She shrugged and looked into his eyes. "I don't understand any of them. They came to me the other day, angry and snarling about how awful I was to try to take you from them."

"They did that?"

She nodded. "They told me I wasn't being a good Christian wife because I wasn't being obedient. They thought to have a battle of Scripture with me until I unloaded a half dozen on them in response."

He laughed. "I can well imagine. I've never known anybody to memorize more Scripture than you."

"I held my temper. I offered them cookies, then suggested tea . . . but still, Cole, they were ugly and rude to me."

"I'm sorry, Dianne. To hear Cordelia and Mother tell it, it's the other way around. It really puts me in a bad spot."

"Why don't you just tell them you're going to sell the place?" she blurted out. "It's your farm now. You own it; the lawyer had all the papers put in order. Tell your mother that she needs to go live with her daughters or even with us, although I can't say I truly desire that be the case."

"But you would tolerate it in order to get home to Montana, eh?" he asked with a grin.

"I'd let Satan himself take a back bedroom if it meant going home."

"You don't mean that," Cole said, moving to where she sat. He reached out and gently pushed back strands of golden hair. He'd noticed she was starting to get a few gray hairs—no doubt they were the result of living in such disharmony. "I know you better."

"Well, perhaps I wouldn't go that far," she agreed, "but honestly, Cole, you don't have a great deal of time. Before you know it, it's going to be time to prepare the fields. I heard Mrs. Meiers at church say they would begin burning off the fields in late February."

"There's no reason I can't help with that. We probably wouldn't head back home until April, maybe May. After all, most of the passes would be snowed in."

Dianne frowned. "Cole, that's a whole lot

longer than I figured on. It's already October. If we don't return before May, we will have been here almost a year." Her voice was edged with such sorrow that Cole could hardly bear it.

"Well, maybe we could try for March. Still, I could help with burning off the fields."

"But why not just sell it now and go home before the heavy winter sets in? If you could find a buyer in the next couple of weeks, we could still get home before the weather turns too bad."

He nodded. "Maybe I'll mention it to Mother. If her health truly is bad, then she definitely should be in town closer to the doctor."

"Exactly," Dianne said, smiling again.

Dianne had to admit she liked the Kansas autumn. The trees were a riot of color and the days were such a contrast from the balmy warmth of summer. Standing outside now, taking clothes from the line, Dianne felt a peace about her that hadn't been there in so very long.

I don't know why I let things trouble me so. Surely Cole will make things right. He'll let his mother know that he wishes to sell the farm, and then we can all go home. Hopefully without his mother in our number. She giggled to herself and managed to drop a clothespin in the wake of her amusement. Bending to pick it up, Dianne was startled to hear the panicked cry of her son John.

"Mama! Mama! Come quick, Mama!"

She pulled up, forgetting the clothespin. "What's wrong?" she asked her boy as he bolted across the yard.

"Grandma is hurting Lia. Hurry!"

Dianne easily outdistanced her son as they raced for the back door. *Whatever is he talking about?* Mary might not like the children, but would she actually seek to hurt one of them?

Dianne nearly pulled the screen door from the hinges as she rushed into the house. "Lia! Where are you?"

The girl's cries could be heard coming from the dining room. Dianne made her way there and found Mary Selby striking Lia over and over. Without thinking, Dianne rushed forward and grabbed Lia's arm, pushing Mary back as she did. For a split second Mary did nothing but sputter incoherent words. Then without warning she threw herself backward against the wall, screaming as she did. Landing in a heap on the floor, she began to weep.

It was then that Dianne realized Cole had stepped into the room behind her. Dianne could see that he was confused by what had just taken place. No doubt from his vantage point, he thought Dianne had thrown his mother to the floor.

"I can explain," Dianne began.

"Don't listen to her," Cole's mother said, her sobs now drowning out Lia's. "I was only trying to discipline Lia for stealing."

"Stealing?" Cole questioned. "Lia?"

Mary nodded and composed herself a bit. Dianne was certain it was only to make her words more audible. "I found my ruby brooch, the one Laurel and her husband gave me, hidden in Lia's things."

"Lia would never steal anything," Dianne contradicted. "You are lying!"

"Dianne, silence," Cole commanded. He went to help his mother up from the floor. "Mother, I can't imagine Lia taking anything, but even so, why would you take meting out her punishment upon yourself?"

Mary moaned and cried out as Cole helped her into a chair. "I fear," she said, sounding much weaker now, "that I'm injured. Your wife was merciless. Would you call for the doctor?"

John seemed to feel the need to defend his sister. "Lia didn't take your old ugly brooch. I saw you put it in her things."

Cole turned to his son. "John, you need to be quiet."

"They're all against me," Mary sobbed into her left hand while her right remained limp in her lap. "I think my wrist is broken, and I'm having double vision. Perhaps I'll die and then none of you will have to worry about me."

Cole sighed. "I'll get the doctor, but first let me help you to bed."

"Don't leave me with them!" Mary pointed her finger at Dianne and the children. "You saw what she did—at least in part. She hit me hard before you came and then threw me backward. What's to keep her from smothering me in my bed? No, you'd best hitch the buggy and take me with you."

"This is impossible!" Dianne declared.

"Dianne," Cole warned, but she would not be silenced.

Dianne advanced on Cole's mother. "I've taken all I'm going to take from you. You were beating my daughter. Not punishing or disciplining, but rather taking out your anger toward me on a helpless child. You are never to lay a hand on my children again, so help me."

"Dianne, calm down," Cole said in a low stern voice. "You shouldn't have hit her. She's just an old woman."

Dianne threw him a look of disbelief. "I didn't hit her. I only grabbed Lia away from her."

"I saw the whole thing . . . well, I didn't see the hitting, but . . ."

She looked into her husband's eyes. He'd been convinced of her guilt without even allowing her to explain the situation. "If you side with her in this, I swear I'll take these children and leave within the week."

"Dianne, be reasonable. I saw most of it." His voice was sad, almost resigned, and she wanted to scream. "Mother shouldn't have hit Lia, but you shouldn't have hit her. You certainly shouldn't have thrown her backward. I'm going to get the buggy and take her to the doctor. Why don't you go upstairs and we'll discuss this when I get home."

Dianne shook her head. "I've lived with this for months now. Her lies and your unwillingness to see the deceit of your family. Children, go upstairs."

John quickly took hold of Lia's hand and left the room. Dianne stared hard at Mary Selby for a moment. She could see the older woman's delight in the way things had played out.

Turning from her, Dianne walked to the door. "Cole, I mean it. I'm going to make arrangements to leave by Friday. Either you come with us or stay here. It's your choice."

Dianne could hear Cordelia yelling even from upstairs. Seeking sanctuary in her small bedroom, Dianne prayed for the nightmare to end. Her own husband would not hear the truth. She tried to explain what had happened, but Cole felt he'd seen enough and it didn't matter that Lia bore a swollen lip and bruised cheek. It only mattered that Dianne had supposedly harmed his mother.

Now Cordelia and Laurel had arrived to sympathize with their mother. Dianne could hear Cole trying to calm them, but they took turns yelling at the top of their lungs about the indecency of Dianne's actions and how the sheriff should be notified.

Dianne felt especially bad for her children. The boys and Lia were congregated at the foot of her bed, wide-eyed and terrified.

"Mama, will they send you to jail?" John asked. "I can tell the sheriff that you didn't hit Grandma. Even if Papa doesn't believe me, the police will."

"No one will send me to jail," Dianne replied, not at all certain if she was telling him the truth.

"Will Grandma come and hurt me again?" Lia asked.

"No. No one will hurt any of you. I plan to sleep in your room with you," Dianne said. "You three boys can sleep together in one bed. Lia and I will sleep in the other. Tomorrow we'll go to town and get our train tickets so we can go home as soon as possible."

"What about Papa?" Micah asked.

"Papa is making his choice tonight," Dianne said sadly. "Papa may not come with us to Montana. If that happens, it won't be because he doesn't love you." For all her anger at the way Cole had allowed himself to be manipulated, Dianne didn't want the children to hate their father.

"It's because of Grandmother Selby," Luke said, his voice tinged with bitterness. "She's a mean old woman."

"Luke, that isn't respectful. We may have had our difficulties with her, but God would still call us to respect her."

"But she lied about you, Mama," John said firmly. "I saw her. You didn't hurt her. You didn't hit her. You didn't even make her fall."

She nodded. "I know, John. And because you know what happened, maybe someday others will know the truth as well."

"I hope Papa will come with us," Lia said, slipping from the bed to come to Dianne. "I get sick on the train."

"I know, sweetheart," Dianne murmured and drew the child into her arms. "But we can't stay here. We aren't welcome anymore." *We were never welcome.*

———

"Don't try to stop her from going," Cordelia insisted. "We want her gone."

"She's my wife and her place is at my side," Cole countered. "If she should go, then I should too."

Cordelia took hold of his arm. "You can't

mean to go now. Not with mother so terribly injured."

He looked at his mother. She seemed completely without strength and very pale against her propped up bed pillows.

"She's a danger to Mother," Laurel added. "You cannot allow her to threaten Mother's life anymore."

"I don't believe she meant to harm anyone," he said firmly. "To hear Dianne's side of this—"

"I don't want to hear Dianne's side of this," Cordelia proclaimed. "She doesn't deserve to have a say. I think we should send for the sheriff and have her arrested."

"Really?" Cole said rather snidely. "You'd put my wife in prison and then expect that I would stay here? You'd best think again. If you do anything to harm her, I'll take my family and leave now."

"Please," his mother said in a low moaning voice. "Please don't leave. I've endured much worse." She sounded weak, and Cole wondered how much damage had truly been done.

"She plans to leave," Laurel stated firmly. "I say, let her go. Let her take her gamins back to Montana and let us go on with our lives."

"Those *gamins*, as you call them," Cole said angrily, "are my children. Children I am quite proud of. In fact, the only reason I dragged them across the country and brought them here was because of that pride. I wanted to share them with my family."

"And you have. We all think they're wonderful," Cordelia said, trying to calm him. "But they aren't civilized. They don't know how to behave in school or church."

"I've not seen them act inappropriately in church," he replied. "If you have a report of this, then you should have that person with a complaint come to me—instead of taking it to my sister."

Cordelia fidgeted. "Cole, the point of this is that Dianne has her mind made up to go. That might be for the best right now. She can always come back at a later date, perhaps after she's had time to think about what she's done."

"I don't think she did anything purposefully," he reiterated.

"Well, we certainly can't take a chance on that, now can we," Laurel said. "I mean, after all, it could take Mother's life . . . next time."

Chester Lawrence had eaten as much dust as he could stomach while moving the cattle to winter pasture. He'd been glad to see that despite the drought and summer fires, the area he'd chosen for his cattle was in good order with tall, dried, undisturbed grasses. There was plenty of water too, although the river was down considerably from previous years.

"You boys get these horses put away, then clean up and get in the house for supper," Chester instructed Jerrod and Roy. He was glad his two oldest hadn't deserted him yet but knew it was only a matter of time. They'd both already told him they wouldn't be at the ranch through winter, and they really weren't all that much help. At least not until Chester promised them both a hefty sum of money. That had put their back into their work.

Chester wasn't at all sure what the future would hold because of this. He'd always figured to have the boys and even their families working alongside him for the years to come. But now that was clearly not going to happen. His hope would have to lie in Elsa. Perhaps she could bear him some sturdy grandsons.

In the meanwhile, Chester had hired an extra twenty ranch hands for the cattle drive, keeping on ten of those to stay out with the herd for the winter. It wouldn't be the same as having his sons there. Sons who stood to inherit the fortune would care about the livestock, maybe even risk their own comfort to see to the herd, but not hired men. He'd be lucky if all ten lasted the winter.

Heading into the house through the back porch, Chester pulled off his heavy coat and gave it a good shake. It would need to be cleaned. He'd have to remember to get someone to see to that. For now, he tossed it onto a peg and went into the house.

"Elsa!" he called in a loud booming voice as he entered the kitchen. He pulled off his hat and gave another holler. "Elsa! Where are you?" He had plans to tell her of his further arrangements with Henry Denig. The only time he'd mentioned her marriage to the older man, Elsa had been livid, spouting off that she'd never marry him. But Chester wouldn't let her slip away from him the way he'd allowed Mara and Joshua to go.

"Elsa!"

"Sir, she's not here," the cook told him as she came in from the dining room.

"What do you mean, she's not here? Where is she?"

"I don't know."

Chester slapped his hat against his leg. "What are you talking about? Has she gone for a walk or a ride? Where is she?"

"She's been gone for over a week. Left just hours after you and the boys moved out with the cattle."

Chester let loose a stream of curses that would make most men pale. "It's that no-good brother of hers, isn't it? He came here while I was gone, didn't he?"

"I didn't see him, sir. I only saw Miss Elsa take out on her horse."

"I know where she's gone," Chester snarled. "And I'm not going to tolerate it. Get supper on the table and be quick about it. I have business in Virginia City and it won't wait."

CHAPTER 16

"I THINK THIS DRESS IS GOING TO BE PERfect," Charity told Mara as she took in the waistband and pinned it securely. "You were certainly wise to heed the Lord in making it."

"It was funny," Mara admitted. "I knew I wanted to marry, but there was no man to choose. Still I felt the Lord direct me to prepare."

"Like the wise virgins in the Bible," Charity mused. "Only with a gown instead of oil."

Mara laughed. "Well, maybe not quite."

"There," Charity said, stepping back. "I think we've tucked and tightened all the right spots. It looks perfect now, and I can easily finish the alterations by tomorrow."

"You still have a couple of weeks," Mara said, trying hard to get a look at herself in the gown. It was difficult to model the dress and see how it fit all at once. Twisting around, she tried to get a glimpse of the bustle. "Is the train lying right?"

Charity checked the back again. "It's perfect. Not too long—just the proper length, and it drapes so nicely. You were quite creative."

"I took one of my older gowns and patterned it after that," Mara told her. "I knew there'd be little chance to buy a real pattern or even have a gown made professionally."

"And why should you when you have such a talent for sewing? You should consider doing this professionally. I hear that Mrs. Danner is looking for an apprentice."

"Truly?" Mara thought it might be a wonderful way to earn money. Then she remembered Zane had already told her they wouldn't be living in Virginia City. At least not for the time. "I don't suppose it would be prudent to begin work with her. Zane plans for us to live in Butte or Anaconda."

Charity nodded. "I'd forgotten all about that. I've not visited Anaconda, but Butte is not at all a nice town. They've torn down all the trees, and the mines and smelters have corrupted the land and air. It's certainly not as lovely as the Madison Valley where you grew up—not even as nice as Virginia City." She leaned forward as if sharing a secret. "And it's full of rowdies and lowlifes who need the Lord."

Zane had already warned her of the town

and its bad air. "I know from what Zane has said that it won't be as nice, but I'll be with him, and that makes up for a great deal."

"Then it must be true love," Charity teased. "For anyone who would willingly move to Butte in order to be with a man must surely love him."

"I do," Mara said, smiling.

"Just keep practicing that phrase for the wedding." She laughed and added, "Although I seriously doubt you need to practice. Sounds to me you have it down to perfection."

———

"Where's the Selby house?" Chester Lawrence demanded at the livery.

"Cole Selby? He lives in that big house up on Idaho, near Warren Street. He ain't there, though. If you had business with him, he's in Kansas right now."

"Kansas?" Chester asked the balding, overweight stable keeper. "Why Kansas?"

"Heard tell his father died. He went back there to take care of his mother. Took his family earlier this summer. Don't know if he's coming back."

"Well, good riddance, I say. Never could stomach the man. What about the others? Are they still living in the house?"

"The sister is still there. Mrs. Sperry and her daughter, Winona. There's also a couple of other folks there. A brother and sister."

"Mara Lawrence?" Chester asked. The man nodded and Chester growled. "She's my daughter."

"Oh, well, then you've probably come for the wedding. Ain't for another couple of weeks, though."

"You certainly know everything about everyone," Chester said, throwing the man a coin. It wasn't in his nature to give money away, but the man might prove useful at a later date and Chester wanted to make sure he kept on friendly terms.

"Thanks, Mr. Lawrence. You want I should put that horse of yours up for the night?"

"Maybe later. Right now I'll need him to get around." Chester reined the horse back toward the street. "Thanks for the help."

He didn't wait to hear the man's reply but instead rode out to find his sons. They were loafing, as usual, in the closest saloon. Seeing that they were well into their second glass of beer, Chester sneered down his nose at them. "It would benefit us all if you were to remain sober long enough to help me retrieve your sister."

"How will it benefit us?" Jerrod questioned.

Roy nodded. "Yeah, how'll it benefit us?"

Chester had suffered their temperaments long enough. He cursed them both and added,

"Stay here and drink yourself to death. I really don't care. In fact, don't even bother to come back to the house. Just head out for whatever parts you were figuring to head out to and save me the touching good-byes." With that, Chester forgot all about having any kind of refreshment for himself. He stomped out of the saloon and mounted his horse, still cursing his children.

Why had his life taken such a sudden turn for the worse? It seemed to Chester that all his best laid plans were being usurped by his disrespectful offspring. It was too late in life to start over. He had no desire to marry again— especially after Portia. He still wasn't entirely sure how he'd managed to let that woman weasel her way into having him marry her. It wasn't like him.

But he had to admit there was something about Portia Langford that had been almost mesmerizing. He supposed he went along with marriage first of all because she made it clear that she'd get rid of his nagging, sickly wife. That appealed in ways Chester couldn't even begin to list.

Then there was something about the power she seemed to exude. She struck him as a female counterpart to himself, so it seemed natural that they should be together. But she was gone now, and Chester had no desire to endure another woman. He wanted the power and glory for himself. He wanted a bigger spread, more cattle, and stronger herds. He wanted it all.

"And I would have left it to those no-good, ungrateful brats of mine—if they hadn't turned traitor on me."

Yet Chester held hope that he'd find Elsa. She wasn't yet twenty-one, so he could no doubt get the law to help him see her returned to the ranch. First he had to locate her, however. No doubt she was hiding out with her sister and cowardly brother. The thought of Joshua sneaking in after he'd left for the cattle drive and stealing Elsa away made Chester want to pummel the boy. No doubt he'd arranged for everything.

"Well, he won't get away with it."

The small town was fairly quiet for a weekday. Chester made his way to a large two-story house on Idaho Street and, seeing it to be the nicest in the neighborhood, figured it must be the Selby house. He dismounted and looked around. The place seemed to be deserted.

He tied off the horse and marched up the front walk to the porch steps. He was about to climb them when Joshua appeared in the doorway.

"Father. I was expecting you."

"Where is she?"

"Where is who?" Joshua asked flatly.

"You know good and well who. Where's

your sister Elsa?" Chester was in no mood to brook the boy's nonsense.

"Elsa isn't here, I can tell you that much. Beyond that, I won't betray her."

Chester charged up the stairs. "I'll beat it out of you then." He raised his fist, but Joshua only crossed his arms against his chest.

"Do what you think right, but I won't tell you where Elsa is. She came to me for protection when you would offer her none. Now she's safe and happy and far away from here."

Chester let out a stream of profanity that made Joshua wince. "She's not yours to protect or hide. I have a business arrangement, and you aren't going to ruin this for me."

"I'm sorry, Father, but I cannot help you in this. You're welcome to come in and have some coffee with me. I'd like to talk with you instead of fight."

"I don't have time for talking. I need to know where my daughter is. If I have to, I'll involve the law."

Joshua frowned. "If that's how you want it. But I can't understand what drives a man to care nothing for his offspring. You could have had our loyalty if you'd only given us kindness and love instead of hatred."

Chester was unmoved by this attack, and that was truly how he saw it. Joshua would fight him with words of love and God, but it would be a fight just the same. "I'm going to round up your brothers from the saloon, and then we're going to find your sister."

Joshua said nothing, but his gaze never left Chester. The old man thought for once his son actually showed some gumption—some strength of character. Unfortunately, it was to Chester's frustration and detriment, instead of his benefit.

———————

"I don't understand why I can't get back to work," Jamie protested as Elsa took away his breakfast tray. His sister, Susannah, came into the room with a basin of warm water and a washcloth.

"You can't get back to work because Mama said you couldn't."

At nearly seventeen, Susannah had taken on the grace and charm of their mother. Her skin was as white as Elsa's, but her hair was dark black like her mother's. Her Blackfoot heritage was hidden in an exotic beauty that had men in Virginia City noticing her much too often for Jamie's comfort.

"I'm tired of being bossed around by a bunch of females," Jamie said, struggling to throw back his covers. "I'm not taking this anymore." He got up and ignored the wave of dizziness that momentarily blurred his vision.

Elsa returned from taking the tray and

shook her head. "You aren't supposed to be out of bed."

"Help him to a chair," Susannah instructed. "I have to change his bedding anyway."

Elsa went to Jamie and looped his arm around her shoulder while taking hold of his waist. If Jamie hadn't been weak-kneed before, this action certainly brought it on. In the days since the accident, Elsa had been at his side, completely devoted to seeing him well. And in that time, Jamie had found himself more and more taken in by her charming attention.

"Come on. Let's get you to the rocker," Elsa said, pulling him along.

Jamie stumbled a bit, leaning heavily on Elsa—maybe more heavily than was needed. He liked the feel of her soft touch, the way she smelled so good. He couldn't help but wonder what the scent was that wafted from her hair, but of course he couldn't ask. That would really be unseemly.

Elsa helped him into the chair much too quickly and released him to retrieve a blanket. "Here, this will keep you warm while Susannah and I see to the chores."

Jamie found it hard to understand the change in Elsa, but he liked it. She'd come to the ranch all spit and tacks—angry and wounded. Now she seemed content, even happy. Perhaps she was one of those people who could easily dispel with the past and look only to the future.

The girls changed the bed quickly and had just finished pulling back the covers when his mother entered the room. "I see you're up. That's good. I think today you may walk around a bit if you like. I want Elsa or Susannah with you when you are up, however."

"He was about to start a rebellion," Susannah declared. "I guess he doesn't like all this good service."

"I don't like layin' around doing nothing. There are animals to be tended."

"Your uncle has been seeing to them," Koko said calmly. She smiled and came to examine his head. "This has healed nicely. I'm confident you'll be able to get back to work in another week or so."

"Another week!"

The girls both giggled. "I wish someone would give me a week without work," Susannah said. Elsa nodded enthusiastically. This wasn't a battle Jamie was going to win.

"Elsa has fixed you a mixed berry pie. She used some of the dried berries we picked up in the mountains earlier in the summer. I'm sure you can smell it baking. If you behave yourself and don't exhaust your body, you may have some at lunchtime."

Jamie tried not to react to the news. The thought of Elsa baking something just for him made his stomach flutter. He wasn't used to having these feelings or even this interest. Talks with his uncle George had pretty much given Jamie the idea he should spend the rest of his life alone, unless he could find a woman of Blackfoot descent who was in the same fix as he was. No doubt they were out there, but Jamie didn't know exactly where. And even if he could find them, he wasn't convinced that was the answer. After all, why would he put his children through the pain and suffering he'd known his mother and uncle, and even himself, to a lesser degree, to experience? But the issue hadn't even come up because there were no girls of mixed breeding to rouse his interest. So far he'd only met snooty white girls whose parents had obviously warned their daughters about his heritage. But now there was Elsa.

Elsa didn't seem to mind his heritage. At least she'd never indicated otherwise. He watched her from the chair while she finished helping Susannah clean the room. Was it possible they could have a future together?

"I've left you a basin of water," Susannah told him. "If you don't feel strong enough to wash up, I'll stay and help you. I can even shave you if you want."

"I can take care of myself!" he insisted, irritated at the comment. His sister was making him look the fool in front of Elsa.

His mother laughed. "Come, girls. Let us

go and leave Jamie to himself."

As much as he didn't want to admit it, Jamie had a hard time washing up and dressing. He felt completely exhausted by the time he worked the last button on his shirt.

"How are you doing?" his mother asked as she peeked into the room.

He grinned. "Well, I don't like to admit it, but I'm beat. I feel like I should go back to bed." His grin faded. "This will pass, right?"

Koko nodded reassuringly. She came into the room and closed the door. "It takes time to recover from a head wound. I didn't want to frighten the others, but you took a pretty good blow. I was afraid you might end up with pressure on the brain, but you bled out good, so I think you'll be fine."

Jamie sank into the rocker and sighed. "I knew it was worse than anything I'd experienced before. Even that time I broke my arm didn't hurt this bad."

His mother picked up his bedclothes and neatly folded them. "So it would seem to me that Elsa has taken quite an interest in your recovery." Her change of subject took him by surprise.

"She feels guilty," Jamie declared.

"I think it's more than that."

"Truly?"

She laughed. "You sound as though you'd like it to be more than that."

He felt his face grow hot and lowered his gaze to the floor. "I guess I was thinking that might be nice. But she's not going to be interested in someone like me—someone with Blackfoot blood."

"Jamie, you have to let the Lord guide your heart and life. If it's meant to be, He'll open a door to that prospect."

"He never seemed to care much about me otherwise. God didn't make it so that I could inherit the ranch or so that I could have my father with me now."

"But He kept you on the ranch by means of your cousin's generosity. In fact, Dianne always talks about this being your ranch as much as hers. And He brought you Uncle George right when you needed him most."

Jamie knew her words were true, but he'd been harboring feelings of frustration toward God for longer than he wanted to admit. "It's not the same."

His mother gently touched his face. "No, it's not. I miss your father more than I can say. I loved him so much. We were so happy here."

Hearing her sadness, Jamie shook his head. "I'm sorry. I shouldn't have said anything. It's just . . . well . . . sometimes things are hard and I feel angry."

"But God isn't the enemy here. Blame the laws of the land or blame the prejudices of people, but don't blame God. You must remember we are people who make mistakes and bear those consequences. I loved your father very much, but should I have forsaken that love because of my heritage? Saved you and your sister the possibility of being Blackfoot?"

"No!" It hurt something fierce, but he refused to back down. "I don't regret being Blackfoot, and I wouldn't have anyone else for my mother."

"Then you mustn't grieve over the way things have turned out. Part of your frustration with God is because of my choice to marry a white man. You have to think these things through and reason them out so that you don't make poor choices. My decision to marry your father was a good one, motivated by love. But again, there was a price to pay. For him. For me. For you and Susannah."

"And for Elsa, if her feelings turn out to be something more than friendship," he murmured.

She nodded. "That's very true. But let her make the decision as to whether or not the price is too high to pay. I don't regret my choices or the price. Talk to Elsa. Tell her about your heritage and about the problems that have come from being part Blackfoot."

Jamie thought for a moment. "I will. It's probably best to do that early on. That way, if there isn't any interest, neither of us will get hurt."

Koko leaned down and kissed her son on the head, opposite his wound. "It's too late for that," she mused. "I'm certain you've already lost your heart."

———

"Your brother is so hard to figure out sometimes," Elsa told Susannah as they hung clothes on the line.

"Why do you say that?"

Elsa looked at the beautiful young woman. She was so tiny and pretty. Elsa felt like a clumsy ox next to Susannah. How could Elsa expect a sixteen-year-old girl to understand these feelings?

"Well, sometimes he seems to want me close by," Elsa began, feeling quite awkward. "Other times he seems unhappy—even annoyed that I've come into the room."

"I think he's still simply trying to recover," Susannah said. She looked up from the clothes basket and asked, "Are you ready to help me with this sheet?"

Elsa nodded and took up one end of the piece while Susannah grabbed the other. Together they hung the sheet across the line and pinned it in place.

"I hope he doesn't hate me for my part in his accident." Elsa sighed. "I didn't mean for him to get hurt. He's such a nice person too."

Susannah laughed. "You didn't think so when you first came here."

Elsa had to smile. "No, I suppose I didn't. He seemed so difficult, like he didn't think I was good enough to be here because I was a Lawrence."

Susannah shook her head and picked up the basket to move down the line. "He probably felt much more inadequate because he has Indian blood and you don't."

This snapped Elsa out of her moody thoughts. "Has it really been a problem for you? You don't even look Indian. Neither one of you."

Susannah said nothing for a moment. She put the basket down and lifted out a pair of Jamie's pants. "It doesn't matter what you look like sometimes, but rather what people know about you—about your past. Folks in these parts knew my father and mother. They know my mother is half Blackfoot. Therefore, they know her children are part Blackfoot as well."

"But that's hardly a reason to punish. It's not like you're a full-blooded Indian."

Susannah looked at her oddly. "And if I were, would you hate me then?"

Elsa realized what she'd said. "I never thought of it that way. I mean . . . well . . . you have to understand how I was brought up. My mother and father hated Indians because of the threat and the troubles they'd seen. My father used to tell stories about entire settlements being burned out because angry Indians wanted to see the whites put off the land."

"I've heard stories from Uncle George that tell of whites murdering Indians for the same reason."

Elsa felt troubled in her spirit. "It shouldn't matter, should it? The blood, I mean. Whether you're part or full-blooded Indian, it shouldn't matter."

Susannah looked at her with great compassion. "It shouldn't, but it does. Mama said that the blood of Jesus should be the only blood we concern ourselves with, but it will probably be a very long time before most white people see it that way."

Elsa felt she'd received a real education that morning. In her heart, she knew Koko and George, though of Blackfoot heritage, to be wonderful people. On the other hand, she knew her own brothers, Jerrod and Roy, to be horrible people—deceptive and cheating. They were as white as the day was long. There wasn't any chance of Indian blood tainting their lineage. But when it came down to a matter of whom Elsa would rather be with, she could easily say that Koko and George were the better choice.

"Susannah, I'm sorry if anything I've said offended you," Elsa said, shaking her head slowly. "I've been raised by people who cared only for themselves. I feel I'm learning everything anew."

Susannah came to her and hugged her for a brief moment. "At least you're willing to learn."

———

Several nights after speaking with his mother, the time to talk with Elsa presented itself before Jamie even realized what had happened. Susannah, suffering from a cold, had gone to bed early and Uncle George and his mother were busy with expense records, sequestered away in the kitchen. That allowed Jamie and Elsa to sit at the far side of the house in front of the fire.

"How's your head?" Elsa asked, toying with a cup of tea.

"It's better. Doesn't hurt as much when I'm up and around."

"I still feel so bad. I'm really sorry, Jamie. I know I've said that before, but I just can't shake my guilt."

He smiled. "You're forgiven. Don't give it another thought." She put the tea aside and looked deep into Jamie's eyes. He felt his heart skip a beat as she leaned closer.

"I know I wasn't very nice when I first came here. I have to be honest with you: I was terrified. I'd heard horrible things about your family."

"My family?"

"I'm afraid so. My father was not very kind about the fact that your mother was part Indian. He said you were savages, all of you. That he intended to see you all on the reservation. Luckily, he got caught up in other matters, namely buying up the valley and everyone else's herds."

"I had no idea." Jamie's heart sank. If she was raised to despise them because they were of Indian blood, what hope could there be to share his heart with her?

"Your mother has been talking to me about God," Elsa continued. "I didn't understand a lot of things. Joshua had helped me to know a bit about Jesus, and Mara has such a strong faith, but I didn't understand."

"I know what you mean. My mother's faith has always been rather intimidating. She talks about Jesus as though He were in the next room."

Elsa laughed. "Exactly. She has a friendship with God that I cannot understand."

"Me either, but I envy it."

"Yes!" she practically gasped. "Me too."

They fell silent for several moments, and all Jamie could think of was how to turn the subject back to his heritage. He wanted to know—needed to know—how Elsa felt now.

"I hope you aren't still afraid of being here," he barely breathed. He held her gaze, searching for the truth in her eyes.

"Oh no, I'm not afraid. I feel the opposite of how I felt then. I've come to love your mother. I hadn't realized how much I missed my own mother until I came here. Your uncle is a fine man too."

"Despite the fact he's a half-breed?"

"Oh, Jamie, I don't even care about that anymore. I've come to realize the color of a person's skin, the ancestors they claim—none of that matters when it comes to the heart. Your sister helped me to see how my family's beliefs were wrong. She and I talked the other day, and I know now I have a great deal to learn. I'm just not all that sure where to start."

He reached over and touched her hand. She didn't flinch or pull away; in fact, her expression warmed and he felt her approval immediately.

"Maybe we could read the Bible together," he said, feeling at a loss for words. "Maybe if we did that every night, we'd find the same kind of faith that Ma has. Maybe we would both learn the things we need to know."

Elsa turned her hand to clasp his. "I'd like that, Jamie. I'd like it very much."

He felt rather sheepish. "I have to admit, I have a long ways to go until I understand why things happen the way they do. I've been bitter most all my life because of my father's death and inability to leave me the ranch. I've often wondered why, if God was the creator of the universe and in control of everything, He couldn't make this one thing right—for me."

"I can well understand that. You know, I don't have Indian blood, but I have Lawrence blood. And around these parts, that's sometimes seen as being even worse."

Jamie looked at her for a moment and considered her words. He'd never thought of it quite that way. He'd been angry when the daughter of his enemy had come to stay with them, but now he felt entirely different. "You know, we have a lot in common."

She smiled and looked at her hands. "I think so too."

"Maybe we can help each other more than we realize."

CHAPTER 17

SHE'S LEAVING. SHE'S TAKING OUR *children and returning to Montana, and there's nothing I can do about it.* Cole kept hearing her words over and over in his head. Kept feeling them slice into his heart.

I could go with her—with them.

"But how can I leave Ma to fend for herself? Especially now with her sprained wrist and bruised hip?"

Cole ran his fingers through his hair. He wanted to pull his hair out by the roots as the frustration of the moment washed over him again and again. *How can she say she loves me—yet leave me?*

Cole had wrestled with the situation ever since the incident in which his mother had gotten hurt. He didn't really believe Dianne had pushed her, even though from where he stood, it looked as if she'd done the deed. John and Lia had both told him what had happened. He hated himself for not letting Dianne have her say when she wanted to, because now she wasn't talking at all. All that remained between them was a look of betrayal in her eyes that pierced him to the core of his being.

"Pa?"

Luke stood at the doorway looking almost afraid. Had his own son come to fear him? To despise him?

"What is it, Luke?"

"Why do you hate us?"

"What are you talking about? I don't hate you. Did somebody tell you that?

Luke shook his head and lowered his gaze. "No, sir."

"Then why would you say such a thing?"

"Well, you never talk to us no more. You don't read us stories from the Bible like you used to. You never come tell us good-night."

Cole was instantly convicted. He was guilty on all accounts. "Son, I've just been busy. It certainly doesn't mean I hate you."

"Mama said you loved us, but you always used to tell me that when you loved somebody you made time for them. That's why you spent time with us, you said. Now you don't spend any time with us, so I figured—"

"Come here, Luke," Cole interrupted.

Luke came across the room and looked up apprehensively. "Yes, sir?"

"Son, you'll be eleven in December. You're old enough to understand that sometimes folks have to sacrifice what's important to them so that they can meet the needs of other people. Your grandmother is sad and she needs me. She's heartbroken over the death of her husband. She feels alone and afraid."

"Mama feels alone too. And she cries all the time, so I know she's sad," Luke said softly. "We need you as much as Grandma does."

Cole knew his son's words were true, but there were no easy answers. No way to resolve this without hurting someone. His wife and children were his first responsibility, but they were all very capable, while his mother was aging and not at all able to tend to the needs of a big farm.

He heard the wagon outside and knew that Cordelia or Laurel had come to care for their mother. This had become a daily event, and Cole hated it because they always insisted on berating him for Dianne's actions.

"Son, my sister has come and I need to tend to the buggy. We can talk about this some more later on."

He nodded. "Mama says we're going home. I sure hope you'll be coming with us." He waited, as if hoping to hear Cole say something in response, but in truth there were no words Cole could offer his son. Luke's expression fell and his shoulders hunched forward ever so slightly as he left the room. *He knows the truth,* Cole thought. *He knows I'm staying here. But why am I staying?*

Cole waited until Luke had gone before heading outside. He wasn't at all happy to have to deal with whatever his sister might say. Both Cordelia and Laurel believed that Dianne was a threat to their mother and had asked on more than one occasion for her to be removed from the house. Cole had already explained that Dianne intended to leave, but she'd taken ill the day after the accident and had been unable to go. *At least until today.* Dianne seemed recovered now and had spent the entire morning washing and packing.

His sisters had told him that her illness was God's punishment for her meanness to their mother, but Cole didn't believe that. Dianne was the light of his life. Her kindness and love had been a comfort to him through all sorts of trials and hardships.

"How can I let her leave without me?" he murmured, heading to the door to take care of the buggy for his sister.

But how can I leave Mother without help—without at least imposing some form of resolution on her regarding the farm?

The questions would not let him be. Neither would they be easily resolved.

To Cole's surprise both Cordelia and Laurel were in the buggy. They were dressed in their city finery, looking for all the world as though they were heading out to a social function instead of visiting their ailing mother.

"We have to talk," Cordelia demanded.

"Yes, Cole. We have to talk."

"Well, talk then." Cole's irritation was evident as he helped them from the buggy. He knew they would simply harangue him again about Dianne and the incident.

"We do not feel that Mother is safe. If Dianne isn't well enough to travel, then put her in a hotel," Cordelia demanded.

"I suppose we could move to a hotel," Cole

said, knowing it wasn't what they wanted to hear.

"We don't want *you* to move to a hotel. Just your children and Dianne. Mother was quite vexed and hurt by Lia's thievery."

"And," Laurel picked up where Cordelia left off, "by the boys' rowdiness and constant noise."

"Then of course," Cordelia continued, "Mother is terrified that Dianne will do her harm while she's unable to defend herself."

"Stop." He put as much force into the word as he could muster. Both his sisters seemed taken aback, but they said nothing. "Stop speaking against my wife in such a manner. She may not always do or say the things you'd like, but she has tried to get along with everyone. I can't say that you've done the same with her."

"Cole, you mustn't be deceived by her," Cordelia said, reaching out to take hold of him. "She isn't the good woman you think. She's had plenty to say behind your back. She's not at all happy with you for keeping her from her beloved ranch, and she's not afraid to speak out about it."

He tried to show no reaction whatsoever. He wasn't sure if Dianne had spoken to them about the ranch and her life here. He couldn't imagine his wife sharing such intimate thoughts with his sisters.

"She isn't happy here anyway. So let her go," Laurel said firmly. "Stop trying to keep her here. She isn't even being a proper wife to you."

"How would you know?"

Laurel blushed. "Well . . . Mother . . . that is, she told us that you two weren't even sharing the same room."

"That's ridiculous," he replied. "Up until the day of Ma's accident we were in the same room every night. I think you must have misunderstood. Even so, it's none of your business."

"Cole, Mother needs you. Laurel and I are happy to do our part, but she doesn't want to live in the city."

"If her health is so frail," he said, remembering something Dianne had told him, "then surely the city is the perfect place for her."

Laurel and Cordelia exchanged a rather panic-stricken expression.

Cordelia jumped in quickly. "She needs to be here on the farm. It's important to her mental well-being. Even the doctor says so."

"Well, it is *my* farm now. I should be able to make decisions about who lives here and who doesn't. I should be able to decide about hiring help and seeing to whatever else needs attention."

"You wouldn't put Mother from her home, would you?" Cordelia gasped, putting her hand to her throat in a melodramatic manner.

"I never implied that." He looked at each of his sisters and shook his head. "There's just no easy answer in this." He climbed into the buggy and looked down at his sisters. "Will you be here long? Should I unhitch the horses?"

"No," Laurel said. "We have other appointments. You might as well know that we feel the need to speak to a lawyer on mother's behalf. We're not at all certain that charges shouldn't be filed against Dianne for her actions. Perhaps she's not entirely in control of her mental faculties. It might be best to let a doctor assess her and then tell us if she's quite safe for others to be around."

Cole jumped down from the buggy, not even bothering to reset the brake. "You listen to me, little sister. If you do go to a lawyer and file charges against my wife or seek to get her forced into some kind of asylum, I'll take my family and leave this state so fast you won't know what happened." He pointed his finger first at Laurel and then Cordelia. "Dianne may not be perfect. She may not even be cordial where you two and Ma are concerned, but I will not stand by and watch my wife, the mother of my children, end up in jail because of some concocted story."

His sisters looked notably stunned by his statement. Cole didn't care, however. He'd had it with their threats and attitudes.

"I mean it," he said sternly before turning to climb back into the buggy. "You do anything to hurt Dianne, and I'll leave with her. I'll sell this farm and pack Ma off to one of you and never return again."

"You're not listening to reason," Cole declared as he followed Dianne and the children down the stairs. The boys and Dianne each carried one of their bags, packed and ready for their train trip home. It was the most difficult decision Dianne had ever had to make. Each step she made tore at her heart. *I'm really going. I'm leaving my husband. This isn't right, but I can't stay here. My children will suffer.* Just yesterday Cordelia had slapped John full across the face for running in the hall.

"I have a hired carriage coming for us," Dianne explained. "You needn't worry about leaving the farm even to take us the short distance to the station." Her tone was pure sarcasm. If she distanced herself enough—made herself mad enough—then the pain would be less, wouldn't it?

"I don't want you to go," Cole said softly.

She turned. "I can't stay. You know that. Your family desires me to leave." She turned to the children. "Go outside and wait for the carriage. Let me know when it comes." They walked solemnly out the door. Dianne's heart pounded as she saw their looks of fear and sorrow.

"Please stay," he said, taking hold of her shoulders. "I know this has been difficult, but you shouldn't just run away like this. Give it another chance. I've told my sisters to leave you alone. I've even spoken to Ma."

"Give them another chance to hit my children—to blame them for things they didn't do?" she questioned. "Give them another chance to blame me for things I didn't do?"

"Dianne, I can't help what happened."

"No, but you could have reacted differently. You could have believed me. You could have acted on the grounds that I've never lied to you—that I've been faithfully true to you, even when it hurt or frightened me. But instead, you chose to misunderstand—to believe what your mother told you."

"I thought I'd seen what happened," he said, his voice pleading. "Please understand, I was wrong. Lia and John both told me what happened, and I figure Ma misunderstood the moment. She probably got worked up and lost her balance and—"

"Stop it!" Dianne said between clenched teeth. "Stop making excuses for her. She wasn't confused. She knew full well what she was doing. Stop trying to make it right, because it will never be right. Your mother has done nothing but manipulate and deceive you since our arrival. I'll pray that God opens your eyes before it's too late, Cole, but I won't stay another day in this house—this town—or even this state."

"You could at least listen to reason," he answered in frustration edged in anger.

"Like you listened to me when I tried to explain?"

"I told you I was sorry."

"I hope you are," she said without emotion. "I hope you regret your choices, because I do. You've been a changed man since the fire—since we lost the ranch. You've been brooding and closed up. I've tried to be a good wife, and I've made plenty of mistakes. But I've tried to seek your forgiveness, to confess my sins to you, and for what? For this?" she said, waving her free arm. "For deception and accusations? For nothing but disapproval and pain?" Tears came to her eyes, making her even more angry. She hated appearing weak. Cole was silent as she wiped her tears with the back of her gloved hand, but his expression had changed from angry to concerned.

"Dianne, look, we've both made mistakes. I just don't want us to make another one."

"I don't either. Staying here another day would be a mistake—at least for me. Subjecting our children to cruelty and accusation would be damaging and definitely wrong. I have to protect them. Do you even realize they can't sleep at night? Lia is so afraid her grandmother will sneak into the room and hurt her that she whimpers all night long. The boys are afraid to even play for fear one of your sisters will punish them."

Cole nodded, much to her surprise. "Maybe you're right," he said with a sigh.

For a brief moment Dianne thought perhaps he would come with them. She was ready to offer to run upstairs and pack his things while he said good-bye to his mother. In her mind, she even deduced that they could trade in their train tickets and leave the following day, then stay the night in a hotel in Topeka, just long enough to let Cole meet with a lawyer and deed the farm back to his mother. But before she could speak on any of these things, he continued.

"Maybe it is best you take the children and go back to Montana. I don't like families living apart, but I don't want to see any of you hurt again. And I don't want there to be any more opportunity for my sisters or mother to accuse you of wrongdoing."

"A noble gesture," she muttered. She clasped her bag more tightly and moved to the door.

"Dianne," Cole said, reaching out to take hold of her bag. "Wait. Please understand, I'm not choosing them over you."

"Funny, for that's exactly how it feels."

"But it's not that way."

Dianne looked into his face, hoping she'd find something there to convince herself that he was telling the truth. She wanted so much to believe that he still loved her the way he used to. But there was nothing there. Nothing but the memory of pain and misery. She had tried so hard to be what he asked of her. Now she had nothing left to give. The great emptiness inside of her had consumed all of her energy and strength.

"Mama! The man's coming with the carriage!" Luke called out from the yard.

"I have to go," Dianne said, tugging at the bag.

"I'll carry this for you." Cole gently pulled the bag from her grasp.

Rather than fight him, she hurried outside and helped her children into the carriage while the driver took their bags and stowed them in back.

"You children be good for your mama," Cole admonished. "I'll be home in the spring. It won't be long—you'll see."

Dianne wondered how he could stay when all of his children were fighting back tears, longing for him to join them. She tried to harden her heart against the devastating pain, but it was no use. She had never hurt like this before, and she never wanted to hurt like this again. *Let him stay,* she told herself. *Let him do what he will. I don't care if he ever comes home. I won't care—it hurts too much to care.*

"I'll see you soon," he told Dianne as he helped her into the carriage. "You'll see. I'll take care of everything here and be home before you know it."

"Don't worry about it. I'm sure we'll manage. We're strong and capable," she said, using his words against him. After all, that's why he said he had to consider his mother's needs over theirs. They were strong and capable, while his mother was weak and old. She shook her head and met his gaze one last time. Speaking more for herself than for him, she said, "We don't need help. We'll be just fine."

It was the middle of the night when Cole awoke from a nightmare. He bolted straight up, panting, feeling the sweat clinging to his neck and his chest. He gasped for air, struggling to calm his breathing. The dream had been so vivid—so awful.

They were all gone. They had left him and he couldn't find them. His children. His wife. Gone.

Reaching out beside him, Cole felt for Dianne. But the emptiness of the bed proved once again he'd not merely dreamed about a thing that could never be. He had only relived the nightmare that was his life.

They were gone.

She was gone.

The catch in his breath turned to a sob as he fell back against the bed. "Oh, God," he pleaded in prayer, "what do you want me to do? What am I supposed to do now?"

CHAPTER 18

DIANNE SAT IN SILENCE WHILE HER CHILdren chattered about the images that passed by the train window. She had never been wearier of travel than in this moment. Even the wagon train journey back so many years ago had been simpler. No doubt it was because her heart had been joyful back then—expectant of the promising future to come. Now she just felt hopelessly empty. She tried to pray, but words wouldn't come.

"Mama, when will we get there?" Luke asked. "The conductor said Corrine was the next stop."

"Shouldn't be long now," Dianne said, stroking Lia's silky hair. The girl had fallen asleep with her head on her mother's lap, but even this didn't offer the comfort Dianne so desperately longed for.

She had wired ahead for train tickets to Dillon. From there they would have to take the stage to Virginia City. She'd been promised seats but knew that if the weather had turned bad and snows had set in, they might very well be waiting a spell before they could reach home. She'd already determined that no matter how difficult, she would take the children straight to the ranch.

I'm not going to stay another minute in town, she had promised herself. *I'll buy supplies and I'll see to it that we make it through without Cole.*

"Mrs. Selby, isn't it?" a man questioned from the aisle.

Dianne looked up to find Christopher Stromgren standing over her. "Good day, Mr. Stromgren. What brings you west?"

"Your sister, of course. Didn't she tell you?"

Dianne shook her head. The man was dressed impeccably in navy blue, with a snug bowler hat on his head. The hat made him look rather comical, but she wasn't sure why. Perhaps it was the way his dark red curls peeked out from under the covering. Maybe it was just that she was far too used to cowhands and their wide-brimmed hats. Even in Kansas she'd seen many of the same conventional hats she'd known in Montana.

"Ardith is scheduled to return with me to New York City. I have her concerts all arranged. She'll make a tremendous amount of money, to be sure. I know she'll be quite popular."

"What of Winona, her daughter?" The boys had lost interest in the window and had come to observe the stranger.

"Is Aunt Ardith really going away?" Micah asked. "I've missed her piano playing."

"As has the rest of the world," Stromgren said enthusiastically. "Your aunt is a wondrous woman. She'll soon be the toast of the town."

"But what of her child?" Dianne asked again.

"As I understand it, she's made arrangements for her daughter," Stromgren said, sobering a bit. "In time, the girl might join her mother, but for now it wouldn't be prudent. The schedule is grueling, and there's no chance to hire a responsible companion for her on such short notice. Then there's the concern of schooling. The child can hardly attend school on a regular basis and travel around the country."

"I see." Irritation mingled with apprehension, for her sister's choice made Dianne even more uncomfortable with the man. She was relieved when the conductor came by to tell them the train would be pulling into the Corrine station in five minutes. "If you'll excuse us, Mr. Stromgren. The children and I have another train to catch and not much time to make our way."

"I'll be traveling with you. After all, there aren't too many other opportunities for getting to the Montana Territory. Allow me to make myself useful and assist you." He glanced around, "Unless, of course, your husband would object."

"My husband is in Kansas," Dianne replied flatly. "Thank you for your help, but I'm sure we can manage."

"I wouldn't dream of it," Stromgren declared. "I'll see to your luggage at the very least."

Dianne didn't have the energy to protest further. Her children were tired, and she was exhausted. Having been sick prior to leaving Kansas, she'd battled nausea all the way home. She was four months pregnant by her own calculations. She didn't want to be pregnant, not now. She thought of Cole and knew she should have told him before she left. She'd meant to, but she didn't want him returning to Montana simply because a baby was on the way. And she knew he would never have let her go alone if he'd known of her condition.

Mr. Stromgren was good to see them cared for. Dianne didn't like what the man represented, but she couldn't argue that his assistance hadn't been superb. He'd even managed to locate box lunches for them all, much to the boys' excitement. As they boarded the train for Dillon, she settled her three boys on one side, then took to the other side with Lia. She was relieved when Stromgren seated himself beside her sons rather than positioning himself beside her.

Before leaving Corrine, Dianne's last point of business was to send a couple of telegrams. She wanted to let someone in Virginia City know that she'd be arriving soon so she could get some assistance in getting home. She'd truly wanted to get word to Koko and George, but there had been little chance for that. No doubt Ardith would think that her arrival would signal Dianne's stay in the house there in Virginia City, but Dianne had already laid plans for her departure. The other wire spoke to Dianne's determination to make the Diamond V a great ranch once again. She wrote to her Texas cattle people and requested five thousand head of prime beef be sent her way in the spring. She knew the decision had been made without Cole's approval, but she no longer felt it was important to consult him. She seriously doubted he'd return in the spring. His mother was gifted with powerful persuasion, and it stood to reason that Mary Selby would somehow convince her son to remain on the farm.

Let him be a farmer if that's his desire,

Dianne thought as she gazed out the window. Tears trickled down her cheek, but she stopped them quickly, unwilling that her children should see her cry yet again.

I must be strong for them. I must be strong.

"She's coming home without him?" Zane asked as he reread his sister's telegram.

"That's what it looks like," Ardith replied. "It says 'the children and I.' There's no mention of Cole."

Zane tossed the paper down and shook his head. "That can't be good. I can't figure her leaving without a reason."

"Maybe," Mara said softly, "Cole thought it would be better for Dianne and the children to be here in Montana than in Kansas all winter."

"It doesn't sound like him," Morgan threw in. "Cole isn't one to see his family scattered to all parts."

"No, he's not," Zane agreed. "I wonder if maybe he changed his mind about staying through the winter and just sent them on ahead. But that doesn't seem right either. He would have been concerned about Dianne traveling by herself with the children. It's mighty dangerous to have a woman going across the country by herself—not to mention it being poor thinking to put a mother by herself with four children. What if one of them gets sick? What if she gets sick?"

"Maybe she had all she could take and left him," Ardith said matter-of-factly. "You've read her other letters. She was miserable. His mother and sisters treated her very poorly. I'm guessing she's quit the whole thing."

"Quit her marriage?" Zane asked.

"Maybe not that, but quit Kansas and the farm." Ardith turned to bring the pot of coffee to the table. They had gathered casually in the kitchen, and little by little she had brought refreshments to the table for their consumption. The coffee was preceded by a fresh crumb cake that she'd intended to be a part of supper.

"It can't be good that she's coming back without Cole," Morgan said before he stuffed a piece of cake into his mouth.

Zane poured himself a cup of coffee. "I agree. There's no telling what she'll have in mind once she's here."

"Well, I know you're concerned about Dianne, but there's something I must tell you. I haven't kept you informed," Ardith announced, "largely because I didn't wish to be chastised or to have you try to talk me out of my plans."

"What plans?" Zane asked.

She drew a deep breath and lifted her chin. "I'll be leaving for New York as soon as Mr.

Stromgren can escort me there. He should be here tomorrow or the next day at the latest."

Zane looked to Morgan and then back to Ardith. "What? What are you talking about?"

"Yeah, what are you talking about?" Morgan asked.

Ardith met their surprised expressions. Even Mara looked stunned. "I've been speaking about this for weeks. Hasn't anyone listened? I mean, I know I didn't inform you that Mr. Stromgren was arriving soon, but you knew I'd been talking about going."

"I figured you'd get it out of your head after a while," Zane admitted. "You have a daughter to take care of. What about her?"

"I was going to send her to Koko. George is due to arrive any day now to pick her up. But since Dianne is coming home, I won't have to send Winona to the Diamond V. She can simply stay here with her aunt."

"But Winona needs her ma, not her aunt or anyone else. How can you just leave her like that?" Morgan asked.

Ardith fumed. "None of you knows anything about me. You don't know what I've endured, and you don't know what I have to live with. Apparently I have a gift for music." She wasn't about to credit God for the gift. Charity had suggested God had given her music as a means of soothing her in her time of loss, but Ardith wasn't about to see it that way. God was the divine thief, robbing her of precious things, stealing away her youth, her husband, her joy. She drew a deep breath. "If you'll excuse me, I need to see to something."

She hurried from the room, unwilling to have them force any more questions upon her. It was a hard enough decision to make without their condemnation. Winona had been her life . . . her will to go on. But now Winona was a living, vibrant reminder of her life with Levi, never ceasing with her questions. Worse still, she had asked her mother about finding her another father.

"As if I ever want to consider that," Ardith muttered.

No, she thought, *the only way to deal with this pain is to put it far from me. If that includes removing Winona from me as well, then that's the penalty I'll pay. I've sacrificed enough in my life, but if God demands it all, then so be it. Let Him steal the last of my hope . . . my heart.*

———

It was good to be home again—at least as far home as Virginia City. Dianne looked around the little town and almost felt as if she could kiss the dirt. The chilled October air exhilarated her in a way she'd not felt since leaving for Kansas. It appeared to do the same for the children, who now ran in great abandon up and down the street.

"Mama, can we walk back to the house?" Luke asked.

"Yes, please," John added. Micah merely nodded.

"I suppose it would be all right. Maybe you could let Ardith know that we've arrived." No one had come to meet them, and Dianne didn't relish the idea of walking home.

"Yeah!" Luke exclaimed. "I'll race you!" he told his brothers, and before Dianne could say another word, the boys went running at full speed up the street.

"Your children seem quite happy to be back in Montana," Christopher Stromgren said with a smile.

"Yes, they are." Dianne looked beyond Stromgren and was surprised to see her brothers Morgan and Zane driving down the street. "Morgan! Zane!" she called out in an unladylike fashion. She'd never been happier to see anyone.

They drew the wagon up close to the freight office, then jumped down. Rushing to them, Dianne put aside her sorrows and embraced them together. "I'm so happy to see you both. I certainly didn't expect you'd be here." Lia joined them and giggled when Morgan lifted her in the air.

"Zane's getting married, and I'm the best man. I had to be here," Morgan admitted.

Dianne pulled back. "Charity mentioned in

one of her letters that you were interested in Mara Lawrence. She's a sweet girl. I must say she'll make you a fine wife."

Zane nodded. "I know she will. So where are your bags?" He looked past Dianne. "And where are the boys?"

"You just missed them. You came down Idaho as they went up Wallace. They're heading up to the house to tell Ardith we've arrived."

"Mr. Chadwick," Christopher Stromgren greeted. "It's good to see you again." He turned to Dianne and added, "This man is the finest guide I've ever had on any hunt."

"Morgan is quite talented," Dianne agreed. She'd had enough of Stromgren's company, however. "If you'll excuse us, Mr. Stromgren, I'd like to go home with my brothers. Perhaps you could call on Ardith tomorrow?"

"Indeed. I will make myself at home in the hotel and see your sister on the morrow." He gave a slight bow and tipped his head at the twins. "Good day."

"I wondered if you two would end up on the same stage," Zane said as he watched Stromgren walk toward where the stage driver had placed his bags. "Ardith only told us of his coming a couple of days ago."

Dianne grimaced. "He was actually quite helpful, and I can't say he was entirely unpleasant company. It's just that I know why he's come, and I cannot approve of it."

"You might as well save your breath." Morgan nodded in agreement with his brother's words. "Ardith has made up her mind. We've tried to talk her out of it, but she's determined to go."

"Well, then, we must let her go," Dianne said sadly. "Sometimes we have to let people go."

"Like Cole?" Zane asked.

"I hope he'll come to his senses, but for now he's made his choice."

"And you've made yours."

"I had no choice," she said with great bitterness. "My choice was made for me."

―――――――――

Very little was discussed amongst the siblings on Dianne's first day home. She was eager to rest and get things ready to head back to the ranch. She hadn't intended to stay even another night in Virginia City, but Ardith had explained that George was coming for Winona, and this gave Dianne reason to delay her trip. If George was coming, that meant she'd have help in getting back to the ranch. It would only be a matter of waiting for him. It seemed as though God had arranged this to ease her burden.

When Dianne awoke the next day, she lay in bed for several moments with her eyes closed. The sounds of the house were familiar, even comforting. Still, she knew that Cole was far away and that the anger between them had forever damaged a precious bond. She put her hand to her abdomen, eyes still closed. A baby grew there—a child that she really didn't want. She grimaced. It wasn't that she didn't love her children. It wasn't that she wouldn't, under different circumstances, have loved another child. But in her present state of mind, this was the last thing she needed or desired. What if Cole never came home? How could she provide for the welfare of five children without a husband? How would it be for a precious baby to come into the world only to know that his or her father didn't care enough to be there for them?

Putting aside her depressing thoughts, Dianne quickly dressed and roused the children. She hoped George would come today. It was imperative she get back to the ranch before the snows set in. She needed to set up her own housekeeping, and Ardith assured her that the Selby cabin was complete. In fact, Mara's little sister, Elsa, had been staying in the cabin, so Dianne knew that it must be fully functional.

At breakfast the children were quite animated, telling Winona about all their adventures. Because it was Saturday, there was no school, so the children gobbled down their breakfast and went out and about to reacquaint themselves with all their favorite things. Dianne was glad to see them happy. She knew they were troubled by their father's absence, but she did all she could to reassure them that the separation was only temporary.

"George is here," Zane announced as he came through the back door.

"Wonderful!" Dianne said. "His timing couldn't have been better."

"Are you sure you can't stick around for the wedding? I mean it's bad enough that Elsa can't be here for Mara."

"Why couldn't she have come with George?" Dianne asked, putting away the last of the breakfast dishes.

"Our wedding is the one place her father is sure to look for her. So far he hasn't been able to get so much as a single clue as to her whereabouts, and we want to keep it that way. She'll turn twenty-one next year and then she won't be under his rule."

"It must have been difficult for her being the only one left with those ruthless men," Dianne said softly. "I'm glad you thought to hide her out at the ranch. She's welcome to stay there, you know."

"Mara figured we'd take her with us to Butte."

Dianne grinned. "Take a little sister along to your new home—barely married and in need of privacy? Doesn't sound ideal."

He laughed. "There's been nothing ideal about our relationship. Mara is half my age and the daughter of our sworn enemy."

"But you love her," Dianne said wistfully. She could remember those feelings of falling in love—of believing in the fairy tale and the dream. Surely it wasn't dead. Surely she could find a way to rekindle all of that in her own life.

"Of course I love her," Zane replied. "I wouldn't marry her if I didn't."

"Good. I'm glad to hear it." Dianne set the dish towel aside to dry and unfastened the ties of her apron. "Let's go find George."

"He's outside talking with Ben and Joshua. You've heard that Ben is going to retire from preaching, haven't you?"

"Charity mentioned he was considering it. It's hard to imagine, though."

Zane nodded and opened the back door for Dianne. She took up her shawl and walked outside. "He's told us over and over that he'll never truly retire, that once a man is called of the Lord, he's in it for life. Still, he's getting tired, and now that Joshua is here and has some experience preaching, well, it seemed God provided the answer."

"So Joshua will take over the church and Ben will still lend assistance, is that it?" They walked around the house to where George had parked the wagon. Dianne saw him glance past Ben and Joshua and smile at her. His greeting warmed her. She waved back, feeling a sense of peace in his presence.

"Hello, George. How are you?"

George's grin broadened. "Doing pretty good. Sure didn't expect to find you here."

"I know, but this is God's providence. I need a ride to the ranch, and here you are with a wagon."

"If you're moving to the ranch, we'll need to get another wagon," he advised. "We'll need to lay in a whole lot more supplies."

"I know. I've already arranged it," Dianne said. "I have the freighters loading supplies even as we talk. I was going to ride out with them, but now that you're here it will be much more enjoyable to travel together."

"You'll need some decent furniture. Jamie and I made a few pieces—beds and such, but there aren't any tables or chairs or anything decent to sit on for comfort. I could probably make some bookshelves or cupboards, but we'd need to pick up the wood."

"Are there curtains at the windows?" she asked.

"Yes. Koko and Susannah saw to that. They figured if you didn't care for them you could always make new ones."

"I'm sure they're fine. What about dishes—pots and pans and such?"

"Nope. The cabin is pretty empty."

"All right, then. I'll pack some things from

the house and buy whatever else I need."

The boys rounded the house, then took off in a dead run. "Uncle George!" They attacked the man with such gusto that George nearly went backward under the sheer weight of their bodies.

"You have grown," he said, looking at each one. "I'm impressed. What have you been feeding them?" He glanced to Dianne with a laugh.

She frowned. "Aggravation and sorrow mostly." Her voice was low enough she doubted anyone heard her. "When will you be ready to head back to the ranch?"

"The sooner the better."

"Can't you stay—at least for the wedding?" Zane asked again.

"The weather could turn bad any time," George said, shaking his head. "The signs aren't looking good. So far we've been blessed, but it's a long trip home."

"George is right, but I would love to be here for you," Dianne said thoughtfully. "Any chance of moving the wedding up?"

Zane looked to Ben and Joshua. "What of it? If Mara is in agreement, could we do that?"

"I don't know why not," Ben answered.

"Wonderful!" Dianne declared with a smile that she really didn't feel, forcing words for which she had no heart. "I'd love to see you married."

Funny how easy it was beginning to be—pretending she was happy. She caught sight of George watching her. His face was sober, his expression intense. *He knows,* she thought. *He knows it's all a game for me. He knows my heart isn't in any of this.* She sighed. If she wasn't careful she'd find herself confiding everything to George, and that could be very dangerous.

"So you're absolutely certain this is what you want to do?" Dianne asked Ardith.

Ardith sat on the edge of Dianne's bed. She had stared at a fixed spot on the wallpaper for the last ten minutes of their discussion. It was clear to Dianne she didn't want to get into the emotional side of the matter.

"Winona will be better with you and Koko. She loves your children, and she needs to be with others her own age. I know this will cause you to take on extra responsibility, what with her schooling and such, but I'll send money home for her upkeep and your trouble."

"The money is certainly of no matter to me," Dianne told her. "I'm more concerned with your daughter's needs . . . those that can't be bought. Like a mother's love."

"She'll always have that," Ardith said, still not looking at Dianne.

"But will she know that—believe that—when you are nowhere to be found?"

"You'll always know where I am. It's not like I'm going to disappear into uncharted territory. It's New York City. Of course I'll be doing some travel, but my residence will be there and you can wire me or send mail to the address I gave you. Besides, you left your husband in Kansas. Do your children believe he's stopped loving them simply because of the distance involved?"

Dianne wanted no part of that question. She instead brought the subject back to Ardith. "I just want to be sure that you understand how hard this will be on Winona," Dianne said, coming to stand between Ardith and her fixed point. "Look at me."

Her sister slowly raised her gaze. "Why? Because you think if I look deep enough into your eyes that I'll change my mind? Don't play such a game with me. You're hurting enough—you're feeling the same sense of loss that I feel. You've run away, so why can't I?"

"I didn't run away," Dianne protested. "I brought my children to safety. They were endangered in Kansas."

"And Winona . . . well, I can't be a good mother right now," Ardith said sadly. "I'm sorry. I'm not as strong as you are. I need to go, and I need you to understand and let me go. You must know how I feel in some small part. Your pain drove you to make a difficult decision—a decision that you never would have made under normal circumstances. Please understand that my situation is no different."

Dianne fought back unbidden tears. She nodded slowly, feeling that she understood her sister's plight for the first time. "I understand. I love you, and I love Winona. I want good for both of you. I'll take Winona with me and love her as my own, but please remember that it will never take the place of your love. Don't make the separation a long one or I'm afraid her heart will be forever broken."

"Your sisters seem so unhappy," Mara said as she and Zane took a long walk to discuss the events of the next day. "I hope they'll be able to enjoy the wedding."

"If they're saddened by it," Zane said, "they'll simply have to understand. We moved the wedding up for them, and we're happy. I won't be made miserable just because they are."

"I know," Mara replied, "but I feel sorry for them. They are struggling with so much. I wish I could help more, but neither one seems to want to discuss the situation with me."

"They don't want to talk to anyone. I tried discussing this with Dianne, and she tells me that because I'm not married, I can't possibly understand what she's going through. Then when I tried to talk to Ardith, she accused me of trying to run her life. So I figured it was safer to keep my opinion and thoughts to myself."

"You can share them with me," she said lightly. "You know I love hearing what you have to say."

He grinned and tightened his hold on her hand. "I never figured to fall in love this late in life."

"It's hardly like you have one foot in the grave," she teased.

"No, but my father was my age when he died. I guess sometimes I think about that."

"But he didn't die naturally—he was killed. It wasn't like his health failed him." Mara stopped and turned to face Zane. "You can't judge your existence by your parents.' Both died tragically."

"I know you're right, but I will always worry about what might become of you if something were to happen to me. I didn't have those concerns before agreeing to take on a wife. I figured if I died, I died. I wouldn't be leaving any grieving widow or orphaned children."

"Zane, you've talked about this before, and I want you to know that I feel a complete peace about this. I'd rather have whatever time together God will give us than to have nothing at all."

He reached out to stroke her cheek. Her skin was so soft. "I want that time too. I didn't mean to despair on the eve of our wedding. I suppose it's seeing the problems around us that brought it all back to me."

"Then put it aside," she said, putting her hand over his. She drew his hand to her lips and kissed it lightly. "I just know we shall have a long and happy life together."

In that moment Zane felt certain of it too.

CHAPTER 19

DIANNE HAD NEVER SEEN TWO PEOPLE HAP-pier to be wed than Zane and Mara. She was taken back in time to her own wedding as Mara gazed adoringly at Zane.

I felt that way once. I loved Cole more than life. I waited for him for such a long time—lived with the fear that he was probably dead. Still, love prevailed. She sighed. Could love prevail this time? Could it cover the multitude of sins that seemed to paint her life like watered-down whitewash?

With their marriage only twenty-four hours old, Zane and Mara were completely immersed in each other. Dianne had already reminded them twice that they needed to get on the road, only to have them mutter something to the effect of, "We'll be right there." She had to laugh. It was good that they were so happy. She prayed that God might never let the interference of others cause them grief.

"Well, at least they have no mothers-in-law to intrude upon their lives," she muttered.

"What was that?" George asked as he tightened the ropes holding the tarp over their supplies.

Dianne shook her head. "Nothing. Nothing of importance, anyway." She looked at her watch piece. Time was getting away from them, and even Daisy, her buckskin mare, was anxious to be on their way. "Should we get going?"

"I think the sooner the better," George said. "But I've been saying that since I got here." He smiled. "If you'll get the children loaded up, I'll make sure the horses are secured to the back of the wagons."

"Do you really think it's wise for Luke to ride? He hasn't had much experience since we moved to town."

"He'll do fine. How else is he going to learn? I'll be with him."

George's kind expression stirred Dianne's heart. Why couldn't Cole care like George? She shook her head. *I can't let these thoughts take me captive. Maybe it's a mistake to go back to the ranch and be around George.* She looked at the man as he walked away to check the extra horses they were taking. *Oh, Father, I don't want this to turn into something sinful. I don't want to turn to George and put Cole from my life.* But George was here . . . and he cared. Cole had made the choice to tend to his mother. She put her hand to her head. *What am I to do?*

"I had to come tell you good-bye," Faith Montgomery said as she came forward with a cloth-covered basket. "Seemed that we never got a real chance to talk. I got this basket from Ardith before she left with that Mr. Stromgren. I filled it with goodies for the trip home."

Dianne took the basket and secured it under the wagon seat. "That was so thoughtful. I know the children will appreciate your cooking."

Faith smiled. "I'm glad you're home but so sorry things aren't as they should be." She sobered and took hold of Dianne by the shoulders. "You know I'll be praying. Charity too."

"Yes, she told me so this morning. I'm glad she and Ben have agreed to move back into the house and live with Joshua. Since Ben wants to groom him to take over the church, it seems logical that they should be together."

"I agree. It should prove to be an amicable solution, and you'll be back on your ranch."

Dianne drew a deep breath and let it out slowly. "Was I wrong to come back? Tell me the truth, Faith."

Faith dropped her hold and her expression changed to sympathetic. "Child, you know God doesn't approve of strife. He doesn't want families divided. The Good Book tells us that His is a ministry of reconciliation, and ours should be as well."

"But it's so hard," Dianne murmured. "You don't know what I was going through."

"But He does," Faith countered. "And He didn't just stick you there without knowing what was coming and without making a provision for you as well."

"Then maybe returning to Montana was the provision. After all, I left with Cole's blessing."

"But not his heart. He knew it'd do no good to fight you on this."

"He didn't even want to fight me on this, Faith. He didn't want me to go, but he also didn't need me to stay."

"Pray, Dianne. Keep taking it back to the Lord. Don't let this become a root of bitterness in your heart. Cole loves you—I know that as clearly as I know my own name."

Dianne knew it too. He might not have responded in the manner in which she would have liked, but she knew he loved her. Right now that love was just being smothered with the vines of his mother's selfish desires to keep him to herself.

"I wish you and Malachi would reconsider and come back to the ranch," Dianne said, changing the subject. "We're going to need a good blacksmith."

"Not for a time. Malachi has good work here, and Cole has trusted him to oversee the freight company in his absence. Our family is happy here. Folks have gotten used to us, and while there aren't many Negroes in these parts, we aren't treated so bad anymore. Not like it used to be. Folks seem to appreciate what Malachi can do for them, and while he's still just a black man to them, they no longer say the ugly things they used to."

"Well, if you change your mind, you know you're welcome. We'll build you another cabin, like we did in the beginning."

Faith laughed and her delight was evidenced in the twinkle in her eyes. "Those were mighty fine times. They will be again. I'm convinced of it."

"I hope so." Dianne's voice was filled with longing. Why did it seem the valleys lasted so much longer than the mountaintops?

Zane and Mara finally emerged from the house. They were dressed in traveling clothes, and Zane carried Lia in his arms while Mara carried a small bag. They were heading back to the ranch with Dianne so they could pick up

Elsa and sneak away with her to Butte. Dianne still thought it a risky idea, but the thought of Elsa living at the Diamond V didn't come without its worries. Just as Zane had figured, Chester Lawrence had been waiting outside of the church after the wedding. When he saw Elsa was nowhere to be found, he spewed out curses at Zane and Mara. Then upon spotting Dianne, he laid into her as well. The moment was still rather startling. Dianne could only imagine that there would be trouble from her neighbor in the months to come.

The boys came running out the front door with Charity coming out of the house behind them. "You boys forgot your cookies!" Charity declared.

Dianne laughed at the antics of her sons as they ran past Mara and Zane, circled around like howling Indians, and raced back to where Charity stood with their treats. Everyone seemed happy and energized. It even looked like the weather would give them a good day for traveling.

"Where's Winona?" Dianne asked as she suddenly realized that the girl was nowhere to be found.

"I haven't seen her," Zane said as he lifted Lia into the place where the children would ride. George had fixed them a sort of covering, and the children were eager to pretend they were on one of the great wagon trains of days gone by. The boys climbed up like kittens scaling draperies and disappeared inside the canvas covering. Zane and Mara were going to drive one load while Dianne drove the other. Poor Daisy would get exercised, but not with a rider. She was tied unceremoniously to the back of Dianne's wagon.

Still there was no sign of Winona. Dianne thought for a moment. "I'll be right back," she told the others and made her way to the house.

"Did you forget something?" Charity asked as she climbed up the steps.

"Sort of," Dianne replied. "I can't seem to locate Winona, but I think she might be upstairs."

"Poor child," Charity said. "She's really hurting. I thought we'd never get her to stop crying yesterday."

"I'll do my best to help her, but she needs Ardith."

"I tried to talk to Ardith, Dianne, but she wouldn't hear me," Charity began. "She loved Levi so much that his loss has crippled her. She's blind to everything but the way she feels."

"I know. She's like a sick person who wants to get well but hasn't the strength to fight off the disease."

"Do you think New York will make her better?" Charity had tears in her eyes.

"I can't say. I'd like to believe that she'll get

there and realize that what she's needed was here all along. I pray that she'll see Winona's love can make things better for her. Winona's and God's."

"She's so angry at God. She blames Him for every bad thing that's happened."

Dianne nodded, feeling a tinge of guilt. "I think we all have a tendency to do that. I suppose it's human nature. A faithless nature."

"He will be faithful, when we are faithless," Charity said. "That's in Second Timothy."

"I remember hearing it. Perhaps from Ben's preaching." Dianne sighed and picked up her skirts. "I'd best hurry. George is anxious to go."

Dianne made her way upstairs and down the hall until she came to the room that Ardith and Winona had shared. She knocked lightly and opened the door. Winona sat in the rocker near the window.

"Are you ready to go?" Dianne asked softly. She came to where Winona sat and knelt down.

"I don't know why Mama had to go away. Does she think I don't love her anymore?"

Dianne looked at the child. She clearly bore her Indian heritage in her dark eyes, black hair, and high cheekbones. She was a little chubby at this age but still quite pretty. "Your mama knows you love her. It's the only thing that's seen her through at times. Your mama is just sad right now, and she can't seem to get any better. Hopefully she'll be able to get better while she's away—maybe see a doctor or get better rest."

"She's going to be too busy to rest. She told me so. That's why I can't go with her." Winona turned away and looked out the window. "She's not going to come back, is she?"

"Nonsense. I know my sister well enough to know she'll be back. In fact, with so many people praying for her to get better, I feel confident she'll be back before we know it."

Winona looked back at Dianne with such an expression of hope that Dianne could only smile as she asked, "Do you truly think so?"

She nodded. "I feel it in my heart."

"And will Uncle Cole come back too?"

Dianne felt as though she'd been slapped. "I . . . well . . . I don't know. I hope so."

Winona frowned. "But you don't feel it in your heart?"

Dianne didn't want to search her heart for that answer. She was terrified of what the response might be. "One problem at a time, Winona. Right now we need to go. The sooner we get on the road, the sooner we'll be home."

"That's where Papa is buried," Winona said softly.

"That's right."

"Do you think there will be any wild flowers left that we can put on his grave?"

"I don't know. It's been so long since I've been home, I couldn't say. But I tell you what. We'll look for them along the way. How will that be?"

Winona nodded and surprised Dianne by embracing her tightly—almost desperately. "You won't stop loving me, will you?"

"No," Dianne pledged. "I won't stop loving you. And neither will your mama."

Please don't stop loving her, Dianne whispered in her heart. *Ardith, please come home to this child and make her feel cared for again.*

They arrived at the Diamond V the next day, with a bitter wind howling down off the Tobacco Root Mountains, leaving the river valley and all its occupants chilled to the bone. Koko was delighted to see Dianne and the children. It was one of the happiest reunions Dianne had ever known.

"I'm so blessed that you have come," Koko declared as everyone climbed out of the wagons. "I have prayed for your safety and your happiness."

"Well, I'm safe," Dianne said with a shrug. "I can't give you more than that."

"We have much to talk about," Koko said, patting her hand. "And look, your children have grown so beautiful and big." She reached down to touch Lia's face. The child clung to

Dianne's skirts like she might be stolen away any moment. "You are quite the beauty, Miss Lia."

Dianne felt a flutter in her abdomen. The baby was moving as if demanding to be introduced. "I have some news," she said loud enough only for Lia and Koko to hear. She put her hand to her stomach. Koko met her eyes and stood.

"When?"

"I think March, by my own calculations. I haven't been to any doctor. I told Faith and Charity. Oh, and Mara too. No one else knows, however, unless they've shared it with the others. Zane might know because of Mara, but Morgan took off so quickly after the wedding that I doubt anyone told him."

"I see. Well, we will do all right together." Koko smiled reassuringly. "You are a strong woman and have done this many times. You'll do just fine."

"I really have no choice but to do fine." Dianne caught sight of Jamie and Elsa together and nodded toward them. "Those two seem rather cozy."

"I know. It's quite a comical tale. I'll tell you over coffee. It's cold out here and we really ought to get the children inside. I'll have George make provisions for the freighters to sleep in the barn, and we'll get you settled into your place. Come along."

"I don't know why you have to go all the way to Butte," Jamie told Elsa. He had become very accustomed to her company. Their Bible reading was proving to be an inspiration to both of them, and Elsa could cook like nobody this side of his mother.

"Actually, we're going to live outside of Butte, in another city called Anaconda," Elsa said, as though that might change his opinion.

"It doesn't matter. It's too far away."

"I don't want to go, but Mara and Zane are being so kind to care for me. My father is sure to find out sooner or later that I'm here. At least in Butte, Zane has friends who can help him with the law. If my father shows up there with his demands, then perhaps it won't be so bad."

Jamie couldn't help but reach out and touch her soft cheek. "I wish it were me protecting you."

She nodded and leaned into his touch. "I wish it were too."

"You two seem mighty intent on something," George interrupted. He smiled broadly and laughed as the couple jumped apart. Jamie felt a sense of frustration at his uncle's appearance but said nothing.

"Did you see the new horses I brought back with me?" George asked.

"Most of them aren't new. Most are the Selby horses from town," Jamie said. "I remember them from before."

"But what about the sorrel? She'll foal in the spring. The bay will as well," George responded. "I figure them good beginnings to building the herd back up. In fact, I'm thinking maybe come spring we could go looking for a few wild horses. They're good with the cows."

"But we don't have any cows," Jamie protested. "At least not many."

"We will come early summer. Your aunt has ordered five thousand head."

Jamie couldn't contain his excitement. "Honestly? Five thousand? That's just like the old days."

George laughed. "And you thought you weren't going to have anything to do all winter with Elsa gone."

Jamie felt his face grow hot. "I could have figured you'd find something for me," he groaned.

Elsa laughed. "I'd better go inside and see if the ladies need help with supper." She left quickly—probably to save herself further embarrassment. At least that's what Jamie figured.

"So is it true love?" his uncle asked.

"As true as I know it to be," Jamie answered, shoving his hands into his pockets.

"What about you, Uncle. Have you ever been in love?"

While George's face had registered pure amusement only moments before, now Jamie watched his expression change to a tense kind of reservation. What did it mean?

"I'd rather not talk about it. You're the one who has the problem right now."

"Being in love isn't the problem. Her leaving for Butte, or rather Anaconda, is the problem."

"Well, if it's meant to be, it'll keep. You're going to have your hands full come spring, and before spring we'll need to prepare. I'm figuring maybe we can build some corrals with the extra wood we had left over from the cabins. We also need to keep working on those horses. Two of those geldings are nearly broke— you've done a good job with them, and they'll be valuable with the cows come spring."

Jamie nodded. No one seemed to care that his best friend in the world was moving a world away. They only wanted him to focus on what was important to them. But he couldn't get away from the question that haunted him. He found it hard to concentrate on anything else, even on the excitement of seeing the Diamond V become a real ranch again.

When would he see her again?

"Did you get the children settled in?" Koko asked as Dianne came into the cabin.

"Yes. Elsa and Mara said they'd see to them while I helped you finish cleaning up."

"Nonsense. You are tired and need to get to bed early. Especially in your condition." Dianne glanced to the far end of the cabin, where George sat by the fire whittling on a stick. She looked rapidly back to Koko as if in question. "I told him. I'm sorry if that was wrong, but you're already halfway along, or very nearly. You won't be keeping it a secret much longer."

Dianne sighed. "True. I just wish it weren't happening."

Koko looked at her oddly. "You don't want another child?"

"Not like this. There's so much anger and hatred going on between Cole and me. I don't want to bring a child into that."

"You don't have a choice."

"Exactly!" Dianne said, her voice a little louder than she'd intended. "I have no choices. No one cares what I want. No one asks me how I'd like to have things."

"So what do you want?" Koko asked, smiling ever so slightly.

Dianne calmed. Her aunt had become such a mother to her. She always seemed to know the right thing to say. "I want my life back the way it was. I want the ranch to function as it used to. I want to know that everyone is safe and happy. I want Ardith back with her child. . . . There's so much I want, but again, it doesn't matter. I have no choice. I'm pregnant with a child that will bring me nothing but heartache."

"Don't look at it that way. Perhaps God has given you this child as a tool of reconciliation. And Cole might already be on his way home in order to be here before the baby comes."

"Cole doesn't know about the baby."

"What? You didn't tell him?"

"I didn't try to keep it from him either. The right opportunity simply didn't present itself to share the information with him. We were fighting almost all the time, and when we weren't fighting, I was too exhausted to care about telling him."

"You need to let him know, Dianne."

By this time George had come to join them. "You have to let him know."

Dianne felt a sense of embarrassment that George had overheard their conversation. But that was the trouble with a cabin like this. Its one main commons area where everyone lived and ate and passed the evening was not designed for privacy.

"I can't very well let him know now," Dianne said firmly.

"You could send a letter back with the

freighters. Or even with Zane and Mara. You need to at least let him know about the baby and your safe arrival. You owe him that much."

Dianne felt exhaustion settle over her like a wet blanket. "I suppose you're right. What time are the freighters heading back?"

"Early. They'll probably leave at first light."

Dianne suppressed a yawn. "If you have some writing materials, I'll pen a quick letter. I didn't think to purchase any for myself in Virginia City."

Koko smiled. "You'll be glad you did. There's nothing to be gained by keeping Cole from the truth."

Dianne laughed bitterly. "I tried so hard to get Cole to see the truth, but it was as if he were blind. I doubt this letter—this news of a child—is going to change anything. There are already four children here who didn't change his mind about coming home."

CHAPTER 20

"THE REAL BEAUTY OF THIS CITY IS IN THE architecture," Christopher Stromgren told Ardith. "Changes are happening all the time, and New York is growing at a rapid pace. Why, just a few decades ago you wouldn't have seen this area developed at all. Now there are a growing number of buildings and new businesses."

They were on their way to an early Christmas party. As Christopher had proven to Ardith, it was a time of social festivities that would leave them with little time to grow bored. Ardith had been whisked from one party to another between her performances, each more glamorous than the one before.

She couldn't even remember the names of the people who were throwing tonight's affair. She only knew that Christopher was quite impressed with their total capital and social standing.

"If you are asked to play," he said, moving on to other topics, "you must agree. But play only one song. They will ask for more, but I will step in and then promote your upcoming concert."

"That seems rather impolite," Ardith said. "After all, it is a party."

"True, but these are the very kind of people we hope to draw. They are from old money, as are their friends. Some are even related to royalty in Europe. Imagine for yourself what that might mean."

The cold was beginning to numb Ardith's gloved fingers. She rubbed her hands together. "I'm not sure what that would mean."

"It would mean traveling to Europe. Possibly to play for kings and queens."

"I can't go to Europe. I have a daughter to raise. I only agreed to come and give this a try. If it proves to be something that I find I'm unwilling to give up, then I must send for Winona."

Christopher sighed. "I've been meaning to talk to you about that."

"What? Is something wrong? Has word come from Montana?" she asked, growing worried.

"No, not at all. I merely wanted to discuss the matter of Winona and her heritage. You wished for your past—your time with the Indians—to remain untold. I can hardly do that with an Indian child at your side. Do you understand?"

Ardith considered his words for a moment.

"I suppose I do. But I cannot leave her there forever. I am her mother and she needs me."

"Of course," he said, almost laughing. "No one means for you to never see her again. Oh, good, here we are. Now remember all that I've told you. You must conduct yourself in such a manner as not to offend."

Ardith nodded and allowed him to help her from the carriage. She was glad the snow had been cleared away from the walk. The delicate slippers she wore were no benefit against the snow.

At the door they were met by a reserved looking man in a dark suit. He took the engraved invitation that Christopher offered and their wraps. He handed the invitation to one man and the coats to another.

"Come this way," the servant commanded. He took them up two flights of stairs, then handed their invitation to yet another impeccably dressed man.

Ardith was breathless from the climb. Her corset was much too tight, but it was necessary in order to do up the buttons on the burgundy velvet gown she wore.

"Mr. Christopher Stromgren and Mrs. Ardith Sperry," the servant announced as they were ushered into the room of party guests.

Ardith was amazed at the way the entire ballroom had been transformed into a feast for the eyes. Holiday greenery had been draped in massive boughs from one end of the room to the other. These were then trimmed in bright red and gold bows. At one end of the room, a Christmas tree, so large it must surely have been difficult to force indoors, stood with lighted candles dripping onto red circular bases.

"Mr. Stromgren, we are so delighted you could come this evening and bring Mrs. Sperry," a woman bedecked in green silk began. "I have so longed to meet this new star of yours."

Christopher bowed and turned to Ardith. "Mrs. Ressler, I would like you to meet Mrs. Ardith Sperry."

Ardith smiled as the woman assessed her. "I'm pleased to be here and to meet you."

"I'm sure you are. Perhaps later you will grace us with some of your music."

"Perhaps she will," Stromgren interjected, then turned to Ardith with a wink. Mrs. Ressler looked as if she would like to continue the conversation, but instead nodded and took herself off to the next guests being announced.

"Her husband is a drinker. He'll most likely make an appearance later, after he's returned from his men's club."

"How odd that he shouldn't be at her side."

"New York and its society is hardly like that of Montana. Money sets the rules, and if you have enough of it you can do most anything you like."

"Except have your daughter by your side," Ardith murmured.

Christopher looked at her oddly. "Remember, you are the one who wished to keep your secret regarding the Sioux. Not I."

He was right of course, but it offered no comfort to Ardith. She couldn't put the image of Winona's tear-streaked face from her mind. She had arranged to send her daughter some beautiful Christmas presents, including a lovely doll and several new dresses, but Ardith was certain they would mean little to Winona. She had severed a precious tie with her daughter, and despite feeling the necessity of it, Ardith was certain she'd long regret it.

———

As Christmas approached, Cole was beside himself with worry over Dianne. He'd heard nothing from her, and even the telegram he'd sent to her in Virginia City had gone unanswered. November had proven a battle of wills with heavy snows setting in around the middle of the month. Blizzards were not uncommon for the prairies or the mountains, but these snows seemed almost unnatural in their intensity and plunging temperatures.

Glancing upward to the night skies, Cole grimaced at the hazy condition. It was almost as if a thin veil had been placed between earth and the stars. It had been like that for several nights and always seemed to precede another bad snow.

"Cole, it's too cold to stand out there gawking. Come back in here," his mother commanded.

He went in against his better judgment, knowing that she would probably just berate him for missing his family. "I think it's going to snow again," he said as he hung his coat on the peg by the back door.

"It wouldn't surprise me," his mother said, pouring him a cup of coffee. "Sit down and drink this. I've also got a couple of leftover doughnuts. I can warm them if you like."

"No, thanks. I'm really not hungry."

"You have to stop moping around," she admonished. Turning, she frowned and practically slammed the coffee down in front of him. "She isn't worth it."

"If you're going to talk badly about Dianne, I'm going to bed," he said, starting to get up.

His mother motioned him to stay put. "If she loved you—truly cared for you, she would have written by now. She would have told you that she'd made it home safely. I think you should consider the truth."

"Which is what—at least by your standards?"

Mary Selby sat down across from him. "She's made her choice. She's taken the children and left. By all legal standards that would constitute desertion. I think you should obtain a divorce and see the thing done."

"Divorce?" Cole couldn't believe she was suggesting such a thing. "You lived for years in a miserable marriage and never once attempted a divorce."

"I couldn't have afforded a divorce," his mother replied bitterly. "Hallam never sent us much money when he was away, and what little I could earn we used for our existence. A divorce was never possible because of the cost involved. Otherwise, I probably would have jumped at the chance."

"But what of your reputation? You know how it would be looked at—how the church would see it. You wouldn't have been accepted in many social circles had you divorced Pa. Besides, Pa returned and tried to make things right. You had a good life together here in Kansas—you said so yourself. Divorce wasn't the answer for you."

"But we aren't talking about me," his mother replied flatly.

"Well, we certainly aren't talking about me." Cole drank nearly half the cup of coffee and then toyed with the cup as he continued. "I've been giving some thought to what needs to be done with the farm." He hoped a change of subject would get his mother's mind off of Dianne and divorcing.

"Good. There are a lot of repairs and improvements we could make," she said, folding her hands on the table. "Of course, Hallam never had enough money for some of the things he wanted to do, but I can tell you all about them, and we can work from there."

"I'm not talking about repairs and improvements," Cole said, fixing his gaze on his mother. He put the coffee cup down. "I'm talking about selling the farm."

"I won't hear any of it. Not with Christmas but two days away. Your sisters and their families will be with us, and it will be a grand celebration. We can talk after that." She got up and marched from the room without another word.

Cole was surprised by her actions. Generally speaking, his mother wasn't one to back down from a fight. Maybe this time she knew she was defeated and merely wanted to delay the event.

———

Christmas wasn't a grand celebration for Cole. It passed, in fact, in relative disgust and frustration. Cordelia and Laurel were spoiled wives, with equally spoiled children. Cole had no idea when his mother had had time to shop for gifts, but she lavished her grandchildren with one bauble after another. When he offhandedly asked if she'd purchased gifts for his children, his mother had turned away, muttering something about there being no sense in it.

It was little things that bothered him as he watched his mother and sisters. They seemed not to consider his feelings at all in regard to his family. They didn't appear to even think that he might be especially lonely for them at Christmas. It was actually the first Christmas he hadn't spent with his children . . . with Dianne. But when he did say something about missing them, during Christmas dinner, his mother immediately changed the subject.

Now that the new year had come, Cole couldn't help but wonder what 1887 would hold in store. He was more determined than ever to get home again, but at the same time, he wondered if he'd even be welcome there.

She should have written something. She should have at least responded to my telegram. But maybe her silence was a response. Maybe it was the only response she intended him to have.

"I'm glad you stopped by, Cole," Ralph Brewster greeted a couple of weeks later.

Ralph was the neighbor who owned the farm just north of the Selby farm. He had indicated at church that he might be open to a proposition from Cole regarding the place.

"Glad you had time to talk."

"Ruth has made us some cake and coffee. Want some?"

"I'd love some. It's mighty cold out there." Cole smiled at the stocky Kansan. The man was in his midthirties, and something about him told Cole he could be a good friend. He didn't seem at all to care about the gossip that went around the church concerning Dianne and the children. His own two boys had played happily with Cole's boys, but only at school. They were never allowed to come over to the farm, because Cole's mother didn't like there to be too much noise. Cole hadn't learned about this until after the children had gone back to Montana. It was one more thing that seemed to support Dianne's comments about how she and the children were being treated.

"We don't stand on ceremony in this house," Ralph told Cole. "We'll just sit in the kitchen. It's warmer there. Ruth has some sewing to do, so she'll be busy in the other room."

"That sounds fine," Cole replied. "I've always liked sitting in the kitchen." He took the chair offered him by Ralph and waited while the man brought the coffee and mugs to the table. Ruth's promised cake was already cut and sitting on two plates, ready to be devoured. Cole had to admit it looked delicious. He and his mother had not eaten nearly as well since

Dianne had gone back to Montana. He missed her cooking.

"I was intrigued by your comments Sunday," Ralph said, pouring them each a cup of the steaming liquid.

"Well, truth be told, with this crazy winter we've been having, I figured I had time to get this situation planned out."

"Did you hear about the areas to the west? Montana, Wyoming, and the Dakotas have already been buried in one snow after another. Now it's spread to Kansas, Colorado, and Nebraska. Doesn't look to be letting up anytime soon. My brother tells me a wire came from Cheyenne saying the storms are heading into their eighth day without sign of stopping. They're afraid the telegraph lines will go down any moment."

"I didn't know it was that bad there. It's been bad enough around these parts. That would explain . . ." He didn't finish the thought. He didn't want Ralph to know that Dianne hadn't written. "Well, anyway," Cole picked up, "I'm glad I don't have a lot of cattle to worry over."

"I'd say." Ralph took his seat and picked up his cup. "There's already reports of hundreds of deaths, both human and animal. The temperatures will probably drop and then we'll really be in for a time. Won't be a chance for ranchers to get feed out to those beasts."

"No, probably not."

"Makes me glad I'm a farmer." Ralph blew out a deep breath. "I surely don't envy those that have livestock."

"It's never easy," Cole admitted. "We used to move our cattle to winter pastures—places of open range fairly close to our ranch—to avoid heavy mountain snows and such. Now much of the land is being bought up and people are starting to fence it off. I doubt seriously too many Montanans are going to take to barbed wire."

"Sure is necessary down here. Of course, this is a state where farming and ranching go hand in hand."

Cole nodded. "There are places like that in Montana as well. Still, it's too wild for most to make a decent living. Like I said, I'm glad I don't have cattle herds this winter. The losses will no doubt be outrageous if everything you've said proves true."

Ralph pushed a plate of the cake toward Cole. "Try this. It's been passed down in Ruth's family for ages. She calls it her chocolate cheer." He laughed. "I have to admit it always cheers me when she makes it."

"It looks great." He forked in a mouthful and gave his approval. "It is great."

Ralph leaned forward as if to share a secret. "I like to put mine in a bowl and pour milk over it most of the time."

Cole laughed. "Well, feel free to do just that. Don't think you have to be fancy on my account."

"Nah, it's good enough like this . . . for now." Ralph took several large bites, nearly devouring his piece before continuing to talk. "So tell me about your proposition."

Cole swallowed and drank down some coffee before he opened the conversation. "You know I inherited my dad's place." Ralph nodded and Cole continued. "You also know I have the ranch in Montana to be responsible for. I need to get back as early in the spring as I can."

"The way it's snowing you may have to wait until July," Ralph joked.

The thought pierced Cole's heart. He'd been worried about getting home ever since the really bad blizzard just after Christmas. Now with Ralph's news about the ongoing storms in Montana and Wyoming, Cole seriously wondered if he would be able to get home before May or June.

"Here are my thoughts," Cole finally continued. "I know Ma wants to stay on the farm, but I can't remain here indefinitely. I'm thinking a hired man could come and stay at the farm and help with odd jobs, milking and tending the few animals, as well as helping with the farming. That's where you would come in. I'd like you to consider farming my father's place.

I'd give you half the profit and hire the man to help when you needed it—like in planting and harvesting. The other half of the profit would have to go to my mother."

"That's mighty generous," Ralph said. "I have to admit, I've been itching to expand, but I don't have the income for such a jump. This would allow me to make a little extra money; maybe I could save it for more land."

"I think the soil is rich. We had a decent profit from last year, and that was during a drought. I can't begin to think of what it'll be like when these snows melt and replenish the water tables."

Ralph finished his coffee and poured himself another cup. "Would you consider one more thing?" he asked, putting the cup aside momentarily.

"Sure, Ralph. What is it?"

"Would you agree in writing to give me first chance at the place if you decide to sell?"

Cole laughed. "You read my mind. I only plan to keep the farm as long as my mother insists on living there. Frankly, I'd be glad to sell it to you now if we could make some agreement to that effect."

"I think we probably could, but again, I don't have the capital it would require to make an outright purchase. And I already owe the bank for improvements on my place. I don't think I could get any more money."

"I'm not in need of money," Cole said, realizing the only thing he truly needed couldn't be bought: his wife's trust and love. "I think we could work out payments. Yearly, after the crops were brought in."

"Well, this is like Christmas all over again," Ralph said, slapping the table. "Wait'll Ruth hears. Oh, and don't fret yourself with finding a hired man. Ruth's brother has been itchin' to get out here from Indiana. I think he'd be mighty glad to come and work for your ma."

God always seemed to have a way of working things out. Cole felt a peace settle on his shoulders like a warm woolen coat. He could finally see hope in his situation. "I think that sounds fine. Go ahead and arrange for him to come. I'll even pay for his train ticket."

"Now that's too generous. The boy's been thinking of coming out here anyway. He's twenty-two and has been saving for five years while trying to figure out what he wanted to do. Let him pay his own way. It'll make him appreciate it more. Pay him a decent wage and it'll be fine by me."

"Will he need to live on my mother's place or do you have room for him here?" Cole asked, knowing that his mother was going to resent the arrangement no matter what.

"We've got plenty of room, and I doubt you could get Ruth to let him live anywhere else. He'll be fine here. He can ride over at dawn each day and work at what needs to be tended, and then come home for dinner and help me. By evening he can go back and take care of anything else that needs to be done. Oh, and if your ma needs him to drive her into town or run errands for her, I'll arrange for him to be free for that as well."

"Ralph, this sounds like the perfect solution. But don't mention this to anyone yet. Except for your brother-in-law, of course. I need to break this to the family gentle-like. They know I plan to leave, but they also think they've somehow convinced me to stay."

Ralph nodded. "Your ma is a determined woman. I've seen her accomplish many things."

"That's a very kind way of putting it," Cole said, lifting his mug. "Here's to a profitable and long-lasting partnership."

Ralph raised his mug. "I'll drink to that."

———

Several days later, Cole thought the perfect opportunity had arisen to tell his mother about Ralph. She was in a very good mood and had even baked that morning. The cake she made was similar to the one Ruth Brewster had served, which was what gave Cole the thought to bring up the topic of the farm.

"You know, I had a nice long talk with Ralph Brewster the other day," Cole said, leaning against the back door, watching his mother frost the cake.

"Oh? How's he doing? How are Ruth and the children?"

"Good. They're all good. I told him how I'd need to be returning to Montana in the spring."

Mary Selby slammed down the crock of frosting she'd been holding. "Why would you tell him that? You know you don't want to go back. You know you aren't wanted in Montana."

"I don't know any such thing," Cole said. "And I wish you would stop saying that I don't want to go back. Do you suppose if you say it often enough it will change my mind?"

His mother narrowed her eyes. "You listen to me, Cole Selby. You listen to what's good for you. That woman you married will do nothing but manipulate you and steal your life from you. You're appreciated here and you have all that you could possibly want."

"I want my family, Ma. I wanted them when it was Luke's birthday. I wanted them at Christmas, when no one else seemed to care that they were gone. I wanted to bring in the new year with them—not with my sisters' spoiled and selfish girls—but with my boys and Lia. With Dianne."

"How dare you say your sisters' girls are

spoiled and selfish. They are your nieces and they adore you."

"They hardly speak two words to me," Cole replied angrily. He strode across the room and stood directly in front of his mother. "You need to get this through your head now, Ma. You need to understand that I am going home come spring."

"This is your home now. You own it," she said bitterly. "You are the selfish one if you consider leaving. I need someone here to run the farm. I won't leave."

"I know you won't, and that's why I've asked Ralph to farm the land. His brother-in-law is going to come from Indiana to live with them, and he's going to come over here and be your handyman. He'll even drive you into town when you need him to."

Mary shook her head vigorously. "I won't have a stranger living here!"

Cole smiled. "He won't be living here. He'll live with Ralph and Ruth and come over every morning, then go home for dinner and work with Ralph. Then he'll come back in the evenings. Like I said, if you need to go to town or have him drive you to church, Ralph said he'll make provision for that."

Mary's face turned beet red. Her expression contorted angrily. "How dare you make arrangements for me behind my back!"

"This is my place now, Ma, as you've

pointed out over and over. I have the right to make whatever provision I want. If you're uncomfortable with it, then you'll have to go live with Cordelia or Laurel, because I intend to make a deal with Ralph that will allow him to buy the place so long as he allows you to live here as long as you like."

"This is all about her," Mary spewed. "That horrible little wife of yours. She's poisoned you against me. Well, I won't have it. You'll rethink this and stay with me. I'm your mother and you owe me this."

"How do you figure that?"

His mother seemed momentarily at a loss for words. Then she seemed to calm before his very eyes. Finally she picked up the frosting bowl and went back to her work but added, "I figure that no one else will have you. Not now—especially not now. Your conniving wife won't think twice about turning you out. She certainly didn't think twice about leaving you."

Her words stung deep. Hadn't these thoughts been a part of Cole's very nightmare? Dianne hadn't written. She hadn't sent so much as a single word to let him know she was safe. His mother said that was because she was trying to hurt him . . . make him so afraid he'd hurry home to her so that she could drive him back out, refuse him a home. Now his mother's words just seemed manipulative, almost deceitful. Exactly as Dianne had told him.

"No one is going to escape this winter unscathed," Dianne said as she put down the curtain. Snows had buried them deep, and for the safety and conservation of heating wood, they'd all come to live in Koko's cabin.

"I've never seen a winter when the snows continued for more than ten days," Koko said, shaking her head. "This winter is fierce. Many cattle and horses are sure to die."

"I suppose we're blessed not to have a herd," Dianne murmured as she took a seat at the table with George and Koko. The children were still sleeping soundly by the fireplace, and though it was dawn, the heavy skies would allow in no light.

"We're very blessed. Had you returned last year like you wanted and brought up all those cows from Texas, we'd be losing them now," George said, looking to Dianne with a somber expression.

"Poor Chester Lawrence," Koko added. "He was boasting a herd of over eight thousand. I don't know if that was true or not, but George heard it in Bozeman when Gus was ill. If he has that many, he'll no doubt see huge losses."

"Serves him right," Dianne said, not feeling the least bit charitable. Her advancing pregnancy was making her irritable. Being buried alive by blizzard after blizzard was making her feel desperate.

"I know Chester has wronged us all," Koko began, "but remember the Bible talks about being kind to your enemy. We don't want to make our hearts like his."

Dianne felt completely chastised. "I know," she sighed. "It's just that sometimes a person likes to see God intervene and take His revenge. When I think of all the people who have suffered under Chester's hand—folks who've lost their ranches and are now long gone—well, it seems this is a just revenge."

"Perhaps, but there is nothing of Christian charity in gloating over the misfortune of others. God doesn't like a haughty spirit and we must guard our hearts."

"My heart is definitely guarded," Dianne said with a heavy sigh. She'd written to Cole about the baby and had heard nothing from him. Of course, the snows had come early and heavy and there could be a letter waiting for her in Virginia City. If so, she had no way of knowing. Either way, she wasn't getting her hopes up. She was, as Koko had admonished, guarding her heart.

Guarding it against further pain.

Guarding it against a future that might never come.

CHAPTER 21

FEBRUARY BROUGHT NO RELIEF FROM THE weather nor the discouragement that seemed to embrace the residents of the Diamond V. Dianne could barely stand her own company, much less that of anyone else. She found herself constantly feeling angry with the children for no good reason.

She'd come to accept the new life she carried and even told herself that it would make things better. The children were quite excited about the baby, and everyone wanted a part in planning for the arrival.

George and Jamie had the boys help them fashion a cradle for the infant, while Koko and Susannah worked with Lia and Winona to make tiny baby clothes. Dianne had tried hard to put aside the distance that separated her from Cole and focus instead on her little ones.

Day after long, cold day, Dianne turned to the Bible for her nightly reading. She knew that God was her mainstay—her fortress of strength. She tried to keep her hope fixed on the fact that He was a God of impossibilities.

But as the winter pressed in closer around them, Dianne worried that maybe her life and the mess she'd created were even beyond God.

The thing that worried her most, however, was that she hadn't felt the baby move all day. Maybe it had even been as long as two days. She couldn't be sure. She'd been so busy with schooling her children and Winona that she hadn't really thought about the baby inside her. Dianne pushed against her abdomen, hoping to stir a little reaction from the child, but there was nothing.

With this concern on her mind, along with a fierce headache, Dianne was hardly up to dealing with her aunt's distress over Winona.

"Dianne, she's deeply saddened by her mother's absence. She's hardly eaten or spoken to anyone for weeks."

"I know," Dianne said, rubbing her forehead. "I'll talk to her."

"Are you feeling poorly?"

Dianne looked up wearily and met Koko's compassionate gaze. "My head hurts, that's all. Just too much white outside and too much darkness inside."

"Mama, when is Papa coming home?" John asked.

Dianne frowned. "And too many questions." She looked at her son and shook her head. "Stop asking me about your father! We're buried in snow, John. Nobody can get through until it all melts and goes away. Hopefully, Papa will come home after that." *If it's important enough to him.* The proof of her irritation rang out in her tone, and John's expression made it clear his feelings were hurt.

"Your mama doesn't feel good, John," Koko told him. "Why don't you go play with your brothers and let her rest?"

John nodded and started to walk away, but just then Luke came bounding up to the table. "Can we go work with Jamie and Uncle George? They're going to go dig us out."

Dianne thought the idea sounded like a good one to help her energetic sons get some exercise. "Put on your warm clothes and your coats. Don't forget your gloves and hats and then you can go outside to shovel snow."

Koko smiled. "Come on, boys. I'll help you."

Dianne sighed as they all went to the back porch. She knew she needed to talk with Winona, but truth be told, she just didn't have the heart for it. What could she possibly say to the child that hadn't been said before?

Making her way to the bedroom that she had been sharing with Lia and Winona, Dianne didn't even bother to knock. Inside she found Winona sitting on the bed, curled up in the corner against the wall.

"I haven't seen you all day," Dianne declared as she went to the bed and awkwardly sat down. The baby was making everything difficult these days. "What are you thinking about back here all by yourself?"

Winona sighed, refusing to look at Dianne. "I miss my mama. I want her to come home."

"I want that too, but sweetie, we've got several feet of snow outside. There's no way your mother could get here now." *Even if she wanted to.* But Dianne feared Ardith had no desire to be here. If she did, she'd already be here.

"I don't know why she had to go away."

Dianne nodded sympathetically. "I know, but sometimes people need time to think things through—to feel better."

"Aunt Dianne, do you think Mama will ever come back?"

The question caught Dianne off guard. "Of course she'll come back." *At least that's what I pray every day.* Dianne wished she could assure the child that there was no doubt about her mother's return. But Ardith's departure had been such a drastic move that it wouldn't surprise any of the family to see Ardith make yet another bad decision. Dianne reached out to touch Winona's leg, but the child only recoiled. Deciding to try again later, Dianne stood.

"You can't give up hope, Winona. The hope within is all that keeps anybody going from day to day. My children miss their father, but they have hope of seeing him again. You have reason to hope that your mother will come home or at least come back for you."

Winona looked at her hands and said nothing. Dianne knew it would do little good to keep talking about the matter. Winona didn't believe her anyway.

By six o'clock that evening, Dianne was certain she was sick. The headache had alleviated a bit, but other aches and pains had come to make up for its lessening. She wished Cole were there. She always felt better just having him close whenever she was sick.

"You've hardly eaten," Koko admonished. "How are you going to keep you and that baby strong and healthy if you don't eat?"

"I'm sorry. I'm not feeling at all well." Nauseous and light-headed, Dianne got up from the dinner table.

"I'm going to lie down. I—" She stumbled and grabbed for the back of her chair.

"Dianne?" Koko asked as she started to stand as well.

George jumped to his feet and came to where Dianne stood. She smiled. "I'm sorry for being a bother," she said just before losing consciousness.

"This doesn't look good," Koko told George. "I'm sure the baby has died inside her.

There's no movement. I think it's making her sick."

"Can we do anything?" he asked, never letting his gaze leave Dianne for even a moment.

"I can give her some herbs. They'll help her start her labor. She must expel the child in order to recover. Her body is filled with poisons now—poisons from the baby."

"So there's no hope for the child?" George asked, saddened by the idea of Dianne losing a baby. She loved her children greatly and was a good mother. He could only imagine how hard it would be for her to lose one of them.

"I don't think so. I think the baby has probably been gone for several days. Dianne started feeling ill two days ago." Koko shook her head sadly. "I'll go get my things. You stay here with her."

George pulled a chair to the side of the bed. He would have been hard-pressed to leave her had his sister commanded him elsewhere. He felt useless and unable to help this woman . . . the woman he loved more dearly than life. Would she perish? Would the child's death also take the life of the mother?

George took hold of her hand. "You have to get well—you know that. Your children need you. They need you, Dianne. You must get well for them." *For me.* He left his thought unspoken. Only his sister would have understood. If anyone else would have overheard his thought, it would have only served to confuse them.

"Mama said to bring this hot water in," Susannah said as she entered the room.

George quickly dropped Dianne's hand and stood to help her. "I'm going to stay here and help your mother. Will you be able to work with Jamie and care for the children?"

Susannah looked at him oddly. "You don't have to help Mama. I can do it."

"No, I think it'd be best if you were there for the children. They need a female for a time like this," George said firmly. "Your mother will understand."

Susannah didn't argue. "All right. I'll let Mama know that you're going to help her." She left the room, her expression telling him that she didn't understand.

Koko came back quickly after that. She said nothing about George's encounter with Susannah but merely held up a glass. "We have to get her to drink this."

"I'll lift her up and hold her for you."

Koko nodded. "Let's get to it then."

As the night wore on, Dianne developed a fever that rose with every passing hour. Koko was clearly worried about the situation; George could read it in her eyes. She usually wore a guarded expression when dealing with injuries or sickness, but this time she was too worried to conceal her fears.

"The baby should come sometime after midnight," she told him. She put her hands on both sides of Dianne's abdomen. After several moments, she said, "The contractions are good and hard. We shouldn't have to give her anything more—at least not for the birth."

But it isn't really a birth, George thought. This child was never going to breathe air— would never cry—would never open its eyes to see its mother. He hadn't realized how hard this was going to be for him. He supposed he'd always thought of Dianne's children as his own, in some strange fashion. He'd always pledged to himself that if anything happened to Cole, he'd see to the welfare of the family. So now, with this baby being stillborn, George felt almost as if he'd somehow failed in his duties.

Dianne would be devastated by this loss. She might have been worried about having a child during a time of marital difficulty, but George knew she would have loved this baby as much as she did the others. Losing the baby would not be an easy matter for her.

Praying silently, a million questions came to mind. Why was she enduring this? Why had God allowed such grief in her life? Why was Cole in Kansas, when she was here? George knew he could never have let her go had he been her husband.

But you're not her husband, a voice whispered

in his heart. *And you cannot desire her as such. She is your friend—as is Cole.* His conscience won over his heart. *I won't do anything to jeopardize our friendship,* he determined as he sat beside Dianne. *I will not dishonor God by thinking thoughts that should never be.*

When the tiny boy was finally expelled, Koko wrapped him quickly in a white blanket and handed him to George. "You'll need to build a small coffin for him. We won't have any hope of burying him until it thaws. We'll have to do what we can." She met George's tear-filled expression. He hadn't meant to cry— truly it was one of only a handful of times in his adult life that he had wept. But this moment, if none other, deserved his tears and more.

He felt the lifeless bundle in his arms and mourned the loss. He mourned for all that might have been but now would never come.

"Will she live?" he asked, barely managing to speak the words.

"I cannot say. She is very ill. It's in God's hands now."

George was glad the children were all asleep as he slipped through the house with the baby. He took up a lantern and headed out the back door. He'd strung a rope between the house and the barn, but the path was fairly clear of drifted snow and overhead the moon shone brightly, lighting his way.

"God, my heart hurts so much for her— for Dianne." He looked down at the blanket. She would ask him about the child. He knew that much. If she survived this ordeal, she would want to know everything.

He went into the barn and hung the lantern from a nearby hook. Drawing a deep breath, he lifted the blanket and looked down at the face of the infant. The tiny face was perfectly formed. The eyes were closed as if in sleep. The boy reminded George of the way Lia looked when she was born. A thought came to mind. George gently placed the baby on a stack of horse blankets and pulled out his knife. With tender care, he cut a lock of hair from the baby's head. "I can't give you your child," he whispered, "but perhaps this will help."

He wiped his eyes and cleared his throat as if to clear away the sorrow. Looking around for his tools and appropriate pieces of wood, George went to work on the casket.

"But what happened to the baby?" Luke asked Koko at breakfast the next morning.

"He wasn't strong enough to live, Luke. He might have been sick; we just can't say for sure."

The children were all very somber, including Jamie and Susannah, who were quite grieved at the thought of such tragedy. Koko knew the family was going to endure this pain for a long time to come.

"Is Mama going to die too?" Lia asked, her lower lip quivering.

"I don't think she will," Koko replied. "I won't lie to you children, though. Your mama is very sick. She will be needing our prayers, and you will need to be extra good so that I can spend my time tending her. Do you suppose you can work with Susannah on your schooling and not argue?"

"We can be real good," Luke said as the head of the family while Lia crawled up onto Koko's lap and began to cry.

"It's a strong man who makes a stand in times of adversity," George said. "You can be a great help to your brothers and sister."

Luke shrugged. "We really need Papa."

"He's right, you know," Koko said, looking to George. "We need to get word to Cole, in case . . ." Her words trailed off. She couldn't worry the children unduly, but Dianne was desperately weak. She couldn't honestly say if Dianne would survive.

"I'll go send a wire to Cole in Kansas. You have the address, don't you?"

"I do, but how in the world will you ever make it through to town? That's a long ways, and the snows have buried everything around here."

"Around here—but there's no telling what

it's done five miles away or ten," George said as he got to his feet. "It's got to be done, and it's my job to do it."

Koko swallowed hard. She knew how much George loved Dianne. But he loved Cole as well. He would never have risked his life otherwise. "I'll pack provisions for you. Will you take a horse?"

"No. I'll take snowshoes and walk. I used to do this all the time when I was Jamie's age. I could run for miles and miles."

"But you aren't Jamie's age anymore."

"I could go with him," Jamie chimed in. "I'm strong and together we can help each other."

Koko didn't want to let her son endanger his life, but it did seem reasonable that two together would be better than one alone. However, before she could speak, George took the decision from her.

"You'll need to be the man of the ranch," he told Jamie. "Your mother and sister and the children will need you. You'll have to tend to all the outside chores on your own and make sure they have enough wood to keep warm."

Jamie seemed to understand the truth of George's words. Koko nodded as well. "How long do you suppose it will take you?"

"If I'm not back in a week . . ." His voice trailed off. If he wasn't back in a week there would be little they could do for him.

"Can you bring the doctor for my mama?" John asked.

"I'll do what I can, John," he promised.

Koko turned from the table. "You'll need to hurry. I'll get your things."

Ardith looked at herself in the mirror. The reflected woman there was a stranger. Dressed in a pink silk evening gown, complete with long train and bustle, Ardith couldn't help but feel out of place. The gown, the room, the life—none of it was hers.

Oh, her money was paying for it, of course, but it didn't feel like it belonged to her. She touched her gloved hand to her fashionably styled hair. The hairdresser had spent nearly an hour on the arrangement, weaving curls and ornaments into a highly impressive fashion.

"Madame Sperry, Mr. Stromgren requests your company in the receiving room," Olga announced. The girl had been assigned to Ardith as her personal maid, and it was no wonder. There was no possible way a woman could dress in all the frippery and layers by herself.

"Tell him I'm coming," Ardith replied, turning just in time to see Olga curtsy.

The last thing she wanted to do was spend her last hour before performing listening to Christopher try to impress her. He constantly felt it important that she know how much money things cost and how difficult it was to associate with certain people. He wanted to stress to her how fortunate she was to be invited into certain circles, but Ardith didn't feel lucky. She just felt tired and lonely. Maybe even more lonely than when she'd been at home. How was that possible? How could one be more lonely in a crowd of hundreds of adoring fans than in the solitude of her room in Virginia City?

She walked from her bedroom into her sitting room, where Olga stood ready with Ardith's cloak and bag. "Thank you, Olga."

Ardith made her way downstairs. Christopher stood to the side, speaking with a rather stocky man. He looked familiar—perhaps someone she'd met after one of the concerts.

"Ardith, my dear, come meet Mr. Roosevelt."

She nodded and extended her hand as she'd been taught. Roosevelt took it and bent over it ever so slightly. "If I remember correctly, you are the sister of Morgan Chadwick."

"I am," she admitted. "Ardith Chadwick Sperry."

"And you are also the divine angel that my sister heard play piano last night."

She smiled. "Most likely."

"Well, we are delighted to have you gracing New York. You must come spend some time with my family. I've already commanded Christopher to bring you by. I've recently returned from my wedding trip, and I know that Mrs. Roosevelt would count me remiss if you were not to come for dinner."

"I will look forward to it."

Christopher laughed. "Perhaps it's a good thing you didn't win the mayoral race, Teddy. You'd be far too busy with city politics to enjoy wondrous new artists such as our Mrs. Sperry."

"That is one way to consider it."

Ardith could tell it was a difficult subject for Mr. Roosevelt. His expression made it clear that he was not at all happy with the result of his campaign—or even with Christopher's bringing up the matter.

"So will you be with us long, Mrs. Sperry?"

She lowered her gaze to the intricately woven carpet and thoughtfully considered his question. "I'm uncertain. There are benefits here to be sure, but there are also sacrifices."

"I know it well. Ah," he said as he seemed to spy someone across the room, "if you'll excuse me, I must speak with that gentleman."

"But of course."

Christopher barely waited until Roosevelt had stepped away before he chided Ardith. "How can you be uncertain about staying? New York loves you, and you're very comfortably situated, are you not? We're both benefiting from this. Don't be too quick to put it aside."

She met his eyes, which seemed dark and brooding.

He leaned closer. "I need you here, Ardith."

She felt a chill run up her spine. There was no reason to be afraid, but she felt fearful nevertheless. Perhaps Dianne was right. Perhaps Christopher Stromgren was more dangerous than she knew.

CHAPTER 22

SNOW BURIED THE KANSAS FARM IN A thick, wet blanket. There was little to be done but stay inside and wait it out. Cole was worried about his family in Montana. He couldn't help but wonder if they were enduring the same fierce storms. He wondered if Dianne had gone to the ranch or if she'd been more cautious and remained in Virginia City.

"She's probably gone to the ranch," he murmured as he let the curtain fall back into place. He wondered if she was happy—if the children had adjusted to the changes.

"What was that?" his mother asked as she brought a steaming platter of food to the table. She didn't even wait for his response before adding, "Dinner is ready."

Cole took his seat and waited until his mother had dished up the baked chicken and noodles before speaking. "Smells good."

"It should suffice," she responded. They bowed their heads in prayer, but Cole couldn't help but feel that for his mother, the prayer was only something done out of habit.

They ate in silence for several minutes. Cole could find no fault with the food. His mother, when she wanted to be, was an adequate cook. Her food couldn't match Dianne's, but then, he'd never had food that could. Dianne just had a way of seasoning and spicing food that set it above the cooking of others. He supposed it could be credited to her eclectic teaching—taking things she'd learned from Faith, Charity, and others in order to make food tasty.

"You aren't even listening, are you?" his mother asked in that curt manner that always set his nerves on edge.

"I'm sorry. I have a great deal on my mind. What did you say?" Cole asked apologetically.

Mary pushed back from the table. "I'm going to get some more bread. Would you like anything else?"

Cole looked at the table. His mother had thoughtfully put out jam, pickled beets, and bread and butter, along with a bowl of hominy. "I can't think of anything."

She nodded and departed for the kitchen without another word. Cole knew she was upset about his plans for the farm. She wouldn't hear him through on any of it, and when he'd come back from town last week with papers showing that the deed was done and that Ralph Brewster now owned the farm, she'd nearly thrown herself into a state of apoplexy.

Cole was about to take another bite of the noodles when he heard a heavy-handed knock on the front door. He was surprised that anyone would risk his well-being to travel in this weather. Getting up, Cole left his napkin at the table and went to answer the door.

"You Cole Selby?" the young man asked, his teeth chattering.

"Yes. Please come in and warm up."

The boy, barely a man, stepped inside. "Thank you kindly. I have a telegram here for you, mister." He thrust the paper into Cole's hands. "Wouldn't have come in this snow, but it was marked as an urgent matter."

Cole reached into his pocket and fished out a couple of coins. He exchanged them for the paper, leaving the boy quite pleased with the generosity. "Fireplace is through here," Cole directed.

Once the boy was warming up at the hearth, Cole opened the message. He felt the blood rush from his head at the words. George had sent the note, and its urgency was clear. Dianne had given birth to a stillborn son and was gravely ill. Possibly dying.

"Why wouldn't she tell me?"

"Pardon?" the boy asked, looking over his shoulder.

"Cole! Where are you?"

"Stay here and warm up. I'll see to it that my mother feeds you, then we can make our way into town together. It's bound to be easier that way," Cole instructed.

"Yes, sir!"

"I'm here, Mother," Cole announced as he came back into the dining room. "There's a young man warming himself by the fire. I need you to give him some food. He's half frozen, and it would do good to get his insides warmed up as well as his outsides."

"Who is he?" she asked.

"Never mind. Just feed him."

Cole left the room, racing up the back stairs as quickly as he could. He tried not to think about the message of the telegram and instead simply focused on packing his things. He wouldn't let himself believe that she was dying. He couldn't. He couldn't even conceive of the idea.

He thought of the children—their children—sitting alone in worry. Wondering what was happening and why their mother was so sick.

"Why didn't she tell me about the baby?" he muttered. Cole found it almost as impossible to imagine another child born to him—yet not born at all. A son. Another boy. A child he would never lay eyes on—never touch, never know.

He threw his clothes into a carpetbag without bothering to fold them. He grabbed what few toiletries and other articles belonged to him and shoved them in with the clothes. The last thing he reached for was his gun belt. He wrapped the holster around the revolver and tucked it in with the clothes.

"What's going on?" his mother asked as she appeared in the door of his room. "What are you doing?"

"The boy downstairs brought me a telegram from Dianne."

His mother harrumphed. "So you're going to go running off to her, is that it?"

"It's important. I don't want to discuss it," he said, working to close the bag. He didn't know what to say that wouldn't come out in tones of anger and frustration, as well as deep worry. His mother would no doubt have little sympathy, despite the death of her grandson.

"It's always about her. She's twisted your thoughts and manipulated your heart. She's no doubt telling you lies. Lies about having another child and how necessary it is for you to return to Montana. Lies about—"

"What did you say?" Cole dropped his hold on the bag.

His mother seemed taken aback by his tone. "You heard me. She's a conniving little liar. She lied about me and your sisters, and now she's lying to get you to rush home. But no doubt once you risk life and limb in these blizzards, she'll simply laugh in your face and refuse you again."

"She's never refused me," Cole said, barely able to keep his voice even. He felt a growing rage build within. He held up the telegram. "I never said anything about a baby. Why did you?"

Mary Selby paled and took a step back. "Perhaps now isn't the best time to discuss this."

He crossed his arms. "I think you'd better be honest with me, Mother. I've tolerated as much as I'm going to put up with."

His mother's anger appeared to overcome any fear she might have had. "I can't believe after all I've done for you that you would go back to her. She doesn't need you like I do."

"She's dying!" he roared. "How dare you

tell me what she needs?"

"She's lying! Just like everything else. She's telling you these tales to get you back into her snare. How could a dying woman send a telegram?"

"She didn't send this telegram," he said, stuffing the paper into his pocket. "The man who sent it wouldn't have lied about this or anything else. Unlike this family, there are still honorable people in the world."

"Cole, you can't mean that," his mother said, moving to where he stood. "I've done nothing but try to protect you."

He was unmoved by her pleading tone. "How did you know about the baby?"

"There's no baby. I'm certain she was just saying that to entice you," she replied firmly.

"I want to know right now how you knew about the baby." He narrowed his eyes and leaned toward her. "Right now, Mother."

She drew a deep breath. "Well, there was one letter. But only one, Cole. She never bothered to write again, and the letter was full of lies."

"When did she write?"

"It came shortly after they arrived in Virginia City. She wanted to let you know they had arrived safely."

Cole shook his head. "I can't believe I'm hearing this out of your mouth. You've deceived me—not only with the letter, but in everything."

"No! I've done only what was necessary."

"To help yourself. Certainly not to be of help to me. You drove my family from here—in truth, you made it clear that you never wanted them here to begin with. Now my wife lies near death, and my children are without their father."

"I'm confident that you'll find it all a deception when you arrive." She straightened from her cowering appearance. "Then you'll see that I was right to keep the letter from you."

"You lied to me," he said, his voice void of emotion. The anger that had so clearly fueled him moments ago had abated in the wake of his fears. Dianne had been right all along. His mother and sisters were manipulating every situation to pit him and Dianne against each other. The excuses he'd made for his mother now soured in his stomach as he reflected on them. How betrayed Dianne must have felt, and now she might very well die with that on her heart and nothing more.

"You need to calm down and think this through," Mary said. "You know very well the trains haven't been running. The entire countryside is buried in snow and there is no chance you'll be able to get far."

"I'll get a room at the hotel. Then at least I

won't have to stay here." He picked up his bag. "I don't know why you ever thought it acceptable to do what you did. If I'd only listened to my wife—if I'd only have returned to Montana with her—I'd be at her side now, where I belong."

"Please don't go, Cole. I need you here."

"You don't need anyone. You've made that abundantly clear." He shook his head. "No, I take that back. You need to make a right stand with God. You need to clear out the hatred and bitterness that you have in your heart, and you need to seek the forgiveness of those whom you've wronged."

She laughed bitterly. "I've done nothing that requires forgiveness. I tried to protect my child, out of a mother's love. I don't want to be forgiven for that."

Cole pushed past her and headed to the door. "Ralph will contact you as soon as the snows melt enough to burn off the field. He owns this place now. I'll send you money as he pays off the mortgage."

"Don't go," she said, pulling at his coat sleeve.

Cole jerked away and stared at her hard. How could he have been so blinded by her schemes? "You have my lying sisters to consort with. Hopefully you'll all get on your knees and pray to God that Dianne lives. There's no hope for my dead son, but the least you could do is pray for her."

———

There was no train out of Topeka that day or the next, but as soon as the tracks were cleared, Cole was headed home. He spent the days of travel in deep prayer and meditation on the Bible. He searched for Scripture passages of hope and restoration. He prayed for Dianne's recovery and for his marriage.

I've made a mess of things, Lord. I got caught up in a problem that wasn't even mine to worry about. If I'd listened to Dianne early on and if we'd prayed on this together and worked together, I might have been by her side. I might have kept her from illness—from the baby dying.

He tortured himself with his thoughts, and no matter how hard he prayed for forgiveness, Cole felt the weight of the situation pressing down on him.

"You travelin' far, son?" the conductor asked Cole as he came to check his ticket.

Cole produced the piece and handed it up. "Montana," he said in a rather dejected voice.

"I'll probably get you as far as Denver but won't promise much more'n that. Snows are bad up Cheyenne way, and to the west it's nigh onto impossible to get through. They've had some luck off and on, but no promises." He handed the ticket back to Cole.

"Thanks."

" 'Course, you should've seen us last year in January. Snows so bad we put eleven engines on one locomotive and still couldn't get it broke loose of the ice. That was around Salina way." The man crossed his arms. "Ain't never seen the likes of it, but sounds like the same thing's hit up north and west. South ain't farin' good either. Last year was the start of the 'big die-up,' as they call it—with Texas losin' lots of steers to the cold and snow. This year don't look much better for them or anyone else."

Cole was discouraged enough without the man's help. "Guess I'll have to pray for a miracle then," he muttered.

The conductor laughed. "Prayin's the only thing that's got us this far. If you ain't been prayin', you'd best get to it."

I haven't been praying enough, that's for sure. I let my life get overrun with worry and fears. Cole remembered the time after the fire took the ranch. He had been consumed with the overwhelming amount of work necessary to put the ranch back in order. He had worried about every detail, until he did nothing at all for fear of doing the wrong thing.

I didn't keep my eyes on you, did I, Father? Guess it's time to stop thinking about myself and focus in on you. I've learned hard lessons about leading things. Forgive me for my pride—my doubt. Help me to move forward with my eyes on you—not on what I can do.

"I'm sick of snow. I haven't seen this much snow since . . . well . . . since never!" declared Elsa Lawrence.

Mara laughed. "At least we don't have to be out in it much. Not like when we were ranching. Zane has provided a nice warm house."

"I'm always cold, even with the fire blazing," Elsa said as she rubbed her upper arms. "I've not been warm since last summer."

"But you have been full of complaints," Mara chided. "I know this isn't an ideal situation, but honestly Elsa, you could show some gratitude."

Elsa plopped down on a chair. She hadn't even bothered to braid or pin up her long brown hair. Her icy blue eyes reminded Mara of their father. She tried not to think about it or let it unnerve her, but sometimes Elsa could sound exactly like him.

"I'm really sorry, Mara. I know I've been a bear to live with. It's just . . . well . . . I miss the ranch."

"Father's ranch?"

Elsa rolled her gaze to the ceiling and laughed. "Goodness, no. I meant the Diamond V. Everybody there was so loving, so kind. I've never known folks like that. They loved each other and worked together. They were so nice to me."

Mara nodded, knowing full well what her sister was talking about. "I never thought families could be like that. I'd never known anything but the anger and ugly tempers shown in our home. When I went to stay with Cole and Dianne, it wasn't that they didn't have their problems, but they always seemed willing to talk and work through things. I've never seen any two people more in love or more happy being parents than Cole and Dianne."

"Do you suppose Cole will come home in time for the baby to be born?"

"It's hard to say. With the weather the way it is, Zane says no one will be coming this direction until it all thaws. I wish it would thaw enough to get some letters through. At least then we'd know when the baby comes and how everyone is doing."

"The thaw could take until next summer by the way it looks." Elsa sighed and got to her feet. "I'm going upstairs to sew. I might as well do something productive."

"Zane will be home for dinner soon," Mara said, standing up as well, "so I'd best get some food warming for him."

"Be sure and ask him if there's any news. I'm positively wasting away for some word of how the rest of the world is doing. At least

Father always had a newspaper or two in the house." Elsa tramped up the stairs, muttering to herself about keeping informed or something along those lines.

Mara smiled to herself. The thing that was bothering Elsa the most wasn't the snow or the lack of newspapers; it was Jamie Vandyke. The girl was positively smitten. Mara giggled and went to open the stove. Feeding in a few pieces of coal, she stirred up the embers and worked to get the stove nice and hot. Next she retrieved some of the roast they'd had from the night before. She had her own well-kept cooler on the back porch. It was better than any icehouse. With the temperatures well below zero most nights, truth be told, the food probably was kept much too cold. But at least there was no worry about spoilage.

Mara had thick slices of warmed bread and roast ready for her husband when he came stomping up the walk. She couldn't help but smile at the way Zane had bundled himself against the sub-zero temperatures. She knew he was wearing several layers of shirts and trousers, but he'd also taken every knitted scarf she could find to wrap around his face and neck and to tuck down inside his coat.

She opened the door for him when he reached it. "Is Zane Chadwick to be found in there somewhere?" she teased.

"Nope, he froze to a freight wagon 'bout an hour ago."

She laughed and helped him to shed his layers. It was rather like peeling an onion—only without the teary smell. "Let me put these by the stove in the front room," she said, taking off with an armload of scarves and his coat. "That way they'll be nice and warm when you have to go back out. You get out of your boots and I'll put them in here too."

"No sense getting your nice wood floor all wet," he called to her.

She came back, shaking her head. "I can mop the floor. I don't want you catching your death. Especially now."

Zane pulled his boot off. "Why now?" He stood there balancing on one foot while trying to pull his other boot off.

"Because we're going to have a baby," Mara threw out without warning.

To her surprise, Zane snapped his head up, throwing off his balance. He fell backward, landing hard on the floor. He sat there in stunned silence for a moment, looking at her as though she'd suddenly sprouted wings.

Mara put her hand to her mouth to keep from laughing out loud at the sight of her big, strong husband on the floor—in shock.

"Did I hear you right?" he asked, still not moving.

She lowered her hand and tried hard to look

quite serious. "You did, Mr. Chadwick. I am going to have a baby. You're going to be a father."

"When?" His voice was barely audible.

She smiled and went to help him get his boot off. "September—maybe a little earlier." She pulled the boot off and picked up its mate. "I'll go put these by the stove now. You get on into the kitchen and eat. There's a plate warming for you on the back of the stove."

She went and put the boots by the stove and checked to make sure it had plenty of coal to keep the fire hot. Closing the stove door with the hem of her apron, Mara straightened to find Zane watching her.

"You're pretty amazing, Mrs. Chadwick. You seem so calm about this whole thing."

Mara fairly danced across the room. She'd never been happier than she was right now. "I am calm about this. I'm calm and excited and terrified all at the same time. But mostly I'm filled with such joy and love. I'm blessed that God has given us this child, and I'm doubly blessed to be your wife."

He drew her into his arms and held her close. Mara put her head against his chest and sighed. "I wish you didn't have to go back out into the snow. I'd much rather stay like this the rest of the day."

"Me too," he said, kissing her forehead. "But it looks like I need to be practical. With a baby coming we're going to need to consider our future."

She pulled away. "Haven't we always considered it?"

"True enough, but now this . . . well, this makes everything different." He looked quite serious, almost worried.

"So you're not happy about the baby?" she asked, frowning. She hadn't even considered that he might not want a child.

He reached out and held her at arm's length. "Of course I'm happy. It's just that I want to do all the very best things for you . . . for the baby. I'm afraid Anaconda isn't the best."

"Then we should pray about what is," she said, relief washing through her heart. "Because I'm convinced that God has the very best planned for us if we will but trust Him to guide us."

"I know. I believe that too. I just need to know where it is He wants me to go—what it is He wants me to do."

Mara took Zane by the hand and led him to the kitchen. "Well, for one thing, I'm sure God would want you to have a good dinner. Now sit down here and I'll bring you your plate. Then we can talk more about what we're to do for the future."

Zane sat, his expression almost bewildered. Mara felt sorry for him. Such news was not to be sprung on a fellow during his noon break. Still, there had been no way she could keep the news to herself once she was certain.

She gave Zane his food and then went to pour him a cup of coffee. Hopefully after getting something warm in his belly, he'd feel more like himself and the surprise of her news would become a little more real to him.

"Elsa was hoping you'd bring home a newspaper. I don't suppose you did," she said, putting the coffee in front of her husband.

"Uh . . . no. Never thought about it." He toyed with the cup for a moment. "I'll try to bring one this evening."

"Good. That will please her. She's as miserable as I've ever seen her. She misses Jamie, to be sure."

Zane nodded, but Mara wasn't entirely sure he would ever even remember this conversation. Smiling to herself, she sat down across from him and reached out to cover his hand with hers. "I love you."

This seemed to penetrate the worry and concern her news had given him. He met her gaze and said, "I love you too."

"Then don't be afraid of what this means," she said softly. "We'll see it through together. God has charge of the entire world. I know He can handle something as little as our becoming parents."

"Parents." He blew out a deep breath.

"Don't know that I'm ready for that kind of responsibility. I think it's probably easier to run a freight company or break a green colt."

"Maybe, but I'm betting the joy is greater still in holding a child made from the love you share with another person. In fact, I can't imagine there being a greater joy for a man or woman."

Zane finally smiled. "I'm betting you're right."

CHAPTER 23

DIANNE DRIFTED IN AND OUT OF CONsciousness for nearly a week. The fever still seemed to consume her, but Koko fought against it with all of her healing knowledge. George, on the other hand, felt helpless to watch the once vibrant woman battle to live. Even his generally optimistic sister wasn't sure what would happen at this juncture.

"I'm going to go help the children with their studies," Koko told George. "Would you mind putting a cold cloth on Dianne's head? Just rinse it out every so often to keep it cool."

"I'll do that," he promised. There wasn't

much he wouldn't do for Dianne. Including deny his feelings and remain the trustworthy friend he'd always been.

To George's surprise, Jamie came to sit with him for a while. The boy had been positively impossible to live with the last few weeks. His mood seemed to change as quickly as mountain weather.

"I think once the snow melts, I'm going to make a trip to Butte," he told his uncle.

"You think that's wise?"

Jamie frowned and pushed back his dark brown hair. "Why do you ask that?"

"Well, it seems to me there's a chance Lawrence could be watching all of us now. He might be looking for any clue that would connect him to his daughter."

"I hadn't really thought of that." Jamie got up and went to look out the window. "It's almost March. Surely this weather will settle and turn warm. When are Dianne's cattle supposed to come?"

"I don't remember—I think June. Of course, if other parts of the country are faring no better than we are, there may not be any cattle to send our way come spring."

Jamie sighed and threw himself back on the chair. "I feel like I'm losing my mind. I hate being cooped up here. I can't even work much in the barn. It's just too cold to be out there for long and we don't dare waste burning wood when we might very well need it here."

George nodded and frowned. He'd long been worried that if the desperate cold continued, he'd have to find more fuel. The only sources of wood they had nearby would be the extra rails they'd kept for the corral fencing, and after that they'd have to start tearing down the buildings. He couldn't let that happen. They'd worked too hard to see them built.

"I really enjoyed reading the Bible with Elsa, but now I don't even want to pick it up. It just reminds me that she's gone."

"You can't build your knowledge of God any other way," George countered. "Reading His book is the only way to learn about Him and see what He has promised."

"It's hard to have a faith like you and Mama. I don't know why it should be so hard, but it is."

"When I was your age, I didn't want to believe such things either. I'd learned from my mother's people that there were many spirits and many things to be done to please them. Now I believe in the one true God. It wasn't easy coming to accept that there was only one Father and creator of all."

"What helped you most?"

"The Bible and your mother. I couldn't read all that well back then, but I learned. I also learned to understand what God was trying to teach me through the Scriptures. Sometimes it's still difficult to discern, but when it becomes clear, there is no other man happier than me."

"Elsa helped me understand some things," Jamie said, "and I helped her. I suppose it would be easier still if we had a regular church to go to. I know we read the Bible every morning, but things were different when Ben preached."

George nodded. "I remember it well. Those were good days when we could go to Madison and hear Ben in the little church."

"Do you suppose those days will ever return? Chester Lawrence is buying up all the land, and that doesn't give me much hope."

"But your hope can't be in land or in what Chester Lawrence does or doesn't do. It has to be in the Lord."

Jamie seemed to consider George's words for several minutes while George rinsed the rag. Then without warning he started up the conversation in another direction.

"I know I asked you this a time back, but you never answered," Jamie began. "Have you ever been in love?"

George's hand trembled slightly as he adjusted the cloth on Dianne's fevered brow. "Why do you ask?" He looked up and met his nephew's eyes.

Jamie shrugged. "I guess I just want to talk to someone who understands how I feel."

"I understand how you feel," George replied, easing back against his chair. "Yes, I've been in love."

"What happened? Did you marry? Ma has never said anything about it if you did."

George laughed. "There were always girls around—girls I fancied myself in love with. They were beautiful and easily captured my attention. You have to remember, I spent much of my youth with my mother's people. There were many lovely young women available to marry."

"So did you marry?" Jamie edged up on his seat. "Was there one special woman?"

"I didn't marry," George said sadly. "I was often away hunting, causing trouble. I've not always lived a life to be proud of. But yes, there was one special woman."

"But you didn't marry her. Why?"

George closed his eyes. He could still see Dianne as a young woman, standing on a stump, refusing to let George's Blackfoot friends steal her beloved pony. He'd called her Stands Tall Woman, and she had earned that name in every way, ever since.

"She was already taken," he said sadly.

"Married?"

"No, but pledged."

"But couldn't you have tried to win her away?" Jamie asked in disbelief. "I mean, if it was true love, why didn't you do something extraordinary to win her over?"

George thought of how he'd rescued Cole for Dianne. How he'd had the chance to put his competition to death and instead showed compassion on the woman he loved more than life. George opened his eyes as Dianne stirred ever so slightly.

"As a Blackfoot, I never had much of value. I had horses that I'd stolen from our enemies to prove my bravery, and I had the knowledge and training given me by the Real People. I didn't have anything else but my honor. A man's honor is not something to take lightly, Jamie. Not ever." He looked to his nephew. "This woman was not in love with me, as I was with her. She loved another. I honored her by not interfering in that love."

"I don't know that I could do the same thing. I mean, if you love someone as you did and you do nothing, then you run the risk of never finding love again. Is that what happened to you, Uncle?"

George felt a sort of sadness overcome him. "I suppose so. I knew I would never love anyone as I loved her. So I never tried to love again."

"That's probably another reason you left the Blackfoot people, eh? That way you wouldn't have to see her every day and see her being happy with someone else. I would have done the same thing," Jamie said as he gazed off to the ceiling and leaned the chair back on two legs against the wall.

George said nothing. How could he ever explain that because of his love for his sister and her need for him to help with Jamie's upbringing, George had put himself in the one place that was a constant reminder of what could never be his? He shook his head and rinsed out the cloth again. Let Jamie think what he would. George could never hope to explain something that didn't make sense even to him.

"I love Elsa. I know that much. I'll fight for her," Jamie finally said, letting the chair smack down on the wood floor. He got to his feet. "Thanks for telling me about her, Uncle. What was her name?"

George froze for a moment, then smiled. "It doesn't matter." He turned to Jamie. "What matters is that you keep yourself honorable— that you keep God at the center of your life."

"I'm trying," Jamie said. "It isn't always easy, but I'm not giving up." He left the room, and George almost breathed a sigh of relief as the door closed.

Dianne stirred, moaning Cole's name. The word pierced George like a knife. She opened her eyes and looked at him. "Oh, you're here. I thought I'd lost you." She closed her eyes and smiled. "Cole . . . why did you leave me . . . why did you let me go?"

George knew there was no sense arguing

with a sick woman. Dianne was still battling a fever—still fighting for her life. She had no idea that he wasn't Cole.

He took hold of her hand. "You must fight to live, Dianne," he whispered.

"Will you stay?"

"Yes."

She opened her eyes. "We're going to have another baby. I didn't want it at first, but now I'm glad. It was just so hard—hard to be without you—hard to wonder if you still loved me." She closed her eyes, then opened them again as if she'd forgotten something. George strained to understand the barely audible words. "I love the baby because it's a part of you. I love you, Cole."

George patted her hand. "Be strong, Dianne. Get well." His heart broke for her— for her inability to understand what had already happened—for the loss of her child.

Dianne's eyes closed and this time she didn't open them again. Her breathing evened out, however, and George thought she felt less feverish.

Kneeling beside her bed, George began to pray fervently for Dianne's recovery. *Please, Lord, let her live. Heal her body, and in time, heal her heart.*

———

That night, Koko was nearly frantic when

she woke up and found Dianne had grown still and cool. Koko thought at first Dianne had died, but then she realized that Dianne was still breathing. Her restless body had calmed when the fever broke.

"Praise be to God," Koko murmured and began tending to her charge. She feared the fever had lasted too long and had been too high. Even now she wondered if there had been brain fever—that destructive state that seemed to tear apart the mind of its victim. Only time would prove that to be the case.

The next day, Dianne opened her eyes, moaning softly as she fought against the heavy covers.

"You need to take it easy," Koko told her. "You've been very sick."

"Where am I?"

"You're in my cabin—on the ranch. Remember?"

Dianne closed her eyes and shook her head. "Where's Uncle Bram?"

Koko bit at her lower lip. What should she tell Dianne? How could she explain the situation and not further upset her? But as it was, Dianne had faded back to sleep and there was no need for explanation.

Koko eased back into the rocker that sat beside the bed. The mention of her dead husband created an ache inside that refused to be ignored. "He's in heaven," she whispered, hugging her arms. "I wish he were here, though. I wish at times like this when things are so hard—so painful—that he were here to tell me that it will all be all right. That nothing is so bad that it won't seem better tomorrow."

She smiled and let out a long breath. "If you could see us now, Bram, I'm sure you'd be shaking your head. You'd be barking out orders, and in no time at all you'd have all our problems resolved."

She looked back to Dianne. "But you can't fix this and neither can I." She gazed to the ceiling. "But I know who can. I know who holds tomorrow, and He is able to do great things—far beyond anything I can ask or imagine."

As March warmed and a chinook wind came across the valley, the snows began to melt almost overnight. In turn, Dianne began to heal. Her first real memories after falling sick were of Koko helping her drink warm broth. After that, her thoughts were consumed with understanding that she'd lost the baby and very nearly succumbed herself.

Sitting by the window now, watching the barren land thaw, Dianne had much to think about. The baby she had carried was gone, awaiting burial as soon as George could dig a grave in the frozen earth. She'd not even seen the tiny boy, but George had told her he looked just like Lia when she was born.

It's all my fault, she told herself over and over. *If I only would have loved him more—wanted him more—he would have lived.*

The children were her only comfort. They would come daily and pile into bed with her, telling tales of their schoolwork and of the ranch. Lia had started embroidering with Koko, and her work, although childish, showed great promise. They were all memorizing Bible verses, and Dianne was quite impressed with how much they'd learned.

Life went on as if nothing were wrong—as if all were perfectly ordered.

"But that isn't true," Dianne said aloud.

She leaned forward to better see outside. It would probably be a month or so before she saw any real signs of spring. Still, the warmth of the chinook made the day feel as if the changes were coming sooner.

"Koko asked me to check on you and to bring you this," George said as he came through the open door. He carried a tray with food and drink. "There's tea and venison stew. Oh, and two big biscuits with jam."

"She's trying to fatten me up," Dianne said, trying hard to sound light-hearted.

"She's trying to make you well," George corrected.

"You've both done a marvelous job of that.

I'm weak, but I know I'm getting better every day." Dianne wished she could sound enthusiastic about it. There was just too much darkness around her. The hope of her future seemed faded like an old piece of paper worn and damaged by the years.

George put the tray down on a small stand and came to where Dianne sat. He pulled up a chair and sat down. "You sound as if you doubt that you are getting better."

She sighed. "It's not doubt. It's just not . . . well . . . I suppose it lacks conviction."

"You don't want to get well?"

"Of course I do," she countered. "I need to get well for the children, if for no other purpose."

"But you're grieving, and it is hard to put a positive effort toward healing when so much energy is given to living in sorrow."

Dianne knew she couldn't maintain the facade with George. "It's my fault the baby died—that Isaiah died." She'd named the baby Isaiah Daniel after two of her favorite books in the Bible. She wasn't sure Cole would have approved, but then he wasn't there to ask and the child needed a name.

"Assigning yourself blame doesn't make the situation any easier to bear."

"It wasn't intended to make it easier," she said, looking at him oddly. "It was merely to state the truth."

He shrugged. "I always figure the Bible to be true."

Dianne felt a great exasperation for his attitude and tone. "Of course it's true. Why do you say such things?"

"Well, the Bible says that the Lord giveth and taketh away. That some things happen that are good and some things happen that aren't so good, but that it all comes through Him before it gets to us. I kind of figure that He doesn't wish to see His children suffering, but that because we live in these bodies—live on this earth where sin abounds—some things are just going to happen."

"But I didn't love the baby as I should." Tears coursed down her cheeks. "I did love him, but . . . oh, it's just so hard to understand. I didn't want the baby because there were so many problems. I didn't even try to love him at first, and that must surely have caused him to suffer."

"You loved him. You told me so."

Dianne studied George for a moment, trying hard to see if he was lying. His expression, however, was completely sincere and she'd never known him to be false. "Why do you say that?"

"When you were sick with the fever you spoke to me. You thought I was Cole. You told me you loved me and that you loved the baby because it was a part of me . . . of Cole," he said, appearing embarrassed. He looked away. "You loved your child . . . but you were lost in your misery and couldn't see how much you truly cared."

Dianne buried her face in her hands and sobbed. She hadn't remembered anything that he was talking about, but something inside spoke to the truth of it. George wouldn't lie to ease her conscience. In the wake of Isaiah's death, Dianne had mourned, believing it was out of guilt—now she was certain it was out of love.

"I have this for you," he said.

Dianne looked up as he extended a small leather pouch to her. "What is it?"

"Look inside. I knew you'd never get a chance to see Isaiah."

She opened the pouch and found a bit of hair bound by white thread. She looked to George.

"It's from the baby. I thought you might want it—need it."

Dianne cradled the tiny memento in her hand. She stroked the edge of the golden-brown piece with great tenderness. "It's the same color as the others had at birth. I suppose there was a lot?"

"Yes. He had a lot of hair—just like the others."

"Oh, George." She looked up, tears dripping down her face. "Thank you for this.

Thank you so much for caring about me—and Isaiah."

"Changes are coming," he said, getting up. "The snows are melting and life will start anew here. You have cattle coming from Texas and a ranch that needs your attention."

Dianne couldn't deny the love that shone in his eyes for her. His love for her had always touched her deeply, but it had always made her uncomfortable at the same time.

"You need to get well so that when Cole shows up, and when the cattle come, you'll be ready."

"What if he doesn't come back?" She dared the question, knowing it was dangerous territory to share with George.

He chuckled. "Oh, Stands Tall Woman, he'll come back. He'll always come back. He loves you, just as you love him. Nothing can separate you two for long. Not the distance, not the Sioux, not the storms of life or blizzards. He'll be back. You mark my words."

In her heart, Dianne felt the first spark of hope that Cole would come home. And she would need to be well when he did. She would need to be strong for the future. Looking again to the tiny bit of her baby's hair, she made a promise to herself.

"I will trust in God. I will be strong in Him, even when my strength is gone. And I will hope."

Ardith had never known such wondrous examples of finery. The table she shared with Christopher Stromgren was set with the finest linen and crystal. The china was edged in gold and splashed with bold colors reminiscent of the Far East. She knew this only because one of the many local art galleries had been hosting a display of such treasures and Christopher had escorted her there only the day before.

If her trip to New York had taught her nothing else, it had taught Ardith that everything of value could be known by its weight and appearance. Crystal, for example, was valued for its cut, its ability to catch color in its pure transparency, and its weight. Gowns were valued for the name of their maker, the quality of their design, and for their materials. Everything was quite efficiently categorized and valued accordingly.

But living in New York had taught Ardith something else as well. For all the finery and attention she had received, it wasn't home. Money couldn't fill the empty hole in her heart. Dianne had once told her that only God could do that, but Ardith was terrified of giving Him a chance.

"Your performance last night was sheer perfection," Christopher said as he returned to their table. He continued eating his succulent prime rib steak, not even realizing that Ardith had barely touched her food.

"I'm glad you enjoyed it, but I'm afraid the performances are less enchanting for me."

"You cannot appreciate what the audience feels." Christopher picked up his wine glass. "It's like this wine. A man with less knowledge of such things could hardly appreciate it as I do."

Ardith toyed with her fork. "I'm going home," she stated without warning.

"Nonsense. You're just tired. You'll have at least a week to rest and put yourself aright. We travel on Friday to Boston, but you'll enjoy the trip, I assure you."

She slammed her fork down. "I'm not going to Boston. I'm going home. I'm not happy here. I thought perhaps getting away from Montana would make me happy—would ease my suffering—but instead, I miss my daughter and I'm no happier."

Christopher, never one to make a scene in public, laughed. "If that's all it is, we'll send for the child. You will have to use portions of your profits, however, to hire a nurse to keep her while you're performing. I think there are several people we could see who might have someone trustworthy for the position. You'll need to hide her away, however, lest your past catch up with you."

Ardith said nothing, and Christopher took

this for her approval. "See there," he said, "a simple solution."

She realized the conversation was going nowhere. Christopher Stromgren was happy riding on the wagon of her success. Granted, he'd known how to manipulate and market her skills to the public. He'd known people in places that could offer them beneficial help. Christopher had indeed been responsible for her success—at least her performing success.

"There now, you see? It's not so bad. We'll go to Boston and you'll give your usual fine performances there, and then we can worry about sending for your daughter." He went back to eating as if the entire matter were settled.

Ardith had held some fear of Christopher ever since she'd made the wrong comments to Theodore Roosevelt. She hadn't been quite sure what Christopher might do if she opposed him in full, and she had no desire to find out.

I've told him my plan, she thought and picked at the chicken breast on her plate. *When he finds me gone, he'll simply have to endure it as best he can. I have my tickets, and tomorrow, I'm leaving for Montana.*

The thought pleased her more than she could say. Soon she would be home. Home to the ones who loved her for more than the show she could give. Home to a daughter and family she loved. Suddenly her appetite returned. *I'm going home!*

CHAPTER 24

"WHAT DO YOU MEAN WE CAN'T TAKE A freighter to Virginia City?" Cole asked one of his employees at the Corrine freight yard.

"I'm sorry, Mr. Selby, but I've been stuck here for some time. The passes are closed, and until things started warming up last week, we didn't even have trains coming in or out. Some of 'em still aren't running all the way through. Believe me, I've been as anxious to get back home as anyone."

Cole calmed as he saw the man's sincerity. Jim Riley had his own family in Virginia City to worry after. "I had a telegram that my wife was ill," Cold told him. "I don't know if she's made it through or not."

"I'm sorry to hear that."

"You will send me word when the pass is open? Even if it's slim pickin's, I'm willing to risk it. I'll move rock or dig out snow, whatever it takes."

"I'm with you, boss," Jim replied. "I'll let

you know the minute we can leave."

It wasn't until nearly a week later, however, that word came to Cole. He was dressing for the day when a knock sounded at his hotel door. He opened it to find Jim Riley standing on the other side.

"You ready to head out?"

Cole laughed. "You bet. When?"

"Next twenty minutes. I didn't know until a little while ago. Had a man come through from up Eagle Rock way. Said it isn't easy, but it can be done."

Cole grabbed his things. "Then let's go."

He was still wrestling into his coat as they made their way into the street. Jim had taken Cole's bag to free up his hands, but Cole was so excited that he could hardly manage his own sleeves.

"I feel like a schoolboy, giddy and worked up about getting my first horse," Cole said as they strode toward the freight yard.

"I have to admit, I feel the same," Jim said. "This winter hasn't been an easy one. Even in Virginia City it's been hard." They approached a group of wagons covered with tarps, and Jim called up to one of the drivers. "You set to pull out?"

"Just waiting on you to take care of the invoices," the man replied.

"Guess we're ready," Jim said, looking to Cole. "How about it, boss?"

"I'm ready!" Cole jumped up into the empty wagon and waited while Jim finished signing off the paper work at the freight office. It would probably take them twice as much time as usual to make the trip, but at least they'd be on their way.

"Excuse me, sir!" a familiar voice sounded from behind Cole. He turned and looked.

"Ardith?"

"Cole! I had no idea of finding you here. I've been trying to get transportation home. The trains aren't running all the way, and the stage refuses to even try a trip north just yet. They said the passes, especially the Malad Hill, have been impossible."

"I know. We've been up against the same thing, but a man came down from Eagle Rock and said it can be done. It just won't be easy."

"Please tell me I may come with you," Ardith said. "I have to get home."

"Of course you can come." Cole reached down to grab the small bag she carried and help her up. "Is that all you've brought?"

She laughed. "I brought the only useful articles I own. I'm wearing three layers of skirts and at least as many petticoats. Most of what I had with me in New York wasn't worth the effort of bringing."

"So you did take that trip to New York?"

"Yes. It was a waste of time. Just as Dianne told me it would be." She frowned. "I thought going away would help to heal my hurts."

"But it didn't?" Cole asked, blowing steam in the chilled morning air.

"I miss my daughter. I realize that while it's painful to endure the memories of what I've lost, it's better than feeling nothing at all. It's far better than finding solace in the company of strangers."

Cole nodded as Jim Riley climbed up on the wagon. "Jim, this is my sister-in-law. I had no idea she was in town, but I told her we'd take her with us."

"Well, I'm sure we're bound to spend extra time on the trail—probably with nothing but the wagons and tarps for shelter. Are you sure she's up to such a difficult road?"

Cole looked at Ardith, and they both broke out laughing. "She's one of the strongest ladies I know," he said. "She'll handle it just fine. Probably outlast you and me together."

Jim smiled appreciatively at Ardith. "Then glad to have you with us, ma'am."

———

The trip was more arduous than anything Ardith had expected, but her thoughts of home and Winona drove her on. She was anxious to see how much Winona had grown—to hear what her daughter had to say about all that she'd endured over the winter. Ardith had purchased several small gifts for Winona that were tucked safely in her small bag, but in truth she hoped Winona was happiest with the gift of her return. The thought of what she had said when she'd left for New York now weighed heavily on Ardith's mind.

That night as they shared shelter in a small roadhouse, Ardith warmed herself by the fire and tried to imagine what she could possibly say that would make things right between her and Winona.

"I've been hoping we could have a quiet moment to talk," Cole said as he came upon Ardith. "It looks like most everyone else has retired for the evening."

"I tried to sleep, but there are just too many things to think on."

"Well, unfortunately, I must give you one more."

She eyed her brother-in-law curiously. His expression was quite grave. "What is it?"

"I didn't want to say anything in front of Jim. I figured news like this needed to be shared in private." Cole motioned her to take a seat at the long table where they'd had supper only hours earlier.

Ardith felt a chill as she settled on the bench, away from the fire. "Please tell me what's happened."

"It's Dianne." He began to explain everything that had happened the previous year. After he told Ardith everything, he sat back with a sigh and added, "I don't even know if she's alive."

There were tears in Ardith's eyes. "I knew Dianne had come back; she was in Virginia City before I left," Ardith admitted. "She didn't want me to leave and we argued, but she finally let me have my way. Now, I wish she hadn't."

"I know what you mean," Cole said, regret dripping in his tone.

"But I didn't know about the baby. She didn't tell me about that. Perhaps it was best she didn't. I'm so sorry the baby died." She reached out to cover his hand with hers. "Death is so hard to reason away."

He nodded. "When my father died, I was saddened, but I expected his passing. I had a chance to say all the things I wanted to say to him before he went. If Dianne has . . . if the worst has happened, so much will have gone unsaid."

"That's why it was so hard with Levi. There was so much I felt was undone. I wanted to tell him one more time how much I loved him. I wanted to hear him tell me the same. I wanted so much more—more time . . . more children . . . more love."

Cole sighed. "I don't know how I'll bear it if she's gone."

Ardith shook her head. "There's no way to prepare for such a thing. No possible way to set things right so that you can reason through the situation. But please know this, I am here to help you no matter what. Things are different now for me. My heart is set upon the Lord again. It still hurts from time to time, but God has seen to mend it together."

———————

After more delays than Cole cared to number, they finally arrived in Virginia City. The trip made him more than a little aware that freighting over the passes was probably soon to be completely passé. The trains now ran from the Union Pacific lines to Butte, while others crossed the entire state of Montana from east to west. Freighting to smaller towns that weren't on the rail line would always be needed, but perhaps it was time to get out of the freighting business altogether. Or maybe just sell out to someone whose real desire was to be in that line of work. For Cole, the long trip home had given him a better understanding of his own passions and dreams.

He wanted to go back to the ranch. He wanted to see it rebuilt—not after the fashion of Bram Vandyke's dreams, but in his own. In fact, maybe he'd even be able to talk Dianne into buying adjoining land and starting their own place, leaving Jamie and his family to run the Diamond V. There were so many possibilities and so much he wanted to talk over with her.

Oh, God, she just has to be alive. Please, please let her be alive.

Cole and Ardith made their way to the Selby house. He was amazed at the warmth of the day. The roads ran with mud and melted snow, making it difficult at best to navigate. Cole hardly noticed, however. He climbed the porch steps quickly, pulling his muddy boots off at the door before bounding inside.

"Hello!" he called.

Charity Hammond peered around the corner from the hallway. "Why, bless us all. Cole!" She ran to him and hugged him tightly. "We didn't know you were coming."

"I realize that and I'm sorry. It's been a long trip. I wasn't even sure I'd make it."

"Do I get a welcome too?" Ardith asked softly.

Charity pulled away from Cole. "Oh, my blessings are double and my prayers are all answered." She went to Ardith and embraced her.

"Where is Dianne?" Cole asked.

"She's at the ranch," Ben Hammond said as he and Joshua came into the room. "Welcome home, son."

"She's at the ranch?" Cole asked, disheartened. "I just knew she would be, but I'd still hoped she might be here."

"No, I'm afraid not," Charity said. "We've been waiting for the snow to melt enough so that we could make our way out there. George said . . ." She stopped and looked at Cole as if to ascertain how much he knew.

"George wired me," Cole said. "He said she was gravely ill—possibly dying. He also told me about the baby."

Charity nodded. "Poor wee boy."

"I have to get out there immediately."

"You can't head out there yet today; it'll soon be dark. Wait until tomorrow and we'll go with you," Ben suggested. "That way if there are problems, we can help each other." Cole started to speak, but Ben cut him off. "I know you're anxious, but you won't change what's happened by rushing out there tonight."

Cole drew a deep breath and let it out slowly. "I know you're right. I just can't stand not knowing what's happened."

"It's a hard thing to bear," Ben agreed, "but the Lord will bear it with you. So, too, will we."

"I appreciate that." Cole looked around the room at the concerned expressions. "Wait a minute. Tomorrow is Saturday. Can you be away from the church on Sunday?"

"Joshua is now in charge of the church," Ben replied. "I just add my help and guidance when needed."

"Which is always," Joshua chimed in, "but

I'm sure I can muddle through for at least one day."

"Don't listen to him," Ben laughed. "He's quite good. The folks love him too."

Joshua flushed in embarrassment at the compliment, and Cole had to laugh. "I never thought I would say anything good came from Chester Lawrence, but it seems there are blessings even from that man."

Joshua shook his head. "My father is a ruthless and hard-hearted man. I can't say any good thing comes from him."

"Well, you and your sister Mara turned out all right."

"Grace of God," Joshua said. "Purely by the grace of God."

The trip home was not going to be easy. The warm weather caused unmanageable roads and swollen streams. It also revealed something no one had been prepared for: hundreds of dead animals were scattered across the barren waterlogged valleys and hillsides. It was as if they had grouped together for warmth, then frozen in place with nowhere to go. The sheep and cattle hadn't stood a chance with the blizzards coming upon them so quickly that many ranchers hadn't had time to make provision.

"This is so awful," Ardith said, her voice barely audible.

Death was everywhere, and Cole couldn't help but wonder if it was a foretelling of things to come. He tried not to be discouraged, but after miles of mucky roadways and having to dig out the wagon more than once, he didn't know that he had much courage left.

The land around them was eerily silent when they stopped that night on the trail. Cole couldn't remember it ever being so still. The warmth of the day had caused the carcasses to begin rotting, and already the stench was building, adding to their restlessness.

The next morning the party moved in slow motion—at least it seemed so to Cole. Charity and Ardith fixed breakfast, but with the smell and sight of death around them, no one felt much like eating.

Ben led them in an abbreviated Sunday service, telling them that their strength would come from the Lord. Cole tried to get his mind around Ben's words, but all around him were signs of hopelessness and destruction.

Yet Ben spoke of hope. "The word is given us in First Peter three, instructing that we should 'always be ready to give an answer to every man that asketh you a reason of the hope that is in you with meekness and fear.'" Ben held up the Bible and read on, "'Having a good conscience; that, whereas they speak evil of you, as of evildoers, they may be ashamed that falsely accuse your good conversation in Christ.'

"We have hope in the Lord. It strengthens us when we have no physical reserves. It lights the darkness when we are discouraged. The hope is Jesus, and we're to stand ready to tell others."

Hope. Cole had abandoned the effort of even considering it until Ben forced his thoughts to focus once again.

"Looking around us today, it's hard to have hope. Everything that could go wrong has seemed to do exactly that. Animals are dead. The land is struggling to recover from the elements. Our loved ones are hurting. It seems a right time to lie down and die."

Ben's words startled Cole. He looked up oddly at the old pastor. Ben smiled. "After all, don't we know when we're defeated? How can we hope to come back from this state of things? How can we have hope when we must bury our children? How can we have hope when we must bury our mates?"

Cole saw Ardith nod, tears trickling down her face.

"Hope is not found in ourselves, friends. It's not found in our bank accounts or in our possessions. There is no hope in this world for us—for we are but strangers passing through." He smiled and the compassion of his gaze began a healing in Cole's weary heart.

"The answer comes in a simple truth—nothing so mysterious or difficult." Ben closed his Bible and began to sing in his weak baritone voice. "'My hope is built on nothing less than Jesus' blood and righteousness. I dare not trust the sweetest frame, but wholly trust in Jesus' name.'"

Charity joined in on the chorus. " 'On Christ the solid Rock I stand, all other ground is sinking sand; all other ground is sinking sand.'"

Cole listened as they continued together. He felt more bolstered in this simple act of worship than he had in all the months of church in Topeka—than in all his pleading and wrestling with God.

"'When darkness seems to hide His face, I rest on His unchanging grace. In every high and stormy gale, my anchor holds within the veil.'"

The couple sang in such perfect harmony that Cole couldn't help but miss Dianne more than ever. Darkness had seemed to hide God's face. It was so very hard to understand why these things had to happen, but it seemed to Cole that Ben was suggesting that understanding wasn't as important as hoping—trusting in Jesus.

Ben and Charity continued, and Cole found himself humming along. "'His oath, His covenant, His blood, support me in the whelming flood. When all around my soul gives way, He then is all my hope and stay. On Christ the solid Rock I stand, all other ground is sinking sand; all other ground is sinking sand.'"

The words penetrated deep into Cole's heart, through the fears of what might lie ahead and greet him at the ranch. *When all around my soul gives way, He then is all my hope and stay.* Through the pain of the last few months.

My hope is built on nothing less than Jesus' blood and righteousness.

The words were a balm—soothing, nurturing, healing. His hope was in Christ, and it should have always been there. How much time had he wasted in seeking other means of support? How long had the answers to his fears been right in front him, only to be ignored?

The hope within was a hope that would never let him down. The hope within was Jesus.

Cole doused the campfire as Ardith and Charity finished loading the last of their things into the wagon. Straightening to face the sorry devastation around him, Cole looked at the land with new eyes. He felt rather like Noah must have after the flood. There was a lot of work to be done.

"Are you ready?" Ben questioned as he came to stand beside Cole.

"I wasn't until just a few minutes ago," Cole said, smiling. "But now I am. Now my footing is different. Now I'm back on solid ground."

Ben smiled. There was nothing more to be said.

CHAPTER 25

THEY SHOULD HAVE BEEN ABLE TO REACH the ranch by noon, but instead it was nearly dark before the muddy wagon pulled into the ranch yard. Cole wished he could better see the place. Two cabins were built to stand about fifty yards apart, with a large barn behind one cabin. The land looked as barren here as it had elsewhere. The only trees to be seen were trunks that had been charred in the fire and small, immature saplings that had more recently been planted. At least there were no animal carcasses to deal with. Perhaps if there could be a blessing in the choices he'd made regarding the ranch, Cole could comfort himself in the fact that they had lost very little in the way of livestock.

Cole forced himself to look to where they'd buried Bram and Levi. He knew from what Dianne had told him that Gus was to be buried there as well. What he didn't know was whether he'd find a fresh grave containing his wife's body.

Cole drew a deep breath and held it while he looked for the graves and their markers. The ground seemed undisturbed. He let out his breath slowly. There were still only three graves.

But that doesn't necessarily mean anything. The ground has been frozen solid. They might not have been able to bury her yet. He grieved, longing to know the truth but terrified of it at the same time.

The door to the far cabin opened and George stepped out. He looked weary and much older than when Cole had last seen him. When he realized it was Cole and the others, he gave a whoop and jumped from the small porch. "It's about time!" he declared good-naturedly.

Cole jumped down from the wagon and hugged the man tightly. "Dianne?" he questioned. He watched George's expression sober and steadied himself for the worst.

"She's all right. She's still weak, but she's alive," George told him without hesitation.

"She's over at your cabin." He pointed to the other place.

Cole started to leave, but George stopped him. "She's been through a lot. She doesn't understand why you didn't come sooner, and I think she was afraid you might never come."

"I never got her letter," Cole told him. "My mother kept it from me. You have to believe me, George. I never knew about the baby. In fact, I never knew whether she made it home safely or not. I sent a telegram that was never answered, so I wasn't sure she even wanted me back."

George laughed. "You and Dianne are two of a kind. She's been fretting all winter that you wouldn't want her any longer—that you'd pick your ma over her and the children."

"I could never do that. I know it seemed that way for a time, but George, I honestly felt the situation was impossible. I wanted to do the right thing by both of them, but then I found out my mother was just as manipulative as Dianne had been trying to tell me, and well . . . I realized I'd been a fool."

"That isn't an easy thing for a man to come to terms with."

Cole shook his head. "Now I'm terrified of seeing her again. What if she tells me to leave and never come back?" He looked past George to the cabin where his wife and children were living.

George pushed him in the same direction. "She'd sooner cut off her arm," he said before turning to greet the other travelers.

Cole didn't bother to waste any time. He made a dash for the cabin and threw open the door without bothering to knock. The startled faces of his children greeted him in stunned wonder. Then as they recovered their shock, each of the children jumped up and ran to his embrace.

"Papa!" they cried in unison.

"I knew you would come," Luke said, wrapping himself around Cole.

Cole fell to his knees and hugged them close, words failing him. How he had missed them. It seemed they had grown up in his absence. Even Lia was taller and so pretty. Just like her mother.

"Are you going to live with us again?" Lia asked as Cole lifted her into his arms.

"Yes," he replied, ignoring the hurt it caused to have to face such a question.

"Only for a little while?" Micah asked. "Or is it forever?"

Cole felt his heart nearly burst with love and regret at the same moment. "Now and forever," he said tearfully.

He glanced past the children to see Dianne standing in the doorway to one of the other rooms. He couldn't take his gaze from her. He'd just pledged to his children that he would stay forever, but what if Dianne didn't want him to stay? George might be wrong. It was a moment that Cole knew would decide his future.

"You children stay here and play. I need to talk to your Mama."

"Mama's been real sick," Lia told him.

"Yes, I know."

"Why weren't you here?" John asked in an almost accusing tone. "Our brother died."

Cole rubbed his son's head. "I should have been here, but we'll talk about it later. Right now, I need to be with your mama."

John eyed him almost suspiciously. "She's been real sick," he repeated, as if a warning to his father.

Cole put Lia down and got to his feet. Walking to where Dianne stood, he pulled the hat from his head. "Please forgive me," he said in greeting.

Dianne shook her head, and his heart nearly failed to beat. "Forgive me," she murmured.

He tossed the hat aside and pulled her into his arms. Tears blinded him as he buried his face in her hair. "I'm so sorry. For everything. Sorry I couldn't see what my mother was doing. Sorry about the baby. Sorry that you were alone."

She cried softly in his arms. "I'm the one who's sorry. I acted completely out of order. A

Christian woman should never have left her husband's side, no matter how ugly the situation."

"Hush," Cole said, pulling away enough to see her face. "You were right to go. It was the only thing that helped to clear my thinking. I couldn't see what my mother and sisters were doing, but when you left it was as if the Lord opened my eyes to see the truth."

"Why didn't you come sooner?"

"Mother kept your letter from me. I never even knew you'd written. I never knew about the baby until George telegrammed me."

"George sent a telegram? But until just a short time ago we were buried in snow and the storms were quite fierce. How could he have ever sent a telegram?" she questioned. "He would have had to . . ." Her voice fell silent.

"He would have had to risk his life in order to do so," he finished for her. Once again George's love for Dianne, and even for Cole, seemed clear. Cole felt shamed by the man's unfailing loyalty to Dianne. *I couldn't give her the same thing,* he thought, the sorrow of it binding his chest, making it hard to breathe.

"I came as soon as I heard," Cole told her. "If I'd known about the baby, I would have come last fall."

"Truly?" she asked him, her eyes searching his for the truth.

He thought only for a moment. "I would

have come. I can't bear it that you went through this alone. I'm so sorry about the baby."

Dianne's tears spilled again. "I was so sick, I didn't even know he had died for a time. Then when Koko told me what had happened, I wanted to die too." She pulled Cole into the bedroom and closed the door before continuing. The look on her face was one of grief mingled with guilt.

"I didn't want the baby—not like I'd wanted the others. I thought you were gone for good and that this child would only be a reminder of sorrow and loss. I couldn't bear to think about it. I just know that my lack of love caused him to die." She walked away from Cole and sat down on the edge of the bed.

He could see her sorrow ran deep. She didn't blame him for the baby's death as he'd feared she would; she blamed herself. That was ten times worse as far as he was concerned. He sat down beside her on the bed.

"You didn't cause the baby's death." His words were gentle but firm. "The devil wants you to wallow in self-pity and misery. He wants you to blame yourself for something you couldn't make different."

"I want to believe that. George said I loved the baby. . . . But I'm not sure the baby knew I did or that I loved him enough. I feel so empty inside when I think about it all. I just want him back, Cole. I want to hold him in my arms—I want my baby." She sobbed uncontrollably.

He had no idea what to say or how to comfort his wife. He put his arm around her and prayed silently for her, asking God to ease her burden.

For several minutes they sat there until finally Dianne lifted her head. "I'm sorry . . . for everything. Nothing has been right since the fire."

Cole tenderly turned her face to his. "We don't need to live in the past. It's gone—behind us. We need to focus on what's here, right this minute. I know that now." He cleared his throat, knowing that he wanted to confess his fears to her for the first time. "I wronged you in keeping you from the ranch. I knew you wanted to be here, but my fears kept me from coming back."

"Fears?" She sniffed back tears. "What fears?"

Cole dropped his hold. "Fears of everything. Of failing to rebuild the ranch to its former glory. Failing you and the children. I was completely consumed by it."

"I didn't know."

He got up and shrugged. "I couldn't face it myself. I couldn't talk to you about it. I knew what you'd say. You would have told me that it didn't matter what I did or didn't do so long as we were together as a family on the ranch. But

I couldn't see it that way. It's your uncle's ranch—even your ranch—but it's not really mine. Then when George and Jamie kept coming out here to work, it truly became their ranch—Jamie's ranch, as it always should have been. I had no heart for it, and I'm sorry."

Dianne wiped her eyes. "I'm sorry. I had no idea. I thought you just didn't want to be here—that you'd decided city life was more to your liking."

"I could never love the city as I do this countryside. There's something about this land that gets inside of a man and never lets go."

She smiled for the first time. "It happens to women too."

Cole knelt in front of her. "We've so much to overcome—to work through. So much needs to be done, but I don't want to do any of it without you by my side."

"I don't want to be anywhere else," she whispered.

"Can we start again?"

"Yes," she agreed, "only *you* pick the place. It doesn't have to be here. I had plenty of time to realize that while I love this place, it's not the same without you. It's not the same anyway, but it's unbearable without you."

He put his head on her lap. "I feel exactly the same." He sighed and realized for the first time in his life that home wasn't a place. It was a matter of heart.

———————

"It reminds me of the old days," Charity said, noting the Vandyke cabin. "You've managed to make it cozy and comfortable, and that's what is important." Ardith glanced around. It was an agreeable little house.

"It served us well through the coldest parts of winter," Koko replied. "George and Jamie built it well."

"That's easy to see," Ben said, taking the coffee Koko offered him. "So how is our Dianne?"

Ardith perked up at this. "Yes, how is she?" Ardith and Ben and Charity had decided to spend the evening with Koko and her family, giving Cole plenty of time to be alone with his wife and get reacquainted with his children. Winona and Susannah were at the table as well, silently observing the adults.

"She's not recovered from losing the baby," Koko said. "I wasn't even sure she had a desire to go on—to live. She was so very sick with a high fever. It left her with little strength and a lack of interest in life. She had the children, but I feared that had it not been for them, she would have given up. Maybe now she will want to live."

Ardith knew how hard it could be to find that kind of strength. "It isn't a strength you get from yourself," she murmured.

"What was that?" Koko asked, offering Charity and Ardith a mug of coffee. They both accepted, and Koko retrieved her own cup before sitting opposite Ben.

Ardith felt uncomfortable but spoke nevertheless. "I was just saying that the will to go on with life isn't something you get from yourself. There's no possible way for a human being to muster that kind of strength. I know that now."

Ben smiled. "We try so hard to wrestle life in the flesh. We strive against all odds, fighting ourselves, our loved ones, and God. It isn't an easy lesson to learn."

"Well, I've learned a great deal while being away from home," Ardith said softly. She looked at her daughter, who was sitting next to her. Winona hadn't even bothered to hug her when Ardith had appeared at the door. She'd been helping Koko with supper and instead of throwing herself in Ardith's arms, she had turned away, frowning.

Ardith continued. "I've learned that you can't fill the emptiness inside. Only God can do that." Ben and Charity nodded knowingly. "And I learned that nothing is as important as family. I missed Winona more than I can put into words."

"Life can be very hard to bear—especially alone," Charity said, smiling at Ardith. "So,

Winona, I'll bet you're glad to have your mother home."

Winona looked at Ardith, then got up from her chair. Calmly she looked at the adults. "I'm not glad. I hate her and I don't want her to be here!" She ran to one of the bedrooms and slammed the door shut behind her.

Ardith felt the full weight of what she'd done to her child. "I'm sorry." She lowered her gaze to her hands. "This is all my fault—I know that. I didn't consider the consequences before I acted."

Charity reached over and patted Ardith's hand. "You'll have to give her time. You'll have to prove to her that you won't leave her again. Trust was broken, but that doesn't mean Jesus can't mend the tear."

"But I don't deserve for it to be mended," Ardith replied and looked up into the faces around her. "I was selfish and made a wrong decision. I know that now, but it doesn't mean that I can undo what's done."

"Winona loves you. That's why she's angry," Koko said with a smile. "You will have to win her over. You will have to put self aside and seek her out. Just like Charity said, trust must be earned, and you will have to convince Winona you are worthy of her trust."

"But maybe I'm not."

"Nonsense," Ben declared. "You're her mother. You need each other."

"She does love you," Susannah Vandyke said. "She spent long hours telling me all about you—all the things she admired and missed. She will forgive you if you ask her."

"That's it," Charity said. "You should ask her forgiveness. Let her see that you acknowledge your mistake. It will mean a great deal to her."

Ardith rose from the chair. "I know you're right." She looked to the closed door. "At least I want you to be right." She smiled weakly.

"It's right because it's what we are called to do. To humble ourselves and seek the forgiveness of those we've wronged," Ben said.

Ardith drew a deep breath. There was much work to be done, but it had to start here. She knew it as well as she knew her own name. She had wronged her child and now she needed to make things right.

Going to the door, she paused and looked over her shoulder. "Pray for me?" Their nods gave her the strength to go to her child.

She opened the door and found Winona sitting on the bed. "I know you're angry at me," Ardith said as she went in, "but I need to talk to you."

"I don't want to talk to you." There was a catch in Winona's voice, as if she might start crying at any moment.

"I know." Ardith closed the door behind her and stood silent for a moment. Her child had been so wounded, partly by her own hand. "I'm sorry, Winona. I'm sorry for leaving you."

Winona didn't even bother to look up. She kept her head bowed, even as Ardith drew up a chair and sat down right in front of her. Ardith wondered if she would ever be able to reach through the child's protective walls.

"When your papa died, I felt like a part of me died too. I'd never loved anyone but you as I did him. Even so, it's a different kind of love between a man and woman, and I knew in my heart I'd never have that again. Levi was such a special man."

Winona looked up and met Ardith's gaze. She watched her mother warily. Ardith continued, pushing aside the years of pain and regret. "We were so blessed to have him in our lives. He was a good father to you and a good husband to me. He didn't care that I'd been a prisoner of the Sioux. He didn't care that you were half Indian. He just loved us for who we were. That meant a lot. I didn't figure to ever have that with anyone but family."

Ardith closed her eyes for a moment and leaned her head back against the chair. "Levi loved you from the very first moment. He was gentle and kind—showing us both the utmost respect and care. He pursued us, but not to harm us as others had. Rather he pursued us to love us."

Ardith opened her eyes and smiled. "I know you don't understand all of this, but I felt it important to tell you. I couldn't talk about him before, because I couldn't handle the memories. I thought they would always hurt me, so I avoided them as much as I could. But when I left here, I realized there was nowhere I could go to outrun the pain. I tried to lose myself in my music. I tried to pretend I was happy with all the attention people were giving me. But everyone wanted more than I could give, and the one thing I desperately needed to have back . . . was you."

Winona looked at her as if she were trying to assess the truth of that statement. Ardith's eyes welled with tears. "I don't blame you for being angry at me, but I want you to know that I'm sorry. I'm sorry for hurting you before I left, and I'm sorry I hurt you in leaving. I was wrong, and I'd like you to forgive me. Maybe not today—but soon. I want us to start over and to have a good life together. We can't do that with hate and anger between us."

Winona finally spoke. "But you'll just go away again."

"No, I won't. Not unless you're at my side."

"But I don't want to go away," Winona said firmly.

"Neither do I, Winona. I want to stay here and be with you—raise you to be a fine woman who knows she's loved with an everlasting love. Will you give me another chance?"

Winona hesitated, then nodded. "But I'm afraid."

The words cut Ardith to the core, but she knew she deserved them. She knew too that this was the very thing she would have to overcome. "I'm afraid too," she admitted. "Afraid you'll never trust and love me again."

Winona threw herself off the bed and into Ardith's arms. "I'll always love you, Mama."

Ardith stoked her daughter's hair for a moment, then took hold of Winona's face and gently lifted it to meet her gaze. There was such hope, such desire in the child's eyes. "And I will always love you, Winona. I won't always make the right decision. I'll make mistakes, because that's what people do. But if we work together—forgive each other—love each other . . . we'll make it through."

———

Jamie helped his uncle put away the horses and clean off some of the mud and muck from the wagon. It wasn't the most pleasant work, but Jamie had noted something in George's mood that made him want to help.

Ever since Dianne had fallen ill, things had been hectic and out of place around the ranch. Jamie felt the tension every day, knowing there was little he could do to help or alleviate it.

Now he felt as if the truth were clear. Having watched his uncle earlier when Cole returned with the others, Jamie finally felt he understood.

"Dianne was the woman you loved, wasn't she?" he asked softly.

George stopped brushing the horse he'd been working on and looked at his nephew in disbelief.

Jamie toyed with the hayfork before sending another pile of straw into the stall. He put the fork aside and came to where his uncle stood. George refused to say a word but watched Jamie with an intensity that made the boy uncomfortable.

"Tell me the truth." Jamie saw the pain in George's expression. "You loved her . . . you still do."

George went and sat down on an overturned bucket. He moved the brush back and forth between his hands. "Yes," he finally said with a sigh.

Jamie went to his uncle and leaned back against the stall fence. "How did it happen? When did you fall in love with her?"

George gave a croaking laugh. "She was just a girl—like Elsa. She was terrified of me and my Blackfoot friends when we showed up here at the ranch. We were on the run, hiding out from our pursuers. She thought we were here to attack, but she tried hard to be brave.

I'd never met anyone like her."

"That's how I feel about Elsa," Jamie said. "Temper and all."

George seemed to recover from the shock of the moment and got back to his feet. He walked to the horse and resumed brushing the animal. "You realize you can never say anything about this. Too many people stand to be hurt."

"Of course. But does she know? Does Cole?"

George smiled sadly. "I think they both know. They also know that I would never do anything to come between them."

"It wouldn't be honorable," Jamie murmured.

George met his gaze. "No, it wouldn't be honorable."

"How do you bear it? How can you be here—seeing her all the time?"

Shrugging, George continued to work on the horse. "I give it to God. I will always care deeply for her, but she is not mine to love. I will never love another, but God has shown me how to bear this."

"How?"

"By keeping my eyes on Him . . . instead of her," George said without hesitation.

Jamie thought on his uncle's words long after they parted company. He'd never known a man with more honor than Takes Many

Horses. Jamie couldn't even fathom what it might feel like to be so deeply in love with someone yet know you could never have them for your own. When he thought of Elsa that way, it tore him in two.

I've lost my heart so completely to her. I can't bear the thought of her not being here with me. He looked to the skies overhead. "God, I know I'm not very good at this praying, but here's my heart. I want to please you. I know I'm a sinner and that I haven't always done things as I should. But I want to try. I want to be yours first and then I want to be Elsa's. I hope that's not a heathen thing to say." He looked away, almost as if God's face might appear before him.

"I love her, Lord. I love her, and I want her to be my wife. I don't want to spend my life like my uncle. I couldn't bear to see her every day and know that she belonged to someone else."

"I want to go back to the ranch," Elsa told Mara. "I hate Anaconda."

Mara laughed. "Not as much as you love Jamie Vandyke." She finished dusting the front sitting room and looked to where her sister was supposed to be sweeping up. Elsa leaned against the broom, looking all moon-eyed and dreamy. Mara shook her head. "I've never seen anybody act the way you do."

"Oh, I suppose you never acted this way over Zane," Elsa said, snapping to attention. She met her sister's laughter by making a face and sticking out her tongue.

"Look, you're twenty-one now. Father has no claim to you. So go back to the ranch and see if Jamie will have you."

"If he'll have me?" Elsa asked in disbelief. "He'll have me. He'd better. He's the one that made me go and fall in love with him. He'd better not back out now."

Mara looked surprised. "Back out of what? Has he proposed?"

Elsa shrugged and looked toward the ceiling. "Well, not exactly. But I know he wanted me to wait for him."

"Sounds to me like you'd better go back to the ranch and see what he really wants. He might have taken on other notions by now."

"You're no help!" Elsa declared, starting to sweep with a vengeance. "You could at least dream a little with me. Encourage me."

"Dreaming gets nothing accomplished, and encouraging folks can be dangerous. You know me to be a woman of action," Mara said quite seriously. "If you intend to marry this man, then you'd best start laying in plans for a wedding. That's what I did."

Elsa stopped again. "You did, didn't you? You made a wedding dress before there was even a husband to marry."

Mara laughed. "Sometimes that's how God works things. Seek Him out, Elsa. Let God tell you what to do about Jamie."

Elsa knew her sister was right. She'd continued reading the Bible every night since she'd parted company with Jamie. She hoped and prayed he'd done the same. It made her feel closer to him somehow.

"Do you suppose Zane would take us to the ranch—I mean, if I pray about it?"

Mara laughed again. "If you pray about it, God can put it on Zane's heart to do exactly that—if it's what God wants for you."

Elsa closed her eyes and prayed with such fervency she was certain God must have heard. *I just want to go back to the ranch and be with him, Lord. I want to be his wife and live our lives together.* She'd no sooner concluded her prayer and begun sweeping again when Zane came through the front door.

"Mara!" he panted. "Mara!"

"What in the world is wrong?" Mara asked, rushing for the door. Elsa was right behind her.

"You need to pack your things. We're going to the Diamond V."

The girls exchanged a look, but Elsa quickly cast her gaze to the ceiling. "That was certainly fast," she murmured.

Mara only laughed. "Sometimes God is like that. Come on—we'd best get packed."

CHAPTER 26

CHESTER LAWRENCE LOOKED AT THE SIX men who stood across from him. The news they'd brought was inconceivable. "You can't be serious," he said in disbelief.

"Boss, it's the same for everyone," one of the men ventured to say.

"It's not the same for everyone!" Chester countered. "Not everyone started the winter out with over eight thousand head of cattle. Now you're telling me that I've lost all but about fifteen hundred."

"There could be a few more. The boys are still in the process of rounding them up," the man offered. "There's no hope for the calves, what few were born. The elements were just too harsh."

"What did I hire the lot of you for?" Chester asked in complete exasperation. He had notes due at the bank by the first of June. He'd depended on that herd to produce in large numbers. He'd figured on at least another two thousand calves being born, and that had been a conservative estimate. Now he faced his financial obligations without enough livestock to sell—even if he auctioned off the entire herd.

"We could hardly raise the temperatures or eliminate the snow," one of the other cowhands snarled. "A couple of men ran off, and we lost a good man out there to the cold. You need to arrange a proper funeral for him."

"I'll arrange nothing! You no-goods have lost me my ranch. Now get out of here."

"You can't treat us like that," a large man said, stepping forward. "You owe us winter pay, and I intend to see you hand it over."

Chester realized he was helpless to fight the man. He hadn't bothered to strap on his gun when the housekeeper had announced that there were men at the front door. In retrospect, he should have done just that. Then these no-account cowboys wouldn't be trying to force his hand. Instead, they'd be staring down the barrel of a revolver.

"Fine," he muttered. "I'll pay you, but I expect you to bring in the remaining herd quickly. I want to see those animals for myself. No doubt they're skin and bones."

"No problem, boss. We're bringing them down and collecting the strays. Shouldn't have to worry much with branding this year—like I said, I don't think any of the calves made it through."

"You get those animals here and then—and

only then—will I pay you," Chester said, staring hard at the big man.

The man who acted as his foreman nudged the larger man. "We'll do that, boss." The men followed their leader's direction and stepped down from the porch and went to remount their horses.

Chester watched them with a scowl on his face. If Jerrod and Roy were still here, those men would have minded their places. *Now I'm just an old man with a bad temper. Few people will even concern themselves with me.* Chester seethed at the thought. All of his life he'd been the man to get attention—to get things done. People respected him . . . or at least feared him. Now he couldn't even get his children to respect or fear him. They'd all left him. He'd figured at least the mean ones would stay on. He'd counted on their greed, but they were gone too. Off to make their fortunes.

"Like I didn't give them more than they deserved," Chester said, then spat as if to rid himself of the bad taste they left in his mouth.

He stormed back into the house, slamming the door behind him. There wasn't enough money to pay those cowhands and be able to come anywhere near paying his notes. If he took everything he could get his hands on, he might be able to at least get the bank to hold off on foreclosing. But he wasn't liked at the bank. Last fall he'd been downright threatening, and the bank president would surely remember his ill temper. Had it not been for Chester's well-known reputation for retribution, he seriously doubted the bank would have agreed to lend him the large amount he had demanded.

Chester went into his office and locked the door behind him. He didn't want to be disturbed. There was a great deal to think about and plans to be made. He intended to maintain his role as the cattle king of southwest Montana. He deserved that title. He deserved to rule his domain with an iron fist.

But there are nearly seven thousand cattle lying dead on my domain. Dead cattle were no good to him. He cursed the weather, then cursed God just in case He really did exist. After all, if He did exist, then all of this was His fault.

It didn't help that Chester realized the Selby-Vandyke group would have come through the winter relatively unscathed. They had very few animals to worry over. It would have been simple to gather them in close to the house and feed them by hand. He knew for a fact that the boy and his uncle had harvested quite a bit of hay over the summer months.

"They had precious little else to worry themselves with," Chester muttered. The very thought of his enemy faring well was more than he could stand.

He pounded both fists down on the desk. "What am I supposed to do now?"

———————

Dianne gently caressed the rough wooden box as though she could somehow reach through to the baby inside. The devastation of the winter months had left its mark on the Diamond V. Perhaps not in the same way as it had to other ranchers, but the loss was just as deep.

Isaiah would be buried today. The ground had finally thawed enough to make that possible. She knew there was no possible way to know Isaiah—to see him—but her heart still longed for that glimpse.

"I'm so sorry you aren't going to be with us," she murmured. "I promise you, you would have been loved. You are loved." She toyed with the locket around her neck. It contained the baby's hair George had given her. It was all she had of this child.

Dianne looked to the crystal blue skies overhead. "Oh, Father, forgive me for all that I've done wrong. Help me to heal. Ease this pain so that I might not lose the joy that I have with my other children."

She dropped her gaze to see her boys climbing up and down on the new corral fence the men had put in place. The boys loved to be busy, and play was hard work. Dianne smiled. Soon they would be young men and then grown. How quickly time could pass. Isaiah would have happily joined them—taking his place beside his brothers—struggling to earn their respect.

"Are you ready?" Cole asked softly.

Dianne drew a deep breath and nodded. She didn't turn around to greet him, but instead leaned hard against him when he came up behind her. His arms encircled her and pulled her close.

"As ready as a mother can ever be for something like this."

"We'll see him again—someday," Cole whispered.

"I've never seen him at all. And that is so very hard."

"It would serve no purpose now. He wouldn't look anything like what you'd expect. It's better to remember him like the others. George said he looked a lot like Lia, so maybe reflect on that."

She knew he was right. She knew, too, there was absolutely nothing she could do to change things. She would have to accept the situation as it was or suffer the rest of her life. There was no sense in that. It wasn't what God would want for her.

"How do you think it works? Heaven, I mean," she said softly. "Is there some great nursery where children go when they die?" She liked to think of her baby son being happy with other children who'd gone before him. Her own sister Betsy and their unborn sibling, Ardith's baby and Faith's lost children. She could well imagine them all being together, tenderly cared for by some celestial being.

"I don't know," Cole admitted. "But I know that God loves us. I know that He loves Isaiah and all other children. I'm sure He has a special place for them—a place where they're cared for and treated real special."

"I just wish I knew," she said. "It's hard not knowing."

He turned her around and stepped back a pace. "But you know your Father in heaven. You know He is always loving. His very nature is love, so we have to know that those babies are loved—they're safe and nothing and no one can grieve them."

"And they never have to worry about being hungry or cold."

"Or tired or in pain."

Tears streamed down Dianne's face. "I know he's gone to a better place. I keep reminding myself of that. But my arms are still empty."

Cole pulled her close. "They aren't now, and they never will be if I have anything to say about it."

———

George saw Luke walking around the outer

edges of the yard and wondered what the boy was thinking. They were nearly ready for the funeral, and George couldn't help but wonder if the boy was feeling out of sorts about it all.

Walking over to the corral and pretending to check on the structure, George motioned to Luke. "You doing all right?"

He shrugged. "I don't know why people gotta die."

George nodded. "It can be kind of confusing."

"My baby brother didn't do nothing wrong. He shouldn't get punished."

"Luke, death isn't a punishment." George squatted down. "Is that what you're thinking?"

"Well, sure. Bad people get killed—like when the law catches them and hangs them. Ma said that people sometimes die when they are doing the wrong thing at the wrong time."

"Both things are true," George agreed, "but death doesn't always come as a punishment. Sometimes people just get old and die. Sometimes they get sick and die. Death is in the world because of sin, that much is true, but God isn't standing by waiting to punish us with it because we're sinful folks."

"My brother wasn't even born when he died. He couldn't have been sinful," Luke protested.

George felt he'd gotten in over his head, but he tried to stumble through. "Luke, some things are a mystery. Ever since Adam and Eve sinned in the garden, there have been consequences."

"That don't hardly seem fair," he said. "I wasn't there. My brother wasn't there. How can that be fair to punish my brother for what Adam and Eve did?"

"I've often wondered that myself. But God knew the choices they'd make—He knows the choices we make. We're sinful by nature, but we can be redeemed with Jesus. Jesus can help us not to want to sin. As for your baby brother, well, I can't say that I have the answer for why he had to die, but I trust that God knows. God isn't trying to hurt us by taking baby Isaiah away, and He isn't trying to punish us. These things just happen because we are human. People get sick and die, like I said earlier. Your baby brother got sick inside your mother. Nobody knew he was sick, so nobody could help him."

"But you said God knows everything—so He knew my brother was sick."

"True, and maybe taking him to heaven was the best way to make him well. Did you ever think about that?"

Luke cocked his head to one side. "You think that's what happened?"

"I think it's very possible. Sometimes God fixes folks right here on earth—like your Mama. She was real sick and almost died, but

God healed her body so that she could stay here and be with you children. Sometimes God takes folks home to be with Him, however. You gotta know that He still loves them as much as the folks he leaves here to keep on living. It's not a punishment, Luke."

"I guess not."

George got to his feet and put his arm around Luke's shoulders. "All through your life there are going to be times when you don't understand why God is doing things the way He is. The Bible says our thoughts aren't His thoughts and our ways aren't His ways. That sometimes makes it hard for us to understand why things are happening the way they are. But God doesn't call us to understand, Luke. He calls us to trust Him. Can you do that?"

He looked up thoughtfully. "I want to."

George smiled. "That's a start. Keep looking to God, Luke. He won't let you down, and someday we're gonna understand why things happen the way they do." He looked across the yard to where Cole and Dianne had just appeared. Cole carried the tiny coffin.

"You ready?" George asked Luke.

The boy nodded and started off to join his parents. He stopped abruptly and turned back. "Thanks, George. My heart doesn't hurt so much now."

The funeral was simple, with Ben giving a loving tribute to the child no one ever knew. Isaiah Daniel Selby was buried beside his great uncle Bram, uncle Levi, and Gus. The day was bright and full of the hope of spring. The children were subdued during the funeral, but afterward they seemed to quickly recover and tore out across the yard with squeals of delight. Luke and Winona seemed more sober, walking together and talking, but even they seemed to be accepting of the event without too much grief.

"They seem to be taking this well," Dianne said, watching them go off to play.

"Children sometimes seem better able than adults to accept death," Ben said as he joined her and Charity. "Sometimes they don't, of course. They expect a father or mother who has died to reappear. Even now, I'm sure the depth of this situation is impossible for them to comprehend."

"True," Charity said. "The baby hardly seemed real to them. It would be different if it were, say, John who'd passed on. They all know him and share memories with him."

"I know it's true even for me," Dianne had to admit. "I can barely stand the pain of losing Isaiah, but the thought of losing Lia or the others would completely devastate me, I'm sure. Like you said, I have memories with them and it would be hard to just walk away from that."

"I'm going to go help get dinner on," Charity said, getting to her feet. "Why don't you rest here and enjoy the spring sunshine? Hopefully the Good Lord will hold off with any more bad weather."

"That would definitely be a blessing," Dianne murmured. She got to her feet and looked to Ben. "Would you care to take a walk with me?"

He grinned. "I'd like that very much." He stood and offered Dianne his arm.

They walked slowly down the trail that long ago had become the main drive into the ranch. Dianne tried hard not to look at the place through the eyes of yesterday but rather with new eyes that could see the promise of what was to come.

"I feel as if I'm walking this lane for the first time," she said softly. "I'm determined to start afresh."

Ben nodded. "It's a good plan, Dianne. There's nothing to be gained in living in the past. God would have you move forward—to make new dreams."

"I haven't bothered to dream in so long. Making plans simply hurt too much. I was always afraid of what Cole would or wouldn't want to do. It's different now. I've learned so much in the wake of losing Isaiah."

"I know you've had it difficult this last year," he said. "It's hard to see times like that as necessary growing periods. Sometimes they come to us out of our own disobedience and rebellion, and sometimes they're just times that come by nature of growing in the Lord."

"I know much of my sorrow has been borne out of rebellion and trying to do things my own way." Dianne pushed back a strand of hair that had come loose in the light breeze. As the land inclined toward her favorite hill, Dianne slowed her pace to accommodate Ben's aging limbs. "I don't know why I always have to learn things the hard way. Just when I think I completely understand how a thing ought to be—how I ought to conduct myself— I manage to mess up everything and make the wrong choice."

"We're only human," he said. "We're fallible and long to be in control of our destinies. But we learn early on that taking charge of such a beast isn't as easy as we think."

"I know that full well," she admitted. "I don't know where God is leading our future. I hope you'll pray with me about it. I worry that starting over here isn't the right choice for Cole and our family."

"Why do you say that?"

"I suppose because of something Cole told me. He talked about being afraid to come back here—afraid to fail—afraid that he wouldn't be able to bring the ranch back to its former glory."

"Perhaps that won't happen," Ben said, nodding slowly. "But it's possible that a new glory would be even better."

Dianne considered his words as they continued to walk. Ben's perspective on the matter helped her sort through the strange out-of-sort pieces that had become her life.

"What if we were to start a new ranch? Maybe find a way to buy land close by or even adjoining? We could arrange for Jamie to take this place for his own. Even if our name remained on the deed, he could treat it as his own."

"Is there land close by that would be available? I thought Chester Lawrence owned most everything to the north and east of you."

"That's true, but there might be something to the west. Many people will be selling out because of their losses. Chester Lawrence might even be considering such a thing, although I'm certain he would never sell to us. Perhaps he might sell to another person, who then in turn might sell to us." Dianne sighed. "I don't like the idea of benefiting off of someone else's misfortune, but Cole feels certain a lot of small ranches will go under from the loss of livestock."

"No doubt he's right. And if those people are determined to sell, you can't let sentiment stand in the way. I see nothing wrong with buying their land so long as you pay them a fair price."

"Most of the folks I don't even know very well. So many left after the fire or over the years since. It almost feels like a new territory—like when I first came here." But as they rounded the final bend in the road and stood at the top of Dianne's hill, she knew the land that spilled out beneath them like the back of her hand. She'd walked most every inch of that valley. She knew the turns in the river, the ravines and rocky crags.

"This was always my favorite place to come," she said. "I could look down on the ranch and see that everything was just right. The land hasn't changed—not really. The trees are gone, but new ones are growing back. The house Uncle Bram built is no more, but new houses stand in its place. Still . . ." She fell silent, realizing that something was very different for her. She still loved this land, but something had happened in her heart.

"Still?" Ben questioned.

She laughed. "I don't feel the same way. The land hasn't changed, but I have."

He grinned. "That's always the way of it. When we're seeking God's heart, our own can't help but be different."

"That's it," she said. "I've been seeking the Lord so hard for these past weeks. Ever since waking up after losing the baby. I don't understand why it should have taken so long to come to this place."

"And what place is that?"

"The place where I can honestly say that so long as I have my family with me, and the Lord guiding, I can live anywhere. I didn't think that was possible. I mean, even now, I don't want to go back to Kansas and Cole's mother, but I know . . ." She paused again, letting her words trail. It was almost as if before speaking she had to test her heart and know that her words would be true. "Yes," she said, "I know that I could do even that—if that was where the Lord wanted us." She grinned and reached out to take hold of Ben's hand. "Because I know He would make it well within my soul. He would be my hope within, and nothing else would matter."

As April came, the devastation of winter passed as the men set bonfires to destroy the dead animals. Dianne felt her health return, and there was great joy in being back on the ranch with her family and loved ones. There was even greater happiness in the new way she and Cole spent time together talking, sharing their dreams.

As a gentle rain fell over the valley and heavy gray clouds moved across the mountains, Dianne and Cole sat on the porch holding hands and enjoying the fading day. They'd talked about the ranch and all the possibilities set before them.

"I think it would be wise," Cole said, squeezing her hand, "to talk this all over with Jamie and Koko and George. Even Susannah, although she hardly seems all that interested in ranching."

"No, I think Susannah has grown weary of ranch life. I thought about talking to Koko and suggesting Susannah could live with Charity in town. She's quite lovely, and no doubt there will be many suitors vying for her hand— despite her Indian heritage."

"She may not care about the ranch," Cole replied, "but the others do and they need to be consulted."

"I agree, but there was no sense in talking to them until we knew for sure what we wanted to do."

"Well, if the news I learned in town is correct, Chester Lawrence is going to have to sell out or find someone who will lend him more money. We need to bide our time and see what that will bring. After all, if he sells in an auction, he can't very well choose who will buy his land. And if he allows the bank to foreclose, then he definitely will have no say."

"I wish we could speak to his children. I know there's nothing to be said between us and the older boys, but Joshua, Mara, and even

Elsa should probably be consulted about their father's situation."

"That's a good idea. Maybe I can ride over to Virginia City later this week and encourage Joshua to come out or at least talk to him there. Maybe we could also get a letter to Zane and Mara."

"And Elsa," Dianne added.

A lone rider appeared at the top of the hill and headed down the road into the valley. His heavy slicker didn't allow for recognition. As he approached, however, Dianne recognized the horse.

"Believe it or not, I think it's Joshua," she said, getting to her feet.

They waited until he had dismounted and tied off his horse before greeting him. "What brings you clear out here?" Dianne asked, laughing. "We were just talking about you."

"And I need to talk to you." Joshua pushed back his hat as he stepped under the porch roof. "Didn't start raining until about two miles south of here. I'm certainly glad for that blessing. It would have been miserable trying to get here in pouring rain." He pulled off his slicker and gave it a shake.

"We watched the rain move across the valley," Cole said. "We quit work early because of it, but I can't say I've minded. Dianne and I've been discussing our future plans, and like she said, your name came up."

Joshua draped the coat across the porch rail and turned to Cole in surprise. "Why would I come up in conversation regarding your future?"

"Well, it's not the best of topics," Dianne said hesitantly. "It's certainly not ideal anyway."

"What Dianne is trying to say is that the winter pretty much ruined your father. We've heard that he's in a bind with the Bozeman bank over all the extra money he borrowed, and we feel pretty certain he'll sell off some or all of the ranch."

Joshua shook his head. "I didn't know. I can't say I've even attempted to know his business. In truth, I didn't come here with him in mind at all. I received a telegram from Zane saying that I should come here and that I should wait for him. He wanted me to let you know that he and my sisters are coming and should arrive within the week. I arranged for one of the elders to take over the services until I can get back, so I'm hoping you can put me up here."

"Of course we can," Cole said.

"They're all coming here?" Dianne questioned. "How wonderful. It'll be good to see them, but I can't imagine why they're coming now."

Cole shrugged. "Maybe they just want to see how we fared through the winter."

"Maybe Elsa couldn't bear to be apart

from Jamie anymore," Dianne teased.

"The telegram said something about news that Cole had been waiting for. I don't know what that's about but figured you did."

"News that I've been waiting for?" Cole said. "I don't know what that would be. Zane and I haven't had a talk since before I went to Kansas."

"I guess we'll learn soon enough," Dianne said. "Then maybe we can talk our plans over with Joshua, Mara, and Elsa."

Joshua looked at her curiously. "You definitely have my attention. Both you and Zane."

———

Zane's arrival was much anticipated, and by the time the trio rode into the ranch yard, the entire family turned out to greet them. The women waited near the house while the men moved forward to offer assistance.

"This is quite the welcome," Zane declared as Cole took hold of his horse. George and Jamie helped Mara and Elsa from their horses. Dianne didn't miss the way Jamie's hands lingered on Elsa's waist nor the look the two young people exchanged.

Dianne looked to Koko and grinned. "It would seem that their time apart has done nothing to quench their interest."

"I think we'll have a wedding soon," Koko answered with a slight lift of her chin. "Elsa's a good woman. She accepts and loves Jamie for who he is." The couple sauntered off together to tend to the horses.

Mara came to Dianne and embraced her. "It's so good to see you again. We took the train and then rode the rest of the way on horseback. It was quite an adventure for us."

"I've had my fill of trains for a while," Dianne told her. "But I'm so glad you could come to visit. It's wonderful to have you here."

"We're soon to have a few more visitors," Zane declared, coming to where his sister stood.

Cole and Dianne exchanged a look, then turned back to Zane. "Who are you expecting?"

"The U.S. marshal and his deputies," Zane replied.

CHAPTER 27

CHESTER LAWRENCE LOOKED AT THE ledger and knew there was no possible way to meet his payments come June. With nothing more than a little over sixteen hundred starving steers and cows, he couldn't possibly hope to even sell the herd to settle his affairs. With great reluctance he had paid the winter wages and sent the cowhands on their way, leaving Chester alone to figure out what was to become of the herd.

He'd never been this far down on his luck, and it confused and frustrated him to no end. How was he supposed to run the ranch this way? Where was he supposed to get the additional capital he'd need?

"If those boys of mine would have just turned out to be reliable, I'd be having a better time of it now," he said, slapping the ledger together. He pushed back all the papers on his desk with more force than he'd intended. The ledger sailed across the room and hit the bookcase beside the door.

Chester got up and began to pace. "I can sell off some land." But who would buy it? Everyone in the neighboring areas had suffered as much loss as he had. They wouldn't have money for land. The Selby name came to mind and he grimaced. "I'd rather lose it all than sell them my property!"

He stormed out of the house, cursing. He'd burn it to the ground and see himself dead before he let a Selby have any part of the Walking Horseshoe Ranch.

Morgan Chadwick yawned as he doused

his campfire. He loved being alone in the mountains—he much preferred it to staying in town, even when he wasn't leading a hunting expedition. He poured out the remains of his coffeepot on the embers, then picked up a shovel. A noise in the pass just behind him caught his attention. He perked an ear to catch the sound, not turning lest he startle whoever or whatever was approaching.

He moved ever so slightly to the left, keeping a tight grip on his shovel. The bushes rattled behind him, and without waiting for further warning, Morgan leaped across the remaining distance, grabbed the rifle, and rolled to the ground. He heard the distinct sound of laughter before bouncing back up to his feet. His shoulder hurt something fierce from landing on the dirt. He wasn't a young man anymore.

"Come on out and show yourself!" he called.

A boy who couldn't have been more than twelve or thirteen appeared in short order. He wore a ragged coat and britches that were two sizes too big.

"What are you doing out there?" Morgan asked in a gruff tone as he lowered the rifle. "Don't you know that's a good way to get yourself killed?"

The boy sobered. "I wasn't lookin' to hurt you, mister. I was just huntin'—trying to find some food for my ma and me. My ma's real sick and she needs something to eat."

Morgan eyed him again. He saw no weapon on the boy. "What were you figuring to use to kill an animal if you found one?"

The boy produced a slingshot and a rock. "I'm pretty good with this. I managed to keep us fed until the bad snow came."

Morgan could well imagine the boy and his mother had gone hungry if a slingshot was all they had to use for bringing down game. "Where do you live?"

"About a mile over that way," the boy said, pointing back to the north.

"So you aren't too far from Virginia City, eh?"

The boy nodded. "My ma said it's a town of drunks and reprobates—my pa bein' the worst of them all before he died last summer." The boy spoke so matter-of-factly that Morgan figured it must be the truth.

"I have family over that way myself. They aren't drunks or reprobates. They're good Christian folk."

"Ma says Christians are people who talk pretty with their mouths but ain't much good for anything else. She said she's never seen a Christian who acted like what they were supposed to."

"I see. Well, I'd beg to differ with her. I know a lot of good Christian folks, and they are loving and kind people."

The boy shrugged, making his small frame seem even more skeletal as the clothes draped awkwardly. "I couldn't say. My ma won't take me to church. She said that's where all the hypocrites are, and she don't want me growing up to be like that."

Morgan smiled. "Tell you what. I'm a Christian, and I'm going to help you and prove to you that not all Christians talk pretty and do nothing else." He started picking up his few supplies. "Can you gather up my bedroll?"

"I reckon so," the boy said, putting away his slingshot and rock.

"Good. You do that, and I'll get my horse saddled. Then we'll go hunting."

The boy went to work and only then did it dawn on Morgan that he didn't know the boy's name. "My name is Morgan Chadwick. What's yours?"

"David. David Nelson."

Morgan grinned. "That's fitting what with your slingshot and all."

"What's that got to do with my name?"

"I'll tell you about it," he promised. "As soon as we're on the trail."

"It's hard to believe all the trouble my father has caused," Mara said sadly. "I knew he and Mother were always conniving, but when

Father married Portia, things just went from bad to worse. I never met anyone more demanding or more hateful. She hated everyone, it seemed." She started the platter of eggs around Koko's big table.

"Everyone but Father," Elsa admitted.

"She may not have hated him," Mara said, "but I don't think she truly loved him either. She treated him with very little respect."

"Be that as it may," Zane began, "we finally have witnesses who are willing to testify against your father and Jerrod and Roy. They were no-accounts who were jailed for other crimes and offered this information to keep from getting a noose around their necks. They were a part of the plot to kill the Farleys, as well as Trenton and Portia's father, Sam."

"I can't believe after all this time that justice can finally be served," Dianne said, shaking her head. "I'd completely given up hope of seeing justice done for Maggie and Whit Farley. It seemed so unfair that they should die and no one pay for what they did to them." She took up a piece of toast and buttered it before taking a bite. The entire matter held her spellbound. "Then, too, I knew in my heart that Portia was at least partially responsible for killing her father and trying to kill Trenton. I could have figured Chester would have backed her up in it—maybe even pulled the trigger himself."

"Cole and I have put a lot of time and

money into tracking down information," Zane told them. "Mostly my time and his money."

Dianne turned to her husband. Here was yet another thing she'd held against him so long ago. Her frustration over his seeming unwillingness to put the Lawrences behind bars had caused much grief in their marriage. "Why didn't you tell me?"

"I couldn't tell you everything," Cole said, looking to the table and sighing. "If Lawrence would have known there was an ongoing investigation of any kind, he would have found a way to rid himself of the evidence. As it was, he sent those two characters who'd helped him to California. Their own stupidity brought them back to Montana."

Dianne looked to the Lawrence children and shook her head. "I'm so sorry you have to be in the middle of this. I wouldn't see you hurt for the world."

"People have to bear the consequences of their actions," Elsa said firmly. "Our father always thought that rule applied to everyone but him."

"She's right," Joshua added. "Father always believed himself above the law. If he couldn't bully his way out of trouble, he'd pay folks off and buy his way out."

"Well, he won't be buying off the U.S. marshal," Zane said. "There's too much evidence against him, and times are changing. The legal system here is becoming more firmly established. The days of interpreting laws to satisfy just one man are soon to be behind us. The officials in Washington aren't going to give us statehood if we can't prove ourselves capable of upholding the law. Mark my word, the old days are behind us."

"I hope that's true," Dianne interjected, "but in the meantime, what's to happen next?"

"The marshal and his men will come here first. I promised them lodging. I hope that's acceptable," Zane said apologetically.

"Of course it is," Koko replied before anyone else could say a word. "But when are they coming?"

"Should be here almost any time. Their plan was to go to Bozeman first, then come here. From here we'll go with them over to the Walking Horseshoe Ranch to meet with Chester. I expect an ugly confrontation. Most likely Chester and his boys won't go without a fight."

"Probably not," Joshua agreed, "but I hope to talk some sense into them. Perhaps if we can just keep things calm, they'll give up without trying to hurt anyone else."

"They've got to realize it won't go well for them in a court of law," Cole said. "If they know that and feel that the worst is bound to happen to them, they probably won't listen to reason."

Zane nodded thoughtfully. "I don't suppose so."

"What will happen to them after that? After they're taken into custody?" Dianne asked. Her heart ached for Mara and Elsa. Joshua might be strong enough to bear the situation, but the girls would surely be troubled by the arrest of their father. After all, they would most likely see him hang for his crimes. Dianne found that such thoughts made her victory over Lawrence seem bittersweet. She'd wanted the man dead—she couldn't deny that. When Trenton had nearly died and Dianne had been convinced Portia and Chester Lawrence were behind the plot, Dianne had prayed for revenge. Now it seemed a hollow victory.

Zane looked to his wife and closed his hand over hers. "We've all talked about this long and hard while traveling here from Butte. We know they'll probably all hang. We can't even be sure that Jerrod and Roy are still there. Lawrence said something last fall about them leaving. We don't know if that happened or if they came back. Guess we won't know until we get there."

"It will be dangerous no matter who's there," Dianne said. "I've long wanted them to get what they had coming, but I feel so bad for you, Mara—Elsa." She looked to Joshua and added, "And you. I know this cannot be easy to reconcile. I hope it won't cause hard feelings between us." She couldn't help but wonder how she'd feel if one of them were responsible for seeing Trenton hang for the things he'd done.

"There will be no bad blood between us," Mara said. "My father and brothers are getting what they deserve. There's no love lost between us, unfortunately. I must admit when Zane first explained what he'd been doing, I felt strange about it. It was like he'd gone behind my back—even used his knowledge of me and the things I could tell him to get what he needed. It wasn't concern about Father or the boys; as I said, they deserve to face the punishment for what they did." She paused and seemed to consider how to put her thoughts into words. "I just felt like Zane had kept this huge secret from me. Then we talked and he explained why it was necessary to leave me out. Upon reflection, I could see the truth in his words. In fact, it might have been in part why Zane hesitated to accept my love in the first place. He knew that he and Cole were working on this and that it would probably lead to my father and brothers' demise." She looked to him and smiled. "He's always trying to protect me. Now more than ever."

"Well, I should expect that of him," Dianne said, smiling.

"She isn't talking about her father and

brothers' misdeeds," Zane said. He met Dianne's eyes. "We're going to have a child."

Dianne forced her smile to remain fixed. "That's wonderful news."

"We thought so," Mara said, blushing. "We hesitated to say anything since learning about little Isaiah, however."

Dianne shook her head. "This is joyous news. My sorrow should not take away from that."

"She's right, you know," Cole said, extending his hand to Zane. "Congratulations."

And so the heartache and sorrow were laced with joy and anticipation of things to come. Dianne thought it all rather fitting and so like God to arrange it all so perfectly. It was hard to imagine Mara giving birth. Her days of motherhood were only beginning, while Dianne's were coming to an end. *Well, not an end,* she thought. *I still have my children, and they are very much in need of a mother.* But she knew there would be no other babies for her and Cole. Koko had told her this much. There had been too much damage—too much bleeding. *Even so, there is peace in my heart. I am content.* She smiled in earnest as she watched her brother and Mara. *I'm happy for them.*

The marshal and his men arrived soon after Zane's announcement. The ladies had already begun to clean up the breakfast dishes when the dogs started raising a ruckus. The men wanted to waste no time in heading out.

"Won't you at least have some breakfast?" Dianne offered.

"No, ma'am. We ate some biscuits on the way out here. Now we need to get this matter in hand. Who's coming with us?"

"I am," Zane and Joshua declared in unison.

"Me too," Cole added. He heard Dianne's sharp intake of breath, but to her credit she said nothing.

"Then let's get to it!" the marshal directed. "I want those men in custody before sundown." That was all the command they needed. The men jumped into action.

Cole saddled his horse, seeing the grave apprehension in Dianne's eyes. He knew she'd rather he not accompany the marshal, but he felt it his duty. Zane and Joshua were going, and it didn't seem right for him to remain behind. Perhaps with the show of force, they could preclude any violence between the Lawrences and the lawmen.

"George and Jamie will be here if you need anything," he assured her. "Ben too. Try not to worry. We have the law on our side, and those deputies look quite capable of dealing with the Lawrence boys."

"I'm sure you're right," Dianne said. Cole

could see she was battling not to say more.

He kissed her good-bye and climbed into the saddle.

The ride to the Walking Horseshoe seemed to take forever. Cole couldn't help but think back to days gone by. He missed working with Trenton Chadwick. His brother-in-law had been a good man, with a big heart. He was hiding from a past that wasn't entirely his responsibility, yet he'd made himself a part of it out of poor choices. Trenton's decision to hide out in the wilds of the northwest was still somewhat troubling to Cole—to Dianne as well. He knew she'd been bothered by her brother's decision but also had encouraged him to go and be safely away from Portia Lawrence. The woman had positively had it in for the man, and all because Trenton knew she was up to no good.

They approached the ranch with caution. There was no telling what Lawrence's reaction might be. He could very well come out the front door blasting away. Most likely he would be working out in the yard—perhaps dealing with the few cattle that remained in his care.

The place seemed unnaturally quiet. Too quiet to suit Cole's taste. The marshal motioned for Cole and the others to remain behind while he and his two deputies advanced. Cole dismounted, hoping there wouldn't be any trouble. Then without warning, Chester Lawrence bounded out the front door.

"What do you want?" Lawrence called out.

"U.S. marshal, Mr. Lawrence. I'm here to arrest you and your sons for the murder of Margaret and Whitson Farley."

Cole could see the color drain from the old man's face. Joshua stepped forward while the marshal waited for a response.

"Father, we don't want trouble. You need to call Roy and Jerrod and have this thing settled."

"Your brothers aren't here. They deserted me long ago, just like you and your sisters. They haven't been here since before winter, not that I would turn them over to the likes of you even if they were here." The man's face contorted in rage as he addressed the marshal. "How dare you come here threatening me! I've done nothing wrong."

"Nevertheless, we're here to uphold the law. Your guilt or innocence is for a judge and jury to decide."

"Hardly! I'm not going to leave my fate in the hands of a bunch of fools." Lawrence surprised them all by retreating back into the house and slamming the door shut. "I won't be taken!" he called from inside the house. "Now get off my property!"

The marshal looked to his deputies and then to Joshua. "Do you think your father is telling the truth about your brothers?"

"Probably. Jerrod and Roy were threatening to leave him. He told me that some time ago. Called them traitors and every other name he could think of. I suppose they finally made good on their threats." Joshua pushed his hat back and scratched his forehead. "I would imagine there's only my father and the household help inside. I could go and try to talk some sense into him."

"You can try," the marshal said hesitantly, "but you also might get yourself killed."

"I'm willing to take a chance." Joshua took a hesitant step toward the house. "I'll do what I can to get him to surrender."

He made it to the porch before glass shattered in one of the side windows. Joshua's hat ripped from his head as a shot whizzed by. He reached up and touched his head but didn't appear to be hurt.

"Father!" Joshua called out. "You need to stop this now. There's no possible way you can hold out on your own against the marshal. You need to sit down and talk with us."

"Talking isn't what your marshal has in mind. You take your friends and get out of here! Get out of here or I'll put a bullet in you," he commanded. He fired again, this time barely missing one of the deputies.

"Take cover!" Cole cried, circling back around his horse. He coaxed the animal to step back with him several feet. The nearest out-building became his refuge then, and he quickly tied the horse to the back corral fence behind the barn.

"What are we going to do now?" Joshua asked, joining Cole. "He clearly isn't willing to reason this out." Zane soon followed suit and tied his horse beside Cole's. The marshal and his deputies were right behind him.

"I want to put a man on each side of the house," the marshal directed. "If he won't come out willingly, we'll smoke him out. He's got both chimneys going," he said, pointing back to the house. The men looked around the corner.

Cole could see the possibilities in the man's plan. "We smoke him out and then what? He'll no doubt be firing his guns as he runs for it."

"I can't help that. It's my order to bring him in dead or alive," the marshal said. "I'd rather it be alive, but I'm not going to put that man in a position to kill us off."

"I could try again," Joshua said.

"The time for talk is behind us. Your father wants no part of negotiating this matter. We'll have to do it my way now."

Joshua nodded and Cole put his arm around the younger man's shoulders. "You did your best. You tried. Your father doesn't want to talk this out or deal reasonably. Probably because he knows in the end it won't matter.

There's never any justifiable reason for the things he's done."

"I feel so inadequate. Pastors are supposed to be men of reconciliation, but he won't even hear me out. It just seems that I should have been able to do something more."

"It always does. Especially when rebellious hearts refuse to yield to the truth."

They took their positions as the marshal directed.

"Here, take my coat and use yours too," the marshal told one of his deputies. "Climb up there and throw them over the chimneys." The man threw the coat over his shoulder and then scurried up the porch rail before hoisting himself onto the roof. Cole kept watch, worried that Lawrence might catch sight of the man and shoot him. The marshal seemed more than aware of this concern as well.

It took only a matter of minutes for the man to accomplish his task. Once done, he jumped from the lower roof and hit the ground without a sound. He was good at his job, Cole had to admit.

"Lawrence, you need to come out with your hands up," the marshal called into the house. "I'm giving you exactly one minute to make up your mind."

Chester broke through another window and fired rapidly. From the sounds of it, Cole figured he was first using his rifle, then his revolver. "And then you'll do what? You charge this house and I'll shoot you down. Now do as I say and get out of here. You won't take me in to hang for something I didn't do."

"I don't care if you did it or not," the marshal called back. "That's not my judgment. Now surrender or we'll be forced to shoot you down."

Laughter rang out from the house, chilling Cole to the bone. Lawrence was clearly crazy. By now smoke was beginning to seep out the broken windows. There was some commotion in the back of the house, and it was only a minute later that one of the deputies called out that the cook and housekeeper were safely out of the house.

"I'll go to them," Joshua said and crawled off toward the back of the house.

"They say no one else is in there but Lawrence!" the deputy called again.

"He won't be in there for long," the marshal declared. "Not if he wants to go on breathing."

Joshua came around the house with the servants and guided them to safety behind the barn. Both women were crying, and Joshua was apparently trying to console them.

Cole knew that left Zane by himself on the west side of the house and a deputy on each of the other sides. He started maneuvering across the yard to join Zane when another burst of gunfire rang out. This was followed by a spell of coughing and swearing.

Cole saw Zane hiding behind an empty wagon. He ran the final distance and joined his brother-in-law. "Reminds me of being pinned down by the Indians," Cole said.

"Reminds me of being in the army, dealing with the same," Zane replied. "Hard to believe one old man could cause such grief."

"One very well armed old man."

Looking around the corner of the wagon to the front of the house, Cole could see that thick smoke roiled from the front window. It couldn't possibly be long now. Then without warning, gunfire sounded again. Only this time it was a single shot and then silence.

The shot seemed ominous in light of earlier assaults. Cole saw Joshua walking toward the house. "Get down, Joshua," Cole called as he moved toward the young man. He seemed not to care about the danger. Perhaps he'd momentarily lost reasonable thought.

"There's no need," he said, continuing his walk toward the porch.

The marshal and Cole both rushed forward. The marshal reached Joshua first, however, and pulled him away from the house and behind the fence. "Get back here. What are you thinking?"

Cole crouched behind the fence. "Yes, what were you thinking?"

"I'm thinking he's dead," Joshua replied. "I'm thinking that single shot put my father out of his misery for good."

CHAPTER 28

"So this fella, David in the Bible, he killed a giant with a slingshot?" David asked in disbelief.

"That's right. When no one else could be found to fight for the Lord, David answered the call. He was very brave, even though he was but a boy."

Morgan felt David shift his weight and his hold. "That's our cabin over there." He seemed to forget about the story. "Do you see it?"

"I see it," Morgan said as he turned the horse toward the rundown shack. "Here, let me help you down and you go inside and let your ma know she's got company. Ladies can be kind of fussy about strangers showing up. She may not be too excited about my being here since she's been sick."

David held onto Morgan's arm and slid to the ground. "I'll tell her. She'll be mighty surprised about that deer you shot. Ain't had venison in a long time."

"Good. Maybe that will help her to feel stronger. I'll get something cooking right away. I can build a fire out here and work on it." Morgan dismounted and looked around. Most places had at least a fire pit for doing laundry outside, but he didn't see any signs of one.

David scurried toward the house like a tiny field mouse. He darted between the broken fence and a pile of discarded junk, calling to his mother as he went. "Ma! You'll never guess what we're havin' for dinner."

Morgan laughed. The boy was more than a little enthused over their capture of the young buck. He hoped the animal's youth would make it easy for the sick woman to digest.

"Mr. Morgan! Come quick. I don't think my ma is breathing!" David called suddenly.

Morgan's breath caught at the thought. He tossed the buck to the ground and headed to the cabin.

"Hurry, mister. I think she's dead!"

A week after Chester Lawrence had been buried in Bozeman, Joshua made plans to return to Virginia City. As he gathered with the others at the ranch for the morning meal, he made his announcement.

"I've been gone from the church long

enough. I know there are good people who've been filling in for Ben and me, but with both of us gone . . . well, I feel as if I've left the sheep to stray."

Dianne chuckled and took her seat at the table while Ardith and Susannah finished bringing in platters of food. "I'm sure it must feel that way, but I would imagine they are fine. They can't begrudge you the time to bury your father and deal with family business."

"Speaking of which," Zane interjected, looking at Joshua, "the marshal told me he had a lead on your brothers. They were seen near Deadwood. I wouldn't be surprised if they got caught soon."

"I hope so," Elsa said. "They're only going to cause folks more pain and misery. They were never anything but mean—through and through."

"So what about you, Elsa?" Dianne questioned. "Will you go back to the ranch and live? What about you, Joshua?"

Both shook their heads. "I want no part of that place for myself," Joshua replied. "It never gave me anything but sadness. I'd just as soon we sold it."

"That's how I see it too," Elsa said, then looked to Jamie with a grin. "After all, I intend to live here."

Everyone looked to the couple, and Jamie stammered to quickly add, "I've asked Elsa to marry me. We were hoping Joshua would stick around and do the job."

Joshua shook his head in wonder. "Two sisters married within a year. I would never have thought it possible."

"Well, we've always been taught to go after what we wanted," Elsa said. "So I went after Jamie." This brought laughter from everyone around the table.

Joshua quickly sobered and looked to Koko and George. "What do you say about this? They are young. Elsa's just turned twenty-one, and I know from what you've said that Jamie will be twenty in May."

"They love each other," Koko replied. "That's enough for me. They are good children with strong backs and loving hearts. They fear God and respect their elders. I think they'll make a good match."

"I believe a love such as theirs should never be denied," George said. "I won't stand in their way."

"And what of their living here?" Joshua asked.

"Where else would they want to live?" Koko said. "This was the ranch Jamie's father always intended him to run."

Dianne thought for a moment on that statement. It was Jamie's inheritance. Just as the farm in Kansas had been Cole's. Only Dianne knew how deeply Bram had felt about this land and about his son inheriting the property. He had gone out of his way to make provision by making Dianne a partner on the deed. All so that Jamie wouldn't lose his inheritance.

"Well, this is exciting news," Cole interjected. "But what of you, Zane? Would you and Mara be interested in taking over the Walking Horseshoe Ranch? After all, it's as much Mara's as it is Elsa's or Joshua's."

"I've no interest in ranching," he said. "You know that. I am very interested, however, in this breakfast. Might we bless it and continue our discussion while we eat?"

Cole laughed. "Of course we can." He offered a quick prayer of thanks, then picked up a platter of ham. While he skewered several pieces, he continued. "Will you and Mara remain in Anaconda?"

Zane was already busy ladling eggs onto his plate. "I don't think so. With the baby coming, I want to get Mara to a place where the air is better and the town less rowdy. Marcus Daly would actually like me to consider working for him in Helena. He wants to see Anaconda become the capital of Montana when we finally achieve statehood. He thinks he can stir up enough folks in Helena to vote for this, but I seriously doubt it. William Clark is fighting equally hard to keep Helena the capital."

"Do politics interest you, Zane?" Dianne

asked. She found it difficult to believe that her brother would hold any true desire for such a proposition.

"Not exactly." He took up the offered ham and helped himself. "I frankly like the line of work I'm already in. Freighting is a good business if you aren't afraid of hard work. I've still got a few more years in me for hauling and lifting." He grinned as Mara elbowed him.

"He'd better. I intend for him to haul and lift our baby around. Maybe two or three babies," she added boldly.

"It would be wonderful to have you living close enough for visiting," Elsa said hopefully. "Couldn't you just move back to this area?"

"Truth be told," Cole began, "I was going to ask the same thing. I kind of had it in mind that you could take over my freighting business."

Zane looked up. "You mean, have me sell out in Anaconda and buy up your business in Virginia City?"

"Why not?"

"I just hadn't considered it."

"Well, I wish you would," Cole said thoughtfully. "There's good work to be had, though maybe not as much as there was in Butte and Anaconda. You might even want to think about moving it all to Bozeman. That town has grown like a wildfire spreading. We could always check into the prospects of putting in a business there."

"That might work well," Zane said. "It would definitely be worth checking into. When they closed down Fort Ellis, I wasn't sure Bozeman would last. But the railroad and new settlers have definitely caused a boom. I'm betting they'll be around for a long time."

Cole took a bowl of fried potatoes from Dianne and put a generous amount on his plate. "And I have another proposition to offer as well."

Dianne was greatly surprised by this. Cole had talked about getting out of the freighting business, for which she'd been quite glad, but she had no idea what else he would suggest.

"Though I haven't had a chance to settle plans with Dianne, I'd like to make the proposal nevertheless." All gazes were fixed on Cole. Even the children seemed spellbound by what he had to say.

"Well, don't keep us waiting," Koko said, laughing.

Cole grinned. "I was just wondering if Joshua and his sisters would consider selling the Walking Horseshoe to me."

Dianne felt her stomach tighten. "Buy the Lawrence property? But why?"

"A good question and here's the answer. Joshua, Mara, and Elsa will most likely sell it anyway. There aren't a whole lot of folks in this valley who could afford to pay a fair price for the cattle and the land. We're in a position to do both. We could then split the cattle between us and the Diamond V and let the animals free-range all summer. Come fall, we can sell off the fattened steers and buy new animals. I don't know what the ratio of steers to cows might be with your father's herd," Cole said, looking to Joshua, "but I think we might be able to make this work—and work well. We might also look into getting some sheep. The sheep didn't suffer nearly as much this winter. They might be a good investment."

"I think it's a wonderful idea," Elsa declared. "I don't want the ranch, but it would be nice to see someone I cared about living nearby."

"I think it's a good idea as well," Mara said, and she looked to Joshua. "What say you, brother?"

Joshua concurred. "I think it would solve a lot of problems. We wouldn't have to worry about finding a buyer or holding an auction. That's always appealing. But wouldn't there be a matter of clearing up the deed and such? I know there are debts owed. Debts that hold the property in lien."

"Which we would pay as part of the purchasing price," Cole said.

"Would there be enough money for that?" Dianne questioned. "You know I bought cattle last winter and took money from our account.

I don't know how many they'll actually be able to bring us, what with the death of so much stock across the plains states as well as Texas."

"There's more than enough," Cole said. "I've already been figuring it all out on paper." He passed the bowl of potatoes to Luke. "There would be a healthy amount of profit for each of you to split between yourselves. It would be a better price than you could get from anyone else—that's for sure." He looked to each of them. "I've been praying a great deal about this and would like you to pray as well."

"But what about the Diamond V?" Ardith asked. "This is your home."

Cole looked to Dianne. She saw the hopefulness in his eyes. She could see him questioning her silently as to whether she could ever call any other place home. Smiling, she knew why God had done such a work in her heart. "My home is wherever my family is," Dianne said softly.

Cole squeezed Dianne's hand and looked back to the others. "The Diamond V belongs to Jamie by rights. I'd like to see him continue on here with his family, and perhaps there will come a time when it won't matter that he has Indian blood and the place can be his in name as well."

Jamie looked stunned. He met Cole's expression and shook his head. "But by law, it's yours to take."

"Or to give," Cole replied.

Koko wiped tears from her eyes. Dianne smiled and caught George watching her. He smiled as well. It was a special moment—one that Dianne knew her uncle Bram would have relished. She and Cole had already talked about checking into possible ways to get Jamie's name on the deed. The laws were changing all the time, and some even suggested that the laws had been misinterpreted to them. It was all a matter of working out the details, but it was possible that Jamie could be the legal owner of the Diamond V sooner than any of them suspected.

"I don't know what to say," Jamie said. "I used to be so angry about the ranch. I couldn't figure out why it was fair to keep a son from inheriting what his father always intended to leave him." He looked specifically to Dianne. "You've always been fair—more than. I don't want you to misjudge me. I never hated you or wished you gone."

Dianne met his eyes—they were a warm brown like his mother's and father's. She saw the gratitude and love expressed in Jamie's face and couldn't help but smile. "I know that, Jamie. You are too much like Bram. You couldn't hate someone who was only trying to do whatever it took to protect you. Cole and I want the Diamond V to belong to you. We want you to raise your family here. To be as happy as we always were. I've always known it would be your inheritance—not mine."

Elsa leaned over and slipped her hand into Jamie's. "We prayed about all of this. We prayed because Jamie wanted to someday run this ranch as his own. He worried that it was selfish, but I couldn't see it that way."

Koko wiped her eyes again. "It wasn't selfish, Jamie. It was your dream. Yours and your father's."

Dianne warmed at the words. They were true, and her heart fairly rejoiced in the moment. It was hard to imagine starting over on the Walking Horseshoe Ranch, but she knew deep inside she could make the place her own. God had given her hope for their future. He'd shown her that no matter where she went or lived, He would be with her.

She felt her old determination and strength return. *I can take that ranch and make it my own. I can wipe away all the old and make it new. It can be a good home for my family and still close to Koko and the others.* Dianne smiled and squared her shoulders. It seemed the perfect answer to their need—to their prayers.

———

Morgan tried to rouse the sleeping woman. It was clear she was still alive, but just barely. "We need to get her to the doctor." He pulled the covers around her and scooped her into his arms. "What's your mother's name?"

"Molly. Molly Nelson," David replied, looking fearful.

"Molly," Morgan called as he carried her to the door. "Molly, we're taking you to Virginia City. We're going to get you help." He mounted the horse with the feather-light woman in his arms. Struggling to balance her against him, Morgan then reached down and helped David to climb up behind him.

"She won't like going to Virginia City," David muttered.

"Sometimes we have to do things to help people that they don't particularly like. I can't give your mother the help she needs," he said, moving the horse out and back toward the trail that would take them into town. "She needs a doctor."

"Ain't no money for a doctor. No one is gonna want to help her. She's just gonna die." There was such resignation in the boy's voice that Morgan felt more determined than ever to see him through the crisis.

"They'll help, and I'll pay for it. And I'll go one step further: I'll pray for your ma. She may not hold stock in it, but I do."

"If you think God will listen to you, mister, you pray as much as you want. My ma is all I got. I can't lose her."

Morgan looked down at the deathly pale woman. "You hear that, Molly Nelson? You've got to live for your boy's sake." He barely whispered the words, but the woman stirred momentarily and opened her eyes. She held his gaze for only a heartbeat, then closed her eyes again. It gave Morgan all the encouragement he needed.

"Hee-ya!" he called to the horse, nudging the beast with his heels at the same time. "Hold on, David!"

———

"May I come in?" Ardith asked as she pushed open the front door to Dianne and Cole's cabin.

Dianne was alone, finishing forming up the last loaf of bread. "Sure. I'd love your company. I'm just putting the last pans of bread into the oven, and then I have to start a roast for supper."

Ardith closed the door behind her. "Winona is playing with the boys and Lia. They wanted to go down to the river to try to catch some fish, but I told them no. I hope that was all right."

"It's more than all right. That river is swollen and running high. I don't want any of them down there." Dianne straightened and closed the oven door. "There." She looked at the clock. "I suppose I have time to share a cup of coffee with you. There's some left over from breakfast."

"No, thank you. You go ahead if you like."

"I'm not really of a mind to have any either. Why don't we sit for a minute?" She led Ardith to the sitting area of the main room. "Times certainly are different from when you first came here. I can't even offer you a decent stuffed chair."

"I don't mind," Ardith said. "I had plenty of luxury in New York."

"I can't even begin to imagine," Dianne said. "Did you wear silk all the time?"

Ardith laughed. "Silk, velvet, sateen. Each gown was more luxurious than the last. Such opulence seemed almost sinful. The people seemed to cling to their things and the value of each piece."

"That's sad. Not that they enjoyed fine things, but that they would make it the focus of their lives."

"You don't know the half of it. So much money was spent on things that were here one minute and gone the next. Why, I was at one party where the hostess, I'm told, spent one hundred dollars to have several ice sculptures created as decoration for her tables. The silly things melted away by the end of the evening. All I could think about was that her money was dissolving before my very eyes."

"I can't even imagine such nonsense. Still," Dianne said with a laugh, "some nice stuffed furniture would be a wonderful change. We weren't able to get much before we came out last winter."

"This is perfectly fine. Stuffed furniture is nice to be sure, but it didn't satisfy or meet my needs then, so I can't imagine it would now."

"So what are your needs?"

Ardith sat opposite her sister and fidgeted with her hands. "That's why I'm here. I wanted to ask you something. I know it's probably a lot to ask, and you can of course say no, but—"

"Goodness, Ardith, just ask. You've no reason to think you can't approach me about anything."

She looked up with a slight smile. "I wondered if Winona and I could come and live with you and Cole when you take over the Walking Horseshoe. I don't want to go back to Virginia City, and I don't want to stay here."

"You silly goose, of course you may come with us. We'd already planned for that. I figured you'd want Winona to be around the children. Besides, if we all leave here, then Jamie and Elsa can have this cabin for their new home."

A look akin to relief washed over Ardith's face. "I know I've made some poor decisions in the past, but I'm striving to make better ones now. I feel that God must surely make a way for even us stubborn children."

Dianne laughed. "I hope so. I'm among

His worst in that area. The Walking Horseshoe has a huge house. There is no reason we can't all live there quite happily, so put your mind to rest. That isn't a poor decision—it's a perfect one."

"I'm so glad you understand. I'm blessed that you've been willing to take care of us since Levi's death—well, even before our marriage you were there. I'll work hard to help you at the new place."

"I appreciate that," Dianne said softly. "I love having you and Winona around. Never forget that."

"Cole might feel differently."

"He might, but he doesn't," Dianne said with a smile. "We've already talked about all of this. Once things are settled on the Lawrence estate, we'll ride over and check out the place. We'll make a list of what we need and get to work on the house. It shouldn't be in too bad of order. The cook and housekeeper are still there, and Joshua said they'd just as soon stay on and work for us if we're interested."

"So we're starting all over again," Ardith said matter-of-factly.

"I guess we are."

———

"I now pronounce you man and wife," Joshua said in a serious tone. He then winked and grinned. "You may now kiss the bride."

Jamie took Elsa into his arms and kissed her tenderly. Everyone in the room broke into cheers and laughter. The children began to dance around Jamie and Elsa, clapping.

Cole put his arm around Dianne and pulled her close. "So, Mrs. Selby, I thought you should know that I love you very much."

Dianne smiled and looked up to catch her husband's loving gaze. "And I love you."

"We've certainly endured a great deal. I suppose we'll go on enduring—that's our nature."

"Yes, but more so, we'll succeed. We aren't mere survivors of our trials, we are conquerors. We'll face whatever comes our way, and with God's help, we'll overcome."

"And nothing will divide us again," he whispered.

"Nothing," she promised.

CHAPTER 29

"I'M AFRAID SHE'S PASSED ON," THE DOCTOR told Morgan and David.

"No! You're wrong. My ma wouldn't die," David cried in near hysterics. He started to charge at the man, but Morgan held him back.

"David, you can't bring your ma back this way. I know this is bad news, but let's hear what the doctor has to say."

David settled against Morgan. Tears ran down his dirty cheeks, leaving stripes on the boy's face. Morgan wasn't sure what to do or say, so he turned back to the doctor. "What took her?"

"Pneumonia. She's probably been sick for some time. Being malnourished didn't help her cause any."

"What's pneumonia?" David asked.

The doctor looked down on him with great compassion. "It's a sickness that affects the lungs. They become inflamed—infected with fluids and such. It's often fatal, especially for the poor."

Morgan felt the boy's shoulders slump as if in acceptance of the news. He kept his arm around David and said, "Thank you, Doc. Come on, David. We'll need to arrange a funeral. I know your mother hated Virginia City, but I think it best to have her buried in the cemetery here rather than take her back out to the cabin."

"I guess so."

Morgan told the doctor that he'd make arrangements with the undertaker, then settled up the bill before he quietly escorted David from the small hospital.

"What am I going to do now?" David asked Morgan. "I ain't got no other family. Can't go live with anybody else."

Morgan realized that the boy was probably telling the truth. If they'd had family, surely his mother would never have lived in the shack alone. Morgan scratched his chin. The bearded stubble there was itching something fierce. "Tell you what. Let's get us a room at the hotel, and we'll talk things over while we have some dinner."

"I ain't hungry," David said, stuffing his hands deep into his oversized pants.

"Well, maybe not. But I am. I was looking forward to some venison steaks, but by now a bear probably has taken our catch. Come on." Morgan nudged the boy toward the street. "We'll think better on a full stomach."

At least that was what Morgan hoped would be the case. He couldn't say that it helped at all, however, as he pushed back from the empty luncheon plate an hour later. He'd been trying to consider the boy's situation and what was to be done, but in truth, it seemed hopeless. As he watched David, Morgan found he was strangely drawn to him. He didn't know if it was a matter of seeing himself in the boy or if he just felt sorry for him, but Morgan couldn't bring himself to walk away.

"Will you take me back to the cabin after we get Ma buried?" David asked.

"I've been thinking on that very thing. I can't hardly see that it would be the Christian thing to do."

David scowled. "Don't want no Christian things done to me. Your prayin' didn't help my ma."

"Well, it may not seem like it now, but I know God heard my prayers and that He cares deeply about you and your ma."

"I don't believe you. God killed my ma as sure as anything."

"Sickness took your mother's life, David. Everybody gets sick now and then. Good folks and bad. It was just her time."

"I don't care." He crossed his arms tight against his chest. "It's not fair."

"No, I suppose it's not."

Morgan watched the boy for several minutes. He liked the child and had enjoyed their time hunting that morning. A thought came to mind. He was alone and now David was alone. Why not remedy that and stick together?

What am I thinking? I'm not equipped to take on a child. But in truth David hardly seemed like a child. He'd probably lived through more than most adults. Morgan took a long drink of coffee and continued to think about the possibility.

I'll probably never marry—never have children of my own. He looked at the boy who by now had bowed his head in complete exhaustion. How long had he been up hunting to find something for his mother to eat?

"David, how old are you?" Morgan asked, sizing up the boy's frame.

"Be fourteen come July."

Another couple of years and the boy would be old enough to be on his own if he wanted. Surely Morgan could endure a couple of years raising the boy and seeing to his needs. If nothing else, Morgan could ask Dianne for advice if things got too complicated. Then Morgan realized that being on the road all the time might not be the best for David. After all, he couldn't very well attend school while camping deep in the wilderness.

"Do you go to school?"

David looked at him and frowned. "Not since I lived here. I didn't much like it, but I can read and write and cipher. Figure that's enough for any man."

Morgan had to give him that much. He'd not enjoyed school himself and had put it behind him at sixteen. David had already managed to retire his education, and who was Morgan to preach at him that he should do otherwise? He took another draw from his coffee mug.

"And you've got no family? Not even back East?"

David shook his head. "Ma said they were

all dead. It was just her and me. Now it's just me."

"So you wouldn't be opposed to maybe signing on with someone else?"

David looked up apprehensively. "I don't know no one else."

"You know me."

"I don't know you much."

Morgan was surprised at the boy's comment. "That's true enough, but I was kind of thinkin' to take on a partner. I do a pretty good business guiding folks on hunting expeditions and such."

"A partner?" He looked rather interested at this aspect. "What would I have to do?"

"Oh, help lead pack mules, dress the game, make camps, care for animals. Things like that. You'd be paid, of course."

"You ain't joshing me, are you, Mr. Morgan?"

Morgan could see the apprehension in the boy's eyes. "Not at all. My business is growing, and I need the help."

The other people in the dining room seemed oblivious to the moment. They were sharing their quiet dinners, immersed in their own discussions. No doubt the young boy and man held little interest for them.

"Most of the time it involves a lot of travel. I hike miles into the mountains. Like a while back I took a man west into the Coeur d'Alene

Mountains. It was probably the worst trails and climbs I've ever made. It took a lot of time and energy."

"I'm good at that stuff," David offered. "I can shoot fair too. Ain't had a gun for a while, though—we had to sell it for food."

They sat across from each other in silence for several minutes. Morgan knew this quick decision might cause him grief down the road, but even now, reflecting on the possibilities, it seemed right. He felt a complete peace about taking on David. After all, what was the alternative? He could walk away and leave the boy on his own, or he could turn David over to the authorities. Neither choice was something Morgan felt he could live with.

"So what do you think?" Morgan asked.

"I guess I don't got nothing else. I'd need a job anyway."

Morgan smiled and pushed back his sandy blond hair. He picked up his felt hat and motioned to the door. "Good. Then let's get to the store and get you outfitted. You'll need some decent clothes and a bath. Oh, and a haircut. I know none of that is much fun, but we have to see to your ma all proper-like."

"How you gonna pay for all that?"

He laughed. "I've been earning money and putting it away since I was seventeen. Don't you worry about me. Now, come on. Let's get over to the general store and see what we can find."

———————

Elsa and Jamie stood just inside the cabin looking with great wonder and gratitude. The open door allowed the warm breeze of the early June day to filter in. "It looks so homey," Elsa declared. "Dianne and your mother surely did a good job of fixing it up."

"I'm glad you like it," Jamie said, putting his arm around her shoulder. "We weren't sure if you'd mind that they brought in some of the furniture from your father's house."

"No, I don't mind," she said. "It makes it look so nice, and after all, it's just material and wood. Remember when we were reading in Matthew about not storing up treasures on earth where moth and rust could corrupt?"

"I do."

"It made me think about a lot of things. Like this furniture. It only has a little material value. It's only important if I make it so. I can't see being foolish or prideful about it. It's here. We might as well use it. Doesn't matter who owned it before us."

Jamie laughed. "You're a wise woman."

"And a happy one." She grinned and embraced him. "I've never been this happy before." And in truth she didn't think it possible to be any more filled with joy.

"Me either. I have you and the ranch. It's taught me a lot about letting other folks help you out, and about trusting God."

She pulled back so she could see his eyes. "Sometimes I think I'll never get that one right. Just when I think I trust God completely, something happens and I act so foolish. God must surely suffer patience with me."

"No doubt with both of us."

"You two gonna stand here and gawk all day?" George questioned as he came up behind them on the porch.

Jamie and Elsa jumped apart as if caught doing something they shouldn't. George laughed in amusement, then turned and pointed up the ridge. "We've got about a thousand head of prime Texas cattle coming this way. I could use your help. After all, this is your place now."

Jamie picked up his hat. "I'm ready."

Elsa's heart swelled with pride. He was the man of the ranch now. Just as his father had been before him. And he was her man.

August 1889

A little more than two years had passed since Dianne and Cole had taken on the Walking Horseshoe Ranch. The time had passed quickly, and little by little they had managed to restore some of the herd numbers, as well as help build better accommodations at the Diamond V. It was rather like a large company, Dianne thought. And in truth, that's what Cole and their sons, along with George and Jamie, had been discussing. The formation of a cattle company.

Now as they journeyed back from a trip into town, Dianne found herself deep in thought. She rode behind the rest, nearly a quarter mile from the wagon her husband drove. Watching her family in amazement, she couldn't help but feel content.

They had promised to drop off some much needed goods at the Diamond V and to stay long enough to further discuss the cattle company. Soon she'd be able to visit with Koko and Susannah, as well as Elsa. It was always nice to have time with her aunt. Koko had become a mother to Dianne over the years.

Dianne's attention was drawn back to her family, however, as the younger boys began playing around, racing back and forth across the open fields on their horses. She laughed at the sight.

Luke, now nearly fourteen, was tall and lean like his father. He rode at the side of the wagon and carried on a conversation with his father. No doubt they were talking about new innovations and projects for the ranch.

Luke worked hard beside his father when his studies were done. Cole was firm that his children should have an education, and since the new school districts had been formed and schools mandated for public education, Dianne had given up teaching the children at home. Luke was a star pupil, as were Micah and Lia. John, on the other hand, seemed to have little interest in education. He rather reminded Dianne of herself.

John and Micah had become good friends and conspirators. They were always the practical jokers. They thought it funny to find ways to pull tricks on their brother and father. Not that Lia and Dianne were exempt, but Dianne had long ago set the boundaries. She made it clear that the boys were to treat women with dignity and honor rather than as "one of the boys."

But the important thing, she thought as she turned Daisy to the right, hoping to avoid the dust of the wagon, was that they were all happy.

The ranch had proved to be a good investment, and before long Dianne had found that the Walking Horseshoe felt like home. She enjoyed the sights and sounds of a ranch again. She loved the bustle of roundup and the quiet evenings in the summer.

The boys came riding at her in a race against each other. They circled her and reined up beside her.

"Ma, we're going to ride ahead so we can

help Pa with the wagon and see if George can teach us how to shoot with his bow after we're done," Micah announced.

"I see Jamie!" John declared. "Let's go!" He was a boisterous ten-year-old who always seemed to have a lot on his agenda.

Dianne halted Daisy as they passed. "Be careful." She watched the boys urge their mounts into a gallop as they went careening down the hillside. Lia had stayed at home with Winona and Ardith while the rest of the family had ventured to Virginia City. At eight years old, Lia was quite the little horsewoman, but a fall two weeks earlier had resulted in a broken arm. Dianne had picked up some special treats for her in Virginia City, hoping they might make up for missing out on the trip.

As was her custom, Dianne halted Daisy on the hilltop overlooking the Diamond V. Dianne sighed. It was still just about her favorite place in all of Montana. She'd contemplated so many things from this ridge.

"We're all very blessed, Lord. I thank you for that." Her family was healthy and well off. Zane and Mara were happy and completely devoted to their nearly two-year old son, Zachary. They were even now concluding some business dealings in Bozeman and would soon move the freighting business to that bustling town. Even Faith and Malachi were planning to move.

Dianne also knew from conversations she'd had with Koko that Jamie and Elsa had grown quite capable with the ranch. Elsa seemed to have a real knack for ranch life. In some ways, Koko said, Elsa reminded her of Dianne.

Daisy whinnied as if to urge Dianne to join the others. No doubt the mare was anxious for a long rest and a rubdown. They would stay here tonight and venture on home tomorrow. She would be a guest on the ranch. It was no longer her home.

"Funny, all the other times coming here, I still felt as if I were a part of it. Now . . ." She let the words fall silent. Dianne shook her head and smiled. "Now it's just a part of me—a part of who I've been—instead of who I'll be."

The sound of a wagon rose up from the north. Dianne turned Daisy, uncertain as to who might be approaching. She put her hand to the brim of her hat to block the sun, but still she couldn't make out the figures on the wagon seat.

She waited there until they drew closer, then gasped aloud when she realized it was her brother Trenton and his wife, Angelina. She urged Daisy forward to close the distance more quickly. Her breath caught in her throat.

"I can't believe it's you!" she cried as she drew up beside the wagon.

Trenton, now showing signs of his forty-four years, grinned. "It's me all right."

"How . . . why . . . I mean . . ." Dianne stammered in disbelief.

They all broke into laughter at her strange greeting, but it was Trenton who sobered first and offered explanation. "I have a great bit to tell you. I've been working on something, and that's part of the reason we're here."

"Working on what?" Dianne asked. All she knew for sure about her brother these last few years was that he was still alive and living in the Washington wilderness with Angelina.

Angelina patted her husband's arm. "Go ahead and tell her first. She should know before the others."

Dianne was truly curious now. "Know what?"

Trenton pushed back his hat and looked down at the reins in his hands. "I've been working with a lawyer. A good man—a godly man. He's trying to secure a pardon for me. He's managed to get witnesses to support my claims of innocence. We have to deal with three different states, but we're hopeful that given my circumstance, we will win. We've also managed to make good friends with a certain state senator."

"Who?" Dianne asked, still in a state of disbelief.

Trenton laughed. "Andrew Danssen."

"You mean Robbie and Sally's father?"

"The same one. He understands what happened to me back then. He's agreed to help."

"Then you're going back to Missouri?" Dianne felt her heart pound more rapidly. Her breathing quickened. What if it didn't work out? What if Mr. Danssen couldn't help— worse yet, what if he changed his mind and all of this was just a trick to get Trenton back in Missouri? They'd hang her brother as sure as anything.

Trenton looked to Angelina. "Yes. We're going back. My lawyer said it was important to our case." He paused momentarily and his expression saddened. "I just couldn't keep running. I couldn't live with myself anymore. I hope you understand."

Dianne heard the pleading in his voice for her acceptance. "Of course I understand. Oh, Trenton, I know this can't be easy for either of you. I have to admit, I'm terrified."

"Don't be," Angelina said. "Trenton and I have long discussed this. Facing up to the past is what's right. It won't be easy, and it might not go our way. We've talked about all the possibilities."

"I hope you know you're both welcome to come back and stay with us." Dianne knew she was saying it more to Angelina in case things did go wrong, but she meant it for her brother as well.

"The ranch doesn't look the same to be sure," Trenton said, nodding toward the valley.

"You don't know the half of it," Dianne said, laughing. "Cole and I now own the Walking Horseshoe."

"What happened to Lawrence and his boys?"

"Chester is dead, and Jerrod and Roy were hanged for their crimes, including what they did to you and Sam."

"I see." Trenton nodded thoughtfully. "I hope God had mercy on them."

"After what they did to you, I'd say that's a very generous thought," Dianne said softly.

"Forgiveness is important. It makes all the difference in how a person can move forward with his own life. I had to learn to forgive."

"I did too," Dianne said. "It hasn't been easy, and in fact, I know I'm still working through matters where the Lawrences are concerned. Though I desire to put it behind me, my human nature is very protective of my loved ones."

"So what happened to the others? Weren't there some girls and another boy in the family?" Trenton asked.

Dianne laughed. "We have a lot to catch up on." It had been over three years since Trenton had written, and Dianne had had no way to share all the details with him since he and Angelina had last moved. "Come on. Let's go join the others. We can talk all night if need be."

The valley was strangely quiet as Trenton and Dianne stepped out onto the porch to talk. It was late, but they'd had little opportunity to be alone. Trenton looked at his sister and shook his head.

"So much has changed. We've all changed."

"To be sure. I hope you'll stop in Virginia City to see Zane and his family before you head on."

"Oh, I will. I wish we could catch up with Morgan too, but that sounds impossible."

"He's always working. His guide business keeps him busy nearly year round. Sometimes he and David come here in the winter to rest up."

"It's hard to imagine Morgan being a father, but from what you said it sounds like he and David are quite close."

"Close enough the boy wanted to have Morgan adopt him proper-like. He's a sweet boy. I can't say I wasn't shocked when Morgan first showed up with him, but now it seems David has always been a part of the family. He just turned sixteen, you know."

"I keep thinking about you when you were sixteen. Remember how you bullied us all into going west?"

Dianne turned up the lantern on the porch

so she could better see her brother. "Bullied? I didn't bully anyone. I merely encouraged."

Trenton laughed heartily. "Your encouragement left little room for negotiation."

She shrugged. "It seemed the right thing to do."

"And so it was. I can't help but think of how different my life might have been if I would have joined you."

"I know," she said, her voice betraying her regret. "I've often thought of that myself. I know you've seen too much of the ugly side of life. I can't even imagine, nor do I try to."

"That's good, because it would serve no purpose. At least no good purpose." Trenton moved to the porch rail and sat down on it. He breathed in deeply. "I really like it here. I love this time of night when everything has settled down. I could lose myself in it."

"I know exactly what you mean." She sighed and leaned against the rail next to him. "Sometimes I can't help but wonder who I would have been if I'd never come here."

"Oh, you'd probably be married to Robbie Danssen and still living in New Madrid. Maybe running the general store. Or maybe Robbie would run for senator like his pa."

"Maybe." Dianne knew it wouldn't be a life she'd want, however. "Don't you find it amazing that God could somehow work everything out to put us here? I mean, there we were born back East and all our family lived there except for Uncle Bram. Most folks never travel farther than ten or twenty miles from home in all their lifetime. Then we up and move hundreds, even thousands, of miles away. I'm still dumbfounded by that at times."

"I know. And I've learned I can't live with regrets—that's why I have to go back and try to make amends. I know I'm not guilty of most of the things the law might try to pin on me, but I have to try to make it right."

"Are you . . . afraid?" she asked hesitantly.

Trenton didn't answer for a moment, and Dianne worried that she'd said the wrong thing. She was about to apologize when he spoke.

"I do get anxious about it sometimes. I just turn it back over to God, though. I can't let my imagination take over. Otherwise, I'd see myself convicted and hanged before I had a chance at getting the pardon." He shook his head. "I don't deserve a pardon. I let innocent people die."

"Could you have stopped it?"

"I doubt it. I mean, the Wilson brothers were meaner than anybody I've ever met. They didn't care anything about life—not even their own lives—or else they wouldn't have lived as they did."

"I'm so sorry that had to be a part of your life."

"It didn't have to be," Trenton admitted. "I made mistakes and deliberately took the wrong path at times. I kept justifying it to myself, but it always came back around to sin. Now those consequences are mine to bear. Even if it takes my life, I'll have a clear conscience before God."

Dianne admired him more than she could say. "You know I'll be praying. God will honor your obedience. Things may not turn out exactly as we hope, but I trust God to make them turn out the way He wants them to be."

"That's the way I see it too. I do hope . . ." He paused for a moment. "I hope you'll take care of Angelina if things go bad for me. She has family, of course, but I think she'd rather be amongst my kin."

"You know that she'll always have a home with us." Dianne fought the tears that threatened to come. "Always."

"I appreciate that. I can rest easy knowing she'll be cared for."

She turned to her brother and hugged him tight. "I'm so glad for this time, Trenton. I miss the closeness we once shared, but I'm thankful that I have that now with Cole and you have it with Angelina."

"We'll always have a special bond," he said. "There will always be a part of me that wishes for those late night talks we used to have." He grinned as Dianne stepped back. "I'll bet you keep Cole up all night like you used to do with me."

She laughed, feeling much better about her brother's situation. "Not all night," she mused. "Just half of it."

CHAPTER 30

"IT'S OFFICIAL!" A MAN DECLARED, WAVING a telegram like a flag. "Montana has just become the forty-first state in the Union!"

The crowd awaiting the news cheered wildly, and a nearby band struck up a lively rendition of a Sousa march. People began dancing, do-si-doing in the streets of Helena.

"Sure seems like a lot of ruckus," David said, looking to Morgan.

"I guess so. Guess November eighth will go down in the history books as being mighty important."

"So what happens now?" David asked as they maneuvered through the crowd and back to their hotel.

"I don't know. I guess we go on doing what we've been doing."

David laughed. "Sure seems like a lot of fuss."

"It's a good thing, I'm sure of that," Morgan said thoughtfully. "Being a part of the United States, having all the rights of a full state, is beneficial for Montana."

"But how does that change things for us?"

Morgan looked to the boy, amazed that they now stood eye to eye. David had grown tall and lean, filling out into a strong, well-muscled young man. "I don't know that we'll see changes for us—at least not right away. I suppose if we owned land or were settled in just one place, we might see more of an impact. I guess we'll have to bide our time to know for sure."

"We still going to Dianne's next week?"

They made it to their hotel, and Morgan stopped for a moment to look up at the two-story structure. "I don't think we should wait. Weather's been acting up, and who knows what next week will bring. Besides, my sister's birthday is coming right up. I think we should buy her a present, then grab our gear and head out. What say you?"

David grinned. "I say let's go. I like your sister's cooking. It's a sight better than ours. And her beds ain't buggy like they are here."

Morgan laughed. "That's for sure." There was something very satisfying in the thought of being with family again. "You go get our things. I'll pay the bill." David darted into the hotel without another word, but Morgan paused as the band struck up another tune. This time it was "Dixie." So many Southerners had come to Montana after the war. He wasn't surprised at all to hear the old song.

That tune made him think of the war and the reason they'd come west in the first place. He's always figured to get a job with the government—exploring and maybe making maps. But instead, his time with the government had passed, and he now found himself content to lead easterners on wilderness sojourns and hunting expeditions.

The music played on, and Morgan remembered the words to the tune. "Old times there are not forgotten." He supposed he'd never forget his upbringing—his mother and father. There were some wonderful memories of childhood that Morgan would always hold dear. He hoped he'd given David some memories that were just as good. For sure he knew he'd given David a sense of family and home. That was something that couldn't be bought or taken by force.

He smiled. He loved David as a son—and in fact had made him that legally. He might not have married the woman he loved or known what it was to hold his own baby, but he and David shared a powerful bond that had been borne out of loneliness and desperation. It was rather like the same things that had brought Morgan to God. He laughed. "I don't regret either decision."

"I hope we can get the house finished before Ben and Charity get here," Dianne told Cole as he and the boys headed out to work. The November winds had brought a numbing cold to the land, and Dianne was grateful for the warmth of her wool shawl.

"Zane should be bringing them in today," Cole said as he pulled on his gloves. "There isn't a whole lot left to do, but with Zane's help, we ought to make the place at least livable. We can always do some of the trimming up later in spring."

"I'm so glad they've agreed to come live with us," Dianne said, following Cole across the yard to where the small house stood. "I hope they like what we've done."

"You know Ben and Charity. They could be happy in a shack in the middle of nowhere, as long as they had each other."

"That's true enough, but Ben's health is slipping fast, and they may not have each other for long. Sometimes that's hard to imagine. I think about it for us as well. I don't like the idea of either one of us dying and leaving the other behind."

Cole stopped and turned. "You worry too

much, wife of mine." He leaned down and placed a kiss on her cheek. "It's all a matter of God's timing. Who are we to question it?"

"I know," she said softly. "It's the way life is."

"But because life is like that," he replied, "we simply need to appreciate what God has given us—who God has given us—and do our best each day. We certainly can't live in the regrets of yesterday or the worries of tomorrow."

Dianne nodded, trying to push her thoughts aside. She would have whatever time God allotted her. Both for her life and the lives of her friends and family. Either she trusted Him with those lives or she didn't.

"Look, Pa! Zane's comin'," Luke called from atop the small house. He and his brothers were already working to finish up with the shingles.

"No doubt Ben and Charity will be exhausted and cold. I'll get some tea on," Dianne said. She leaned up on tiptoes, and Cole met her lips with his own. "Be careful," she whispered before turning to the house.

It wasn't long before Dianne found herself seated at her dining table with Ben and Charity. She offered them freshly baked bread and butter, along with their tea.

"I'm sorry I don't have any cookies. The children exhausted our supply yesterday."

"Well, I can certainly help with that," seventy-seven-year-old Charity declared.

"And I can help too," Ben threw in. "Eat them, that is."

Dianne laughed. "I get plenty of help from Cole as well."

"I'd love to help with your chores," Charity said, growing serious. "We're much obliged to you taking us on here. Obviously there was never much money to put aside for our later years."

"I'm honored for the opportunity. I miss having my parents to care for. I know we'll have lots of time for talking and sewing," Dianne said, pouring more tea into her cup. "And I think it will be a blessing for the children to have you here. Oh, did I tell you that Cole's mother went to live with one of his sisters?"

"No," Charity replied, shaking her head. "I would imagine Cole is glad for that."

"I think he is relieved. His mother wrote him saying that she couldn't abide someone else farming the land. Personally, I think she finally realized Cole wasn't coming back and that the farm had no hold on him."

"But she knew he'd sold the property," Charity said. "Why would she wait two years for something that could never be?"

Dianne shrugged. "I really don't know. She's certainly stubborn. I wrote her a while back and apologized for anything I'd done to offend her. I told her I was sorry that we hadn't been better friends and hoped that maybe we could be in the future. I thought maybe in hindsight she'd write to apologize, but she never has. I suppose some people simply can't or won't change."

Ben picked up a second piece of warm bread and began slathering it in butter and jam. "Hard hearts aren't easily softened."

"No, they aren't. I can testify to that first-hand," Dianne said, still sometimes feeling a twinge of guilt for the way she'd comported herself with Cole's mother. "Only God has the ability to do the job right."

They fell silent and continued eating. Dianne often wondered if there might still be some way to reach Cole's mother, but so far she'd not come up with anything.

"So you've no doubt heard we're finally a state," Charity submitted.

"Oh, yes. Several of the cowhands were in Bozeman for the celebration. I guess it was a grand time."

"In Virginia City, too," Ben said. "It's a wonderful thing for us. For the country too. There will no doubt be more folks who will come west to settle now."

"New people and new problems," Dianne said, not at all enthused about what it might mean.

"Still, it would be nice to have things grow a little," Charity said. "I mean, wouldn't it be useful to you to have a town nearby that you could make a quick trip to without having to spend days on the road?"

"Certainly, but I also cherish the simplicity and privacy we have." Dianne shrugged. "I've lived in cities, and I don't think a whole lot of them."

"Ma! Ma, come quick! Uncle Morgan and David are headin' in!" John called.

"Uncle Morgan's coming!" Lia announced as she burst through the front door. She had become quite the belle of the family. She looked completely feminine in her pink gingham coat. Her brothers doted on her as if she were their favorite pet, and Lia enjoyed their attention.

"I thought he might come in a week or two. That's what his last letter indicated," Dianne said, getting to her feet. "You two go ahead and enjoy your rest. I'll go greet the travelers."

She took her shawl from the back door peg and walked outside with Lia bouncing up and down at her side. The child seemed to skip or run everywhere she went.

Dianne waved to Morgan and David as they rode up the lane. They waved back and urged their horses into a trot.

"We didn't expect you so early, but you know you're welcome!" Dianne called as they came to the hitching post.

They dismounted quickly, but instead of tying the horses up, Morgan instructed David to take them to the barn. "If that's all right with you," he said, looking to Dianne.

"You know it is. You'd best hurry too. From the looks of the clouds, I'm betting we'll have snow before much longer." She looked to see that the shingling of Ben and Charity's house was finally complete. "The men are inside the new house," she said, motioning. "Zane's here. He brought Ben and Charity up. That's going to be their place."

"You gonna build one for me when I get too old to guide folks around the mountains?" Morgan teased.

"You bet I will," Dianne said, hands on hips. "I'll build one for you and one for Zane and one for Trenton."

"Speaking of which, has there been any news?"

"None to speak of—not since the last letter Angelina wrote. They met with the governor, and the response was good. He seemed to believe the witnesses and understand the circumstances. Our friend Senator Danssen has been extremely helpful, and people seem to hold his word in highest esteem. Angelina believes they'll drop the old conviction of murder. At least that was how she read things."

"Good. We've been praying that it would be so."

She hugged her shawl closer as the wind picked up. Gazing to the west, she could see that the clouds had grown dark. "If you and David want to come warm up by the fire, that would be fine. If you'd rather go visit with the boys, feel free to do that. Dinner won't be for another hour or so. I'm going to fry up some chickens we killed this morning."

"You sure know how to treat a fellow," Morgan said, stepping closer to kiss Dianne on the cheek. "Sure glad you're my sister."

"I am too," she replied. It was so good to have Morgan home. Even for a short while. "How long can you stay?"

"The dudes have been scarce since the weather turned cold. I think we're just going to take it easy this winter. I am getting older, you know."

She laughed. "Yes, I know. Same thing's been happening to me." She picked up her skirts. "Well, you know you're welcome for as long as you like. Take the back two rooms like always, and bring me your dirty clothes." She grinned and added, "And a bath wouldn't hurt you either."

"Yes, ma'am," Morgan said, giving her a slight bow. "I'll see to it."

Dianne giggled all the way back into the house.

The snows held off, veering to the north and leaving them dry. The next day they celebrated Dianne's forty-second birthday. She was completely surprised when Koko and George showed up with Jamie and Elsa. Susannah had long ago convinced her mother to send her to a finishing school in Denver, so she was the only one absent from the party.

Koko, Ardith, and Charity created a wonderful supper, complete with a large chocolate cake, Dianne's favorite. Adding to Dianne's surprise were all the presents she received. Ardith and Winona, now as close as they ever had been, gave Dianne a new brush and mirror set. Ben and Charity had bought her a new George MacDonald book. Morgan and David surprised her with a bolt of cloth they'd purchased in Helena. It was a lovely shade of turquoise and had a delicate floral print. She thought it perfect for a new gown.

Luke, Malachi, and John had worked with their father to make a new china cabinet. The delicate piece amazed everyone at the party.

"I can't believe how much work you must have put in on this," Dianne declared as the boys maneuvered it into place with Cole and Zane's help.

"We worked for about thirty years on i" John said, causing everyone to laugh.

Dianne had known there was to be a special gift from them, as Cole had often rounded the boys up after supper to go to the barn for their extra work. But the boys had been silent about the project, not even telling Lia.

Lia had worked on a piece of embroidery with Dianne, telling her as they made the small table runner that it was for someone special. Dianne had presumed Lia would give it to Charity or Koko but was moved to tears when she opened the piece and realized she was the someone special.

"Mara made this for you," Zane announced as he handed Dianne a gift wrapped in brown paper.

Dianne undid the string that held the package and was surprised to find a lovely white knitted shawl. "Oh, this is perfect. I've needed one just like this. Please tell her how much I love it."

Elsa and Jamie gave Dianne a little wooden box for trinkets, and Koko and George completed the celebration by giving Dianne new saddlebags. They were beautifully designed, tanned to a rich reddish brown, with decorative markings burned into the leather.

"This is lovely," Dianne said, holding up the bag to inspect it. "Thank you so much. I can see that a lot of hard work went into this."

"A lot of chewing leather," George teased. It was their ongoing joke.

Dianne grinned. "I hope you didn't have to lower yourself to do women's work, George."

"Not me. I did the designs."

"I hope you use them for many years to come," Koko said.

"Hear, hear," Ben declared and raised his glass. "Many years of health to you, Dianne. Many years of blessings and happiness."

Dianne looked at her friends as they toasted her. She couldn't have asked for better people with whom to share her life. She couldn't have known more happiness than in that moment.

"Speech! Speech!" her brothers chanted in unison.

Dianne blushed and got to her feet. She looked down the long, very crowded table. This had once been the house of her enemy— a house of sadness and hatred. Now it was a home of love and friends.

"Thank you all. You are such an important part of who I am," she began. "For most of my life I've known all of you. For all of my life, I've known some of you." They laughed and she couldn't help but join them before continuing.

"I've been blessed beyond all that I could have anticipated. My life hasn't always been easy—the storms and trials have been difficult. So much so that at times I despaired of making it through. I can't say that if I had the chance to do some things different, that I wouldn't jump in and do it. There are things that I would have gladly changed—but you aren't among those things."

She looked down the table at each person—the love they held for her evident in their faces. "We face a new era of statehood. A new life that is sure to bring changes. Some of those changes will be good, while others will be less beneficial. But most important, we'll face them all together. There is nothing worse than to be in this world without a friend." She looked to David, the newest member of their family, and smiled.

"There's nothing harder than to live without love." She moved her gaze to Cole. He smiled, and his expression warmed her.

"And there's nothing more devastating than to live life without hope. The hope of Jesus—the hope within."

She looked to each of them and cherished the affection she found on their faces. This was her family—her life. They were the heirs of Montana. Heirs to a vast fortune of land and liberty and love.

"To hope," she said, lifting her glass.

"To hope!" they cheered in unison.